Fiction
Delacroix, Claire
Honeyed lies

Jacot
pain
of in
around

"I meant no harm," she admitted huskily as his fingers tightened at her admission of guilt.

"And I had expected a pretty denial," he bit out with a derisive laugh. Rebecca flicked another glance upward to discover that, remarkably, his anger seemed to have dissipated, his expression now one of ironic amusement. His mood had changed suddenly, that much she could see, but she had no idea how or why.

"Truly I underestimated you," he mused, his tone as warm as the fingertip that now gently traced the line of her jaw. Rebecca shivered at his caress, and Jacob smiled a predatory smile, his strong fingers slipping into the tangle of hair at her nape and pulling her unerringly toward him. . . .

Dear Reader,

Welcome to another great month of the best in historical romance. This February brings us four great titles sure to add spice to your Valentine's Day!

First, don't miss *Defy the Eagle,* the long-awaited reissue of Lynn Bartlett's enthralling saga of epic passion and ancient rebellion. Caddaric, a son of Britain, and Jilana, a daughter of Rome—lovers by destiny, enemies by birth.

For those of you who enjoyed Deborah Simmons's *Silent Heart,* her new release, *The Squire's Daughter,* is sure to please. Marquis Justin St. John is cursed by a tragic past, but when he marries Clare Cummings in a marriage of convenience, his new wife begins to unravel not only his heart, but an old mystery, as well.

If you've got a penchant for the exotic, have we got a book for you! Set in the Mediterranean during the medieval era, Claire Delacroix's *Honeyed Lies* weaves the tale of Rebecca, a young widow who accidentally finds a mysterious book everyone seems to want—including the honorable and handsome Jacob.

And last but not least, in *Dylan's Honor* by Kristie Knight, patriot Honor Richmond is determined to unmask the Tory spy operating out of her tavern— but Dylan Alden's smoldering passion keeps her guessing if he is friend or foe.

We hope you enjoy all our February titles. Next month, keep an eye out for our 1994 March Madness promotion, featuring four exciting new books by up-and-coming first-time authors.

Sincerely,

Tracy Farrell
Senior Editor

CLAIRE DELACROIX
HONEYED LIES

Harlequin Books

TORONTO • NEW YORK • LONDON
AMSTERDAM • PARIS • SYDNEY • HAMBURG
STOCKHOLM • ATHENS • TOKYO • MILAN
MADRID • WARSAW • BUDAPEST • AUCKLAND

ISBN 0-373-28809-3

HONEYED LIES

Copyright © 1994 by Deborah A. Cooke.

This edition published by arrangement with Harlequin Enterprises B. V.

® and TM are trademarks of the publisher. Trademarks indicated with
® are registered in the United States Patent and Trademark Office, the
Canadian Trade Marks Office and in other countries.

Printed in U.S.A.

Books by Claire Delacroix

Harlequin Historicals

Romance of the Rose #166
Honeyed Lies #209

CLAIRE DELACROIX

An avid traveler and student of history, Claire Delacroix can be found at home when she has a deadline, amid the usual jumble of books, knitting needles and potted herbs.

**For my mom and dad,
who have had their own adventures in Spain**

Prologue

Toledo, Andalusia—June 1084

The heat of the summer sun made Rebecca's black veil feel more oppressive and she rued anew the fact that her only dark kirtle was wool. Surely this could not last much longer, she reasoned, her heart sinking as yet another man stepped forward to deliver a few parting words.

Ephraim would have loved all the fuss, she conceded to herself, casting an assessing eye over the size of the group assembled in the bright sunlight. Men of wealth and learning crowded the tiny cemetery, their eyes downcast and countenances solemn, so many beyond the circle of close friends she had expected.

Yusuf caught her eye from the far side of the crowd and she must have made some sign of her surprise to see him in attendance, for he nodded once and smiled slowly, as if amused by her preconceptions, before he glanced tactfully away. Surely by now she knew better than to try to guess what he would do. And he and Ephraim had been friends, regardless of the differences in their faiths.

"Beloved friend and noted scholar," the rabbi continued, and Rebecca closed her eyes so that none might see her response or lack of one, choosing instead to review mentally the preparations made in such unholy haste.

She was certain that all the mirrors were covered, that the few brass ornaments she possessed were put away, that the

Torah was lying appropriately open to the Kaddish. Regardless of her feelings on the matter, she would read that for Ephraim, if only out of respect for the kind of man he had been. The red candle they had received as a wedding gift would suit for the mourning, and there was a kind of irony in using it now that appealed to Rebecca.

With a sigh, she admitted that sitting *shivah* was going to be a relief after all the bustle, but only if she could manage to avoid having a lot of visitors. An entire week without going out and running into people she barely knew who wanted to express their sympathy would be an improvement, and surely the visitors would stop coming after the first day or so.

Her neighbors meant well. Rebecca knew that in her heart, but how could they ever understand how little had really changed in her life? She had always been alone, almost as far back as she could remember, and living with Ephraim had not changed that, whatever her expectations to the contrary had been two years past.

And no one could tell her that it wasn't easier this way.

Maybe now she'd finally get those tiles in the patio cleaned. Goodness knows they had been driving her crazy since she and Ephraim had moved into the house. Strange how he had always managed to appear with some crisis that needed solving or a problem only she could mend whenever she settled with a bucket of soapy water to tackle those tiles. She wondered now whether that had been purely coincidence, or whether the disarray of the patio had appealed to some romantic side of his personality that she had seldom glimpsed and certainly never really known.

It was interesting in a way how little she had known about him, and she wondered as she gazed unseeingly over the assembled mourners how much Ephraim had known about her. Had it ever bothered him? Somehow she suspected not, just as she had not found their lack of intimacy disturbing. It surely was impractical to expect anything more than mutual respect from an arranged marriage.

"Blessed be the true judge."

Rebecca's head snapped up guiltily as the group intoned the words together, and she glanced furtively around in the hope that no one had noticed her lack of attentiveness. She quickly made the requisite tear in her garment, making the hole near a seam so it could be easily repaired. Absently she planned the stitching that would be required before she realized the callousness of her thoughts and pulled herself up short with shock.

Ephraim was dead and she could think of no more than mending her sleeve.

That she should be so unfailingly practical at this moment in her life upset her more than the events of the past few days, and unwieldy tears rose to blur her vision. Had she truly become so shallow? Could she not find some vestige of regret within her heart for her husband's untimely passing?

And was she doomed always to be alone? Once given rein, her emotions could not easily be checked, and the upset of the past few days was quickly eclipsed by her uncertainty of the future.

It was already more than clear that Ephraim had left less than nothing, her own family was long gone, her small dowry had been spent ages past and her ties to the community here in Toledo were meager at best. She would manage and she knew it on some level, but still she could not check her tears. They spilled over her cheeks and she bit one finger to keep herself from making any sound, old Isaac, another of Ephraim's close acquaintances, throwing a sympathetic look in her direction.

Realizing that the scholar had misunderstood the source of her anguish and feeling a traitor amongst all these well-intentioned souls, Rebecca turned abruptly away. Ignoring the sympathetic clucks rising in her wake, she virtually ran from the sun-dappled cemetery in a futile effort to escape her troubling thoughts.

Chapter One

Tunis
Several weeks later

"Ooh, a lovely fat letter from Dalia."

Jacob spared a sharp glance up from his books to find Judith's dark eyes twinkling merrily as she paused inside the library door and visibly waited for his reaction.

"Dalia is a shameless gossip," he stated flatly so she wouldn't be disappointed, her delighted giggle making him smile as he tallied the column once more.

"Of course," she agreed good-naturedly, sweeping into the room, dropping into the chair beside him and tucking her plump feet beneath her trailing skirts. "But she tells the most *interesting* stories," she added, playfully tapping him on the shoulder with the missive. Jacob chuckled despite himself.

"All lies, undoubtedly," he argued, but Judith only grinned wider.

"Who cares?" she demanded pertly. "I don't know most of these people and it's unlikely I'll ever meet them. And it makes for lively reading on a dull day." Jacob glanced pointedly around his crowded library and put his quill down on the table with deliberation. Judith met his eyes unflinchingly, the sparkle deep in her own telling him that she anticipated his next comment.

"Are you honestly telling me, Aunt Judith, that you have nothing to read?" he demanded in mock incredulity, and gestured to the crowded bookshelves that surrounded them.

Judith cocked a skeptical brow in turn, then leaned over and plucked a book from the closest shelf at random. "*Sefer Yetzira*—the Book of Creation," she read solemnly, tossing the considerable weight of the book experimentally in one hand and fixing Jacob with a steady look. "You know how I hate this kind of frivolous nonsense."

Jacob smothered a smile at her sarcasm and returned to his numbers. "It's actually quite interesting," he commented mildly, not missing Judith's grimace.

"You seem to do well enough turning dross into gold in the *souk* without finding some sort of mystical justification for it," she snorted, and Jacob spared her an indulgent look.

"It's more than that and you know it," he chided gently, underlining the grand total on his parchment with a flourish. It had been a good year, that much he had to admit. Maybe not dross into gold, but certainly silk and good steel, Jacob thought as he smothered a smile.

"And besides, the alchemical works are interesting," he added when he realized Judith was still watching him intently.

"You don't know *interesting*," she shot back as she unceremoniously dropped his book, scooping up his letter opener and slitting the envelope with a dramatic flourish. She settled her bulk more comfortably in the armchair, rustled the paper theatrically and cleared her throat. "Are you listening?" she demanded imperiously when Jacob dipped his quill once more, and he shook his head tolerantly.

"I'm all yours," he declared as he set his pen aside, and his aunt snorted.

"Despite my best efforts to the contrary," she muttered under her breath in typical fashion, but Jacob, equally typical, chose to ignore her. When her words provoked no response, she snapped the parchment once, her eyes scanning the spidery handwriting quickly. "Oh, this *is* good," she murmured, and Jacob cleared his throat.

"Well, I'm waiting," he pointed out evenly, and his aunt shot him a mischievous look that made him suddenly uneasy. Then she turned back to the letter and his sense that she was brewing something he wouldn't like evaporated as quickly as it had appeared.

"Dalia says that the weather is good and that the orange crop is really spectacular this year," she began, and Jacob threw a longing glance to his discarded quill.

"I thought this was supposed to be interesting," he commented dryly.

"I'm getting to that," she pointed out, and he watched her skip ahead over the lines until her eyes brightened. "Here's something—Ephraim died last month quite unexpectedly." Judith put the letter down and pinned Jacob with a sharp look. "You remember him? That scholar son of my cousin Eliezer's?"

"Didn't they visit Father once?" Jacob asked, his uncertainty evident in his tone.

"That's right!" Judith declared, tapping one finger victoriously on the corner of his desk. "You boys got into trouble in the *souk...*"

"*That* was Ephraim?" Jacob demanded in surprise, the recollection of that particular afternoon still able to make him uneasy despite the passage of years. Ephraim, to his memory, had been a sneak of the worst kind, and Jacob could still see him lying barefacedly to old Hakim, denying that he had stolen the pomegranate that visibly bulged out the back of his clothing. Hopefully Ephraim had gotten more clever about his deceptions before his untimely demise, Jacob thought wryly to himself, suspecting that his fundamental dishonesty would not have been easily erased.

"Yes, such a handsome boy he was. I remember him well. And clever." Judith rolled her eyes and Jacob decided to hold his tongue regarding his own somewhat less flattering memories of Ephraim.

"Dead, you say?" he asked mildly instead, shaking his head at his aunt's quick nod of assent. "He couldn't have been much older than I."

"No." Judith frowned first at him, then back at the letter. "And Dalia's wording is odd, too, come to think about it. As if there were something strange about the whole business." Before Jacob could ask what she meant, his aunt emitted a little cry as she read ahead.

"Oh, the poor lamb. Dalia says his wife was so distraught that she ran from the funeral in tears." She shook her head sadly and Jacob knew the words had launched a barrage of Judith's own memories. "The poor soul, and no little ones to keep her mind off her loss."

"I expect she's better off without children now that Ephraim's gone," Jacob commented practically, and reached surreptitiously for his quill.

"What a cruel thing to say!"

"I simply meant that she'll probably have a difficult time making ends meet without a husband," he elaborated in a matter-of-fact tone.

"How true that is," Judith agreed, nodding sadly, and Jacob tallied another column to give the older woman a moment alone with her thoughts.

"You know, we *are* family," she mused finally, and he glanced up, having long ago learned to distrust this thoughtful tone.

"We are *not* taking this widow in," he said firmly, unappeased when Judith launched a sunny grin in his direction. "We don't know this woman at all." He felt obligated to continue, even though he was unable to shake the sense that he had already lost this round. "She is somewhere in Andalusia, which is not exactly convenient, and you have already taken in enough strays to last a lifetime."

"What a ridiculous idea." Judith dismissed the thought with a wave of one hand and Jacob regarded her suspiciously. "And besides, Andalusia is not that far—you go there all the time."

"Here it comes," Jacob muttered under his breath, finally seeing the path of his aunt's thoughts. She leaned forward to press her advantage and he waited for the idea he was certain to dislike.

"Oh, come on now, Jacob. You said yourself this very evening that you have to get up to Toledo for swords before the autumn squalls. Didn't you?"

"Yes, I did," he agreed almost inaudibly.

"Well, this Rebecca just happens to live in Toledo and it would certainly be rude not to visit her and pay our respects to Ephraim. Blood is thicker than water, you know, and it wouldn't be right to leave her in a bad situation when you and I are in a position to do something about it."

"Do something about it?" he demanded warily, certain that he was not about to get away with so little as a sympathetic visit. His aunt flushed and looked away, her gesture feeding his suspicions. "Out with it," he said more sharply, and she flicked a glance at him.

"Well, there's no need to be so surly about it all." She said, flustering with uncharacteristic discomfort, "I simply thought that she might need some financial help and..." Judith gestured vaguely with one hand. "Well, you know that I don't have any money."

"You want me to give her money?" Jacob demanded skeptically, and Judith drew herself up proudly.

"It certainly wouldn't kill you to inquire politely as to the state of her finances while you're there," she shot back. "It's the least we could do for my second cousin's widow."

That was it? A bit of money? Jacob spared a quick glance up from his books to find his aunt nodding to herself with satisfaction, and his suspicions of some elaborate plan quickly dissolved. One visit, perhaps some cash. He could handle that. Relief flooded through him and he agreed so quickly that Judith shot him a sharp look.

"If that's what you want."

"You'll really go?" she asked softly, and he nodded once.

"You have only to say it to make it so," he teased, and Judith swatted his arm.

"A likely story," she chortled. When he didn't respond, she reached across the leather blotter to pat his hand in a proprietary way that always made him smile. "You're off this week?"

"Right after the Sabbath," he confirmed, and Judith rose to her feet in a self-righteous swirl of sheer skirts.

"I'll write a letter of regret tonight so you can take it with you," she told him, and when Jacob nodded, she spun on her heel and happily trotted from the room.

He really ought to know by now that there was no arguing with his aunt at all when she had her mind set on something, Jacob reminded himself with a wry smile as the last trailing skirt hem disappeared out of sight. It was that stubbornness that had seen Judith through all the ordeals of her life and helped him through a few of his own. Once again he felt a glow of pride that he was able to provide for his father's favorite sister in the way she deserved.

And she was asking for a small thing from him, regardless of his suspicions to the contrary. He was going to Toledo already, for goodness' sake; it wouldn't even be out of his way. A little money for a destitute relation and an hour of his time—he shrugged in easy acceptance in the quiet room. If that was all it took to please Judith, he would willingly pay the price.

"Jacob?"

He looked up at his aunt's soft question to find her head poked around the door again and he raised his brows inquiringly.

"Thank you," she murmured, and he inclined his head in acknowledgment, barely catching a glimpse of Judith's impish grin before she disappeared.

There it was again, he thought as he stared at the spot she had vacated, unable to shake the sense that his sweet aunt was up to something and that he wasn't going to like it.

* * *

By the time Rebecca reached the courtyard with the bucket of soapy water, she was certain her right arm was longer than her left. She dropped the bucket a little too quickly and the water sloshed over the side, soaking her kirtle while she groaned in frustration. At least it was an old one, she concluded philosophically, wringing the cloth out with one hand as she toyed with the illusion that she had a marvelously rich and varied wardrobe.

Would nothing go right today?

The matchmaker had been by already this morning and it was all Rebecca could do to keep her temper with the woman. Not two months since Ephraim had been buried and it seemed all anyone could talk about was her remarrying. It wasn't Berta's fault that she was having a hard time summoning the interest in getting married again and she could understand that Berta was just looking for business, but Rebecca was beginning to feel that six or seven refusals ought to convince Berta of her decided lack of enthusiasm.

And the woman's coy comments that she must be missing a man in the evenings got on her nerves. As if anyone could miss sex. It was difficult for her to imagine anything more boring or uncomfortable and she thanked her lucky stars once again that Ephraim had had little use for the activity, either. The only good thing she could say about it was that its duration was mercifully short.

If and when she did remarry, it would be for purely financial reasons. And remarkably, she was doing a little better than she had expected, being on her own. There had been a bit of her dowry left after all, and the sewing she did brought in some income. Trading a few luxuries for her privacy had been an easy choice for Rebecca to make and she saw no reason to change her situation soon.

She discarded her veil and tied back her hair, surveying the dirty tiles in the little courtyard with a critical eye. And what else was a man good for? A quick glance at the broken tiles around the perimeter of the courtyard revealed

Ephraim's complete lack of interest in household mainte-
nance, and Rebecca pursed her lips in annoyance. Ephraim could never have been called ambitious and their
household finances throughout their marriage had always
been precarious.

Not that it had ever seemed to bother him if they ate
plain paella every day of the week, that much she had to
concede. Ephraim had constantly been in a world of his
own and one far above earthly concerns. His books absorbed him completely and she often fancied she could still
hear him mumbling in Arabic downstairs when she lay in
bed at night, struggling to sleep.

Funny how she had trouble sleeping now, knowing that
the house was empty. Ephraim had seldom come to bed
with her, but somehow just knowing that he was in the
house and hearing occasional snatches of him talking to
himself had given her a sense of security, although she
hadn't known it at the time. She smothered a smile and
dropped to her knees, wondering what Berta would say if
she told her that she missed a man's mumbling about the
place.

There had been good times and she couldn't forget those:
the way Ephraim made her laugh when he remembered she
was there; his disarming charm when he detected that she
was in a sour mood and set himself to right it; the calen-
dulas he had pinched for her from old Dalia's garden that
long-ago summer day, such an unexpected surprise.

Could they have been closer if time had been on their
side? Probably not, Rebecca thought, seeing now that after an initial burst of intimacy they had both been drifting
further into their own worlds. But wasn't that how it had
always been with everyone in her life? The only one she had
to rely upon was herself and the only time she found herself in difficulty was when she forgot that simple fact.

Rebecca sighed, shoving up her sleeves before plunging
her brush into the hot soapy water, pausing in admiration
when some brief scrubbing revealed the intricacies of a
bright pattern on the tiles. The tiles gleamed wetly in the

sunlight and she sat back on her heels for a moment and
spared another glance for the broken ones along the wall.
Perhaps she could find a glazier who could match the pattern, she mused, bending back to her work with a vengeance.

It had been well worth the trouble, Rebecca told herself
as she looked around the courtyard with satisfaction some
hours later. Her kirtle was soaked to the knees, she smelled
like a common laborer, and as she wiped one hand across
her brow she noted the filth accumulated under her nails,
but the tiles were glorious now that they were clean.

The sunlight positively danced on the gleaming white
surfaces with their blue, red and yellow patterns. She had
even managed to match up some of the broken pieces
around the walls and lean them where they belonged so it
wasn't immediately noticeable how many tiles were broken.

Her gaze swiveled to the center of the courtyard and
locked on the fountain there, which she had never seen in
operation. The basin was choked with old leaves, and she
straightened her shoulders at the challenge it presented. Its
days of inactivity were definitely numbered, she resolved,
and carried her trusty bucket into the fray.

Hauling out the decaying leaves revealed a sizable crack
in the bowl, which dashed some of Rebecca's early enthusiasm. Refusing to be daunted, she scrubbed the stone bowl
clean and tackled the dried algae on the central spire of the
fount itself, pleased to find an elegant gray marble underneath the grime.

Another hour of industrious scrubbing left the fountain
considerably cleaner than it had been, the large crack in the
bowl the only disappointing discovery. Rebecca pushed up
her sweaty sleeves for the hundredth time, frowning at the
straight line of fissure.

It almost looked as if one side of the bowl could be lifted
away. The crack itself was just large enough to accommodate her fingers and she fitted them impulsively into the

space, her eyes widening in astonishment when the heavy stone lifted easily out of the way at her urging.

At the sound of a click, she felt the weight of the stone supported by something other than her hands. She tentatively released her grip, amazed when the curve of the bowl remained locked vertically. A quick glance revealed a sophisticated hinge hidden in the rim, holding the inner bowl open like a door. The fountain had a double-walled bowl, Rebecca saw now, the lifting of the inner bowl revealing a space within the base of the fountain.

Excitement bubbled inside her at her find. A secret hiding place! Maybe there was some ancient treasure locked away in her courtyard!

Rebecca shook her head skeptically at her childish optimism and smiled, certain that the previous owners had left nothing more exciting than a rusty old spoon behind. She peered into the shadows, her heart leaping when she thought she glimpsed something much larger than a spoon jammed into the space.

The musty scent of mildew and decaying leaves filled Rebecca's nostrils as she leaned over the hole and she tried not to imagine the kind of crawling creatures who lived in such damp holes as she reached into the darkness. Her fingers encountered something quite firm and she grasped the bulky package, grunting as she struggled to pry it from its hiding place. She gritted her teeth and pulled and the package came loose unexpectedly, sending her sprawling on her backside on the newly cleaned tiles.

Curiosity making her oblivious to her tumble, Rebecca turned the dark green bundle over thoughtfully in her hands, weighing it assessingly and trying to justify untying the twine that tightly bound it. Secret treasure of some kind, she speculated as she tucked an errant strand of hair behind her ear and hefted the weight of the bundle in her hands. Who did it belong to? And who had left it here?

And did she have any right to open it? Rebecca frowned at the package, seeing the care with which it had been bundled. It had been important to someone, that much was certain, the way it had been dipped in wax to protect it from the dampness of the fountain both an indication of that concern and a curse to her objectives. There was no way she could open the package without the wax cracking and showing her deed.

But this was her house now, she reasoned, her fingers still hesitating as she reached for the knot in the twine. No one could rightfully come for this now and it had probably been hidden away there for years. She held the title to the house, so she had the right to everything on the premises. It was that simple.

She took a deep breath and resolved to open the package just as the bells at the front door jingled.

Visitors? Her head shot up and she stared toward the door as if she could see right through the walls to the front of the house. Who could be here now? Without intending to do so, she clutched the package protectively to her chest and its waxy damp smell brought her back to her senses.

She had to hide the package again and quickly.

In an instant she was on her feet, jamming the bundle back into its hiding place, cursing under her breath when it seemed to take on a life of its own and defy her attempts to replace it. The front bell jangled again and Rebecca gave the package a fierce shove that sent it into the dark recess without further argument. She studied the hinge on the bowl for one wild minute before simply pressing it downward with the flat of her hand, catching her breath when the stone dropped smoothly and elegantly into place.

The crack was barely visible now but she had no time to study it for the bells jingled once more, their ringing lasting longer as her visitor clearly was losing patience. Without a thought to her appearance, Rebecca ran down the narrow hall and threw open the front door, only to find herself staring into the annoyed gaze of a total stranger.

For a moment she couldn't place his faith and occupation by his unfamiliar clothing, the realization unsettling her as much as his unwelcoming expression, until she saw that the long white *tallith* draped over his shoulders had a pair of blue tassels at each end. A Jew, then, for although the shape of the shawl was unusual, it could be nothing else. His chausses were black and cut slightly full to a fitted ankle, and his full-sleeved shirt of a fine white cotton was barely visible beneath his indigo tunic. His black burnous was draped over one shoulder and the *tallith* over that.

Although Rebecca was surprised by how much black he wore, and absently wondered whether his evident poor temper was due to how uncomfortably hot he must be, it was his headgear that completely astonished her. He wore a turban of some fine white cloth, much as the Berbers did, and it was wrapped around what seemed to be a small red velvet cap, the sliver of red visible above his forehead seeming all the more vivid for the absence of any other color in his garb.

Rebecca tore her gaze away from the patch of red to find that his expression had changed from impatience to disdain, his disapproval of her clear by the way those dark eyes swept over her disheveled appearance. With an effort she checked the impulse to smooth her hair and tipped her chin stubbornly to meet his eyes.

Who on earth was this insolent man? And what gave him the right to judge her?

"I hope I didn't disturb you," Jacob commented dryly, thinking that if he had ever had a servant as tardy as this one, he would have sent her packing. She was pretty enough to be sure, he acknowledged with another appraising glance at the way her damp kirtle clung in some intriguing places, but the way she met his gaze as though they were equals was unacceptably bold.

"Perhaps you could fetch the lady of the house," he suggested when she didn't move, determined to get this over with as quickly as possible. If he didn't return to that sword merchant before the sun reached its zenith, the man would sell the blades to another, he was sure of it. His buyer in Tunis would pay a good price for that steel, especially with those motifs in the carving.

The girl folded her arms defiantly across her chest at his request and Jacob added "rude" to his mental list as he met the challenge in her dark eyes, flatly refusing to recognize how her gesture shoved the fullness of her breasts into prominence.

Filthy, he noted in the back of his mind, wondering how this Rebecca could manage not to see the state of her help's clothing and hands. And uncovered hair to boot, as though she would advertise her virginity, the thick mane no cleaner then the rest of her, though it was long and thick.

"I do not know you," she said flatly, and he raised his brows in surprise at her audacity. When he did meet this Rebecca, he would ensure that she knew exactly the way her servant greeted visitors.

"One would hardly expect any different," he shot back, and an unexpected flush rising over her cheeks almost stopped his next words. "However, you go too far to assume you know everyone your mistress knows," he added bluntly.

She stared back at him as though she couldn't believe his censure, then swallowed visibly, the gesture drawing his attention unwillingly to the creamy length of her throat.

"I only meant that perhaps—" she fumbled for a moment and Jacob almost regretted his harsh words "—perhaps my *mistress* does not know you, either."

"Well, it is highly unlikely that she does, should that reassure you at all," he conceded tightly, flicking a glance up to the sky. Clearly he had been overly optimistic to think that Judith's mission for him could be accomplished quickly or easily. "Is this the home of Ephraim's widow?" he demanded, and the girl looked taken aback at his directness.

"Yes," she confirmed simply. Jacob withdrew his aunt's letter from his pocket and offered it to her.

"Then you will see that she gets this letter of introduction, and also tell her that I will return this evening to speak with her."

With that, he bid the apparently dumbstruck woman good-day and strode back toward the market and his appointment, marveling all the way at the tolerance of the Andalusians. He had never been one to beat his household servants, but that one—he gritted his teeth—*that* one would test a man's patience.

Rebecca turned the thick missive over in her hands, flicking one last glance down the street to find that the man's broad shoulders had disappeared into the crowd. She pursed her lips and picked at the red wax seal as she stepped back inside and closed the door, leaning her back against it as she considered the handwriting on the outside. Her name was scrawled there and no more.

What news could possibly come to her in this abrupt manner? Nothing good, of that she could be certain, she told herself, easily recalling the coldness in the man's eyes.

Arrogant creature, assuming that she was a servant. It served him right that she had played along with his mistake. She winced at the thought that he would be returning this evening, then smiled slowly in anticipation of his learning that he had been wrong. It would be interesting to see how he apologized for his gaffe.

If he did apologize. The image was admittedly hard to conjure up.

Rebecca frowned and forced her attention back to the message. She squinted at the seal but could make no sense of the mark, slipping her fingers beneath the flap and opening it as she strolled back out into the courtyard. She might as well know the worst of it now, she reasoned as she dropped cross-legged onto the tiles bathed in sunlight.

The contents of the chatty letter inside were so unexpected that Rebecca had to read it twice, and still she couldn't believe the words.

A certain Judith, who had been some distant relation of Ephraim's, sent her regrets, a thoughtful and gracious gesture. But the truly remarkable part of the letter followed.

My heart goes out to you in your new circumstance as I, too, have worn the widow's weeds and found them most confining. Do not misunderstand when I tell you that your best choice is to find another man while you are yet young, even though the loss of your first love must have been a terrible blow.

I would tactfully suggest that you consider my nephew, Jacob ben Solomon, who will be delivering this missive to you. A trader he is, and well situated here in Tunis, an eligible man with no children out of wedlock or other responsibilities. He is a good man and is of an age to be in need of a wife and children. There is not a doubt in my mind that you will agree with me once you have seen Jacob's charm.

If that was his charm, it was no small wonder he was without marital prospects! Rebecca thought as she read the words once more, only able to recall the man's frosty demeanor. Who on earth would want to get close to such hostility? Charm? Rebecca stifled a chuckle. He had about as much charisma as curdled milk.

Clearly Judith was not a subtle woman, for she continued cheerfully in the same vein.

In anticipation of your agreement and to expedite matters, the *ketubah* has been drawn up here in advance and you have only to sign to make it legal. The ceremony can be held there in Toledo or once you arrive in Tunis.

Rebecca turned the page and examined the marriage contract, her disbelief showing no signs of fading even with repeated exposure.

The contract itself was perfectly standard, the stock phrases familiar to her from her previous agreement with Ephraim. It was the uncompromisingly bold strokes of Jacob ben Solomon's signature above those of the witnesses that she found so unsettling, and she touched the space left for her own signature with a dubious finger. She would never have imagined him a man come courting from his manner this afternoon and she wondered at his motivation.

She scanned the letter again, knowing that there was no possibility that she had misunderstood Judith's words but unable to accept what lay before her. These people knew nothing about her, they had never even met her. She had not employed a matchmaker and she had no dowry or inheritance of any kind. In fact, paying a glazier to fix the tiles in the courtyard was apt to be a financial challenge.

Who did these people think they were? Deciding her fate without even the common courtesy of consulting her feelings on the subject? To be consulted and disregarded was something she was used to, but to be presented with a signed agreement to wed a man she had never even heard of was quite another matter.

Did they honestly think that she was docile enough to go mildly along with the plan?

Rebecca shook her head and folded the letter up with shaking fingers, uncertain what to make of this development. Could it perhaps be some sort of ill-conceived joke? Not that Jacob appeared to have much of a sense of humor. It was unfortunate really that he had such a cold way about him, for otherwise he might have been an attractive man.

But those eyes. Never had she felt such scorn. Rebecca shivered in recollection and knew that she could never follow Judith's suggestion, regardless of how it might solve her current difficulties. Should she decide to remarry, there were lots of men right here in Toledo who didn't, well, didn't *unsettle* her so, and surely the kind of accommodating companionship she had shared with Ephraim was the basis of any stable home.

She looked around the courtyard with unseeing eyes, wondering what on earth she should do. Perhaps she could ignore the letter and hope she didn't see this Jacob again. Tunis, the letter said, so clearly he wasn't from near here.

That would explain his dress. And presumably, at some point, he would leave town.

But he was coming back this evening, she recalled with dismay, and rose quickly to her feet, her pulse pounding in her ears. And if she hadn't quite lied to him, she had certainly misled him, she acknowledged with growing annoyance, the audacious thought that followed close on the heels of that admission making her gasp aloud.

Perhaps she could make that work to her advantage and settle this matter once and for all.

Chapter Two

By the time Jacob made his way down the same narrow street later that evening, his normally even temper was restored. He had made a better deal than anticipated on the weaponry and had had a few drinks at a tavern with the swordsmith to celebrate the conclusion of their business. He whistled tunelessly, smiling to himself in recollection of the smoky look one petite dancer had sent his way as she swung her hips provocatively, and hastened his footsteps down the quiet street.

A few minutes to conclude this business of Judith's—he snapped his fingers—and he'd be back at the tavern before that dancer knew he'd even been gone. And in the morning, he'd head back south.

Jacob nodded to himself in satisfaction. There was nothing like a quick, successful trip. He spared a glance to the darkening cloudless sky and began to whistle again as he rounded the last corner. And all neatly concluded well before the autumn storms on the Mediterranean.

He really had to hand it to himself this time, he thought as he tugged the cord beside Rebecca's door with a jaunty gesture and heard the resultant ringing inside the house. This trip had to set a record for success in a hurry. He listened and grinned anew when he caught the faint sound of quick footsteps, certain that the servant's haste was a direct result of Rebecca's presence.

Maybe he wouldn't get the girl in trouble with her mistress after all, Jacob reasoned, his success of the day making him feel a little more generous than he had earlier.

The door swung open, and at the sight of the woman framed there, Jacob flicked a glance at the door and the front of the house before his gaze swung uncertainly back to meet hers. A knowing glint flashed in her dark eyes at his hesitation before she dropped her gaze, and that as much as anything convinced him of her identity, although he still scanned her features once again, unable to reconcile this woman with the unkempt girl who had greeted him earlier.

"Good evening," she said when he didn't speak.

Jacob cleared his throat, wondering why he hadn't noticed the husky timbre of her voice before. "Good evening," he responded evenly, and forced himself to return to his usual businesslike tone. It was undoubtedly the wine that was affecting him, he concluded, reminding himself that he wasn't used to the strength of foreign spirits.

"I trust your mistress is at home?" he asked formally, and the woman shot him another of those knowing glances for some enigmatic reason.

"No, she is not," she responded stiffly, and Jacob stifled a twinge of annoyance. Had he come all the way back here for nothing? Hadn't she delivered his message? Something of his frustration must have shown, for the woman continued hastily before he could demand an explanation.

"She is visiting her family...in the north," she said, her voice oddly tremulous in adding the last detail. Jacob had an uncanny sense that she was lying before she abruptly straightened and looked him right in the eye. "She will be gone for some weeks," she asserted in a tone that brooked no argument, and he held her gaze stubbornly, trying to catch some vestige of hesitancy again.

"But you saw no reason to tell me this earlier?" he demanded sharply, surprised when the woman flushed slightly under his regard. She dropped her gaze and he noted how the thickness of her dark lashes swept her cheeks, how soft her skin looked in the evening light. She was discreetly veiled tonight, but he easily recalled the lush ebony tangle of her hair and imagined how, brushed and clean, it would gleam in the evening's shadows.

"You gave me no chance," she maintained haughtily, the ice in her narrowed eyes when they snapped back to meet his summarily dismissing his thoughts. Jacob reviewed their afternoon conversation quickly in his mind, certain that she had had more than ample opportunity to set the record straight, then braced his hands on his hips.

"That hardly seems reasonable," he charged softly, watching her lips set mutinously at his words. "And now you have doubly wasted my time."

"You should have asked," she shot back, and made to close the door, but Jacob raised one hand quickly, stopping the heavy wooden door with the flat of his hand. The woman's eyes glinted dangerously but he held his ground, amused at the reluctance with which she conceded defeat.

"When will she be back?" he demanded, leaning closer as if to compel her to answer, the soft scent of her body and his instinctive response to it catching him completely off guard.

"Two months," she retorted breathlessly, and made to close the door again, but Jacob braced his foot against it, something in her tone convincing him that she was being less than truthful.

"You're lying," he charged in a low voice, not at all certain of the fact until she flushed absolutely scarlet.

"No," she insisted, but there was little conviction in her tone and they both were aware of it. Jacob stared in silent amazement at her nerve and she eyed him warily, clearly uncertain as to how he would proceed.

Sensing that he was back in control of the conversation, he stepped onto the threshold, smiling to himself in satisfaction when she took a reluctant step backward and released her hold on the door.

"She's here, isn't she?" he demanded to press his advantage, but the woman shook her head wildly.

"No, she's out," she informed him, her voice lower than it had been before. Either she was telling the truth now or she had realized that her tone had given her away before. Jacob regarded her for an instant and she took another step backward, her dark eyes widening in surprise when she backed into the wall opposite the door.

Intent on getting the truth, he leaned over her once more, bracing his knuckles on the wall on either side of her shoulders so she couldn't disappear on him in the recesses of the house.

"Where?" he asked quietly, and she shot a hostile glance upward at the threat underlying his tone.

"I don't know," she pronounced firmly, her eyes daring him to challenge her again, and their gazes locked for a long, charged moment.

"Maybe I should wait for her," Jacob murmured, not knowing where the idea came from, fascinated by the answering flash in her eyes.

"I should think not," she spat indignantly, and he chuckled under his breath, noticing now the fine quality of her veiling.

Jacob picked up the trailing end of the sheer dark silk and rubbed it speculatively between his fingers, not missing her sharp inhalation when his hand came close to her shoulder. Her breasts heaved in indignation, tantalizingly close to his hand, and Jacob tore his gaze away from that ripe curve with an effort, only to be arrested by the wary expression in her dark eyes. He had an urge to reassure her somehow, firmly dismissing the notion before he had the chance to act upon it.

"Such finery for an evening out from under your mistress's thumb," he mused, something twisting inside him as he recalled how quickly she had answered the door. And her hair was covered now, hinting that his earlier conclusions about her maidenly state might have been incorrect. "Perhaps you are expecting a guest?"

"How dare you?" she snapped, and her chin shot up, her eyes bright with unchecked anger. "Never have I met such an insolent, overbearing, rude..."

She got no further before Jacob gave in to his impulse to kiss her.

She struggled briefly, but he was ready for that, locking his arms around her waist as she twisted, savoring the bite of her nails in his shoulders for that instant before she recognized the futility of her struggle and changed her strategy. She went limp and he admired her perseverance even as he set out to overcome it, his fingers spreading to span and stroke her back, his lips teasing and encouraging her to respond.

The sweet taste of her was intoxicating, and when she finally parted her lips with a soft sigh and shyly slipped her hands around his neck, Jacob thought he would come completely undone. Instead he backed her into the wall again and lifted her against him, letting her feel his response to her as he drove his tongue between her lips.

She *was* inexperienced and he found the realization curiously satisfying, cajoling her gently as she gradually opened to his caress, his own response almost overwhelming in its intensity. She moaned and trembled within his embrace and he tightened his grip on her, his head swimming with the taste of wine and honey, the tempting scent of her response.

The sound of a donkey's leisurely hoofbeats on the cobblestones reminded Jacob that the door was still open behind them and brought him reluctantly back to his senses long moments later. He broke off the kiss and took a deep breath, feeling his pulse pounding in his ears as he opened his eyes to find the woman in his arms looking as dazed as he felt. Her lips were soft and swollen and the knowledge that he was responsible almost sent him back for more, but the look of outright fear she shot up at him stopped that thought dead in its tracks.

"Perhaps I shouldn't wait," he teased huskily, her mortified expression confirming his suspicions in an instant.

Warmth suffused his heart and he grinned down at his virginal temptress, unable to resist planting one last kiss on the tip of her nose.

"I'll be back," he whispered into her ear, delighted when she shivered at the ruffle of his breath there, and he boldly licked her earlobe, savoring her indignant gasp before he released her and strode back to the door.

She had folded her arms defiantly across her chest by the time Jacob glanced back over his shoulder, and he noted with pleasure not only the curves he had seen earlier but the tiny shadows cast by her erect nipples. The wariness in her eyes bothered him not in the least, for he knew her passionate response had taken both of them completely off guard.

He had only to kiss her to melt her reserve, and the expression in her eyes revealed that they were both thoroughly aware of that fact. Jacob smiled in anticipation of the merry chase she was sure to lead and winked at her jauntily before he closed the door in his wake, his grin widening when he heard the bolt slide unceremoniously home.

Maybe there was no need to leave Toledo just yet, he concluded as he swung up the street, giving free rein to his whistling again.

Rebecca slammed the bolt with a vengeance, falling back against the door, her heart still tripping unsteadily from that unexpected kiss. Of all the unmitigated nerve! Never had she been so assaulted, and certainly not within the walls of her own home. What sort of barbarians were they in Tunis to tolerate such behavior?

She exhaled raggedly and knotted her fingers together to stop their shaking, not ready yet to confront the kiss itself. If she had had any doubts about Jacob ben Solomon's role as a man come courting, he had more than adequately laid those to rest, she forced herself to acknowledge, and her heart sped once again.

Although somehow Rebecca doubted that Jacob's intentions tonight had anything to do with marriage contracts. She straightened her shoulders and shook her head disapprovingly, tugging off the veil he had so casually fingered and tossing it aside in disgust. Odious man. She dismissed the image of those long fingers moving gently against the cloth, so close, too close, to her breast, and refused to recall the soft brush of the day's growth of his beard against her skin. Calculating barbarian. To think that he intended to seduce the servant before wedding the mistress.

Not that she had been that discouraging, she was forced to admit, feeling her color rise in the darkness. What sort of spell had he cast over her to make her respond so wantonly? She and Ephraim had kissed a hundred times, a thousand times even, but it had never been like that. Rebecca's fingertips rose tentatively to her softened lips and she shivered, feeling inexplicably hot and cold at the same time. She remembered Jacob's promise to return and her stomach leapt unexpectedly before she sternly quelled it.

Ridiculous. The man's behavior was shocking, immoral even, and she would be a fool not to discourage him flatly should he return. She had simply been surprised tonight, Rebecca told herself firmly, resolving not to make such a mistake again.

High-minded resolutions were well and good, but Rebecca soon realized that they weren't going to help her get to sleep. She tossed and turned restlessly, her skin curiously atingle, her mind fabricating wildly improbable scenarios at a furious pace. Sooner or later her thoughts relentlessly returned to the *ketubah* on the desk downstairs, and in the privacy of the inky darkness, she even dared to let herself imagine signing the document and what would follow once she did.

Had she been missing something? Was it possible that marital obligations didn't have to be tedious? This evening had shown that kissing had a hidden dimension Rebecca had never guessed existed, and her bones positively melted when she extrapolated from there.

After all, she was a widow. Who would be the wiser if she indulged in one tiny, short indiscretion?

This was insane. The second kiss would never be as earth-shattering as the first. How many times had she tasted a dish and found it delicious, only to be disappointed the next time she tried it? Closing her eyes with a sigh, she forced herself to accept the fact that she was never going to kiss Jacob again to find out.

Never. Not under any circumstances. After all, he was insufferably arrogant.

She tried to summon Ephraim's face in her mind's eye to cement that point but found instead Jacob's square-jawed visage filling her inner vision, his brown eyes darkening almost to black with intent as he leaned toward her. Rebecca's eyes flew open in shock and she stared at the ceiling, unable to shake Jacob's image despite her best efforts.

It was no consolation to know that she had been right in her suspicion that he would be attractive when the coldness left his eyes, and she reviewed now a myriad of details she didn't even realize she had noted. The wavy thickness of his dark brown hair spilling over his collar, the dusting of silver at his temples, the uncompromising line of those firm lips and the way they softened when he smiled that wry smile.

And his hands. Rebecca closed her eyes and saw their tapered length playing with her veil again, felt their strength splayed across her back, and she smiled despite herself when she recalled how gentle his touch had become when she capitulated to his kiss.

As if she ever had a choice. The man undoubtedly knew what he was about.

She shook her head and forced herself to think clearly. Just because Jacob had marvelous hands, and perhaps rather attractively broad shoulders, was no reason for her to lose her head over things. Maybe her fingers did itch to tangle in that unbelievably soft thickness of his dark hair, but the man was bent on seduction, no more, no less, and he would be gone as soon as that occurred. It was her moral duty to remain steadfast in the face of his advances.

An indiscretion could result in a child and how would she explain that? Ephraim's child born almost a year after his death? It was unlikely that she would be able to convince her neighbors of that.

She thought of the *ketubah* again and shook her head determinedly in the darkness.

Never. Not under any circumstances. Not even to find out about *that*.

After all, what did she know about the man? Was she to take this unknown Judith entirely at her word and meekly move to Tunis with this single-minded man? Certainly his assumption that she would sign a marriage contract without even discussing it with her showed his high-handedness, and he was undoubtedly, insufferably sure of himself.

Rebecca remembered the imprint of those strong hands curving around the back of her waist and bit her lip in indecision.

Besides, she told herself firmly, there was the minor complication that she had outrightly *lied* to him about her own presence—or absence, as it were. There was no way that she could set matters straight without looking like a fool. And she wasn't willing to do that for him or any man. Rebecca ran one hand through her loose hair and rolled over with new resolve, noting that the moon had already set.

She really had to get some sleep. Lazily, she weighed the relative merits of getting up, lighting a fire and warming some milk against staying comfortably in bed, her thoughts scattering abruptly when something rattled in the courtyard below.

Rebecca sat up with a jolt, her gaze flying to the single door that led to the narrow balcony overlooking the courtyard. Her heart positively stopped when the rattle grew louder, then was followed by a crash of breaking tile.

Any remaining doubts that someone was in her house were summarily dismissed when a man cursed gruffly and thoroughly under his breath.

"You'll wake her up!" growled another deep voice, and Rebecca almost gasped aloud.

Two men! In her house!

What was she going to do?

Her heart began to pound in her ears and she scanned the familiar contents of her room, looking for some sort of weapon but finding nothing. Think, think, think, she scolded herself as the men muttered to each other in incomprehensibly low voices.

Men in her house. Intending to do what? She told herself not to panic and strained to hear their words. Whatever they were saying, they seemed to have no plans to come upstairs.

Emboldened by that thought, she crept silently across the room, determined to eavesdrop on their conversation if she could. She picked up a brass plate on her way, tucking it under her arm, although she had no idea what she would do with it if pressed.

Having its cold weight against her side made her feel braver, though, and she hugged it tight as she gained the door and crawled on all fours out onto the balcony. The half wall facing the courtyard was solid stucco and Rebecca appreciated its lack of openwork for the first time, leaning her back against the cool plaster and straining her ears.

"If I *knew* what we were looking for, I'd *tell* you," one man rasped in evident exasperation, and the other sighed with annoyance.

"How are we supposed to know if we find it?" he hissed, and Rebecca heard tiles click as they were moved. They must be looking behind the broken tiles she had stacked against the walls, she reasoned, wondering what on earth they were hoping to find.

"He said we'd know when we found it," the first muttered, and the other fairly growled in response.

"Oh, that narrows it right down," he snarled. "And you think it's in the courtyard."

"I told you that already," the first snapped impatiently, and something slid across the tile. That terra-cotta planter in the corner, Rebecca concluded, her curiosity slowly overcoming her.

What were they looking for?

"Look around," the second man growled impatiently. "The courtyard is completely empty."

"Then it must be hidden," the first explained in a tone he might use with a particularly slow child.

"Hidden?" the second repeated skeptically, and Rebecca could almost feel his eyes scanning the small courtyard. "I'll bet it's *hidden* somewhere else," he concluded, his words almost sending Rebecca scurrying back to bed as she visualized him heading for the stairs.

"Forget it," the first commanded sharply, and as if they had just realized how loud their voices had become, they both shushed each other simultaneously.

"You're going to wake her up," the second warned, his voice so low that Rebecca could barely catch the words.

"That's why we can't go looking all over the house," the first explained patiently.

"She doesn't know?"

"No, and *he* wants it to stay that way."

What didn't she know? And who wanted to keep her from knowing? Rebecca pursed her lips and frowned into the darkness, trying to fathom a guess at what the two were looking for.

The first man sighed. "We've looked behind all these broken tiles," he commented with frustration. "The only other thing is the fountain and—" he grunted "—it's fastened down pretty thoroughly. I'm going to check the library."

"We have to keep looking," the second insisted, but the first man's words had brought Rebecca bolt upright.

Of course! They were looking for the secret package in the fountain! It must be valuable after all!

And she had to make sure they didn't find it, her frenzied mind concluded within a blink of an eye.

Her first impulse was to leap to her feet and declare her presence. Fortunately, her practical voice shouted that idea down, pointing out that she was outnumbered and didn't even know whether the intruders were armed. She slumped against the wall in dejection and the brass plate slipped down to tap against the floor, drawing her gaze as her eyes slowly widened.

It just might work.

She crawled back to bed as silently as she could, picking up all of the other brass ornaments and trinket boxes in her room along the way. She piled them all on the plate and set it carefully on the side of the cushions that made up her bed, taking a deep breath as she took her place on the cushions and kept the plate steady with one hand.

It was now or never, she reasoned over the pounding of her heart, holding her breath as she deliberately flipped the plate so that it and all upon it tumbled to the floor in disarray.

The brass rattled and clattered and banged much more satisfactorily than she could have anticipated. In the flush of success, she impulsively moaned aloud, wailing "Oh, no!" in the groggiest voice she could manage.

With satisfaction, she heard two muffled oaths in the courtyard below and leaned back against the pillows, grinning victoriously at the sound of stealthy footsteps racing through the hall below and out into the cobbled street.

Victory was notoriously short-lived however, the results of the intruders' activities obvious even in the smoky shadows of the predawn. Some of the bigger pieces of tile were broken, much to Rebecca's annoyance, although her displeasure grew into outrage when she saw the damage the rest of her home had sustained.

Ephraim's study adjoining the kitchen was a disaster, books tumbled haphazardly to the floor, their spines cracked and pages awry, the shelves swept clean. Rebecca picked her way through the mess and replaced a few books before she gave the task up for the moment, the sight of such wanton disregard for the value of the volumes sickening her.

The few trinkets on Ephraim's desk were cast aside, and the contents of the single drawer spilled haphazardly across the surface, a bottle of ink on its side slowly leaking a dark shadow across the white parchment. Rebecca righted the bottle and scooped the stained document out of the way, seeing as she did that it was the *ketubah* from Tunis and finding this unexpectedly upsetting.

She carried the document into the kitchen and made as good a job as she could of wiping off the ink, though the damage was already done. In the process she managed to get some of it on her thumb and the front of her chemise.

While she was casting around for something to wipe her hands on, she noticed the door.

The heavy wood slab had been cut so that the bolt was carved right out of the door, and Rebecca marveled that she had heard nothing. She caught one fingertip under the lip of the door and it swung easily inward, leaving the bolt and the small section of the door attached to it hanging pointlessly from the frame as she stared out into the silent street.

Broken tiles were one thing, but this would have to be fixed immediately, and Rebecca gritted her teeth in anticipation of the cost. She glanced back over her shoulder to the courtyard and sent the door shut with a flick of her wrist. She lifted one of the small stones from the handmill in the kitchen with a grunt and dropped in on the floor behind the door. The stone needed grinding anyway, she reasoned as she pushed it against the door with her toe and turned to pace determinedly back into the courtyard.

It was about time she had a look at the package that was causing all this trouble.

A few more stray leaves had gathered in the bowl of the fountain and Rebecca cleaned them out, noting that she was barely able to discern the crack in the early morning shadows. Reluctant to light a lamp and show her neighbors that she was awake, she ran her fingers over the cool stone and found the hairline crack that marked the secret compartment.

There was no way to get her fingers in the space when it was shut so tightly and Rebecca scrabbled at it with her fingernails for a moment before she admitted that it was unlikely to work. She scanned the courtyard for inspiration, finally fetching a knife from the kitchen and trying to pry the compartment open with that. The door wouldn't budge and she made one last heroic effort, grunting as she leaned her weight on the knife handle and snapped off the blade.

Rebecca sat back on her heels and swept her hair out of her eyes impatiently. There had to be a clever way to do this, she reasoned, squinting speculatively at the stubborn bowl, its bulky silhouette becoming clearer as the sky lightened and the shadows were dispersed.

A catch. There had to be a latch or a trigger of some kind. Inspired anew, Rebecca ran her hands around the bowl, searching for something that wasn't smooth. She tried to wiggle every little ornament on the carved central fount, twisted, fingered and coaxed everything that looked like even a remote possibility, but all to no avail. The sun peeked over the roof of her house and shone down in the courtyard, only to find her scrambling on her belly under the bowl in an attempt to find the secret latch.

Finally she sat back on her heels and fairly spat at the enigmatic fountain in frustration. She crossed her arms over her chest as she glared at it and wondered if the marble could mock her. Too bad she hadn't just secreted the bundle somewhere else, for she was not likely to lay eyes on it again at this rate.

But then, the two intruders might have found it if it hadn't been so safely hidden. She wondered then if they would be back and recalled the state of her door, pushing to her feet and looking down at the state of herself with dismay.

Yusuf.

Yusuf knew everyone and everything and he would know who would fix her door without asking too many questions or spreading too many rumors.

And by now, he would already be drinking mint tea down at the market, so he would be easy to find.

Jacob's buoyant mood had not been dispelled by the morning. In fact he was looking forward to seeing Rebecca's servant again and already formulating a plan in the back of his mind for that encounter. How Judith would laugh to learn that he was having romantic thoughts about a servant!

Jacob grinned to himself as he made his way to morning prayers in the synagogue, conceding that it might be time he heeded his aunt's urging and found a wife. Marriage might not be such an ordeal with a woman that fired his blood as this one did. She undoubtedly could manage his household if she was already doing that for Rebecca, and he dismissed the issue of their class differences easily.

After all, who would even know her origins if he brought her to Tunis?

Her innocence was obvious from her startled response to his kiss, and Jacob's heart warmed at the recollection, his determination to woo her properly growing the more he thought about it. He should send a message to Judith and let her know that he would be delayed. After all, Jacob admitted with a smile, he could make the excuse that he was waiting for Rebecca's return.

When he did unexpectedly see Rebecca's servant later that morning, all his gallant ideas scattered like the leaves in the wind.

Did the girl have no shame at all?

She was sitting at one of the cafés that faced onto the crowded market, and even cloaked and veiled, he had no doubt that it was her. A dark-skinned man of Berber descent sat opposite her, a Muslim by his green turban, and Jacob was shocked to see how Rebecca's servant leaned confidentially toward the man to speak as though they were on very intimate terms. Unable to help himself, Jacob stepped back into the shadows of a stall overflowing with textiles, where he could watch the scene unfold without being observed.

Perhaps he had been mistaken to assume that Rebecca would employ a girl of her own faith within her home, he speculated. Maybe Jews ran their homes differently here in Andalusia, although he knew Judith would have plenty to say about this, if it were truly the case. The woman twisted in her seat and Jacob saw the yellow circle on her cloak that marked her of the same faith as he. He summarily dismissed the thought, watching with narrowed eyes, confused by the way she was veiled like a married woman.

Was it possible she was wed to this Berber? He had heard that the faiths mixed here in Toledo, but that explanation simply didn't make any sense, given the situation. Why would she be working as a servant, then? And why would they be sitting together in a café? He knew well enough how possessive Muslims were of their women and how uncommon it was to see them in public. A quick glance around the *souk* confirmed his conclusions; the few women visible were either Christians or Jews by their dress.

Perhaps women simply veiled themselves in public here out of modesty as Frankish women did.

Jacob quickly saw that the serving woman was begging the man seated opposite her for something, the very sight of her appeal turning Jacob's stomach. There was no question that it was the same woman and less question that she was very familiar with the Berber. The Berber wore the flowing trousers of his people that Jacob knew well from Tunis; his mocha skin creased into a network of lines around his eyes that bespoke of time in the sun, and his every gesture was studied and slow. The woman looked almost feverish in contrast, her insistence on some point making the man appear even more lethargic than he probably was.

Rebecca's servant laid her hand on the man's arm as Jacob watched in amazement, and the man smiled calmly, slipping his own dark fingers over hers and giving her hand a meaningful squeeze that explained everything to Jacob. Scandalous behavior. The woman leaned back in her chair with a catlike smile, apparently satisfied about whatever had been negotiated, while her companion waved easily for his tab.

Jacob had no doubt what had been negotiated. He blinked and feigned interest in the woven goods of the stall before him, trying to fit this revelation into his previous conclusions while the vendor extolled the virtues of his goods. Had he completely misread her response to him? He had been certain that she had been inexperienced, that she, too, had been surprised by the intensity of their kiss. Jacob flicked a glance across the square, his chin snapping up when he found the table they had occupied empty.

An assignation? In the morning? Jacob's lips thinned and any plans he had been harboring for his next encounter with the woman took a decided turn for the worse.

"You truly heard nothing?" Yusuf demanded once again in his melodic voice, and Rebecca shook her head as she scampered along behind him, feeling as completely graceless as she always did in his presence.

"Nothing at all," she insisted, determined not to reveal anything of what she had overheard the previous night. Yusuf shot an assessing glance over his shoulder and she did her best not to squirm, unable to do more than hope she had been successful, when he arched one brow and turned to watch his step again.

"You must show me the damage," he commented quietly, and Rebecca nodded hastily in agreement.

In a few moments they were back at the house, Yusuf's lips tightening almost imperceptibly as he assessed the damaged door. He leveled a look at her and Rebecca folded her hands together, certain he was going to ask her more questions. Mercifully he let the matter drop.

"You need a new door," was all he said, and she agreed. "It would be best if we stayed here," he added, beckoning to the neighbor's boy and dispatching him to a murmured address. The boy scooted off down the street, intent on his mission, and Yusuf's strikingly green eyes lifted to meet hers again.

He knew she had lied.

Rebecca's fingers twisted together nervously even as she knew that Yusuf would simply wait for her to explain. How well she knew that he could weasel information out of her by studying her thoughtfully until she was so self-conscious that she blurted out the truth. At moments like this, she thought it decidedly unfair that he could so easily see through her harmless little lies.

"Would you like some tea?" she offered for lack of a better idea, and Yusuf smothered a smile before gesturing gracefully for her to proceed him into the house.

There was absolutely no doubt what that was all about, Jacob told himself wryly as he leaned back against the wall around the corner, wondering why it bothered him so much that Rebecca's hired help was making use of the house in her mistress's absence. It wasn't exactly uncommon, even in Tunis, where Judith maintained that things were much more rigid. But to think that she was so bold as to take a man into the house in broad daylight!

And a Muslim! It was unthinkable that she should stray outside her faith for her... satisfaction. That word didn't sit well with Jacob at all and he pursed his lips thoughtfully, wondering how to proceed. His errant mind supplied an image of the man's fingers splayed against the woman's long creamy neck and he shoved away from the wall in annoyance, pacing back to the *souk* with such a dangerous expression in his eyes that the few souls who dared to cross his path took but one look and quickly scurried out of his way.

"Did Ephraim say anything to you before he died?" Yusuf inquired softly as he methodically stirred sugar into his mint tea.

Rebecca glanced up in surprise, squinting against the bright sunlight in the courtyard where they sat.

"Say anything like what?"

Yusuf shot her an enigmatic look. "You tell me," was all he said, and she frowned into the reflections in her tea as she tried to recall.

"He asked me to fetch the rabbi," she said slowly, flicking an upward glance in time to catch Yusuf's methodical nod. "I thought he just had indigestion, from eating at the tavern, because he hadn't been sick." She turned the cup around and around with one fingertip, easily recalling the bizarre events of that night and her own confusion.

"He thought differently?" Yusuf asked in a low voice, and Rebecca nodded quickly.

"Yes," she admitted, still puzzled by Ephraim's conviction. "He was certain that he was going to die and I couldn't understand why he would think that," she mused, almost to herself.

"But he insisted," her companion prompted, and Rebecca shook herself away from her memories.

"Yes," she agreed with a frown, and shrugged her shoulders. "So I went to the rabbi, but when we came back, he was already dead."

She took a quick drink of hot tea to cover her discomfort at that recollection, painfully aware of Yusuf's gaze resting steadily on her and the feeling that the sun was unaccountably warm for this time of year. He stirred his tea one last time, then removed the spoon, carefully tapping it once on the side of the cup before placing it smoothly on the table.

"Where did he die?" he asked quietly, and Rebecca began to point to the fatal spot behind Yusuf before she remembered the package. She almost checked her gesture, but then continued as if nothing had occurred to her, hoping that Yusuf didn't perceive her hesitation.

"On the threshold to the kitchen," she answered with a sweep of her hand, which was almost true. "I assumed he had come downstairs to find help."

Only now she wondered whether Ephraim had made his way downstairs to hide the package in the fountain. But what could Ephraim have had of value, especially that she wouldn't have known about? Rebecca's gaze trailed of its own volition to the stone structure cast in morning sunlight and she wondered. She looked back to Yusuf and he glanced quickly down at his cup, the expression in his eyes veiled by his lids, and she wondered how much he had observed, how much he knew.

Was she reading too much into every little gesture? Rebecca had no idea and her lack of sleep was not helping her judgment at all. Mercifully, she had been spared the ordeal of meeting Jacob ben Solomon again this morning.

An uncharacteristically awkward silence stretched between the two of them and Rebecca cast around her mind for something neutral to say to fill the quiet.

She was saved from having to find another topic of conversation by the shout of the neighbor's boy in the street. Both she and Yusuf rose of one accord to greet him and Rebecca wondered fleetingly who was more relieved at the termination of the conversation.

Chapter Three

The hour was late when a firm tap came on Rebecca's new door and she briefly considered not answering. She sat back on her heels in the courtyard in the soft darkness and looked toward the door, chewing her lip indecisively, her fruitless search for the secret latch momentarily forgotten.

The bells jangled impatiently and she jumped to her feet, suddenly certain that she knew who had come to call and finding herself halfway to the door before she realized what she was doing. Against her better judgment Rebecca opened the door, shoving her hair back with an impatient gesture, and met the anger simmering in Jacob's eyes with surprise.

"Good evening," she began uncertainly, but he was in no mood for formalities, judging by the way he swept into her house and abruptly pulled the door from her numb fingers, closing it resolutely behind him.

"Good evening," he returned in a dangerously low tone, folding his arms across his chest and positively glaring down at her. He was taller than she remembered and that realization did little to reassure her. Beyond a doubt, he was spoiling for a fight, and Rebecca's heartbeat accelerated in trepidation.

"Good evening," she managed to say again, relieved to note that her voice did not waver. Jacob pursed his lips and eyed her assessingly for a moment before he continued smoothly.

"There's something we need to discuss," he said, his countenance set like stone, and once again Rebecca had the sense that she was not going to like whatever it was he had come to say.

"Perhaps in the morning," she suggested in a rush, attempting to gesture him politely toward the door, but Jacob was having none of that.

"Now," he confirmed flatly. Rebecca stepped hastily back from the door at the resolution in his tone, determined to leave as much space as possible between them.

The foyer suddenly seemed suffocatingly small and she made to retreat into the bigger courtyard, but Jacob's fingers closed immediately around her upper arm and pulled her to a halt as if he thought she intended to flee. She dared to flick a glance upward and recoiled at the cold fury in his narrowed eyes, but he did not release her.

"You misled me," he fairly growled.

Confronted with such a bald statement of truth, Rebecca did not know what to say. She could hardly deny it, and whatever justification she had thought she had now seemed painfully inadequate. Would she not be annoyed in his place? It had been a childish game she had played and now she could only feel ashamed at her own behavior.

She looked down at the floor, opened her mouth and shut it uneasily when no facile explanation came to mind. There was nothing she could say to appease his perfectly justified annoyance at her deception. Jacob's fingers tightened on her arm as though he would prompt the words from her, and she jumped when his other hand gripped her chin, forcing her to look up.

"Why?" he demanded bluntly, and she stared back into his eyes helplessly, painfully aware of his proximity and the sense of intimacy created by the shadows pressing around them. Her gaze strayed to the uncompromising line of his lips and she watched in fascination as a muscle twitched in his jaw.

"I meant no harm," she admitted huskily, and his fingers tightened at her admission of guilt.

"And I had expected a pretty denial." He bit the words out with a derisive laugh and Rebecca flicked another glance upward to discover that his anger remarkably seemed to have dissipated, his expression now one of ironic amusement. His mood had changed suddenly, that much she could see, but she had no idea how or why.

"Truly I underestimated you," he mused, his tone as warm as the fingertip that now gently traced the line of her jaw. Rebecca shivered at his caress and Jacob smiled a predatory smile, his strong fingers slipping into the tangle of hair at her nape and pulled her unerringly toward him.

Rebecca sighed with satisfaction as Jacob's lips closed over hers possessively and she surrendered wholeheartedly to his kiss, immeasurably relieved that he wasn't angry with her anymore. That she had the unexpected chance to taste him again was no small benefit, either, and she reveled in his caress, opening her mouth to his exploring tongue. He groaned deep in his throat at her submission and gathered her closer, his hands gentle now, his breath feathering over her throat as he kissed and nibbled, and Rebecca was swept away once more by his touch.

Jacob's hand cupped her breast and she gasped in delight as her body responded of its own accord, the nipple tightening even while the flesh seemed to swell to fill his hand. He gently pinched and rolled her responsive nipple between his finger and thumb through her kirtle and Rebecca moaned involuntarily. His smile flashed in the shadows before he nudged aside the fabric and bent to take the rosy bud in his mouth.

He suckled her gently at first and she shivered at the unfamiliar sensation, arching toward him, tangling her fingers in his hair and straining to her toes. Jacob lifted his head and she noted the speculation in his eyes, but before he could speak she framed his jaw with her hands and kissed him with all her pent-up passion. Never had she imagined that she was missing so much and she was seized by an irrational urge to see this intimacy through to its climax, the very thought making something melt within her.

Jacob trailed a row of burning kisses along her jaw and outlined her ear with his tongue, and Rebecca shivered before she mimicked his gesture. His arms tightened around her and he pulled her to the tips of her toes, his lips returning to plunder hers once again, and she felt more alive than she ever had before.

Rebecca forced her tongue between Jacob's teeth and he growled as something ripped, but she didn't care, the feel of his rough hands on her bare breasts making her moan in anticipation. Jacob pressed her against the wall and she felt the unyielding cold plaster against her shoulder blades, her heart tripping erratically at the imprint of his erection against her hip.

"This is madness."

The muttered words didn't sink in until Jacob pulled away and Rebecca shivered at the sudden absence of his warmth. He exhaled raggedly and ran one hand through his hair before he took a deliberate step backward, studiously avoiding Rebecca's eyes.

"No," she whispered, and his hot gaze flicked to her, his nostrils flaring as he cast a glance over her. Rebecca could feel the cool air on her bare breasts, her tight nipples straining against the darkness, her breath coming in short gasps and her hair falling in disarray over her shoulders. Jacob looked similarly disheveled and she reached up to wind her fingers into the thick curls of his hair. His dark eyes locked with hers and she caught her breath at the fire burning there.

"I don't want you to regret anything," Jacob murmured in a low voice, only a slight waver in his tone revealing what the words cost him.

Rebecca's heart wrenched that it was concern for her that brought him to a halt, and she couldn't bear the thought of him leaving. Not now, when every fiber of her being was alive as it had never been before. Not yet.

Not before she finally *knew*.

"I want you," she whispered, and his eyes blazed though he didn't move.

"No regrets?" he demanded quietly, and Rebecca closed her eyes against the meaning behind his words. This night was all she could ask of him. She took a deep breath and forced herself to consider the implications of that, easily concluding in her aroused state that it was enough.

It would have to be.

She saw the flicker of surprise in Jacob's eyes as she reached for him, then his dark lashes settled on his cheeks and he groaned as she drove her tongue between his lips. His hands cupped her buttocks and she ground her hips against him, determined to have this night and the consequences be damned. He murmured something unintelligible against her throat, then scooped her up into his arms and strode purposefully into the house.

When he hesitated in the courtyard, Rebecca directed him to the stairs with a gesture and up to her room, barely noticing how his lips thinned when he carried her over the threshold of the room and cast an appraising eye over its contents.

Jacob set Rebecca unceremoniously on her feet and disposed of her kirtle with an efficiency that took her breath away. The coldness she had glimpsed in his eyes, which might have made her regret her impulsiveness, gradually thawed into a grudging admiration as he stared at her nudity in the shadows.

"Your turn," she whispered shyly into the silence, fighting against an urge to cover herself, and his lips twisted, his eyes holding hers as he quickly stripped off his own garments. In an instant he stood nude, as well, not an arm's length away from her, and Rebecca dared to tear her eyes away from his and look.

He was magnificently well proportioned, a vision of lean muscled strength, dark hair thick on his chest and scattered over his legs and arms. Her gaze landed on his erection and it seemed to grow under her perusal, that realization sending a heated flush over her cheeks, and her gaze scampered back to meet Jacob's eyes.

"Changing your mind?" he asked, his voice low and teasing, the warmth in his tone dismissing all of Rebecca's doubts.

She shook her head slowly, liking the way his eyes darkened with intent, and she stepped closer, brushing her fingertips experimentally across the end of his masculinity. He inhaled sharply and she smiled at this acknowledgment of her effect on him, her pulse pounding in her ears as she leaned forward and tentatively licked one of his flat nipples. Jacob's arms closed around her, his breath warm in her ear as he lifted the weight of her hair out of his way.

"Temptress," he whispered raggedly, and she smiled against his skin, lifting her lips for his kiss. His fingers gripped her hair and held her captive beneath his questing lips, his other hand meandering over her breast, her stomach, her hip, and finally diving into the nest of curls between her thighs.

Rebecca parted her legs to accommodate him and he growled against her throat, the touch of his fingertip sending her arching against him. He chuckled with satisfaction into the soft spot behind her ear, his kiss demanding, his sure touch setting Rebecca writhing against him.

She found herself suddenly on her back, wedged very satisfactorily between the softness of the cushions and the uncompromising solidity of Jacob. He slipped his weight between her thighs and she sighed in capitulation, savoring his strength as she grasped his shoulders and stared up into his eyes.

His fingertip teased and cajoled her hidden pearl even as his lips did the same to her mouth, and Rebecca dug her nails into his flesh when an unexpected flush stole over her skin. She tensed when she felt Jacob's bulk nudge against her, but he murmured reassuringly, threading the fingers of her one hand carefully between the strength of his.

With a slow smile that launched a drizzle of honey through her veins, he slid their entwined hands beneath her neck and Rebecca smiled back as she relaxed, reaching up to touch his face with her free hand as he slid carefully within her. She traced the line of his jaw beneath it, his ear, the threads of silver at his temple, as she adjusted to the pleasing weight of him inside her.

Jacob seemed to sag against her for a moment before he leaned his weight on his elbow and his fingers resumed their caressing, his lips wandering over her throat and shoulders as he began to move slowly within her. Rebecca shuddered beneath his experienced assault, barely able to press intense kisses against his flesh as her senses were overwhelmed by sensation.

She barely had time to acknowledge that she had been missing something marvelous before her heartbeat raced suddenly. She sensed her body reaching for something, her eyes widening in surprise as her womb contracted and a jolt tripped along her veins.

Rebecca looked to Jacob leaning over her in the shadows and he grinned, the brightness of his eyes and the tight grip of his fingers around hers the last thing she knew before the world startlingly exploded into a thousand sparks of light and she heard herself cry out.

Jacob rolled to his back with a groan as the last spasm emptied him completely, taking the woman with him so that she sprawled atop him, her thick hair falling across his face and tickling his nose. He closed his eyes and let his senses fill with the smell of her, the softness of her pressed against him, the almost imperceptible sound of her breath as she slept.

He flicked an affectionate glance down at her and was filled with a proprietary pride that he had been the first to show her the fullness of making love, absently admiring the dark crescent of her lashes against her creamy skin. Carefully he untangled their fingers, spreading hers across his chest, liking the look of their delicacy against his skin.

Sweet as honey, he mused, and felt his body respond to the very thought of her writhing beneath him just moments before, her eyes wide with surprise. An innocent seductress. Jacob swept one hand gently across her cheek, marveling anew at the softness of her, and she stirred sleepily against him, burrowing her nose into his chest hair as if to demonstrate that she had no intention of moving.

Who would have thought that such a sweet conquest would come so easily? He ran his fingers through the thickness of her dark hair and spread it over the two of them with a wry smile, recalling the jolt that had tripped through him when she had confessed that she wanted him.

She had redefined "irresistible" when she had said that, standing before him with her breasts bare, her hair wild, her eyes smoky with passion, and he knew that the image of her would live in his memory forever. No suspicions of what she had done with the Muslim could have kept him from her at that moment.

He spared a downward glance and smothered a smile. Completely irresistible, he corrected himself, his hand straying to caress the smooth curve of her breast. She murmured something against his skin but did not awaken, positively purring as she resettled herself into the indent of his shoulder.

She was a study in contradictions, of that much Jacob was certain. A wanton who knew nothing of the ways of lovemaking. A deceiver who honestly confessed her guilt when confronted with it. He frowned into the darkness, his fingers playing idly with her ebony hair, and wondered whether he would ever know what she was really thinking before he caught himself.

What was he thinking? One night was all that they had promised each other and one night would be the extent of this little liaison. Tomorrow he had to head back to Tunis.

Hadn't they already agreed that this would be no more than a pleasant diversion?

And hadn't she readily agreed to his condition? Jacob's lips thinned and he forced himself to give her the benefit of the doubt. After all, he had proposed the one-night liaison, and he would not be the one to have regrets before it was even over.

Fortunately the dawn was long away. Jacob grinned in anticipation and hugged the woman tighter as he planned how he would wake her up, resolving that he would have to find out her name just before he fell into a satisfied slumber.

She was gone when Jacob stirred sleepily, though the indent that his hand strayed to of its own accord was still warm. He stared at the darkened ceiling, acknowledging that it was still early in the morning, and listened for some hint of what had awakened him at such an hour.

He caught the low rumble of a masculine voice and came fully alert at the sound. Rolling silently to his stomach so he could see the door, Jacob spotted the woman sitting on the balcony outside. She was evidently listening to what was going on below, her dark brows pulled together in a frown.

She sensed the weight of his gaze upon her and flicked a glance in his direction, lifting one finger to her lips in a gesture for silence when their eyes caught and held. Jacob nodded, and to his annoyance she seemingly dismissed his presence as she returned her attention to the muted sounds drifting up from below.

He crept from the bed and found his chausses, silently donning them and checking that he had his knife before he crawled pantherlike across the tiled floor to her side. That she was aware of him he had no doubt, for she tensed as he drew closer and shot a quick glance in his direction when he reached her side. That made him feel a little better and he settled himself carefully against the wall beside her.

Amazingly she had a large brass plate tucked tightly under her arm and Jacob couldn't help but smile when he saw it. He lifted one brow inquiringly and she flushed so crimson that he could see it even in the shadows. His heart swelled affectionately and he slipped one arm reassuringly around her waist. When she glanced up at him in alarm and resisted his gesture, he tapped the scabbard of his knife pointedly, and she smothered an answering smile, resolutely hugging her plate even tighter as she leaned against him.

A resounding crash from below sent them both upright with a jolt, bringing Jacob abruptly back to the present. His arm tightened instinctively around the woman and it seemed to him that she nestled closer when men's voices rose unmistakably from below.

"Now you've done it!" muttered one man, and with difficulty Jacob resisted the urge to peek over the edge of the balcony.

"Me? You're the one who keeps slipping. What are you going to do when she wakes up?"

"We'll do what we have to," the first retorted grimly, and the woman before Jacob stiffened at what was clearly a reference to her.

"Sure," the second sneered. "*He* said to see she wasn't hurt."

"There won't be a choice if she sees us and you know it." The words sent a chill through Jacob, and the way the woman went completely still before him told him that he had correctly understood the threat. He pulled her closer, spreading his fingers to span her ribs.

"What if she knows where it is?" the second man argued now. "If we don't find it and she's dead, I wouldn't want to face him."

"She isn't going to wake up," the first hissed again, and dropped his voice so that Jacob had to strain his ears. "Not unless you keep shouting and breaking things."

Their voices dropped to an incoherent rumble and they seemed to move away. Jacob bent over the woman and murmured one word into the curve of her ear.

"What?" he asked, and she shook her head immediately. Either she didn't know or she wasn't going to tell him, he concluded, wondering if these intruders had anything to do with Rebecca's absence.

Had Rebecca gotten herself into some sort of trouble and left town, callously abandoning her servant to deal with the matter? He leaned back against the half wall with narrowed eyes, letting his mind work through the possibilities, disliking how much the thought of this woman being poorly used bothered him, especially since he had resolved never to see her again.

Impatient with the path his thoughts were taking, Jacob shoved to his knees, ignoring the restraining hand the woman placed on his arm. Slowly he rose until he could just barely see over the edge of the half wall, praising the shadows that shrouded his presence as he watched the two men below.

The woman made to rise beside him but he held her down with one hand and a firmness that brooked no argument, relieved when she struggled only briefly against him before conceding the point and settling back to the floor. Jacob glanced at her, not surprised to find her arms folded stubbornly across her chest and her lips set mutinously, but he looked quickly away before she could catch his eye.

The intruders' behavior was curious, he had to acknowledge as he watched them poke and prod the tiles of the courtyard. They tugged experimentally at the stone cornice carved into the outside wall, tapped on the graceful pillars that faced the narrow arcade that ran around the perimeter of the courtyard. Jacob frowned and shook his head in confusion, wondering what they sought in the house.

"What are they looking for?" he asked almost silently as he leaned over the woman again. She shot him a sharp look.

"I don't know," she mouthed with flashing eyes, hugging her plate tighter to her chest. Yet again he had that uncanny sense that she wasn't being totally honest with him.

"You're lying," he mouthed back, stunned by the fear that shot through her eyes before she resolutely looked away. He reached for her chin with one finger, wanting only to look into her eyes, but she jerked away, scooting an arm's length down the wall. Jacob frowned at the floor, trying to guess the source of her fear, surprised when he glanced up to find her watching him warily.

"They've been here before?" he guessed, and the way she bit her lip nervously and nodded was more than enough to send that curious protectiveness raging through him again. Without another thought, Jacob crept toward the stairs.

"Stay right here," he told her firmly when he drew alongside her, holding her gaze for a long charged moment until she reluctantly dropped her eyes.

Unable to resist the temptation, Jacob leaned over and kissed her thoroughly, tasting her fear on her tongue, seeking to reassure her with that one short embrace. After a moment of resistance, she melted against him and he almost forgot what he had intended to do. When he pulled away, Jacob didn't trust himself to look at her again before he continued down the stairs.

He gained the courtyard without his presence being detected by the two intruders, so intent were they on their task, and he paused for a moment in the protection of the shadows, planning his strategy. One of the men, the slimmer one, advanced into the arcade near him, and his pulse raced even though the man was completely unaware of his presence.

Jacob bent and silently retrieved a fist-size stone from the closest flower bed, gripping it carefully as the man drew nearer, studiously bent over the tiles lining the base of the wall. He tapped each one, fiddled with its corners, scratched at the grout surrounding it, then slipped a little closer to Jacob to examine the next tile similarly.

One tile at a time, he progressed with mind-numbing slowness. Jacob waited impatiently, certain the man would be able to hear his heartbeat each time he drew closer, cursing the man's methodical progress and the band of moonlight that shone traitorously into the space between them.

Finally Jacob could wait no more.

He stepped forward and lifted the stone quickly, his heart stopping when the man sensed his presence and cast a look over his shoulder.

"What the...?" he cried out, and Jacob writhed inwardly at his failure, leaping forward to finish the deed.

The intruder moved just before Jacob struck him, the blow only grazing his temple. Momentarily dazed, the man fell back against the wall and lifted his hand to his head, but Jacob had already turned to confront the second thief.

"Who are you?" the man demanded sharply, but Jacob only drew his knife in response, watching a cold gleam settle in the man's eyes as he drew a similar blade.

He really ought to have practiced more of this, Jacob thought wildly as he dodged the man's first attack in the nick of time. Years of trading along safe routes had made him soft and much slower than he used to be, but this was not a good time to speculate on whether or not he had become too slow.

He jabbed and his blade grazed his opponent's forearm, the resulting rush of adrenaline sending Jacob lunging after the man with strikes in rapid succession. Despite the fact that he didn't connect again, the man suddenly cast aside his blade and threw up his hands in defeat.

Too easy, Jacob concluded, and turned to see his woman slam her brass plate with a resounding crack over the head of the man he had thought no longer a threat. Jacob watched as the man crumpled to the ground, a wicked little knife slipping from his limp fingertips, and found himself fighting against mingled gratitude that she had been there and annoyance that she had deliberately disobeyed him.

"Behind you!" she shouted, and annoyance won the day.

Jacob spun on his heel again, cursing his own stupidity as the other intruder divested him of his knife with a quick kick to his wrist that he had turned too late to avoid.

Damn her for being right and damn himself for being slow.

The blade skittered across the tiles and the men faced each other weaponless, circling silently in the moonlight as each awaited the other's move. Jacob gritted his teeth, knowing that he had to be victorious in this particular encounter.

A glint in the other man's eye warned of his impending move and Jacob deflected the kick easily with one of his own, catching the intruder in the crotch by accident. He landed a solid right when his opponent buckled over and the man stumbled backward, losing his balance and tumbling into the dysfunctional fountain with a groan that stopped short when his head hit the rim of the bowl.

Jacob prowled around the courtyard uneasily, picking up the three knives and jabbing them into his belt abruptly, ensuring that both men were down and that no more lurked in the shadows. He stared around himself impatiently, seeking some outlet for his fully roused ire in the wake of the fight and finding only his woman watching him from the base of the stairs.

"I told you to stay upstairs!" he hissed as he jabbed an accusing finger in her direction. Her chin shot up at his harsh tone and he immediately regretted the words, but saw that she was not about to let the matter go without a fight.

"Don't tell me that you would have handled this all by yourself," she commented archly, her assurance and its justification hitting a nerve.

"It doesn't matter," Jacob growled, unable to shake the vestiges of his anger, and she shook her head in disbelief. "You should have stayed upstairs."

"You would have been dead twice over," she pointed out, the fact that she was right doing little to appease Jacob's wounded pride, her next words rubbing salt in the wound. "You *ought* to thank me," she added with a toss of her hair, and the unexpected thought of how he could show her his gratitude summarily dismissed the remnants of his anger.

"You promised me you would stay upstairs." He tried another tack as he advanced toward her with measured steps, but she only shook her head stubbornly, setting all that shining ebony hair in fascinating motion again.

"No promises," she denied flatly, and he had to concede that point even as he drew close. For an endless moment he held her gaze, watching her defiance fade as she became aware of his arousal. Her expression softened and she spared a thoughtful glance down at the brass plate, now swinging between her fingers, before her eyes sought his again.

"And no regrets," she added quietly, the sadness behind the words sending a pang through Jacob's heart.

"No regrets," he reiterated firmly despite his qualms, threading his fingers into her hair and pulling her to her toes to kiss her possessively. The ardor with which she responded emptied his mind of everything except the feel of her and he drew her closer, fitting her against him as though he would meld their very flesh together.

A scuffle behind him reminded Jacob of the two intruders when he would have preferred to have forgotten them, and he broke his kiss reluctantly, noting with pleasure the way she tipped unsteadily toward him. That it was the same for both of them pleased him immeasurably and he ran his thumb across her reddened bottom lip, savoring the way she trembled beneath his touch.

"Upstairs," he murmured, and she nodded, pressing a kiss beneath his ear before she darted up the stairs. Jacob allowed himself to watch the provocative sway of her hips before he turned his attention back to the awakening intruders and found the courtyard empty.

Not that he was in the mood for a fight, he concluded philosophically. At least not anymore. He stepped into the foyer to find the door gently swinging ajar, but a quick glance out to the street revealed no one.

Jacob listened and fancied he caught the sound of running footsteps fading in the distance. Shaking his head, he closed the door and fastened the drop latch. There was no point in chasing them now for they had too much of a start through the twisted streets. And he doubted they would be back tonight.

He frowned at the latch, certain he had heard a bolt slide home the previous night but strangely not finding one on the door. He would have to talk to her about that, he resolved, knowing that it was far too simple for a would-be-thief to lift a drop latch from the outside. He frowned at the gap between the door and its frame and shook his head disapprovingly. Far too easy.

He looked around the foyer for something to wedge the door more firmly shut and spied a piece of parchment lying on the table in the kitchen. Even though he knew that it was none of his business, his curiosity propelled him forward and he scanned the document with amazement.

It was unmistakably a marriage contract, albeit an ink-stained and grubby one, but what riveted Jacob's attention was the sight of his own signature gracing the bottom. The space for Rebecca's agreeing signature was noticeably empty and he turned the document over speculatively, his stomach going cold when he recognized Judith's writing on the reverse side.

This was the letter she had entrusted him with, the "letter of condolence" she had asked him to deliver to Ephraim's widow.

Despite himself, Jacob chuckled in the darkness. His sweet aunt had a nerve, of that there was little doubt. He peered intently at the parchment, confirming that it was in fact his signature and wondering how on earth Judith had fooled him. As if by magic, he recalled suddenly how she had interrupted him when he was working over a particularly thorny accounting problem the week before he left. He smiled at the memory, knowing that he would never again be so quick to trust her assurances when he was busy.

Especially now that he knew Judith was intent on marrying him off.

Jacob fingered the document thoughtfully before replacing it on the worn table. Hopefully Rebecca would be no more enamored with the idea than he. Jacob could only wish that the space for her signature remained blank. Judging from the tale he had heard from Judith, she and Ephraim had been close and he could appreciate her unwillingness to jump immediately into another marriage.

He cast an appraising glance around the comfortably equipped kitchen, nodding thoughtfully at the inevitable conclusion that she was adequately well established and didn't need to make a match right away. That would reassure Judith.

This document might well explain both her absence and her maid's discomfort telling him of it. Briefly Jacob considered taking the *ketubah* with him or destroying it, but the idea that he might get the woman upstairs in trouble with such a move brought him to a halt. Undoubtedly she would not want her mistress to know she had entertained him this night, he admitted, reluctantly leaving the document on the table as he knew Rebecca would miss it.

Certainly Rebecca would not have any inclination to sign it, so he had nothing to worry about. Despite his conviction in the truth of that last, Jacob couldn't help sparing one backward glance toward the piece of parchment as he reached the foot of the stairs, instinctively disliking leaving anything with his signature around.

Not that it really mattered, he reminded himself. After all, he was leaving in the morning and he would never see the woman again or meet her mistress. That thought didn't sit as well as it should have and he frowned, deliberately reminding himself of their agreement.

No regrets.

After all, she was a servant, a woman beneath his station. And more important, in spite of her delightful lovemaking, she was not a blushing virgin that he could take to wife without consequence.

But at least he could leave the *ketubah* and spare her Rebecca's irritation. After all, it wouldn't do for her to think he had been snooping around the house. To be sure, he had already left her alone too long. At that thought, Jacob retrieved the stone he had used in his battle from the tiled courtyard and quickly wedged it against the base of the door.

Grinning in anticipation, he strode up the stairs and cast such serious musings from his mind. He still had some things to teach his fetching lover, and with luck, there would be enough time before the dawn.

Chapter Four

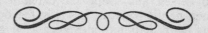

He was gone.

Rebecca didn't have to get up and check to know the truth. She could feel Jacob's absence as tangibly as she had felt his presence, and she rolled onto her stomach, closing her eyes against the brightness of the morning sun streaming through the doorway and the courtyard beyond. The ache between her thighs made itself known and she shook her head silently against the pillow as tears rose behind her eyelids.

What had she done?

Or more accurately, what *hadn't* she done?

Rebecca stumbled to her feet and ruefully acknowledged the sticky reminders of her passionate night, the dampness staining the lavishly embroidered cushions, the pervasive scent of lovemaking that seemed to fill the corners of the achingly empty room. She flipped the weight of her hair over her shoulder and tiredly drew a surcoat over her shoulders, her heart dropping lower with every step down the stairs to the garderobe.

No regrets. Rebecca shook her head dismissively at that thought, wishing she was pragmatic enough to follow through on their agreement. She had found out what she wanted to know, hadn't she? Not only did she know unequivocally that she *had* been missing something with Ephraim, but she had experienced that wonder, as well. Surely that should be enough.

But he hadn't even said goodbye.

Rebecca started the fire on the hearth and hung a kettle of water over the fitful blaze, staring blankly into space while she waited for it to heat. She reflected upon her impulsiveness. God knew, Jacob had given her enough chances to change her mind and she had no one but herself to thank for her insistence to see things through.

She stirred herself and found the battered tin of tea, placing a pinch of the precious leaves in the bottom of a crockery mug with habitual movements, a glimpse of something white on the table catching her eye. The instant realization of what it was brought tears to her eyes anew.

What would have happened if she had just signed the *ketubah?*

The thought made her heart jump until she recalled Jacob's accusation when he arrived the previous night. He had called her a liar. He had *known* who she was and still he had insisted on a one-night liaison. There was only one possible explanation for his scorn and she couldn't imagine how he could have uncovered that particularly dark little secret. Rebecca had pursed her lips and frowned for an instant before she dismissed her confusion over that with a philosophical wave of one hand.

Maybe she was jumping to conclusions. Who knew what had made him change his mind? She certainly had never claimed to understand men, she acknowledged with more than a little frustration, disregarding the water that spilled onto the flagstones as she filled the crockery with unsteady hands. He had signed a *ketubah* without having laid eyes on her but decided against it once he did meet her, although apparently she was still desirable enough to merit a sleepless night like the one just past.

Jacob's attitude was more than a little insulting, now that she thought about it. What kind of person did he think she was? Rebecca grimaced and faced the painful truth that she had managed to fulfill all of those unflattering expectations, regardless of her own markedly higher perception of her character. She absently stirred her tea while it brewed and frowned unseeingly out into the sunny courtyard, wishing she could turn back time and start the entire encounter with Jacob again.

Having no regrets was proving dangerously difficult to accomplish.

The sight of the broken tiles reminded Rebecca abruptly of the intruders the night before and she straightened suddenly in alarm. Stupid to be thinking about Jacob, she chided herself, especially when someone seemed quite intent on breaking into her home each and every night.

Ephraim's study was still in disarray from two nights ago and she spared a glance to the discreetly closed door, wishing now that she had remembered to clean it up. It seemed somehow disrespectful to leave his study so disorganized and she felt a considerable twinge of guilt, which she quickly attributed to her thoughtlessness and nothing else.

What would happen tonight? Rebecca bit her lip, unconvinced that the victory she and Jacob had claimed the night before would completely dissuade the thieves. Clearly they intended to have that parcel, and being alone again made her fear anew for her own safety.

But whom could she ask for assistance? Yet again Rebecca cursed herself for making so little effort to get to know others in the community since she had moved here with Ephraim. Yusuf she knew best, and only because he had spent so much time in the study with Ephraim over the last year, peering over old texts and arguing about translations.

There were others, like Isaac, who had been cronies of Ephraim's, but most of them she hadn't seen very often and didn't know well enough to ask a favor. She spoke pleasantly to the other women in the street and knew them by name, but never one for gossip, she had not made the effort to seek out their company. It seemed she knew the elderly matchmaker as well as anybody and she almost laughed aloud at that thought. Certainly Berta visited her more often than anyone else.

Sobering as she scanned the broken tiles once more, Rebecca frowned at the realization of how few ties she had to Toledo. Maybe she shouldn't even stay. That would solve the problem of the break-ins rather easily.

But where would she go?

Her family was long gone, her hometown of Madrid no longer hospitable to Jews since the Reconquista had reclaimed it for the Castilians and Christ. Her gaze flicked to the contract on the table and darted away again; she flatly refused to speculate on that option.

What was she going to do?

When no answer immediately came to mind, Rebecca set down her tea and pushed up her sleeves, determined to restore Ephraim's study to rights today if she accomplished nothing else. There had to be some way out of this muddle and a little manual labor was the best way to put her thoughts in order.

Jacob had already hired two boys and their donkeys for his return trip when he had the unshakable sense that he was being watched. He straightened from checking the lashing securing a vessel filled with olive oil and glanced around the market with a casual air, his gaze locking solidly with that of the Berber perched in the opposite café.

The two men stared at each other warily, Jacob noting that the other man was sitting at the same table where he had been talking to Rebecca's servant the previous day. A tall glass of some dark beverage, probably mint tea, sat forgotten before him and Jacob almost squirmed beneath the knowing expression in the man's eyes.

He couldn't possibly know what had happened the previous night, Jacob knew that for a fact, but something in the man's expression made him wonder. More than wonder, positively writhe, for his casual encounter with a woman who did not take payment for her companionship was already pricking at his own conscience.

Feeling as though he had little choice when the Berber cocked a brow suggestively, Jacob bade the boys wait for him and strolled over to the café. A gleam of amusement had appeared in the man's eyes by the time Jacob stood before him, and he gestured elegantly to the empty seat opposite before his lids dropped and veiled his expression.

"Jacob ben Solomon," Jacob introduced himself, extending his hand to the other man, only now seeing the chessboard on the table with its men in disarray from a previous game. A game the Berber had apparently won, he concluded from a quick scan of the position of the pieces.

"Yes." The Berber acknowledged his name without surprise, flicking a glance up to Jacob, who still stood. Jacob lifted his brows questioningly and the man smiled for an instant before extending his own hand leisurely. "Yusuf Khudabanda," he supplied, and Jacob nodded as they shook hands, the other man's grip strong and sure within his own.

"Please join me."

Jacob sat down, watching despite himself as Yusuf methodically began to line up the chess pieces, the man's fluid movements mesmerizing in their simple grace. What had he intended to say? And why had he come over here? He owed this Muslim no explanation for his behavior. In fact, he was in somewhat of a hurry to get out of town, although his haste had *nothing* to do with a certain dark-haired woman.

Autumn was in the air, after all.

Jacob took the opportunity to study the other man while his attention was diverted, wondering in the back of his mind what the Berber wanted to talk to him about.

Yusuf's skin was dark like that of the Berbers in Tunis, his face creased with a myriad of tiny lines that made it impossible to guess his age. Despite his turban, Jacob could tell that his hair was jet black by the fact that his brows and lashes were that same shade. Yusuf flicked another glance upward, the startling crystalline green of his eyes accented by the shade of his turban and catching Jacob unaware. Yusuf's lips twitched with something that could have been amusement before he returned his attention to the chessboard.

The board was well made, Jacob noted with his merchant's assessing eye, and he mentally placed a hefty price upon it, the contrasting squares apparently of ebony and ivory and fitted together in cyclic alternation. The pieces were carved from onyx, an alabaster shade for one side, a smoky ambergris for the other. The men themselves were fabulously detailed and obviously the work of a skilled craftsman, the elephants' tusks and eyes clearly distinguishable, the knights' postures fierce, the *shah's* garments richly ornamented, the powerful *vizier* piece complete with an uncanny expression of calculating intelligence.

What should he say? Too late Jacob heartily regretted his impulse to join this man and wondered how he could tactfully make his departure. The awkward silence between them seemed curiously emphasized by the bustle of the awakening market only footsteps away, and Jacob spared a glance to his two hired boys to ensure that both they and their donkeys still waited for him.

"Do you play?" Yusuf demanded quietly without looking up, his words so low that Jacob wondered for an instant whether he had imagined them. The other man deliberately placed the last elephant on its square and fixed Jacob with a steady eye.

"Regrettably I do not have time today," Jacob declined politely, gesturing to the boys awaiting him, but Yusuf shook his head minutely.

"I assure you that the game will not take long," he murmured with such confidence that Jacob could not let the challenge pass. He was a rather good chess player himself and for some reason he had no interest in leaving this man's air of superiority unchallenged.

"No, I don't suppose it will," he responded firmly as he settled himself back into his seat and gestured to the board with an impatient finger. "Whenever you're ready."

Yusuf closed his eyes and inclined his head once in deference. "Please," he countered smoothly, that same smile stealing once again over his lips. "You are my guest."

The two men's eyes met once again and held for a long moment before Jacob nodded and reached without hesitation for one of his pawns.

"You want to ask me about the woman," Yusuf accused lightly. He gracefully moved his *shah* precisely where Jacob had hoped he would after they had played silently for a while. Three more moves and the game was Jacob's. Belatedly, he took in the other man's words and met those knowing green eyes with suspicion.

"I saw you watching us here yesterday," the Berber continued smoothly, and Jacob's heart took an unexpected leap.

"Yes, I did see you," he confirmed nonchalantly. He folded his hands together and frowned down at the board as though concentrating on his next move, his mind racing as he tried to assess the reason for Yusuf's questioning. The Berber remained respectfully silent and Jacob finally moved his right elephant three squares diagonally as though slightly uncertain of the wisdom of his move.

Yusuf regarded the board, his eyes flicking quickly over the arrangement of the pieces as he stroked his bottom lip thoughtfully. Moments passed before he reached leisurely for one of his castles and slid it forward to take Jacob's elephant, falling for the feint and putting the castle right where Jacob wanted it.

The men's eyes met over the board, Jacob hoping his thrill of victory didn't show in his expression while the Berber held his gaze. Yusuf smiled slowly and Jacob thought the day lost until the words fell from the other man's lips.

"She is a lovely creature, is she not?" Yusuf mused, and Jacob was surprised by the way his gut tensed at the casual reference to Rebecca's servant. His mind supplied an image of her indignantly tossing her mane of hair over one shoulder in the courtyard, her sheer chemise barely shielding her from his view, her eyes snapping as she pointed out that he ought to thank her. Everything within him tightened in recollection of how things had progressed from there, and he anticipated the increasingly familiar refrain before it played one more time in his mind.

They had had their one night and that was that, he sternly reminded himself for the hundredth time since he had crept out of Rebecca's house before the dawn. At least he was considerably less surprised by this point at his mind's insistence on pointing out that there was no earthly reason why it had to be just one night.

But that had been their agreement. And Jacob ben Solomon didn't break his word.

Ever.

"Indeed she is," he responded, amazed at the evenness of his tone as he frowned again at the board, checking that everything was as he had anticipated. He cursed himself for having trouble focusing on the business of the moment, a distracting vision of long dark hair as smooth as silk invading his thoughts.

"And a clever woman," Yusuf added in a speculative tone. Jacob looked up and the other man nodded sagely. "It is rare for Allah to grant both beauty and intelligence to a single soul," he clarified sagely.

"You seem to know her quite well." Jacob satisfied himself with that seemingly idle comment while he calmly moved his knight into position for his last play and unobtrusively held his breath.

"Oh, yes," Yusuf confirmed, and Jacob instinctively disliked the ease of his response. "We have known each other for quite some time." He flicked another look in Jacob's direction, the way his gaze sharpened making Jacob wonder if his reaction to those words had been detected.

"That is, of course, why I must inquire as to your intentions," Yusuf added unexpectedly, his voice dropping lower as he continued confidentially. "You see, I also know what it means when a man watches a woman as you watched her yesterday."

Jacob stared at the Berber, amazed at the man's audacity. "Why would I owe you an explanation?" he demanded, barely checking the tide of anger that rose hot in his chest, Yusuf's slow smile doing little to appease him.

"She is alone and I would look after her interests," he offered in a low voice, but Jacob was not convinced.

"And just what are *your* interests in the matter?" he shot back, surprised at how territorial he felt about this particular woman's fate.

"My interests are quite respectable," Yusuf returned archly and Jacob snorted.

"I should hardly think so," he shot back, not in the least discomfited when Yusuf grinned outright.

"I wondered if that might have been you," he mused with a knowing glint in his eye, and Jacob felt heat suffuse his neck that his presence had been detected when he had followed the two of them.

"So, you do not deny it?" he demanded, wanting to wring the Berber's neck when the man simply smiled with maddening deliberation.

"A man must use whatever means come to hand to win a lady," he commented thoughtfully, another one of those sharp looks making Jacob fidget inwardly. "Surely you would not argue with that?"

Jacob opened his mouth to defend himself, stopping a claim to honorable intentions before it was voiced. Certainly his behavior forbade any such claim and he hesitated, unsure of what to say instead. Yusuf watched his struggle with poorly concealed amusement, reaching out to pluck his *vizier* from the board and place it with a flourish on the empty square adjacent to Jacob's *shah*.

A square he had thought perfectly protected.

"*Ash-shah mat,*" Yusuf whispered with evident delight, and Jacob scanned the board in shock, trying to find his mistake.

Checkmate. It was a move he had never seen before, but Jacob told himself that he still should have anticipated it, hindsight making the other man's strategy painfully clear. But understanding came too late, for no matter how he

studied the board, Jacob saw that it was a checkmate without reprieve.

"I mean to wed her," the Berber added in that same low
melodic voice, and Jacob looked up at him through the
haze of surprise.

"It would be most *unwise* of you to complicate matters," he advised, those green eyes narrowing to hostile slits
before he smoothly rose and swept out of the café, leaving
Jacob struggling against his unwarranted and surprisingly
intense response to that threat.

No regrets. One night had been his own condition and he
was going to live by it. What did it matter to him if she
married the Berber?

He should go and talk to her, Jacob thought wildly, his
gaze lifting to the opposite side of the *souk,* where he knew
the little street wound its way crookedly up to Rebecca's
home. He should tell her how he felt. That he already
longed for the taste of her on his tongue, that the way she
spoke her mind piqued his interest, that he wanted to know
why her hair was so soft. He should find out whether she
felt the same way, find out how she felt about this Yusuf.

Shocked at the path his thoughts were taking, Jacob
curtly dismissed any and all errant suggestions from his
mind. He should leave Toledo, he told himself, and the
sooner the better. He swept one last glance tinged with disbelief over the chessboard before he rose to his feet in turn.
That move he would never forget, he told himself with no
small measure of admiration as he committed the posi-
tioning of the pieces to memory.

As for the rest of Toledo, he thought as he scanned the
market, beckoning to his two hired boys, the rest of Toledo was best put out of his mind for good. They had made
an agreement and he would stick to it, he concluded, forcing himself to ignore the shadow of guilt that crept over his
heart at the recollection that he had left her without saying
goodbye.

And he still didn't know her name.

But Yusuf could have the woman and welcome to her, Jacob resolved viciously as he strode out into the sunlight and summoned the boys with a curt snap of his fingers. After all, the Berber had had her before, too, hadn't he? And how a woman like that would laugh to know that he was nursing tender thoughts of her, he chided himself, resolutely clamping down on the voice of protest that rose right on cue within his chest.

Ceuta, he reminded himself grimly. Ceuta, and what awaited him there, would quickly clear his mind of unnecessary gallantry.

Rebecca's heart leapt to her throat when her doorbell jangled near noon, but she told herself sternly that she should know better than to expect Jacob to return. Despite that admonition, disappointment flooded through her at the sight of Isaac standing on her portal when she opened the door. The older man smiled with pleasure at the sight of her and Rebecca immediately felt guilty, hoping that he hadn't noticed her first response to the sight of him.

"Good afternoon, Isaac." She returned his greeting and he grinned even wider, revealing the gaps where he had lost a tooth or two.

"Ah, Rebecca, I was so hoping you would be home," he gushed, and Rebecca smiled despite herself, leaning against the door frame indulgently while she waited for him to get to his point. He was a dear old man and she had never minded talking to him. In fact, now that her initial disappointment had passed, she admitted that it was quite nice to see him again. They exchanged pleasantries about the weather and the shocking increase in the price of saffron, then she sensed that Isaac was getting to the reason for his visit.

"You know, my child, I must tell you that I have been looking for something of mine for a long time, without success, I might add, and it just occurred to me—" Isaac broke off midsentence and flexed his knee, wincing theatrically.

"Are you all right?" Rebecca demanded in concern, laying one hand on his arm, but Isaac shook his head slowly before meeting her eyes.

"It's just age, child," he conceded with a ragged sigh. "My legs aren't what they used to be and standing out in the sun is so difficult now."

"Why don't you come in?" Rebecca suggested, unwilling to admit that she was glad of the distraction from her troubling thoughts.

"No, no, I have no wish to be any trouble," Isaac protested weakly, but she would have none of it.

"Nonsense," Rebecca retorted, taking his arm to help him up the step and guiding him into the kitchen. "You're not feeling well and should sit down for a few minutes."

"You mustn't trouble yourself, child," he argued, even as he meekly accepted her assistance and leaned on her for support. "No one cares about an old man like me and you mustn't either. After all, it's none of your concern whether the pain is more than a feeble man can bear."

They shuffled into the kitchen together and Isaac settled himself into one of the chairs before the hearth with what seemed to be satisfaction. When his bright gaze fixed pointedly on the kettle, Rebecca realized that she had been manipulated. She swallowed a smile, wondering what the elderly man would say if he knew that she was as appreciative of his company as he was of hers.

"Would you like a cup of tea?" she asked, and he nodded vigorously in agreement before recalling his "weakened" state.

"Oh, yes," he said in a more feeble tone. "That might be just what I need to get out of your way. Bless you, Rebecca, for your thoughtfulness." He mused for a moment while Rebecca filled the kettle and stoked up the fire, his surprising words freezing her motions midgesture.

"You'll make some man a good wife, as you did Ephraim," he said thoughtfully. Rebecca felt her color rise, glad for both the relative darkness of the kitchen and her decision to hide the *ketubah* upstairs.

"Well, there's no rush for that," she commented briskly, thinking that she had recovered quite well until she turned and met the knowing glimmer in Isaac's dark eyes.

"You're too young to be alone," he argued, sparing her a bold wink that gave her an unexpected glimpse of a much younger, more roguish Isaac. He must have been a devil when he was a young man, she thought, and caught herself before she smiled.

"I'll talk to Berta if you can't bring yourself to do so," he concluded conspiratorially, but Rebecca shook her head adamantly.

"Berta and I have talked a number of times in the past few months," she argued.

"And she hasn't found anyone for you yet? For shame. I'll have to have a talk with her," Isaac decided with a shake of his head. "She used to be the very best, you know, but obviously I'm not the only one getting on."

"There really is no need," Rebecca countered, her voice sharper than she had intended. "I have told Berta that I am in no rush to take another spouse," she added to make sure her point was clear, and the older man pulled himself up with dignity.

"I only meant to help," Isaac retorted huffily, and Rebecca felt thoroughly chastised for her tone, knowing that she had overreacted. Why was she so touchy today?

"I'm sorry, Isaac," she apologized softly, and he peered up at her from beneath his bushy brows as though he would assess her sincerity. "Perhaps it's just too soon," she lied, and he held her gaze for a long moment before nodding in apparent satisfaction.

Rebecca had the uncanny sense that he hadn't accepted her explanation, although she was quick to credit that thought to her guilty conscience and the certainty that *everyone* knew what she had done the previous night. Casting around for a neutral topic of conversation as she made the tea, she recalled something Isaac had mentioned when he arrived.

"You said you were looking for something," she prompted, feeling a little better when the old man noticeably brightened at her reminder.

"Yes, yes," he agreed, latching on to the topic enthusiastically. "*That* was why I came by to see you, I remember now. It seems that I cannot find an old text of mine no matter how much I look, and it occurred to me this morning that I might have lent it to Ephraim."

When Rebecca didn't comment, he continued. "So, it seemed like a possibility at least that Ephraim could have borrowed it. There really is nothing more frustrating than not being able to remember things anymore and I sincerely hope that you never get to this point, child. But I do recall that Ephraim had expressed an interest in the subject and, well, frankly, if I didn't lend it to him, then it must have sprung legs and walked away, because it is not to be found anywhere."

"Is it a valuable text, then?" Rebecca asked quietly, reassured when Isaac shook his head quickly and chuckled.

"Goodness no, child. I haven't the money for collecting rarities like some." Isaac chewed his lip for a moment as if deciding whether or not to confide in Rebecca, before catching her eye sheepishly. "To tell you the truth, it has a bit of sentimental value for me," he confessed in a low voice. "It's the inscription that I want more than the book."

"A token from a lady friend?" Rebecca teased, surprised when Isaac looked quickly away and nervously stirred his tea.

"It was a long time ago," he muttered in discomfort, and she impulsively leaned over to pat his hand reassuringly.

"Say no more, Isaac," she assured him. "You're more than welcome to look in the study and see whether it is there."

"Thank you, child," he said with a grateful grin, and Rebecca wondered whether she had imagined the gleam that lit his eyes briefly before he looked away.

"I remember when Ephraim bought that bowl from my nephew," he commented before she could speculate further. Rebecca followed his gesture to the dish reposing alone on the table as though she held it in high esteem, and she winced inwardly.

"I didn't realize your nephew had made it," she said warily, and Isaac threw her a mischievous look that made her suspect he had guessed her thoughts.

"I seldom admit it," he confessed with a twinkle in his dark eyes. "The boy throws some of the ugliest bowls to ever see daylight."

Rebecca laughed aloud before she could stop herself, the old man's words echoing her own assessment of the bowl. "Ephraim was quite insulted when I told him it was the most horrible piece of work I had ever seen," she confessed, and the old man chuckled along with her.

"Clearly you haven't seen the boy's studio," he joked, rolling his eyes to indicate his own opinion, and Rebecca laughed even harder.

"Did Ephraim keep books anywhere else?" Isaac inquired impatiently, and Rebecca looked up from her seat at Ephraim's desk in surprise. The ink stain on the surface had proven to be difficult to dislodge and she berated herself once again for giving it such an opportunity to set.

"Isn't your book here?" she asked, evading the question.

Isaac shook his head. "No," he responded, frowning as he positively glared at the shelves. "No, and I can't imagine where else it could be," he continued peevishly. "I was *certain* that Ephraim had it."

"Well, perhaps you've left it somewhere else," Rebecca commented mildly, surprised by the intensity of Isaac's glance when its full weight landed on her.

"I *said* I was sure it was here," he shot back testily. "Are you quite certain that Ephraim didn't keep any books elsewhere in the house?"

Rebecca straightened slowly, not liking the older man's sudden change of tone. "I think that I have been quite accommodating of your request, Isaac," she told him quietly, and he had the grace to look momentarily shamefaced. "Certainly I have given my neighbors food for thought by having you in my house for so long," she added icily, and he seemed to soften beneath her censure.

"Oh yes, you have, my child," he conceded easily. "I apologize for losing my temper, but I was so looking forward to finding that text and reading that inscription once again."

Rebecca's heart wrenched and she regretted her sharpness with the older man. It must be tremendously frustrating always to be forgetting things, she told herself, and managed to summon a smile.

"I'll keep an eye out for it," she told him, and he smiled softly at her reassurance, pushing himself out of his chair with no small effort.

"Thank you for your patience, child," he murmured. Rebecca showed him back to the door, puzzled by the glance he shot up the stairs when they passed the arch to the courtyard and wondering if she imagined that Isaac was less amiable now than he had been.

He was tired, that was all, Rebecca told herself firmly as she shut the door behind him, unable to dismiss a growing sense of trepidation. That feeling of disquiet seemed to intensify when her gaze fell to the fountain illuminated in the last rays of the sun. Knowing she was being foolish, she lifted the kitchen knife from the table and slipped it into her girdle as the shadows lengthened.

Chapter Five

There was absolutely no way she was going to sleep, so convinced was Rebecca that someone was going to barge into her home at any moment. At least, that was the excuse she preferred for her insomnia, the way her skin heated when her thoughts turned to a certain man not worthy of consequence in her estimation. She sat up, deliberately loosening her grip on the kitchen knife, not realizing how tightly she had been holding it. She shook her head at her own foolishness and rubbed her cramped hand as she frowned into the darkness.

Enough was enough. If this package was going to cause so much trouble, she at least ought to find out what was in it.

Even if she had to break the fountain to get it.

Rebecca dressed quickly, shoving her feet into a pair of sandals and pushing up her sleeves with determination before picking up the knife and stalking down the stairs to the courtyard. She left the knife in the kitchen and propped her hands on her hips, considering her marble opponent so innocently cast in silver moonlight.

There had to be a trick, she told herself resolutely as she stared at the uncooperative fountain, discarding all of the options she had tried so far. She wasn't strong enough to force it open, that much she had learned. And nothing attached to the fountain had triggered the latch as far as she could tell.

No doubt about it, it was time to widen the scope of her search. Somewhere in this courtyard, something opened that latch, and if she searched methodically enough, there was no reason why she shouldn't find it.

Even if it took her all night to do so.

The eastern sky was lightening when Rebecca finally lost her patience. This was nonsense. It was completely unreasonable that her safety should be endangered for something she could not even get hold of. Not to mention the fact that a valuable treasure would come in handy now that she was alone.

Knowing that the gesture was childish, not to mention futile, she stuck out her tongue at the fountain. The act seemed to sum up her frustration perfectly.

Not in the least appeased, Rebecca spun on her heel and stomped across the courtyard to head back to bed. With luck she could get some sleep before the dawn, she thought sourly, although she was in no sweeter a mood than she had been when she got up.

Thoroughly dissatisfied with her complete lack of accomplishment in the long night, Rebecca leveled a solid kick at one of the stone pillars supporting the arcade as she passed. Predictably the tile that took her blow rattled as though it would fall off and she rolled her eyes, but to her relief and surprise it merely teetered, then reverted to its original position.

Before she could marvel at this strange occurrence, an audible click echoed behind her, followed by the sound of stone sliding against stone, the combination bringing her to a shocked halt.

Rebecca turned around slowly, as if moving quickly would dispel what she instinctively knew would greet her eyes. She grinned outright at the widened gap in the bowl where the crack had been and barely restrained herself from whooping with delight. She bent and experimentally flipped the tile back and forth, realizing now that it was on some kind of hinge. Laughing aloud, she positively danced across the tiled courtyard to the fountain to examine her discovery with unrestrained glee.

Just as before, she easily hooked her fingers beneath the stone and lifted the door until it locked in place. Her heart gave a little leap when she saw the parcel lying exactly as she had left it and she hauled it impatiently out of the crevice.

It was heavy for how small it was, Rebecca acknowledged as she cradled its weight in her hands, her fingers exploring the wrapping in the hope that she could determine its contents by touch alone. Visions of handfuls of gold dinars and rubies as big as her thumb filled her mind as she let herself speculate on what someone would want to hide so thoroughly.

It just *had* to be valuable.

Rebecca shook her head at her own foolishness in trying to guess the contents when she knew full well that she was going to open the package anyway. She carefully closed the hidden compartment, teasing herself by postponing the inevitable a little longer. Now she heard the accompanying click that echoed from behind the tile at the base of the pillar as the door closed, and she nodded in silent admiration before gathering the parcel to her chest and making for the kitchen on quick feet.

Her fingers trembled as she lit the lamp and she felt their chill when she jammed her hair impatiently behind her ears. She took a deep breath and carefully slipped the kitchen knife beneath the twine that bound the package.

Did she really have any right to do this? Second thoughts assaulted her, but she shoved her doubts away and deliberately cut the cord. She had a right to know, didn't she?

It seemed that the first gesture was the hardest, for no sooner was the twine cut than Rebecca was tearing at the waxed paper, her anxious fingers making quick work of the paraffin seal as they found the seams. The paper ripped resoundingly as it was unceremoniously parted from the contents of the package, and in the twinkling of an eye, she stood holding a book.

A book?

That was undoubtedly what it was and Rebecca stared at it in mingled disappointment and surprise. It wasn't even very big, she conceded ruefully, turning the simply bound red volume over in her hands.

Why would anyone bother to hide a book?

She exhaled slowly and leaned her hips against the table, flicking open the tiny tome with disgust. A book, of all things. All this trouble over a little book. Well, she hoped it was at least about something interesting.

Rebecca stared at the pages in amazement, unable to believe her eyes. With a frown, she turned to the next page, then the next and the next with greater and greater speed, her disappointment rising and threatening to choke her.

It wasn't fair! she thought wildly, fanning the pages of the book now but finding no relief from the rolling script. She closed the book abruptly and slammed it onto the table as frustrated tears rose in her eyes.

All of this effort and she couldn't even decipher the text!

Rebecca could read but this was not Hebrew, and she opened the book again, certain she must have been mistaken, but only ended up shaking her head at the strange characters. Probably Arabic or Persian, she decided, pursing her lips in annoyance as she studied the text anew and positively growled under her breath. Nobody wrote in any other languages, except maybe Latin that the Christians used, but Ephraim had always said that they didn't know anything worth writing down anyway.

Rebecca drummed her fingers on the table impatiently and flipped slowly through the pages, seeing now that there were many symbols interspersed with the enigmatic words. And there were charts and what looked like notes scribbled in the margin.

Was this Ephraim's handwriting? She squinted at a scrawled note and couldn't be sure, not that it mattered anyhow. It was only a little book. Feeling completely let down, Rebecca closed the book with a sigh.

It was unbelievable that she had put out so much effort for a silly little book. She yawned and covered her mouth with one hand, peering out into the courtyard to find the morning already dawning. She ran one hand through her hair and scowled down at the book, disappointed that she had wasted an entire night's sleep for nothing. Obviously she had been wrong about the package. Thieves would hardly break into her home for a plain old book like this.

If it had had an inscription, she might have thought it was Isaac's book. After all, it obviously wasn't valuable, Rebecca thought as she turned the volume over in her hands. She should know better than to let her imagination run wild. Hidden treasure indeed. Some previous owner's child had probably hidden the book in the fountain as part of a game and either forgotten about it or forgotten how to open the latch.

Philosophically, she gathered up the discarded paper and twine and threw it into the grate, considering the book for a moment while she decided what to do with it. It hardly seemed worth hiding in the fountain again and she had irreparably torn its protective wrapping.

Books belong in the library, she thought with a rueful smile, and tossed the little book in one hand as she nudged open the door to Ephraim's study with her toe.

"La ilaha illa-Llah! La ilaha illa-Llah!"
The *muezzin's* plaintive call summoning the faithful to prayer carried out over the water and Jacob gripped the ship's rail in anticipation, drinking in the sight of Ceuta nestled into the rocky coast. The second pillar of Hercules rose sharply toward the clouds behind the squat white buildings of the town, the lone minaret seemingly echoing its skyward gesture, the entirety cast in the tangerine flush of the setting sun.

A salt-tinged breeze ruffled Jacob's hood as he noted the cluster of ships anchored in the harbor, and he knew that he should have good luck finding passage east in the morning. It was late in the year for most travelers, and pricing for transit would be competitive to say the least. He tapped the rail with a satisfaction he was far from feeling as the ship was maneuvered into its berth, and he called to a boy on the quay.

Arrangements for storage of his goods were quickly made and the shadows were barely drawing long by the time Jacob was striding down the narrow cobbled streets on a familiar path. The *souk* was abandoned when he reached the square, the daily stalls removed, the permanent ones locked and shuttered against the night. A few boys huddled together on the far side of the square but Jacob had no time for their mischief, his boots crunching firmly on the gravel of the tiny route that wound out of the other side of the market.

Laughter rose in the distance, the clink of cheap glassware carrying to Jacob's ears along with the beat and jingle of tambourinelike *tars*. He caught the tantalizing smell of *mechoui* on the wind and hastened his pace, his stomach making its demands known as the golden light of the tavern he sought appeared and beckoned him onward.

The tavern was smokier and noisier than he had recalled, the old turbaned men sitting cross-legged on the other side of the room with their water pipes barely visible through the haze they had created. It was hot inside and Jacob removed his burnous as soon as he crossed the threshold, his gaze darting immediately to the tiled expanse left open for the dancers, surprised that he was not more disappointed to find it empty.

"Jacob!" a gravelly voice called from beside him. He turned to have his hand pumped by the grinning proprietor. "Happy New Year to you!" Husayn added enthusiastically, and Jacob smiled in return.

"And to you," he returned. "Can it be *Achoura* already?"

Husayn laughed and clapped him on the shoulder. "And I thought it was the promise of Fatima's *mechoui* that brought you to our door for the holiday."

"The smell of it certainly brought me more quickly," Jacob conceded, and Husayn waved him to a seat, snapping his fingers and calling out in Arabic to a young boy. The boy nodded once and disappeared into the smoky haze.

"It will take but a moment," Husayn supplied matter-of-factly, and Jacob nodded as he settled back in his chair with pleasure. He always had a sense of having come home when he crossed the Mediterranean and first set foot on the soil here, and this return trip was proving no different.

"What brings you our way so late in the season?" Husayn inquired, and Jacob spared him a quick glance.

"A message that Judith wanted to send to Andalusia before the winter," he responded, and the other man nodded in understanding, a smile of recollection curving his lips.

"And how is our feisty Judith?"

Jacob smiled despite himself, immediately thinking of his aunt's latest scheme. "Still up to her old tricks," he commented, and Husayn chuckled as he poured a shot of *eau-de-vie* into a short glass and placed it before Jacob.

"Still trying to marry you off?" he teased, and Jacob chuckled along with him as he quaffed the drink, savoring the way it burned right down to his toes.

"And she's getting more underhanded," he said with a grin a moment later.

Husayn wagged one plump finger at him. "One of these days, she will outsmart you," he warned, and the two men chuckled together.

"It was close this time," Jacob admitted, his trouble-some mind quickly supplying yet another image of Rebecca's servant, and he dismissed the memories that had plagued him all day with an effort.

"Perhaps it would not have been so bad," Husayn mused, his bright eyes as perceptive as ever. "You are getting too old to be alone and you never know what will come of an arranged match." He gestured vaguely in the direction of the kitchen. "Like you, I fought marriage when my parents told me the contract was made, but now I cannot even begin to imagine living without Fatima and her cooking." He shrugged, but Jacob shook his head quickly in disagreement.

"This match would have been a disaster, no doubt about it," he stated flatly, producing a gold *dinar* for the boy who was placing a steaming bowl of lamb stew liberally strewn with raisins and almonds before them. "Is Alifa working tonight?" he inquired casually, sensing he had said the wrong thing when Husayn remained silent.

"Yes," the portly keeper confirmed tersely, his gaze sobering as he watched the younger man eat. Husayn looked as though he would say something further and Jacob lifted his brows inquiringly, but another customer shouted for service and Husayn merely shrugged his shoulders before he moved quickly away.

The clash and jingle of a dozen *tars* drew every man's attention immediately to the space left open on the floor, and Jacob swiveled on his stool along with the rest. The jangling of the tambourines rose to a crescendo, and somewhere in the shadows a three-stringed *rebab* was plucked as a dancer stepped out onto the floor, her entire body swathed in multicolored layers of sheer silks.

Her kohl-lined eyes were visible above her veil, her feet bare as they tapped the floor in time to the music, the curves of her figure faintly silhouetted beneath the shimmering cloth. She spun on one heel and swung her hips temptingly, the accompanying tinkle and flash beneath the rose-hued veil that draped around her middle revealing the coins stitched around her hips.

The dancer lifted her *tar* over her head and began to tap a slow rhythm with her fingertips, some of the men tapping their feet in time to the beat as they murmured approval to one another. Jacob watched the dancer's gaze slide assessingly over the assembly, as though she were estimating her take from this crowd, until those dark eyes met his own and held for a heartbeat. Something about the way she coquettishly flicked one shoulder as she turned away told him that it was Alifa who danced before him.

Surprisingly neither the realization nor the look she slanted in his direction sent the thrill through him that he had expected, and Jacob finished his dinner in ill humor. The men cheered and he cast a glance toward Alifa just as she discarded the cerulean veil that had been draped over her shoulders, spinning like a dervish as her pace increased infinitesimally. He considered the bare curve of her left shoulder for a moment and could only think of a soft shoulder of a slightly lighter hue beneath his hand.

Jacob clapped impatiently for a *narghile*, reminding himself that he had come here specifically to see Alifa as he dispassionately watched her hips sway. The pipe would cure him of this unusual lassitude, he told himself as the boy lit the *narghile* and sucked the water pipe to life. He had simply become unaccustomed to rich food in Andalusia, that was all.

Alifa discarded the second veil with a dramatic flourish, proudly revealing the golden expanse of her belly, and Jacob met her eyes once more, wondering whether she had gained weight. Certainly that expanse of bared flesh was less appealing than he had anticipated it would be. He took a deep drag from the pipe, savoring the taste of tobacco and molasses, not at all comfortable with his growing certainty that it was not the *mechoui* that lay at the root of his disinterest.

By the time Alifa had shed all seven of her veils, Jacob was dreading their inevitable encounter. There was no way that he could simply slip out into the night, for Alifa had seen him, the hot looks she was sending his way telling him that she expected the evening to progress as it usually did when he visited the tavern.

Only tonight, Jacob found he had absolutely no interest in Alifa's abundant charms.

For the life of him, he couldn't imagine why he had even come here, why he had found Alifa's gently rounded curves attractive, how he could have been interested in a woman who belly danced with such abandon for an entire tavern of strangers every night. True enough, she was a skilled lover, but he wondered how he could ever have believed that she burned only for him. It seemed as though the scales were finally lifted from his eyes and he realized that he had been a fool to imagine that Alifa extended her favors to him alone.

How many of the other men here had sampled her wares?

She sent one of those seductive smiles winging his way as she finished to the men's applause and Jacob knew the moment he had been dreading was almost upon him. Silver flashed through the air, the tinkle of coins falling onto the tiled floor like spring rain, and two boys in Husayn's employ darted forward to gather them for Alifa while she disappeared once more. She paused on the threshold of the back room that the dancers used to send one last longing look in Jacob's direction and he cringed inwardly at the knowledge that he was being summoned.

He might as well get this over with, he reasoned as he pushed to his feet with a sigh. He glanced up to find Husayn watching him and could not think what to say to the man. Jacob satisfied himself with a shrug and saw something like sympathy dawn in the other man's eyes before he turned away.

The tavern reverted to its previous noise level, men arguing over politics, trade and the caliber of Alifa's dancing as Jacob shoved his way through the throng to the curtained back door. One of the boys, his hands full of coins, preceded him, sparing Jacob a censorious glance before he stepped out of his way in recognition. Jacob pushed through the curtain and paused to let his eyes adjust to the change in atmosphere.

The back room seemed warmer than it was, the golden glow of a number of small lamps and the pervasive scent of feminine perspiration making the air seem positively steamy. Thick Persian rugs layered on the floor added to the heat of the room, and red and gold cushions were strewn against the far wall between a pair of large mirrors with ornate brass frames. *Tars* had been dropped on the floor amidst a jumble of discarded veils, and a low table before the cushions sported a tray of confections gleaming with honey in the candlelight.

Two dancers reposed on the cushions, their chatter stopping abruptly as soon as Jacob entered the room, although he noted that they made no effort to cover themselves. They regarded him with interest, one nudging the other and arching a brow pointedly in Alifa's direction. The second nodded in understanding, letting her gaze slide appreciatively over Jacob as she slowly sipped a glass of juice. Her tongue darted into the juice, her eyes knowing, and Jacob looked away.

Alifa stood in the other corner, as yet unaware of Jacob's presence, her golden skin gleaming with a thin sheen of perspiration, her dark brows drawn together in a frown as she argued heatedly with the boy who had preceded him. She tossed the tightly crimped mass of her hair over one shoulder impatiently, her heavy gold earrings rocking as she scolded the boy for pocketing some of the silver. He protested his innocence and the corners of Alifa's rouged lips turned downward in a decidedly unattractive way.

And how had Jacob managed to forget this familiar scene?

The *rebab* player in the tavern behind plucked out a telling pattern of notes and the dancer with the glass of juice rose languidly to her feet, her gaze still fixed on Jacob. She drained the glass before she placed it on the table and he was uncomfortably aware of the way she was watching him. She scooped up a pair of veils and draped them around herself in a practiced gesture, retrieving a *tar* before she strolled toward Jacob.

"Excuse me," she murmured as she very deliberately brushed past him, and Jacob shook his head at the obviousness of her approach. He would have said something but she pursed her lips, touching her finger to her own lips and then his. Surprise effectively prevented Jacob from speaking, and she smiled before she darted out to meet the applause of the tavern clients.

"Darling!" The woman's movements had evidently attracted Alifa's attention, and Jacob spun to find her closing in on him with outstretched arms.

"Good evening, Alifa," Jacob said simply, finding her heat unexpectedly in his arms and taking a step backward. Undeterred, she stretched up and kissed him proprietarily, a move as much for the other dancer's benefit as his own, Jacob was sure, the cynicism of that thought making him pull deliberately away.

"What's the matter, darling?" She pouted prettily, playing the role of the ingenue, and Jacob shook his head, still amazed at his own naïveté.

"I wanted to speak to you," he explained, and Alifa chuckled under her breath.

"So, it's *speaking* now, is it?" She laughed, flicking one finger across his lips. "It's not like you to be so indirect about things, darling," she purred, and Jacob shook his head stubbornly.

"No, Alifa, I do need to speak with you," he repeated, and she pulled away slightly, her gaze assessing as she studied his features. Jacob thought that she knew what he intended to say even before he was entirely sure of it himself, but her expression became coquettish once more.

"But, darling, I'm finished for the night," Alifa said in a low voice, her lips curving into a suggestive smile as she ground her hips against his. "Why don't we go somewhere more private for our chat?"

Jacob stepped quickly away, bracing his hands on her shoulders, and the dancer's eyes narrowed, giving her a catlike air.

"Something *is* the matter," she accused, a thread of steel in her tone now that there was distance between them.

"I came only to say goodbye," Jacob said quickly, wanting nothing better than to escape this place once and for all, the words surprising him when they fell from his lips. But they felt right, he acknowledged with growing conviction, certain that this was what he needed to do.

"Goodbye?" Alifa repeated sharply, ignoring the soft snicker from the woman reclining on the cushions and watching the exchange with interest. "But I thought you were happy," she said almost to herself, her fingers closing around Jacob's wrist as she peered up into his eyes.

"What have I done?" she demanded, but he only shook his head.

"Nothing," he admitted.

"Then what haven't I done?" she countered, her tone dropping with sexual intent. Jacob flicked a look to her face to find her eyes dark, her lips curving into that secretive smile he had previously found so seductive, and he simply shook his head again.

"It has nothing to do with you," he said in a low voice, putting her deliberately away from him. "I must go."

Alifa's eyes narrowed and she propped her hands on her hips as Jacob turned away. "You've met someone else," she charged sharply just as he reached the doorway, and he glanced back over his shoulder in surprise.

That was exactly what had happened, he realized with a start, knowing with unexpected certainty that Rebecca's servant would not be easily purged from his mind. Even now, he realized that he was unconsciously comparing Alifa's ripe curves with his woman's sleek slenderness, Alifa's seductive games with her complete lack of sexual guile, and finding Alifa curiously wanting.

"Yes." He acknowledged the truth simply, staring at the pattern in one of the carpets for a moment as he came to terms with himself.

"Yes, I suppose I have."

His low words hung in the air between them. Jacob risked a glance to Alifa's face to find her fighting against her tears. Had he really hurt her so much? It seemed hard to believe, yet her emotion seemed genuine enough and he was suddenly sorry he had come here at all.

"I suppose she's no tavern dancer," Alifa spat, the venom in her tone shocking Jacob.

"No, she does not dance," he confirmed quietly, the fact that he could not testify to his woman's chastity chafing at him yet again. Alifa's face crumpled and she turned abruptly away, her gesture making Jacob regret that he had felt compelled to be honest with her.

"I'm sorry, Alifa," he added quietly, feeling the words were hopelessly inadequate, and when she didn't respond, he turned and left.

Rebecca awakened to the unmistakably cold bite of steel pressed against her throat.

She blinked once against the impenetrable darkness and inhaled slowly to counter the racing of her heart, the change in the weight of the blade telling her that her assailant knew she had awakened. She strained her eyes against the shadows as her palms began to sweat, trying to determine some clue to her attacker's identity.

An uneventful week had convinced her that the threat to her well-being was past, but she now saw the error of that line of thinking. Frustrated by her inability to see anything at all, she licked her lips and made to speak.

"What—" she began, only to have the blade angled more deeply into her throat.

"Say nothing," a muffled voice advised quietly, and Rebecca swallowed the lump in her throat with difficulty.

"We have been patient," the voice warned, and she shivered at the malice in the hushed tone. "But you have not come forward with what we want."

What did they want? And who were these people anyway?

"Who are you?" she managed before the knife dug into her flesh again, and she fancied that her assailant tut-tutted under his breath.

"Not for you to know," he responded instantly.

"What do you want?" she rasped.

"Too talkative," her attacker criticized sharply. "You know what we're looking for, and even if you don't have it, you know where it is."

Unwilling to risk having that knife press even deeper, Rebecca silently shook her head, and the man made an impatient sound deep in his throat.

"Where is it?" came the sharp question, and the weight of the blade was eased for an instant so that she could respond.

"What?" Rebecca demanded impatiently.

"You *know*," the voice insisted silkily, and she shivered involuntarily. "Make no mistake, we mean to have it and you would do well to cooperate." The blade traced a lazy path across Rebecca's throat, leaving little doubt in her mind as to the assailant's intention.

"I don't know what you mean," she insisted breathlessly, and he seemed to consider that for a moment before responding.

"Perhaps not," he mused, "but it doesn't really matter. Either you will produce it shortly or you will die."

Rebecca caught her breath at this and it seemed her attacker chuckled to himself.

"This is no game, Rebecca," he whispered confidentially, and she sensed that he leaned closer. Instinctively her hand slipped beneath the pillows, and she cursed herself when she recalled that she had left the knife in the kitchen again.

This was no joke. These people meant to have something and were willing to kill her to get it. And she had no idea what it was.

Was it even remotely possible that they wanted that silly little book?

"I don't have it," she insisted boldly, taking a gamble as her numbed mind finally came to life. Judging from the man's attitude, this would be her only chance to negotiate for time, and she knew better than to forsake the opportunity. With her life already threatened, she hadn't much to lose. And she was worth more to him alive if he thought she knew where the mysterious item was.

"Ah, but you know where it is?" he demanded, excitement in his tone. Rebecca took a deep breath and nodded once in the darkness, immediately sensing the change in the man's attitude.

"Very good," he congratulated her smoothly. "I knew you would see this our way sooner or later. How quickly can you get it?"

Rebecca cast around wildly in her mind for an answer. She had to buy herself time and as much of it as she could get. "Two months," she answered breathlessly, and the blade bit deeper again.

"One," the man shot back.

"It will take two," Rebecca insisted as she gambled for more time to figure out the puzzle, not daring to breathe while the man seemed to consider this.

"I'll be back in six weeks," he warned at last. "See that you have what I want by then or you won't live to tell about it."

Six weeks. Rebecca closed her eyes in relief as the weight of the blade left her throat.

By the time she took a deep breath and opened her eyes, she knew the man was gone. Every fiber of her being limp, she rolled over and touched her throat with trembling fingers, grateful that the blade hadn't broken the soft skin. She listened to the silence of the house for a moment, then took a shaky breath and stumbled to her feet, finding her trunk easily in the darkness and striking a flint to light the lamp.

There was only one thing to do, only one way that she could protect herself.

The golden halo lit the contents of the chest when she threw back the lid a moment later, her fingers landing on the *ketubah* without hesitation.

Rebecca fetched a quill and a pot of ink from the other side of the room and signed her name beside Jacob's with an unsteady hand before she could reconsider her decision. On impulse, she scribbled a postscript on the bottom, staring at the fallacy for a long moment before she hastily sealed the missive.

Forgive me, Jacob, she thought to herself, knowing that there was no one else she wanted to trust but disliking the fact that she was making this decision on instinct alone.

Chapter Six

"Well, where is she?" an imperious voice demanded from the top of the stairs. Jacob stared up into the darkness of his home as he gratefully shed his sodden cloak and gave it a shake that launched raindrops all over the foyer, flashing like jewels as they fell.

"Surely you weren't so thoughtless as to leave the woman out in the rain? Honestly, Jacob, I thought that your father and I had managed to teach you some manners, but I can see that I was sadly mistaken."

The bulky silhouette of Judith's figure became visible in the shadows as she trotted energetically down the stairs. Jacob grinned as he shook the water out of his collar, hauled off his wet boots and shed his soaked turban. He found the lamp in its customary place and struck a flint, almost laughing aloud at the outraged expression on his aunt's face when the lamp flickered to light.

"For your information, Rebecca was not interested in your idea," he told her archly by way of greeting, and Judith's outrage turned to shock. Her eyes narrowed thoughtfully and she tipped back her head to give her nephew an appraising look.

"You, of course, were naturally charming?" she demanded skeptically. He laughed, leaning down to give her an affectionate hug.

"I didn't even meet her," he admitted, and Judith drew back to look at him again.

"She wouldn't see you?" she demanded incredulously, but Jacob shook his head.

"Her servant said she was away," he supplied, waving one finger imperiously in the direction of the kitchen as he picked up the lamp and headed there.

"Oh, my dear, of course you must be hungry. I've quite forgotten myself." Judith plucked the lamp from his hand and scurried off to the kitchen in front of him. "The girls are asleep, so we'll have to fend for ourselves," she whispered conspiratorially.

Jacob nodded agreement, knowing how she disliked disturbing the help for every little thing. And this way, they could talk in privacy. There were a few things he and Judith needed to sort out.

"What do you want to eat?" Judith turned abruptly to confront him and Jacob almost ran her over, grasping her shoulders to steady himself, but his aunt apparently didn't notice.

"Something warm—I'm chilled to the bone," he said simply, and Judith held the lamp higher to study his features, pinching the flesh of his cheek assessingly as she frowned. Jacob tolerated her perusal good-naturedly, grinning again when she shook her head in evident disapproval. Even if he had gained weight while he was away, he was sure she would still have been convinced that he had not eaten well.

"No wonder you're cold, you've got not a scrap of extra flesh on you," she scolded as she hurried ahead and poked through the contents of the pantry. "I thought you liked Andalusian food," she commented over her shoulder, and Jacob could only nod as he dropped to one knee to stoke the fire. No need to tell her that the seas had been rough and the trip from Ceuta unpleasant. Judith had already seen that in his coloring, he knew.

"Of course, it can't hold a candle to your cooking," he teased gallantly, and Judith giggled like a young girl.

"You'd have done well to show Rebecca a bit of that charm," she chided, and Jacob spread his hands wide in concession as he rose and turned to face her.

"I told you, I didn't even get to meet her."

"But you could have waited until she returned," Judith countered pertly, emphasizing her point with a jab of the bread knife in his direction. Jacob chuckled and dropped onto a stool, running his hands through his damp hair and letting his exhaustion take hold now that he was home.

"You don't give up, do you?" he mumbled, and Judith laughed as she crossed the room. She chucked him under the chin and handed him a brimming kettle of soup with a mischievous wink.

"You're getting too old for me to be able to afford subtlety," she shot back, and Jacob groaned as he hung the kettle of soup over the fire for her. "We're running out of time, after all," she whispered impishly, darting away when he shot her a dark look.

"Why is everyone intent on reminding me how old I am?" Jacob growled, seeing too late that he had piqued his aunt's interest by the way she cocked her head.

"Everyone?" she demanded brightly, handing him a thickly buttered slice of bread.

"Well, Husayn said much the same thing when I stopped in Ceuta," he informed her, fixing his aunt with a suspicious look. "Are you two in league together?" he asked with narrowed eyes, and Judith laughed delightedly.

"Of course not." She dismissed the accusation easily. "I haven't seen Husayn in years. How is he?"

"Fine," Jacob answered, staring sourly at the growing flames. "He asked after you and I gave your regards to him and Fatima."

"They're wonderful people," Judith commented as she stirred the soup, sending a speculative glance her nephew's way when he simply stared into the fire. "What's the matter? Feeling your age?" she teased.

Jacob met Judith's sparkling eyes and sighed in exasperation, shoving to his feet as he bit into the bread and pacing across the floor. "I'm only thirty-two, you know," he muttered from the other side of the room, and he thought Judith smothered a smile as she turned back to the kettle.

"A fine age for fatherhood," she commented under her breath, and Jacob was sure he heard her stifle a chuckle when he groaned in response. To his immense relief, she unexpectedly changed the subject and he welcomed the reprieve, although he knew it wouldn't last.

"We had lentil soup tonight. It seemed good weather for it with the rain rolling in from the sea, and it does stick to your ribs on these damp nights." Judith chatted idly and Jacob nodded as he sat down heavily at the table and held out his hands to the fire, suddenly aware of how tired he was.

"That's fine," he agreed, closing his eyes and letting the warmth soak into his bones, barely listening while she chattered on about the neighbor's maid getting pregnant and the local speculation on the identity of the father. On some level, he felt that she had deliberately chosen the topic of the gossip she would share with him, but he dismissed that thought as overly sensitive, just as her words faded and the heat of the fire permeated his chilled skin.

"Why didn't you wait for her?" Judith demanded abruptly, her voice startlingly loud. Jacob opened his eyes with a jolt to find her placing a bowl of steaming soup before him, her eyes bright with curiosity. Had he dozed off?

"I... ah, I thought she wasn't really away," he answered, the soft muddle his thoughts had become making it impossible for him to avoid the question.

"Now, why on earth would you think something like that?" Judith asked skeptically, shaking her head as she dropped into the seat opposite him. "What possible reason would the woman have to avoid you? Honestly, you men really have some silly ideas sometimes," she chided, breaking off a piece of challah and popping the bread into her mouth while she pertly waited for his response.

Knowing she was not about to let him off the hook, Jacob deliberately put down his spoon and linked his fingers together like a tent over the steaming bowl as he fixed his aunt with a steady eye.

"When I first went to the house, Rebecca was out," he explained carefully, determined not to reveal anything to his perceptive aunt, "so I left your message with her servant and said I would be back that evening. When I came back, the serving woman said she was away, but the *ketubah* was open on the kitchen table." Jacob held Judith's gaze for a long moment until she flushed guiltily, then returned his attention to his soup.

"A *ketubah* that apparently neither one of us expected to see," he added, just to make sure his opinion on the matter was clear, but Judith grinned unrepentantly as she propped her chin on one hand.

"You seem to be taking it rather well for such an *old* man," she teased, and Jacob chuckled despite himself.

"I've had a week to come to terms with it," he shot back with a grin, but Judith had no intention of taking his displeasure seriously.

"You really think that she was avoiding you?" she inquired, and Jacob gestured vaguely with one hand.

"What other explanation could there be? You said that she was shattered by Ephraim's death—maybe she isn't ready yet."

"Hmm." Judith frowned at the table and traced a vein of wood with one fingertip before shooting Jacob a bright look. "I was so *sure* that I had written a convincing letter," she mused, and he almost laughed aloud at her disappointment.

"It wasn't bad," he conceded with a crooked smile, regretting the words the minute Judith's sharp gaze landed unerringly upon him.

"And how did *you* have the time or the opportunity to read it?" she demanded. "I thought you didn't even get into the house."

To his chagrin, Jacob felt the heat rising on his neck and he made a great pretense of eating his soup, not knowing what to say and distrusting the silence across the table. Judith was thinking and he knew well enough that that was dangerous.

"The soup is good," he said in an attempt to divert her thoughts, but it was too late, for his aunt spoke the same instant.

"The serving woman," she hissed, the delighted giggle that immediately followed telling Jacob that he had unknowingly made some small sign of acknowledgment. "Oh, Jacob, you are your father's son, that's for sure, and no mistake about it."

"Now wait a minute," he tried to interrupt, but she had already launched into her tirade.

"A womanizer," she charged with one finger pointed at him across the table. "And a dangerous business that is, for such men are completely unprepared for an assault on their hearts. Your own mother took Solomon utterly by surprise, for he had never thought to let his heart belong so completely to another. I remember the day he first saw her as clearly as if it were yesterday. The man could talk of nothing else." Judith leaned across the table and tapped Jacob on the end of the nose as if he were but a small child.

"He never had a chance," she whispered conspiratorially, her eyes twinkling in the darkness as she shook that finger at him. "But luckily for him, Tamar was a good woman. Beware the day you fall in love, Jacob, for that woman will have a hold over you well beyond that of most wives, and if you should be so unfortunate that she is not a good woman, she could be your ruin."

Judith folded her hands on the table, her words ending abruptly as some unhappy thought occurred to her. For his part, Jacob struggled not to wonder whether Rebecca's servant was a good woman or not. Indications so far were not in her favor, he was forced to admit, not liking that conclusion, or the fact that it disturbed him so, one bit.

"And how short a time Solomon and Tamar had together," Judith murmured almost to herself, shaking her head slowly. Too late, Jacob wished he had been paying attention so that he might have diverted the memories of his uncle that were now inevitable. Judith's voice dropped even lower as she continued, and Jacob could only listen to her sad words. How often he had wished that he could ease that shadow on her generous heart.

"As did my husband and I," she murmured, closing her eyes for a moment. "Fate can be so cruel." Judith raised her chin and Jacob saw the tears glazing her eyes when she met his gaze.

"Love can be such a fleeting thing," she mused, reaching out to stroke his cheek with affection. "You must promise me that you will grasp it when you can."

Jacob nodded to please his aunt, chewing his bread thoughtfully and staring down into his soup as though he could divine the future within its depths. He felt the change in the air as soon as she had composed herself and cleared his own throat before he met her bright eyes again, considering her for a moment before he spoke.

"How do you know when you fall in love, Aunt Judith?" he asked quietly, marveling at the light that transformed her features when she smiled in recollection, a light that gave him an inkling of how she had looked thirty years past.

"Oh, Jacob, you shouldn't have to ask," she enthused with a heartfelt smile, grasping his hands with hers and pressing a kiss to his knuckle. "Trust your instincts," she urged. "Listen to your heart, for it will always tell you the best path to follow."

Impulsively, Jacob leaned forward and kissed Judith's cheek, tasting the saltiness of her tears against his lips as her grip tightened momentarily on his hand.

Someone tapped on the door and Rebecca jumped at the sound, sternly telling herself to settle down as she took a deep breath to compose herself. She still had a month left to figure out what was so marvelous about this silly book, and being so edgy all the time could only cloud her thinking.

And it was far too soon to expect an answer from Tunis.

She forced her skittish heartbeat to slow as she slipped the book back into its place on Ephraim's shelf, smoothing her kirtle with both hands as she walked to the door with measured steps.

Yusuf stood on the threshold, his eyes flicking to hers and away with uncharacteristic speed. Impossible that *he* could be nervous, she concluded, discarding her first impression without another thought. She noticed immediately the care Yusuf had taken with his clothing, certain she would have remembered this beautiful crimson silk burnous with the filigree of gold embroidery on the hem or the gleaming boots of fine cordovan leather. Had she ever seen them before.

"Good afternoon, Yusuf," she greeted him, wondering what made him stop at her door if he was en route to an important appointment. "How can I help you?"

"A moment of your time, no more," he responded smoothly, and Rebecca nodded, stepping back from the threshold to welcome him with a gesture.

"My home is yours," she said, extending the customary greeting, and Yusuf inclined his head politely as he stepped into the foyer. Fully aware of the unusual tension in the air, Rebecca closed the door, turning to find Yusuf watching her speculatively.

"Perhaps the courtyard?" he suggested smoothly, and she managed to smile in agreement, wishing she knew what this was all about.

Gratefully, Yusuf came immediately to the point once they were seated and her offer of refreshment had been graciously declined.

"There is something of import I would discuss with you," he said, and Rebecca's eyes flew to his, something in his tone revealing the importance to him of what he was going to say.

"Please do," she said when some reply seemed necessary. Yusuf licked his lips and frowned quickly, once again giving Rebecca the inexplicable impression that he was uncertain of himself.

"I know this to be somewhat unconventional," he began slowly, studiously avoiding her gaze, "but you must know that I have long held regard for you." Those sharp green eyes swiveled to meet hers and Rebecca swallowed awkwardly, certain she had not been aware of any such thing and not knowing how to respond without insulting Yusuf.

"Actually," she said with a self-conscious wince when he waited, "I had no idea."

One of Yusuf's dark brows shot skyward and his lips twisted. "You think that I see to household repairs of all women in town?" he demanded curtly, and Rebecca made a vague gesture with one hand.

"I thought you did it out of respect for the friendship you had with Ephraim."

Yusuf leaned forward and propped his elbows on his knees, his eyes boring into hers as though he would read her very thoughts. Rebecca caught a whiff of his body scent, a heady mix of cardamom and musk, and marveled that she had never noted his potent masculinity before. She was suddenly aware of his proximity and the fact that they were alone in the house, and she straightened her posture edgily.

"Surely you know that Ephraim and I ceased to be such good friends near the end," Yusuf said slowly, his voice low and melodic. Rebecca tried to fit that idea in with her own recollections, grateful for the opportunity of something more mundane to occupy her thoughts than Yusuf's sexuality.

"I know you visited less often this year," she recalled with a frown, shooting a glance to Yusuf to find him nodding slowly, "but I simply thought you had other commitments."

"It was Ephraim who made the change," he informed her calmly, and Rebecca felt her surprise show on her face.

"He sensed my feelings and preferred my absence," the Berber concluded, and Rebecca sat back to absorb this news.

How strange that she had had absolutely no idea that Yusuf nursed tender feelings for her. Usually she was so perceptive of other people's feelings, but Yusuf was admittedly difficult to read. She met his eyes again and he almost smiled.

"Your mourning is over," he commented, and Rebecca nodded, fingering the brilliant blue of her favorite kirtle. "It is fitting that you wed again," Yusuf continued in that same low tone, and suddenly she knew what he was going to say. Rebecca tensed, scarcely able to believe it when Yusuf took a deep, unsteady breath and folded his hands together carefully.

"I would ask that you consider my offer for marriage," he said, his words falling with uncharacteristic speed, and Rebecca's hand rose to her lips of its own accord.

"But," she began to protest, and Yusuf held up one finger for her silence.

"The *Qur'an* permits this," he countered, before she could object to the difference in their faith. "It is written that all those who hold the Old Testament in esteem are kindred souls. Surely you know that a Muslim can take to wife one of the People of the Book?"

"Well, I suppose," Rebecca conceded, the notion familiar enough that she knew Ephraim must have told her about it once when she wasn't paying particular attention. "But wouldn't I have to convert?"

"Perhaps if we were in the Eastern Caliphate, you would be pressured to do so, but not here," he said with typical caution.

Unable to believe they were discussing the religious ramifications of a match she couldn't even imagine making, Rebecca rose and paced across the courtyard in confusion. What on earth should she do? What if she didn't hear anything from Tunis? She rubbed her temples and chewed on her thumbnail as she paced.

And what about this business with the book? Yusuf could read Arabic—should she trust him to read the book to her? Rebecca shot a quick glance across the courtyard to find him watching her patiently and increased her pace without meaning to. That this was completely unexpected was an understatement to say the least, and she simply couldn't think everything through fast enough to give Yusuf an answer as he deserved.

To marry a Muslim. Such a thing had never occurred to Rebecca, although she had heard that people did it all the time, and she couldn't believe that it would be as simple as Yusuf claimed. But he must have high regard for her even to suggest such a thing, and it would be terribly rude of her to decline after he had taken such a chance.

"I see that I have surprised you," he commented softly, and Rebecca stopped, spinning to face him uncertainly.

"Yes," she agreed simply, and Yusuf nodded, staring across the courtyard for a long moment before he shoved to his feet and walked toward her. Sweeping aside his glorious crimson cloak, he dropped to one knee and kissed her slipper.

"Yusuf, I am not of rank," Rebecca hissed in shock, laying one hand on his shoulder, but Yusuf spared her a wry smile.

"I am your servant," he murmured, lifting her hand from his shoulder. His grip was gentle, his skin pleasantly warm, and Rebecca stood stock-still as he rose gracefully to his feet again. "And I will await your acceptance," he added huskily, brushing his lips across her fingertips before releasing her hand. *"In sha' Allah'."*

May God grant it.

Rebecca swallowed with difficulty as she watched Yusuf stride from her sunny courtyard and disappear into the shadows of the foyer. A patch of light appeared as he opened the door, silhouetting him for an instant before the door closed and he was gone.

* * *

Pregnant?

Jacob turned the *ketubah* over in his hands in astonishment but there was nothing other than the single line added below Rebecca's neat signature.

> I beg you to make haste. The babe arrives in the spring.

In the spring. Jacob snorted and tossed the piece of parchment aside, running one hand through his hair in annoyance. Who did Ephraim's widow think she was? Summoning him to stand sire to another man's child? He did a quick calculation only to find that this could not possibly be Ephraim's child, and his lip curled in disgust.

He was being taken advantage of and he knew it, cursing his own mislaid gallantry in leaving the contract when he had had the chance to remove it. Had he ever made such a stupid error in judgment? Truly that serving woman's passion had clouded his thinking, he admitted as he dragged a sheet of parchment across the desk impatiently to make his terse response.

There was no way he would be coerced into making this match now, Jacob told himself determinedly, his grip on the quill a little tighter than necessary in his attempt to dismiss the sensation of silky dark hair beneath his fingers. He glared at the *ketubah,* hating the knowledge that there was no way he could deny that that was his signature, whether he had made his mark willingly or no.

After all, he couldn't deny that he had delivered the document to her door. And the paternity of the child would be a question of her word against his. Undoubtedly Rebecca had neighbors who would testify that he had spent considerable time in her home. A court would find in the widow's favor on the basis of the document alone, and Jacob drummed his fingers on the desk with annoyance, knowing that he was trapped.

Unless he could persuade Rebecca to abandon the idea. And that would be better achieved in person.

The thought of making another trip to Toledo to press his case had immediate appeal, but Jacob told himself that it was the prospect of travel that made his blood quicken, not the possibility of seeing Rebecca's servant again.

Although it wouldn't hurt to find out her name, he told himself as he rose purposefully from his desk, barely noticing that his decision had launched a satisfied smile across his lips.

Jacob's horse came to a stop of its own accord as Toledo came into view, the three other merchants with whom he had traveled from Algeciras also pausing to survey the change in the landscape. The wind howled down from the plains and Jacob pulled his dark hood tighter around his face, the damp chill of Andalusia's early winter weather penetrating right to the bone.

The Alcazar fortress with its high square tower still dominated the landscape, the broad sweep of the Tagus River winding down from the east to bend south, then wrap north again, surrounding three sides of the town before it continued west to the sea. The arch of Toledo's great gate marked the end of the single wide bridge that linked the walled city to the opposite shore. The city itself was ancient, the bridge and walls containing vestiges of Visigothic construction, the well-engineered road they had taken from the coast a survivor of the Roman Empire.

But there were differences that immediately captured the men's attention, not only the heavy grill of an iron portcullis dropped across the opening of the gate in the middle of the gusty afternoon, but the vast array of what could only be invading troops camped on the floodplain south of the town.

Despite the relative silence, Toledo appeared to be under siege.

Jacob urged his horse onward, half-anticipating that their progress would be halted before they reached the gate, but the camp remained oddly quiet as they traversed the remaining segment of the road. The silence was disquieting and the four men threw more than one glance of trepidation over their shoulders, only to find the striped silk of the knights' tents in the distance ruffling innocently in the wind.

"Who goes there?" growled a voice in Arabic when they reached the gate, and Jacob relaxed slightly at the sound of the very earthy voice. He identified himself and his companions, listed their goods and business as requested in the usual fashion. The gatekeeper named the toll and the men dug in their purses for the necessary coin.

"You're sure you want to stop here?" the gatekeeper demanded skeptically, his words bringing the merchants' heads up in collective surprise.

"Toledo steel is of great renown," Jacob hedged, wondering what the man was getting at, only to hear a derisive snort in response.

"All you Jews ever think about is money," the man commented with unconcealed disgust. Jacob cast an admonishing glance to one of his companions when the man reached for his knife, and to his relief the statement was allowed to pass without challenge. Obviously Jacob's companion was not used to the antagonism of the mozarabic Christians, and Jacob thought he would do well to grow a thicker skin before passing through the city gates.

"What is going on? Is the city under siege?" Jacob asked calmly, and the keeper stepped out of the shadows of his post to scan the army camped beyond the river.

"Not yet," he said gruffly, his eyes narrowing against the buffet of the wind. "They're waiting for Alfonso himself, according to the gossip, but he's off celebrating Christmas somewhere up north."

"Alfonso of Castile?" Jacob demanded, unable to think of another who could summon such a force, and the gatekeeper shot him a sharp look.

"That's right," he conceded, clearly surprised that Jacob knew that much about regional politics. "He rode clear down to the Mediterranean last year,'' he added quietly, and Jacob nodded in agreement.

The tale of the King of Castile ravaging the Muslim kingdom of Seville, then riding straight into the surf at Cape Tarifa, declaring that his kingdom extended to this point and calling himself Emperor of all Spain, had been told in taverns all the way to Tunis and probably beyond. It had seemed to be empty boasting at the time and had been greeted by a round of wry chuckles. There were hundreds of leagues of territory held by Muslim *taifas* between Alfonso's crown lands and the Mediterranean. Jacob followed the gatekeeper's gaze to the seemingly endless array of tents and wondered if perhaps they had been too quick to dismiss Alfonso's ambitions.

"How long have they been here?" he asked, and the gatekeeper shrugged.

"A month, more or less." Again he shot Jacob one of those piercing glances. "You sure the profits on Toledo steel are worth risking your life?" he demanded archly, but Jacob again declined to take the bait.

"I'll take my chances," he countered smoothly. The gate rose with a creaking groan and the four men entered the city, the raging turbulence of the Tagus behind them echoing the uncertainty in the gatekeeper's voice.

Let the man think what he wanted, but mere money could not have induced Jacob to take a chance on getting out of the city alive. Something far more valuable drove him forward despite the lateness of the season and the difficulties of the voyage past. During this trip, he had come to an unexpected decision, but some sixth sense told him with unflagging certainty that it was a good one.

He suspected that sixth sense might be his heart. And after all, he *had* promised Judith that he would follow its bidding.

Chapter Seven

Rebecca didn't recognize the cloaked stranger on her doorstep and almost closed the door before she recalled the last time she had confronted someone wearing so much black.

Someone just as tall and forbidding.

Her heart leapt and Jacob extended one hand to her, the relief that flooded through her at the sight of those familiar strong fingers making her gasp aloud. Then he stepped across the threshold, his grip closing proprietarily on her waist, and Rebecca pushed back his hood to see his eyes as he lifted her for his kiss.

It was insane, or maybe magical, the way her blood rose in response to his slightest touch, and all her determination to greet him coolly was forgotten the moment his lips met hers. He smelled of dust and salt and horseflesh, and the tip of his nose was cold against her cheek. She arched against his strength in pleasure, sliding her fingers into the thick hair at his nape, all her worries of the past month dissolving before his caress.

Jacob had come! He was here, solid and real, his lips trailing a path to her earlobe and making Rebecca sigh in capitulation. And he wasn't angry with her. He captured her lips again and she ardently returned his embrace, reveling in his presence, barely daring to believe that something had worked out so well.

How could she have doubted her impulse to summon him? Simply having him here on her threshold made Rebecca feel safer than she had since he left, and the certainty that Jacob could resolve everything grew stronger with each passing instant.

"Where?" he murmured huskily, and she shivered at the ruffle of his breath against her throat, the implication behind his words making her heartbeat race in anticipation.

"Upstairs," she responded, and Jacob seemed to hesitate for just an instant before he swept her into his arms as he had once before. He kicked the door to the street closed with an irreverent gesture, sparing Rebecca a heart-stopping grin, and she realized she had not seen him smile like that before.

He looked tired as he headed purposefully for the courtyard, she noted, scanning his features with affectionate concern. There were telling blue smudges beneath his eyes and lines of tension bracketing the corners of his mouth. Rebecca reached up and touched his cheek, still trying to convince herself that he was actually here, and Jacob flicked an indulgent glance her way, the way his lips twisted making her wonder if he had read her very thoughts. She would ensure he had some sleep, Rebecca resolved, stretching up to kiss a corner of his mouth.

But first things first.

Her complete lack of response when she opened the door had been unsettling, to say the least, but that flash of recognition in her dark eyes had been worth the wait, Jacob told himself as he crushed her against his chest and drank deeply of her lips once more.

She was even more intoxicating than he had recalled, and he leaned dizzily back against the wall, certain for a moment that he would stumble on the stairs and send them both plunging to their death. Not now, not when he had so much to tell her, not when the blood surging through his veins told him beyond a shadow of a doubt that he had been right to trust his instincts. There was something rare and wonderful at work here between them and he would have been a fool to turn his back on it.

The spark between them hadn't existed solely in his imagination, Jacob marveled, closing his eyes against the gentle pressure of her fingertips splayed against his cheeks as she framed his face and kissed him sweetly. He felt her heartbeat against the palm of his hand, and its quick pace reassured him that he was not alone in losing his head. His own heart was clamoring and he was suddenly glad of Judith's advice, certain that following it could not possibly lead him false.

Everything was working out perfectly.

Jacob's conviction made him playful and he tumbled onto the pile of cushions on the bedroom floor with her, tickling her as they rolled together, his turban falling away unnoticed. She giggled and twisted in her futile efforts to escape him, her veil losing its hold in the melee, that tangle of hair, which fascinated Jacob so, spilling loose around them. He rolled her beneath him and sobered as he fingered the dark silky strands, staring down into her eyes. She tried to catch her breath from their frolicking as she held his gaze, and Jacob found himself more than casually aware of the fullness of her breasts heaving against his chest.

"I missed you," he murmured, knowing it suddenly to be so. In that moment, Jacob wasn't sure whether he wanted to make love to her or talk to her more, his mind filled with a thousand questions he wanted to ask her. Her features softened and he watched a telling blush tinge her cheeks, her gaze darting away for an instant before she met his eyes shyly once more.

"I missed you, too," she whispered, and her color rose still more. Jacob grinned and leaned down to kiss her lingeringly. She slipped her tongue coyly between his teeth, her gesture summarily deciding him in favor of lovemaking first.

"All of me?" he teased when she shifted beneath his hardness, chuckling when she flushed scarlet.

"Beast!" she accused with sparkling eyes, unsuccessfully trying to stifle her own laughter as she chided him. She swatted him across the shoulder and Jacob rolled away as if mortally wounded, lying absolutely still on his back with his eyes closed until she leaned over him cautiously.

"I didn't hit you *that* hard," she murmured, a thread of concern in her tone as he felt one fingertip prod his shoulder experimentally, and Jacob grabbed her suddenly, laughing aloud as she squealed in shock. She laughed as they tumbled together again, and he nibbled on her ear, closing his eyes against the soft sweep of her hair against his cheek.

"I missed all of you," he whispered against her skin when she was pinned beneath him again, and she simply stared up into his eyes with a slowly dawning smile. He deliberately unfastened the neck of her kirtle and bent to take her nipple in his mouth to illustrate his point, savoring the way she arched toward him with an incoherent little moan as her smile died, her nipple swelling and hardening between his lips.

"All of you," Jacob repeated huskily as he swept her kirtle out of the way and kissed the underside of her breast, the outline of each rib, the indent of her waist. His tongue teased her navel and she squirmed, giggling, until his lips traced a path from there through the tight tangle of curls at the juncture of her thighs. She gasped and twisted but he granted her no respite, the very act of giving her such pleasure arousing him beyond what he could have imagined possible.

This was real, he told himself, knowing that they were making this magical connection on a purely instinctive level and that that could only bode well for every other facet of their lives. They were in harmony in this most fundamental act, and Jacob knew in that moment that they could conquer any obstacle from such a firm foundation.

A shiver raced over her skin as she approached her quickening and he shivered with her, deliberately slowing his caresses to extend her pleasure. She made a little cry that was drawn out into a moan, the blood rush darkening her skin as her fingers gripped his hair convulsively, and he felt a thrill of victory that she rose so intuitively to his touch.

"Please," she gasped, and Jacob needed no second invitation, his chausses torn open in record time, everything inside him melting with satisfaction as he buried himself in her with one smooth gesture.

Jacob reached between them when she shifted to accommodate him and touched her with one thumb, gratified when she immediately gripped the botom of his shaft. She wrapped her arms around his neck and her legs around his waist as she pulled his head down for a long wet kiss. The smell of her, the softness of her wrapped around him, overwhelmed Jacob, each caress adding to his sense that he was completely surrounded by her honeyed warmth.

She contracted around him as he began to move and Jacob wanted to lose himself with her in that instant, the tiny smile of mingled wonder and pleasure that curved her lips when their eyes met sending him racing for the summit and right over the edge.

"You still have your boots on," Rebecca complained drowsily sometime later, rubbing her foot lazily against the offending leather. Jacob propped himself up on his elbows and stared down at her as he tunneled his fingers through her hair, his bemused expression prompting her to smile in response.

"You weren't complaining earlier," he pointed out mischievously, and she laughed, unable to believe she had ever thought those brown eyes cold. To think she was going to spend a lifetime making love like this.

They were never going to get anything else done, Rebecca thought, and almost laughed aloud.

"Hmm," she mused by way of an answer, sparing an assessing glance along the length of Jacob and realizing with surprise that he was still fully dressed. "At least you took off your turban," she commented wryly. Jacob chuckled in turn and Rebecca watched, fascinated by the laugh lines that fanned out around his eyes. He really should laugh more often, she concluded, liking the rich sound of his chuckle.

"I guess I am overdressed," he conceded, and she nodded sagely, finding his unexpected playfulness intriguing.

"Maybe just a little."

Jacob sighed theatrically and rolled to one hip, bending to tug off his boots, nipping at Rebecca's buttocks as he discarded them. Intent gleamed in his eyes for an instant as he leaned over her and she barely had time to wonder what he was up to before he was kissing her with that shocking thoroughness. When he released her, Rebecca was gasping for breath, her pulse picking up speed when she saw that that impish gleam in his eyes was as bright as ever.

"Better?" he asked innocently, but she shook her head decisively.

"More," she demanded, and he obediently unfastened the clasp of his burnous. The heavy wool slipped from his shoulders, but when he bent to kiss her again, Rebecca stopped him with one fingertip planted in the middle of his chest.

"More," she repeated huskily, and caught a glimpse of his grin before he rolled to his feet and peeled off the rest of his clothes in quick succession.

"How much more?" Jacob asked when he stood nude before her, his gaze meandering suggestively over her.

"More than you're up for," Rebecca teased, and Jacob chuckled, lunging after her across the cushions when she took flight. Laughing like children, they cavorted around the room, the way Rebecca managed to feint and get away each time Jacob cornered her making her suspect that he was letting her escape.

She tripped on his burnous and his arms closed around her from behind before she could fall, his very proximity confirming her suspicions. Before she could accuse him, her eye fell on a piece of parchment with cursive writing on its face that was hanging out of a pocket in the discarded cloak.

"What's this?" she demanded, but Jacob didn't even spare it a glance.

"Nothing important," he murmured. Rebecca felt his lips on the nape of her neck and almost melted against him, only the realization of where she had seen that parchment before making her resist. That was her name inscribed on its front, she was sure of it.

"It's the *ketubah,*" she declared, and Jacob straightened, stretching out one toe to shove the parchment back into the folds of the dark wool.

"Like I said, it's nothing important," he murmured, and would have returned to her neck if Rebecca hadn't pulled abruptly away.

"What do you mean, it's nothing important?" she demanded, her ire thoroughly roused.

What sort of game was he playing here? Of course it was important. The signed *ketubah* was the entire reason she had let him back into her bed so easily. Jacob looked confused and Rebecca felt a niggle of doubt that her plan had really worked as well as she had thought.

"It has nothing to do with us," Jacob argued, running one hand quickly through his hair in agitation, and Rebecca couldn't understand what he meant. She propped her hands on her hips and tossed her hair impatiently over her shoulder as she stared him down, determined to have the truth before they went any further with anything.

"What on earth are you talking about?" she demanded, pointing to the partially hidden parchment. "That is a signed *ketubah,* a legal and binding document, and I fail to see how you can simply dismiss it as though it were irrelevant."

"It *is* irrelevant," he declared, and Rebecca's heart sank. Jacob's lips drew into a harsh line and his jaw set as he glared down at the parchment. "That is a *ketubah* that I signed without realizing," he said flatly, "and I have no intention of honoring it."

"What?"

"You heard me," Jacob retorted frostily, moving with pantherlike grace to scoop up the parchment. He wagged it under her nose, his eyes flashing in anger. "My dear aunt tricked me into signing this," he informed her, and Rebecca's heart went cold.

"Then you won't adhere to it?" she asked in a small voice, not in the least appeased when Jacob shook his head stubbornly.

"Maybe once I would have, but not now," he declared, the warmth in his eyes as his gaze lifted to hold hers confusing Rebecca anew before she followed the train of his thought.

Why buy the cow when he could have the milk for free? Her blood boiled at his assumption that her morals were loose, and she took a step closer to him to shake one finger angrily beneath his nose.

"If you think that I will be your mistress—" she began testily, but Jacob crossed the space between them with two strides and cupped her shoulders in his hands.

"I want you to be my wife," he interjected quickly, and Rebecca's heart leapt before her confusion got the better of her once more.

"But you said the *ketubah* wasn't important," she pointed out cautiously, not liking the way Jacob's lips thinned when he flicked a glance to the document in his hand. He straightened away from Rebecca, holding her gaze as he deliberately tore the contract in two. She gasped, but Jacob seemed to take no notice.

"This is for Rebecca and her bastard babe," he said in a low voice as he tossed the torn parchment aside. The relentless expression in Jacob's eyes softened as he studied her features. "And this is for you," he murmured, cupping her face in his hands before he bent to kiss her.

"Wait a minute," Rebecca demanded, pushing him aside when his lips were a finger's breadth away from hers. Something didn't add up. She paced across the room to put some distance between them so she could straighten things out in her mind.

Jacob still didn't know who she was.

Rebecca glanced in his direction to find him looking appropriately bewildered and knew she was right. She writhed inwardly in anticipation of his response to what she had to tell him, but she knew she couldn't let this continue any longer.

"You said before that I misled you," she began cautiously, not liking the way his eyes narrowed as he watched her.

"About your virginity," he retorted, folding his arms across his chest as if he sensed that she had some news he wasn't going to like. Rebecca frowned at his words.

"I never told you I was a virgin," she pointed out, but Jacob arched one brow skeptically.

"Your hair was loose when we met," he countered, and she spread her hands, palms upward.

"But I was home alone and cleaning," she explained, watching Jacob's jaw tighten as he gritted his teeth.

"But you kissed like you never had before," he accused tersely. Rebecca felt her color rise, finding herself suddenly aware that they were arguing in the nude.

"Well, I hadn't," she admitted awkwardly, looking longingly at the surcoat that hung from the hook on the wall behind him. "At least, not like that," she added hastily, certain that she was blushing from head to toe, but Jacob merely watched her coldly.

"What did you think I was talking about?" he demanded abruptly, and she saw that once again he had become that stranger with the hostility in his eyes.

"I thought you had found out who I was," she admitted, holding his gaze for an instant before she looked away. The silence stretched between them and Rebecca crossed her arms across her chest, wishing she could get that surcoat.

"Who are you?" Jacob asked deliberately, his tone dangerously low. Rebecca swallowed awkwardly before she answered.

"I'm Ephraim's widow, Rebecca," she answered quietly, feeling that the words were sticking in her throat. She lifted her chin to meet Jacob's eyes, but he had turned away.

He stalked out to the balcony, bracing his hands on the railing as he glared down at the courtyard, annoyance clear in every line of his body. Rebecca winced at his reaction and took the opportunity to grab her surcoat, shivering in the silence as she slipped its welcome warmth over her shoulders.

"You should have told me." Jacob spun on his heel to confront her with an abruptness that took her breath away.

"I thought you knew," she shot back, distrusting the way that muscle twitched in his jaw.

"I don't believe you," he retorted sharply, and Rebecca's mouth dropped open in shock.

"I am telling you the truth," she insisted, but Jacob only shook his head.

"You knew I thought you were a servant," he charged hotly, and his eyes flashed with anger. "You *had* to know. Why else would I insist on one night without regrets?"

"I don't know why," Rebecca was forced to concede shakily, calling herself a liar but unwilling to add yet another revelation when he was still reeling from the first one. Jacob snorted with derision.

"Yet I don't recall you asking," he accused.

"Oh!" Rebecca gasped in indignation, certain he had gone too far. "Oh, as if I had a chance to ask you anything! I didn't even have a chance to think, you so completely overwhelmed me. Do you really think that anything I might have said would have stopped you from having me?" she challenged.

"Not once you said you wanted me," Jacob shot back, and Rebecca colored, recognizing the truth when she heard it.

She turned to face the window so he wouldn't see her tears rising and paced to the other side of the room. He was right. She had acted like a wanton and he had had every right to take what she had offered.

"What kind of man do you think I am?" Jacob asked quietly into the silence behind her, but Rebecca could only shake her head mutely.

"I don't know," she whispered, more to herself than to him, unable to believe how everything she had envisioned was falling into chaos around her. "I just don't know."

She heard the rustle of cloth behind her as Jacob hauled his clothes on and she closed her eyes, wishing that they could begin again. How had everything become so entangled? How could her instinctive trust of him have been so utterly misplaced?

How was she going to make it through the day knowing that he was never coming back?

"Did you lie about the baby, too?" he demanded tightly, and Rebecca's breath caught in her throat. If she admitted to that, he would walk out of her life, of that she had little doubt.

Was she ready to abandon this magic that they created between them? No. And despite the ordeal of the past few minutes, something deep in her heart told her that this was the man who could help her. Despite their rocky start, despite all the lies that hung between them, there had to be something at the root of this instinctive attraction they had for each other.

Rebecca was surprised by how much she wanted to know what that something was. She couldn't hand him an excuse to leave.

"No," she lied softly, and felt Jacob's gaze bore into her back.

"Turn around and answer me," he insisted in a low voice, and in that moment she hated him for being so perceptive.

Certain she would be unable to deceive him, her heart in her throat, Rebecca turned to find him wearing only his chausses. His arms were folded across his broad chest and his lips were thinned with anger. She lifted her chin, knowing only that she had to convince him of this, and looked right into the forbidding coldness of his eyes.

"I bear your child," she stated with what she hoped was unshakable certainty. Jacob's eyes narrowed for an instant as he studied her face, then he lifted one brow and pursed his lips thoughtfully.

"I've never left any bastards behind and I won't start now," he informed her softly. "We will draw up a new *ketubah.*"

Relief flooded through Rebecca at his words, but Jacob was not yet done. He stepped forward and gripped her chin, compelling her to meet his eyes as he glared down at her.

"Recognize that I'm doing this only for the child," he added in that low tone she found so threatening, and Rebecca managed to nod, despising herself for wishing he would seal their troth with a kiss. Jacob smiled wryly as though he had read her thoughts, and his thumb slid lazily along the edge of her jaw. "Just so neither one of us has any illusions about our marriage," he added, and Rebecca found her voice.

"I have no illusions that *you* possess any tender feelings," she charged, disregarding the warning flash in his eyes.

"You've proven yourself an adept liar several times over," he shot back. "And I don't trust liars."

"While you've proven yourself a shameless womanizer," Rebecca retorted. "And I'm not interested in having your mistresses underfoot." Something gleamed in Jacob's eyes that almost made Rebecca regret her impulsive words, but it was too late to take them back.

"Don't worry," he taunted, and her heart went cold at his calculating expression. "We seem to be compatible enough in that area that I won't need one."

With those words he pulled her closer and kissed her. Rebecca tried to pull away but to no avail, her own body betraying her as Jacob expertly coaxed her response. His touch was irresistible to her and he knew it, just as he had to know that she was cursing him as he nibbled on her neck, his breath in her ear making her shiver right on cue.

At least this could not be sullied, Rebecca consoled herself, resolving to take what was good between them and work from there. She leaned against Jacob, submitting willingly to his touch, only to be mortified when he pulled immediately away.

"Yes," he observed thoughtfully, his steady voice in marked contrast to Rebecca's own shattered emotions. "Yes, I suspect we will be able to come to terms on that issue."

Jacob spun on his heel and walked out of the bedroom, scooping up his shirt on the way and never looking back. Rebecca heard his footfalls on the stairs and in the kitchen, her angry tears not breaking until she was certain he wouldn't hear her sobs.

She had lied to him! With difficulty Jacob resisted the urge to break something, knowing that if he had stayed upstairs any longer, he might have wrung her pretty neck. Had he ever met a more annoying woman? Or a more distracting one? He would have handed her the surcoat himself if he'd thought she would put it on and give him a chance to think without those rosy nipples dancing before his eyes.

She was Rebecca.

It was almost impossible to believe and Jacob gritted his teeth as he paced the circumference of the kitchen restlessly, forcing himself to calm down and think this through rationally. The woman that Judith had plotted to have him marry and the woman who had occupied a sizable percentage of his thoughts this past month or so were one and the same.

The entire situation might have been funny if he'd been in a better mood.

Casting around for something to occupy his hands, Jacob bent to stoke the flowing embers of the fire. Had she really thought that he knew who she was? He reviewed all of their exchanges and conceded that that might have been the case, although he couldn't imagine why she would have agreed to the terms of liaison.

Her charge that he had shown himself a shameless womanizer had hit home, all the more because he would never have made such a condition if he had known her real identity. In fact, he would never had made such an offer to any woman if he had not been so completely and unexpectedly inflamed by her touch. What was it about her that drove him beyond reason?

Jacob frowned at the flames, unable to reconcile the way she had offered herself like a courtesan yet responded to his touch as though she were discovering lovemaking for the first time. Then there was the contrast between her deception of him, however deliberate it had been, and the forthrightness with which she had just now insisted on clearing the confusion between them. She was an intoxicating mixture of opposites, and as much as he disliked the way her presence scattered his thoughts, he couldn't have walked out her door now to save his life.

What kind of woman had he agreed to wed? Jacob recalled Judith's warning and felt a shadow of dread, knowing with frightening certainty that he couldn't break his word. He was committed to see this through, one way or another, and he was forced to admit that it was not only his sense of duty to his unborn child that propelled him onward. He was fascinated by this woman, determined to sort out the paradoxes in her behavior and find the woman of whom he had had such telling glimpses.

And there was the matter of his honor, he reminded himself, emphasizing that thought with a jab of the poker into the flames. He would prove to this woman that he was good to his word, that he was not some shameless womanizer, if it was the last thing he did.

After all, if Ephraim had grown into a man even remotely like the child Jacob recalled, Rebecca would be well justified to have a low opinion of men.

* * *

A tempting smell rising from the kitchen coaxed a reluctant but hungry Rebecca from her room as the streets fell into indigo darkness. She dressed and slipped silently down the stairs, hesitating on the threshold of the kitchen as she watched Jacob stir something over the fire. He wore a full-sleeved white shirt and she saw now the pack he had discarded inside the door when he arrived. His movements were unhurried as he cooked with practiced ease.

"I can't find the saffron," he complained without turning, and Rebecca knew her presence had been detected. She squared her shoulders with determination, his thoughtfulness making what she had to do even more difficult, and walked to the tall cupboard against one wall.

"Up here," she said, reaching up onto the top shelf and retrieving the glass vial with its few golden threads of spice. Their fingers brushed as she handed him the container and Rebecca pulled quickly away, not knowing what to think when Jacob leveled a calm smile in her direction.

"You need some more," he commented idly, his gaze holding hers as he shook the vial between them. "I'll pick some up tomorrow at the *souk.*"

"Oh, no," she protested, the words out before she thought to stop them. "It's too expensive." Jacob glanced in her direction, then turned deliberately to the pot simmering over the fire as he dropped in the last three strands of saffron.

"We're going to be married, Rebecca," he commented with some measure of amusement in his tone, and her heart thumped at the first sound of her name on his lips. "I think it's not that inappropriate for me to buy you some saffron."

"Do you think that's such a good idea?" she blurted out, her carefully planned words disappearing.

"You definitely need saffron," he pointed out dryly, but Rebecca shook her head.

"Not that."

Jacob looked up and studied her silently, his expression telling Rebecca that he had followed her thoughts.

"Our child will be legitimate, Rebecca," he informed her softly, and she felt her lie threatening to choke her anew. Tears of frustration rose as she desperately tried to summon the courage to tell him the truth, only to find Jacob's strong hands gently cupping her shoulders.

"You mustn't let our argument upset you," he murmured with a tenderness that completely dissolved her determination. "Everything is cleared up now and it will all work out fine. Tomorrow I'll talk to the elders at the synagogue, and as soon as we're married we'll head back to Tunis. All right?" He tipped her chin up with one finger and Rebecca could not have hurt him with the truth in that moment for anything.

"Now come and have something to eat, for the baby if nothing else." Jacob ushered her to the table and Rebecca let herself be cajoled. The paella smelled marvelous and she *was* hungry, baby or no baby.

She realized that Jacob was making an effort to give them a fresh start, and who knew what that concession was costing him. Rebecca glanced in his direction in time to see his brows pull together in a quick frown of concentration as he checked the simmering pot. It would be churlish of her not to reciprocate when he had made such an effort. And surely there would be better moments to discuss this in the weeks to come.

Chapter Eight

It was downright disconcerting how charming Jacob could be when he put his mind to it, Rebecca admitted with a frown as she watched the door close behind him the next morning.

She could find absolutely no flaw with his behavior since dinner and it was more than a little unsettling. He had been the perfect gentleman, thoughtful of her to a fault, unfailingly polite. Rebecca retrieved the broom from the corner and attacked the hearth with a vengeance, telling herself that he must be up to something and hearing the accusation ring false in her own ears.

Why did he have to be so nice when she had resolved to confess to her terrible lie? A lie she had declared not once or even twice but *three* times. It simply wasn't fair.

If she had thought she might whisper the truth in Jacob's ear during the night and clear her conscience, she had been in for a surprise. She had been stunned when Jacob had made it clear that he had no intention of sharing her bed again until they were wed. Stunned, relieved and surprisingly disappointed. It had seemed to her in that moment that the flicker of amusement in Jacob's dark eyes was a result of him perceiving all three of those responses, although Rebecca couldn't imagine that she was that easily read.

Terrific. Now she had to tell a man with *ethics* that she was a liar.

Rebecca had been certain that she wouldn't be able to sleep, so worried was she about her deceit and its repercussions. There was also the matter of whether Jacob would be good to his word, and she fretted as she heard him walking around downstairs, even as she wondered why she was so concerned. It would hardly be calamitous if Jacob made love to her after all they had already done together, but even knowing how foolish her concern was, she hadn't been able to shake it.

The distinctive creak of Ephraim's favorite chair in the study had soon revealed Jacob's whereabouts. Rebecca had closed her eyes and exhaled slowly to force herself to relax, telling herself to trust that he would be good to his word and not disturb her.

The low rumble of a man's voice had carried to her ears unexpectedly and her eyes had flown open in the darkness. Admittedly it had been Hebrew that Jacob read aloud to himself, not Arabic, but Rebecca had smiled to herself nonetheless, immeasurably reassured by the soothing sound. She had listened carefully but had been unable to make out the words and had closed her eyes once more, the sound of his voice the last thing she remembered before the morning sun had slanted through the doorway and awakened her.

And Jacob had made the tea and heated some water for washing before she came downstairs. It was almost too much to believe and Rebecca had shot a suspicious glance in his direction, only to earn another of those wry half-smiles.

Of course, the inevitable result of this was that she was unable to tell him the truth about the child, and even knowing it was irrational, Rebecca couldn't help but blame Jacob for thwarting her good intentions. When he had pressed a chaste kiss to her forehead before departing this morning, and bade her be careful, she had stifled a healthy urge to kick him.

How dare he be nice to her when she had something vile to confess? Especially when it was something that was sure to infuriate him.

Something that would throw the very idea of this marriage into jeopardy.

And that was the crux of it. Although marrying Jacob and moving to Tunis would undoubtedly solve the entire issue of whatever that thief had demanded and insisted he would return for, Rebecca had to admit that the concept had more appeal than that. Even since the previous night, she had seen a side of Jacob that increasingly intrigued her, although what she had seen—or more accurately felt—before that had been admittedly far from unattractive.

She liked the fact that Jacob had cooked, that he had tried to give them a fresh start. She liked the way he paid attention to things, focusing on whatever occupied him, whether it was checking the paella or listening to her when she showed him the house. It was a trait that would have been completely foreign to Ephraim, who had always been thinking of three or four things at the same time in a distracted way and had never had a clear grasp of what was happening right at the moment.

Rebecca liked the way Jacob's lips twisted wryly when he found something amusing but thought it tactless to laugh, and found it amazing how often she knew exactly what had piqued his sense of humor. She liked how aware she was of her own femininity when she felt Jacob's gaze on her, and she knew without a doubt that she could very quickly get used to this growing trust that he would do exactly what he said he would. Unlike Ephraim, who had promised anything just to please her and then promptly forgot it as soon as he opened a book and lost himself in its pages.

It was a kind of consideration that Rebecca found particularly appealing, having spent most of her life fending for herself. The very idea that Jacob was concerned about her and her wishes was intoxicating in itself. As if that weren't enough, there was something fundamentally appealing about him, something that made her want to do things for him.

She checked that dangerous thought with the reminder that she still had to tell him about the void in her womb, knowing the news would not be well received. She ignored the little pang that jolted through her heart in response.

Judith had been right, Rebecca admitted to herself as she vigorously swept out the kitchen. Jacob was a good catch and she would be a fool to let him go. She sighed wistfully and the frenzied pace of her sweeping gradually slowed. If only there was more than this tenuous pretense of a child holding them together.

If only she could tell Jacob the truth without the risk of losing him.

The response to Jacob's inquiries at the synagogue was not at all what he had expected.

As a stranger in town, he had anticipated some question to his marrying Rebecca and had brought letters of introduction from Tunis to counter that objection, even though he had thought then that he was marrying a mere servant. He also had letters of credit to attest to his financial situation and even one document ascertaining the trustworthiness of his character. And there was the obligatory letter from Judith, detailing their admittedly distant family connections in Andalusia.

Jacob had expected to be grilled on his own household arrangements and his intentions with regard to this young widow under the elders' jurisdiction. He had fully anticipated that they would want to review the new *ketubah* that he had had Rebecca sign this morning to ensure that her interests were protected.

To his astonishment, the bearded older men seemed more interested in the fate of Ephraim's house than his widow, a fact that Jacob found both shocking and distasteful. His carefully bound pile of parchment was almost completely disregarded as the men locked on to what was apparently the matter of most concern.

"What do you intend to do with the house?" was the first inquiry after Jacob introduced himself, and he met the eyes of the elderly man named Isaac with surprise.

"I really hadn't thought about it," he demurred while he tried to shift his focus from woman to domicile. Had he missed something of import? Although Rebecca's home was comfortable, it hadn't struck him as remarkable in any way, and he couldn't understand what about it would engender such interest.

"It will fetch a good price," assured another, whom he thought had been introduced as Samual.

"Really?" Jacob commented, unable to hide his surprise.

"Excellent location," Isaac assured him with a pat on his arm that set off all of Jacob's warning alarms. Unless people in Andalusia had a vastly different idea of a good location, that was an outright lie. The house was in the Jewish quarter, but it was far too close to the public bathing houses to be in an entirely reputable neighborhood.

Definitely there was something else in the wind and Jacob struggled not to show his awareness of that fact. Let them think him ignorant or stupid. Perhaps then they would unwittingly reveal more.

"I suppose you're right," he admitted slowly, managing to summon a passably genuine smile. "I had only been thinking of Rebecca, but the house will be of no use to us when we move."

"And good coin is always welcome with a new bride," Isaac confirmed cheerfully, to which Jacob could only nod.

"And what of the books?" inquired the rabbi himself, but Jacob shrugged.

"I have no interest in books myself," he confessed mildly, surprised when the assembled men immediately shook their heads in unison.

"You won't be wanting to move all those books to Tunis," asserted Samual.

"Too much shipping weight," Isaac added sagely.

"And the cost of transport these days," contributed the rabbi, rolling his eyes theatrically.

"And they could become damaged with this wet winter weather," Samual observed.

"What a waste that would be," Isaac confirmed with a sad shake of his head. "All that expense for nothing."

"Perhaps you're right," Jacob conceded, amazed at the interchange before him. His suspicion that all was not as it seemed was confirmed when the rabbi clutched his sleeve.

"We have a custom here of offering first to the synagogue elders," he explained huskily, his eyes so bright that Jacob had no doubt the "custom" had been invented on the spot.

"Really?" he confined himself to commenting mildly, and the rabbi nodded assertively.

"And I'm sure Rebecca would want to adhere to the customs of the town," Isaac added, his expression sharp with what Jacob would have called avarice in any other situation.

"It would seem tactless to do otherwise," Jacob acquiesced quietly, watching with interest as a ripple of anticipation rolled over the group of men.

Their curiosity satisfied that nothing would be leaving town, even though Jacob had been careful not to commit himself to that, the elders were perfectly content to return their attention to the pending wedding. Jacob concluded the arrangements for the following Friday, accepting Isaac's recommendation of an inn near the *souk* for his accommodation in the interim.

The rabbi assured Jacob that the local matchmaker wouldn't mind staying with Rebecca and helping her make ready, especially as she had no other family, a fact that Jacob hadn't known. It hadn't even occurred to him that Rebecca might be leaving family by moving to Tunis and he cursed his own thoughtlessness in not asking her opinion, resolving that he would ensure she felt welcome in his own home.

Relieved to have the arrangements made, he shook hands all around, his curiosity unabated as he made his way out of the synagogue and spared a glance to the darkening sky. He needed to tell Rebecca what had been decided before he moved to the inn, and he set a quick pace through the winding streets so he might arrive before the rain began. Perhaps they would eat together first, Jacob thought with a smile as he recalled the precarious new start they had made. Trusting his heart was proving to be much easier than he had thought.

But what was in that house or those books that the elders wanted so badly? He recalled suddenly the thieves in the courtyard on the first night he had spent with Rebecca and wondered if she had ever found out what they were after. He would have to ask her, although judging by the mutinous way she had regarded him this morning, Jacob was not at all certain that she would tell him anything she knew.

One thing was certain: Jacob had no intention of selling a single book or moving out of the house until he found out what was going on.

A soft rap at the door brought Rebecca's sweeping to a halt and she was momentarily dumbfounded to find Yusuf on her doorstep.

"I believe you have had adequate time to consider your response," he said calmly, and it took Rebecca a second to understand what he was talking about.

His proposal! Rebecca felt her color rising in embarrassment at her gaffe in not answering him more quickly. She stepped back and nervously invited Yusuf into the house. His eyes flicked over her expression and she realized that he hadn't missed her response, the way his lips thinned telling her that he had probably already guessed her answer.

"May I offer you some tea?" she said, wishing she could make things right so simply. Yusuf shook his head slowly.

"I thank you, but it is not necessary," he declined politely, indicating the courtyard with a sweep of one hand. "Perhaps we could simply sit," he suggested, and Rebecca nodded before she preceded him and took a seat on one of the stone benches. She spared a glance to the sky, distrustful of the low hanging clouds, but it was not raining for the moment at least.

Yusuf folded his hands carefully in his lap, his gaze fixed on them for a moment before he lifted his lids abruptly and impaled Rebecca with that piercing green gaze that saw too much.

"I suspect you intend to decline my offer," he said softly, and Rebecca thought she saw a shadow of disappointment tinge his eyes when she simply nodded. Feeling terribly cruel, she leaned forward and covered his hand with hers.

"You must understand, Yusuf, that I had already signed a *ketubah* when you made your offer," she explained hastily, and he frowned at the news.

"Why did you not tell me of this?" he inquired with some measure of confusion, and Rebecca looked away with discomfort.

"I was not certain that anything would come of it," she admitted, disliking the sound of that but not having any other explanation. She dared to look at the Berber and found his eyes narrowed assessingly.

"It was not a local arrangement, then?" he demanded. Rebecca was compelled to shake her head, a response that apparently did not meet with Yusuf's favor.

"What do you know about this man?" he asked, his voice sharper than it had been, and Rebecca shrugged.

"He's a merchant, a Jew. He lives in Tunis." Her voice faded before her companion's disapproval and she met Yusuf's frown with a question in her eyes, not understanding the reason for his apparent concern.

"Where did you meet him? Here in Toledo?" Yusuf bit out the words and Rebecca could only nod, mystified at the source of his anxiety. "Was he introduced through friends, acquaintances, family, a matchmaker?"

"No, he came to extend his aunt's condolences over Ephraim's death," she explained quickly, not at all liking his tone. "Yusuf, I don't understand why you are so concerned about this," she continued haughtily, but he cut her short, leaning forward to grip her hands tightly between his.

"You don't understand?" Yusuf made a sound under his breath that Rebecca might have thought an obscenity if she hadn't known him as well as she did. "Do you know this aunt well enough to recognize her signature? Do you know her at all? Had you even heard of her existence before this man came to your door? Rebecca—" He tugged impatiently on her hands. "Don't you see that you have no way of knowing whether this man is telling you the truth? He could be anybody, a thief, a murderer, an adulterer with wives in seven other cities, for all you know."

"But I trust him," she protested, hearing the telling waver in her own voice. Was she being unreasonably naive? Jacob certainly had gone out of his way to charm her, that much she had to admit, but could Yusuf's accusations possibly be right?

"But you mustn't marry him on the basis of simple trust." Yusuf made a sound of frustration deep in his throat and fixed his gaze on her once again. "Understand, Rebecca, that I am only concerned for your safety and that I am not spreading doubt simply because you refused me." He held her eyes for a long moment and she was convinced that he was telling her the truth, although his concern was misplaced. Hadn't she always been a good judge of character?

"Yusuf," she began firmly, unsuccessfully trying to extricate her hands from his grip. "I appreciate what you're saying, but I think that you are reading too much into the situation. I married Ephraim without ever having met him."

"But a matchmaker arranged the marriage," he argued, and Rebecca shrugged in concession.

"Yes, and I knew her. But she hadn't ever met Ephraim, either. These things happen all the time, and although it's very sweet of you to worry about me, I assure you that I'll be fine.''

"In Tunis? And who will defend you there if you find out that you're wrong?'' he demanded skeptically. "Or maybe you won't make it that far. The old road is long to Algeciras and has many quiet stretches where travelers often go missing." Rebecca's heart twisted at Yusuf's words, but she refused to let herself be intimidated.

"Now I know you're being foolish," she chided him. "What possible reason would anyone have to kill me? If I was a wealthy woman, your worries might have some merit, but as it is, Yusuf, I have nothing but myself to offer."

He regarded her silently for a moment, as if debating the wisdom of continuing, before he leaned forward to speak again. "I would not dream of undervaluing your charms," he insisted gallantly, "but you have much more to offer than that."

Rebecca almost waved off what she thought was a gratuitous compliment, but the somber expression in Yusuf's eyes made her pause.

"Yes," he insisted softly, nodding as he noted her hesitation. "You possess something of great value, something you may not even be aware you have. Something many would kill to acquire."

The courtyard seemed suddenly much colder than it had been, the conviction in Yusuf's tone making Rebecca shiver. The sky brooded darker, more threatening than it had been when they took their seats, the fitful gusting of the wind rattling the roof tiles and telling her that the storm was almost upon them.

Yusuf's manner reminded her uncannily of the intruder in the night and the mysterious object she had promised to produce. An obligation she had almost forgotten in her relief over Jacob's return. Only two weeks now, Rebecca calculated wildly, hoping against hope that she and Jacob would have left Toledo by then.

"I don't know what you mean," she said unsteadily, but Yusuf touched one warm fingertip to her lips.

"I don't need to know what you know," he whispered reassuringly, leaning so close to her that she could feel his breath brush her cheek as he spoke. "Do nothing foolish, Rebecca, I entreat you. Ephraim knew something, something powerful, something that may have led him to an early grave. I do not doubt that he hid some vestige of his knowledge, and should you find it, do not make his mistake. Reveal it or its presence to no one. Trust no one." Yusuf's voice dropped to a hoarse whisper and Rebecca leaned closer to catch his words, her pulse tripping in her ears.

"Your very life may depend upon it." Yusuf held her gaze with an intensity that she couldn't challenge, his warning making her very blood run cold. Was it true? Would someone kill her for something Ephraim had hidden here? She almost darted a glance to the fountain, wondering anew what she had missed in that seemingly inconsequential little book.

"I can't imagine..." Rebecca began to protest, but Yusuf's grip tightened on her fingers so that she almost cried out.

"Promise me," he hissed, and his eyes blazed with a determination that seemed completely at odds with his character. Rebecca stared into those green depths and nodded helplessly, feeling compelled to make the gesture solely by the weight of his will.

"By all means, don't let me interrupt."

Rebecca jumped at the sound of a man's voice and closed her eyes against the familiarity of that sardonic tone. She pulled her hands from Yusuf's grip and rose quickly to her feet, feeling her cheeks heat as she met the condemnation in Jacob's eyes, Yusuf's enigmatic words still echoing in her head.

Before she could collect her thoughts enough to say anything, Yusuf stepped forward from behind her and extended one hand to the new arrival.

"I believe we have met before," he said smoothly. Rebecca's heart sank as she saw Jacob's lips set and he shot her a positively glacial look. He was angry, that much was clear, and she had little doubt who was the focus of that fury. But what had she done to earn his condemnation?

"Yes," Jacob rasped, making short work of the obligatory handshake as though he found it distasteful.

"It seems my congratulations are in order," Yusuf added conversationally, seemingly unaware of the hostility crackling in the air, and Rebecca wished he would simply leave. Unfortunately, Yusuf didn't seem to have any intention of departing, for he gestured that she should sit again, and when Rebecca sank to the bench, he followed suit.

Jacob flicked a sharp glance to Rebecca and she almost cringed beneath his regard, tilting her chin stubbornly to meet his eyes instead. Honestly, he acted as though he had found the two of them locked in a passionate embrace. She would willingly admit that she and Yusuf had been closer than might be considered proper, and alone in the house, but there were extenuating circumstances. She had just declined the man's proposal, for goodness' sake.

"Yes," Jacob replied tersely, his tone sounding as though he were reconsidering the wisdom of taking her to wife. "The arrangements are being made."

"And you will be moving to Tunis after the wedding?" Yusuf prodded, apparently seized by an uncharacteristic bout of curiosity. Jacob arched one brow at his inquiry and folded his arms across his chest.

"You have had a long chat," he commented in a low voice. "You must have been visiting for quite a while." It seemed to Rebecca that he placed unnecessary emphasis on the word "visiting" and her ire rose at his implication.

"Yusuf is an old friend," she informed Jacob frostily, and he met her gaze squarely.

"Clearly," he conceded softly. "However, my concern is not with your past friendships, but whether those habitual alliances will continue in the future." With this, he turned to Yusuf and the two men practically glared at each other.

"As I have told you before," Yusuf said quietly a moment later, "I have only the lady's interests at heart."

"It would seem that both her heart and her interests should be solely my concern now." Jacob bit out the words and Yusuf inclined his head in concession.

"Yet you do her the disservice of assuming the worst," he pointed out. "Hardly a commendable way to start." Jacob's eyes flashed and Rebecca laid a restraining hand on the Berber's arm, unable to believe that he had gone so far.

"Yusuf, that's enough," she murmured under her breath, earning herself a hard glare from her fiancé. Well, what did he expect her to do? she thought as a ripple of anger coursed through her. She was damned if she let Yusuf talk and damned if she tried to stop him!

"As you say," Yusuf agreed a long awkward moment later, but Rebecca had no chance to draw a breath of relief. She felt her color rise, all too aware of Jacob's disapproval when Yusuf rose from the bench, then dropped to his knee in that elegant gesture and brushed his lips audaciously across the toe of her slipper.

Rebecca closed her eyes, certain she would die of mortification at his inappropriate display and not having the nerve to watch Jacob's response. She could practically feel his disapproval washing over her and couldn't begin to imagine what he would have to say about all this. What had possessed Yusuf to embarrass her like this?

"I remain your devoted servant," he murmured for her ears alone, but Rebecca had no doubt that Jacob had heard the soft words. It was quiet enough in the courtyard to hear the flagstones breathing. Yusuf looked up and met Rebecca's eyes with an intensity in his expression that surprised her.

"Remember your vow, Rebecca," he admonished in a low voice, and her eyes widened briefly in acknowledgment. Why on earth had she made that promise?

With that, Yusuf turned and strode out of the courtyard, the embroidered hem of his burnous swirling dramatically in his wake.

Thunder rumbled overhead and Rebecca knew it was going to rain any minute, but she didn't trust herself to stand, couldn't even think of slipping past Jacob into the house. Yusuf's words returned to haunt her, feeding her own doubts about how well she knew this man she had committed to wed.

Jacob was considerably bigger than her, she realized now, and his controlled tone hadn't fooled her about the extent of his anger. He was furious, she knew him well enough to know that, although she couldn't fathom why.

"I had no idea you had such devoted admirers," Jacob observed dryly a silent eternity after the Berber had gone.

As if all of this were her fault! Trust him to find her responsible for that sorely misplaced display of masculine head butting! The derision in Jacob's tone gave Rebecca the strength she needed to face him, and the judgment he had made without even asking for an explanation fueled her own anger. Yusuf had been right: he did her a disservice by assuming that she was guilty.

"Yusuf Khudabanda is an old friend," she snapped, risking a glance at Jacob to find him resolutely folding his arms across his chest once more.

"So you've said," he countered tersely, and she felt at a distinct disadvantage from her seat on the bench. "I'm wondering just how *intimate* a friend he is."

"How dare you!" She rose regally to her feet, Jacob's insinuation making her angry enough not to care what he did to her. Her anger adequate to meet his, Rebecca advanced on Jacob and jabbed her finger at his chest to punctuate her points. "You, who bedded me within minutes of our meeting—*you* dare to stand there and make moral judgments on a man who has always been gracious and kind to me." Jacob snorted with unconcealed disbelief.

"I wasn't born yesterday," he informed her icily, gesturing to the abandoned stone benches with one finger. "*That* was past friendly, my sweet, and I've no doubt that if I'd been a bit longer, I would have found you being friendly on your back!"

"You vile, despicable man!" Rebecca cried, inflamed by the injustice of his accusations. "How can you even say such a filthy thing?"

"I saw what I saw," Jacob maintained coldly, his eyes narrowing. "And don't forget that I know well enough how enthusiastic you can be in showing your friendliness."

Before Rebecca could find the words to express her fury, he stepped forward and gripped her shoulders, lifting her to her toes despite her struggles and compelling her to meet his eyes. A flash rent the sky overhead and thunder crackled in the distance. The clouds broke open and the long-threatened rain began to splash on the tiles around them with increasing intensity.

"What's past is past," Jacob rasped, seemingly oblivious to the rain drenching them both, and Rebecca recognized that dangerous tone. "But from this point on, you will be my woman and mine alone. I have no interest in sharing your charms, whatever your feelings to the contrary. Understand?"

"You will not tell me what to do," she hissed between her teeth, and Jacob's eyes flashed angrily as his grip tightened on her shoulders.

"You will yield on this," he informed her, and Rebecca felt the weight of his will upon her as surely as she felt the rain on her head and shoulders.

"Or what?" she prodded, unable to let the matter rest, and his nostrils flared.

Something flickered deep within her and Rebecca was shocked to realize that she was becoming aroused by their arguing, that she wanted nothing more than to make love to him here and now. She imagined his strength within her, the cool slick tiles pressed into her back, the rain pouring over their entangled bodies, and she licked her lips unintentionally, some sense of her own sexual power flowering when Jacob's gaze brightened and he watched her gesture hungrily.

"You know the punishment for adultery as well as I do," Jacob growled, but his words lacked the angry undertone they had had just moments before.

Rebecca sensed that he was approaching the limits of his control and deliberately held his gaze, her frustration of the past few hours finding some kind of vindication in testing him like this.

"Would you cast the first stone, Jacob?" she murmured in challenge, not knowing what devil had taken command of her but unable to stop herself from leaning forward to nip the tender spot beneath his earlobe. What possessed her in this man's presence?

Rebecca felt Jacob shudder and smiled to herself, reaching to roll her tongue in his ear before she continued in a whisper, "Or would you rather ensure that I have no time to wander?"

Jacob's arms closed around her so quickly and so tightly that all the breath was crushed out of her lungs, but Rebecca didn't care. Every fiber of her being was singing in victory as he kissed her with an intensity that was sure to leave her bruised. She speared her fingers through his hair, knocking his turban askew and feeling the rain soak into the thickness of his curls. Water ran over her fingers, her hair, her face and flowed in a chilly rivulet between her breasts, but she was aware only of the fire of Jacob's touch.

She sighed with satisfaction when she felt the wet tiles against her back and opened her mouth to Jacob's tongue. His erection pressed into her hip and she purred with pleasure, welcoming the cool beat of the rain as his fingers closed around her exposed nipple.

"Oh, Jacob," she murmured, still unable to believe the magic he wrought when he touched her. Her utterance seemed to recall him to his senses. Jacob lifted his head and stared down at her, his breath coming in short gasps as Rebecca watched the amazement dawn in his eyes.

The moment was past, she realized as the heat in his gaze was shuttered away, and the disappointment welling up inside of her threatened to swallow her whole.

"This is madness," he muttered, and she sensed his withdrawal before he moved, gasping a denial even as he extricated himself from her embrace. Jacob rose to his feet and stared away for a moment before he turned back to offer her his hand, and Rebecca's heart sank at the coldness in his eyes.

"Why?" she asked, genuinely confused and feeling less than graceful as she got to her feet. He touched her cheek as if in regret, then his lips thinned anew and she forgot that there had been any softness in his expression.

"You will not make me break my vow," he informed her tersely, and Rebecca drew a deep breath of indignation.

"That sounds like an accusation," she retorted, not liking the way he merely lifted one brow in response.

"At least we understand each other," Jacob shot back in acknowledgment, and Rebecca's hand darted out of its own volition to slap his face. He caught her wrist easily and pulled her against him, and she felt the anger emanating from his every pore.

"I keep my promises," he informed her huskily, and Rebecca scanned his features for some vestige of tenderness to no avail. "Just as you will keep the one you made to me by signing that *ketubah.*" Capturing her chin in his other hand, he kissed her hard. Rebecca tried to squirm away unsuccessfully, almost falling backward when he abruptly released her and stepped away.

"Berta will be staying with you until the ceremony on Friday," Jacob informed her coldly. "Try to behave yourself until she arrives."

"You beast!" Rebecca flew after him as soon as she absorbed the words, but he was gone, striding through the house and out into the street without another word, leaving her pounding the door in frustration in his wake. She shivered, suddenly aware that her kirtle was soaking wet and clinging to her like a second skin, then exhaled shakily in an effort to compose herself.

How like Jacob to blame her for what had almost happened! He was determined to see her as some kind of seductress of the highest order, when ironically enough, he was the only man who had ever inflamed her to such wanton behavior. It would have been funny if it hadn't been so tragic, and Rebecca felt hot tears slip over her cheeks.

What had she let herself in for?

Chapter Nine

He was going to kill her one of these days, Jacob told himself, still clenching and unclenching his hands reflexively as he strode blindly through the streets of Toledo.

Although it was a lot more likely that he'd spend the rest of his life in bed with her. That last thought almost made him smile and took some of the edge off his anger. He took a deep breath and forced himself to relax.

Had anyone ever been able to make him so angry? He hadn't even been able to think when he found her there with her hands clasped in the Berber's and the two of them staring into each other's eyes like moonstruck lovers. He could have cheerfully killed Yusuf in that moment and the man had seemed not only to sense it but to dare him to follow the urge.

And if he had had any intention of discovering the truth once the other man left, Rebecca's attitude had done little to encourage that. Daring him to keep her too busy to be unfaithful. He snorted and shook his head, unaware of the falling rain. Did the woman have any idea how close he had come to shaking her until her teeth rattled? Jacob smiled grimly to himself and sidestepped a woman bent over double as she ran through the rain. He'd have no trouble keeping Rebecca occupied in bed, of that much he was certain.

Judith had been right, he conceded wryly, knowing that he couldn't have walked away from Rebecca now, regardless of what she did. That thought made him deeply uneasy and Jacob felt his gut twist as he splashed through the growing puddles. What kind of woman was she? Did he even know? Every time he thought that he caught a glimpse of a sweet and sensitive woman he could easily come to care for, the image twisted and she took on the role of harlot with consummate ease. And it was considerably less than encouraging that she fascinated him either way.

There was no doubt about it: Rebecca held his heart right in those slim fingers of hers and Jacob could only hope that he had not misplaced his trust in granting her its burden.

Not that he had had any choice in the matter.

If only she didn't act as though they were inventing kissing every time they touched, as though it were a new drug of which she couldn't get enough, he thought with frustration. If only she didn't fire this possessiveness he hadn't known he was capable of; if only she didn't inflame him so that the most remote possibility of her even looking at another man made him see red.

It was ridiculous and as much a product of his own twisted thinking as her actions, and Jacob knew it, but there was nothing he could do when the passion took hold of his gut and made him act the part of the jealous lover as though the role were written for him alone. And it wasn't helped by the fact that Rebecca seemed to know precisely what to say to push him even further.

Almost as though she enjoyed provoking him, if that was possible.

But what was he thinking? How could he doubt her intentions? After all, Rebecca carried his child. Their child. The thought dispelled the last of Jacob's anger like mist before the morning sun. That fact alone should be enough to allay his jealousy, that she had chosen to take the baby to term in the face of a thousand other options, without even knowing whether he would come to her when she had sent him the *ketubah*. The woman obviously held him in some regard, for bearing a child with or without a spouse was to risk her own life.

Had anything happened between her and the Muslim? It didn't really matter, Jacob resolved with his newly cleared thinking, telling himself that they both deserved the opportunity to start fresh. He smiled to himself in recollection of Rebecca's challenge and wondered if she had known what she was bargaining for in suggesting that he ensure she have no time to wander.

That was a challenge he planned to make good on and he doubted either one of them would regret it.

It was late afternoon before Berta arrived. Rebecca found the older woman on the threshold, already in midsentence.

"—so exciting, dear. Look at this rain. Can you believe it hasn't stopped all day?" Berta shed her cloak and handed it to Rebecca, continuing on into the kitchen without missing a beat. "You know I always love a wedding, and to help with organizing one is my greatest thrill. Not that it's any commentary on you, but you certainly can't do it all without any other family to help you." Berta tapped Rebecca lightly on the arm.

"Not to be tactless or anything, dear, by reminding you of that, but this is a time when a woman naturally counts on her family, and I want you to know that you can count on me to help you get everything ready. Four days! Can you believe it? The man appears anxious to have things settled, although I can't blame him, dear. You look as lovely as a spring flower. I don't suppose I dare to hope that you have something to wear already?"

Berta gazed expectantly at Rebecca, but the bemused younger woman took too long to reply and missed her opportunity to speak. The matchmaker snapped her fingers in inspiration and was off at a run again as she bundled her belongings into the kitchen, Rebecca following helplessly in her wake.

"Of course, the kirtle you wore when you and Ephraim were wed, I'm sure you still have it, dear. We could change the trim, make a few adjustments here and there and it would be absolutely perfect. And not in poor taste at all, what with the price of a new kirtle these days, and with the few days we have left, it's a relief to have that resolved at least. Trot upstairs, child, and let's have a look at the kirtle so we can see what needs to be done.''

"I won't wear it," Rebecca interjected firmly, and the older woman spared her a surprised glance.

"Why ever not?''

Rebecca considered telling her the truth, but one glance at Berta's intense expression told her that the woman would make mincemeat of her excuse. And it was an excuse, Rebecca knew, but she simply didn't want to wear the same kirtle. It seemed inappropriate to her somehow and not in fitting with making a new start, regardless of whether she hastily changed the trim. Jacob would never know the difference, it was true, but she would, and for some inexplicable and wildly impractical reason, Rebecca wanted to start this marriage in a different, and perhaps less ill-fated, garment.

"I gave it away," she lied, and Berta tut-tutted under her breath.

"Such a generous girl you are," she said with a sigh, patting Rebecca on the shoulder in an attempt at consolation. "But I suppose you never thought that you would need it again and no one can blame you for that." She sent a glance winging up the stairs. "Well, let's have a look at what you have and maybe we can make something do. Come along, dear, time is wasting away and goodness knows we have enough to do before Friday, what with all the food to be prepared.''

"Most of my kirtles are a bit worn," Rebecca admitted reluctantly, and the older woman fixed her with a bright eye. "Actually, I haven't bought anything since my wedding and I didn't buy much then," she confessed, reassured when Berta clucked sympathetically under her breath, immediately understanding the implication of her words.

"Well, you can only hope that Jacob is more aware of such things than Ephraim was. A smart man Ephraim was to be sure, but he never did have a firm grip on the realities of this world and I've not a doubt that you had a challenge in keeping hearth and home together without his assistance. This Jacob seems much more a part of the here and now, if you follow my meaning, and I fancy that as a merchant, he'll be more aware of the kinds of things you'll be needing, dear, so don't be worrying too much about this match you're making. I've seen a lot of matches made in my day and it seems to me you've made rather a good one, even if I must admit that I had nothing at all to do with it.''

Berta spared Rebecca a smile and she could only return the gesture, wondering in the back of her mind whether the woman would talk incessantly until Friday.

"Now then, dear, about the food. You know the rabbi likes a good meal after he does his work and I've no doubt you've a big gathering planned, so we should figure out exactly what we'll have time to prepare and what we'll have to ask the neighbors to help with before it's too late to ask politely."

"Actually, I expected the wedding to be rather small," Rebecca ventured when Berta took a breath, only to be greeted with a look of open shock. "I mean, my family is gone and I'm sure Jacob's family is in Tunis, so I thought we would have a small ceremony here."

"Nonsense, dear." Berta dismissed her objections regally. "The entire community will come to salute you, you know that. And even if many don't know you that well, Ephraim was well established here and they'll want to set their minds at ease that his widow is well situated. Now, if we have the wedding here at the house, we can use the courtyard, and if we push this table in the kitchen back to the wall and borrow stools from your neighbors and—''

Rebecca was spared this orgy of organization by a jingle of the doorbells and darted away with an excuse she was sure Berta hadn't even heard.

It seemed her anger had cooled, as well, Jacob noted with relief as Rebecca opened the door, even though she hadn't been out walking in the rain. Before she could say anything, he pulled the bouquet of flowers from behind his back and presented them to her, feeling a thrill of victory when she smiled and that enchantingly elusive dimple made its presence known.

"I'm sorry I got so angry," he apologized quietly, and Rebecca shot him an embarrassed glance.

"I'm sorry I kept goading you," she returned as she fingered the flowers, and Jacob felt his brows rise in surprise.

"So, I didn't just imagine it," he acknowledged, liking the way Rebecca flushed as she giggled guiltily.

"No. I really don't know what got into me, but I just couldn't leave it alone," she admitted all in a rush, and Jacob found himself grinning in relief as he leaned against the door frame. It was somehow reassuring to know that she felt the same thing humming to life between them.

"Me, neither," he confessed, and in the warm glow surrounding the two of them, the rain that he had been cursing as it soaked him to the skin seemed no more than a beneficent silver mist. As if suddenly made self-conscious by the companionable silence between them, Rebecca buried her nose in the white-and-yellow blossoms.

"I don't know much about flowers," she said quietly. "What kind are they?" Jacob smothered a grin.

"Chamomile," he replied, and when she looked mystified, he explained, "My aunt always said that chamomile grows stronger the more it is tread on." He watched an answering smile light her eyes. "Somehow it seemed appropriate," he teased, and Rebecca laughed aloud.

"I like that," she agreed, and their eyes met and held in one of those long moments that he ought to be getting used to by now. Finally, Jacob stirred himself, remembering what he had intended to ask her earlier.

"I know this is a strange question, but what exactly did Ephraim do?" he asked, and Rebecca shrugged.

"He was a scholar. He taught a few people and did some translations of works he was interested in," she answered blandly, and Jacob had to admit there was nothing un-

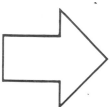

NO COST! NO OBLIGATION TO BUY!
NO PURCHASE NECESSARY!

PLAY "LUCKY 7"
AND GET AS MANY AS FIVE FREE GIFTS...

HOW TO PLAY:

1. With a coin, carefully scratch off the silver box at the right. This makes you eligible to receive two or more free books, and possibly another gift, depending on what is revealed beneath the scratch-off area.

2. Send back this card and you'll receive brand-new Harlequin Historical™ novels. These books have a cover price of $3.99 each, but they are yours to keep absolutely free.

3. There's no catch. You're under no obligation to buy anything. We charge nothing—ZERO—for your first shipment. And you don't have to make any minimum number of purchases—not even one!

4. The fact is thousands of readers enjoy receiving books by mail from the Harlequin Reader Service®. They like the convenience of home delivery . . . they like getting the best new novels before they're available in stores . . . and they love our discount prices!

5. We hope that after receiving your free books you'll want to remain a subscriber. But the choice is yours—to continue or cancel, anytime at all! So why not take us up on our invitation, with no risk of any kind. You'll be glad you did!

This lovely Victorian pewter-finish miniature is perfect for displaying a treasured photograph. And it's yours FREE as added thanks for giving our Reader Service a try!

DETACH AND MAIL CARD TODAY

THE HARLEQUIN READER SERVICE®: HERE'S HOW IT WORKS

Accepting free books puts you under no obligation to buy anything. You may keep the books and gift and return the shipping statement marked "cancel". If you do not cancel, about a month later we'll send you 4 additional novels, and bill you just $3.19 each plus 25¢ delivery and applicable sales tax, if any.* That's the complete price, and—compared to cover prices of $3.99 each—quite a bargain! You may cancel at any time, but if you choose to continue, every month we'll send you 4 more books, which you may either purchase at the discount price . . . or return at our expense and cancel your subscription.

*Terms and prices subject to change without notice. Sales tax applicable in N.Y.

usual about that. Then why all the interest in Ephraim's house?

"What did he teach?"

Rebecca bit her lip as she thought. "I know he was teaching Yusuf to read Hebrew," she said, shooting a quick glance at Jacob when she realized whose name she had inadvertently mentioned. He smiled and shook his head at once, indicating to her that she should continue, and she spared him a grateful smile. "I think he might have taught some mathematics and astronomy, but I'm not really sure." She spread one hand in a gesture of concession. "Mostly he read and translated. He was always in his study, it seemed."

Jacob nodded and scanned the street, unable to help wondering what had so engrossed Ephraim. What could he possibly have had that anyone else would want as badly as those elders this morning? He certainly hadn't been an affluent man, by all indications, and most scholars were anxious to share their knowledge, if that had been the source of all this interest.

"Is anything wrong?" Rebecca asked with concern and Jacob turned back to give her a half-smile of encouragement.

"No," he said firmly. "I was just curious." He gestured down the street and cleared his throat. "I'll be staying at the inn near the *souk* until Friday. Do you know it?" She nodded and he pursed his lips, intending to take his leave. It was about time he got out of these wet clothes.

"You can reach me there if you need me for anything," Jacob added, and flicked her a quick look as he recalled something else. "I don't know whether I mentioned that Berta was coming to stay with you."

"She's here already," Rebecca whispered, the way her eyes widened in mock horror making Jacob chuckle.

"It can't be that bad," he teased, and something mischievous flashed in her eyes before she grabbed the front of his tunic and practically dragged him across the threshold. "Wait a minute," he protested halfheartedly, but it was too late.

"Berta! Look who's here!" Rebecca called jubilantly.

"Why, it's the groom himself!" chirped a matronly older woman as she popped around the corner from the kitchen, her kindly face wreathed in smiles. She gripped Jacob's hand and pumped it enthusiastically, her words flowing more quickly than he would have believed possible.

"And it is a pleasure to finally meet you, Jacob, although I must say I've heard so much about you that I feel I know you already. You know, my sister's husband's family are from Qayrawan, which isn't really all that far from Tunis, at least not in relative terms, if you'll pardon the pun, and I quite naturally had wondered whether you knew them or knew of them. And oddly enough, his cousin's boy is also involved in trading, although I seem to remember that most of his business is in slaves . . ."

"I know no one in the slave trade," Jacob interjected flatly, hoping to halt the woman's words, but he found he was completely unsuccessful. A glance at Rebecca assured him that she was finding his predicament tremendously funny. She held up four fingers with a dramatic wince and he barely kept from laughing aloud.

True enough, she had to listen to Berta for four days. He could at least survive a few moments.

"Well, that's certainly to your credit," Berta continued, "for it is a most *unsavory* way to make a living, if you ask me, but of course, my sister's husband's cousin's boy never did ask for my assessment of the matter, probably because they could guess what I would have to say about it."

"Jacob has quite definite ideas about the wedding," Rebecca managed to slip in when Berta took a breath, and he watched with growing trepidation when the matchmaker turned on him with unconcealed delight.

"Really!" she exclaimed. "It's so rare for a man to take an interest in these things. In fact it's been years, positively years, since I've spoken with a groom about the arrangements, although I don't have any problem in doing so, you understand, it's just so unusual—"

Jacob caught Rebecca's eye, watching as she held up one hand and closed the space between her index finger and thumb while she mouthed the word *small*. So there was a method to her madness, he acknowledged, granting her an almost imperceptible nod to let her know he had understood.

"You do realize that we will only be having a very small ceremony here in Toledo," he informed Berta in his most efficient tone, hating the way he had to interrupt her but knowing already that there was no other way to say anything to the woman. She regarded him with shock, evidently having some difficulties absorbing this piece of news as her mouth worked silently for a moment.

"Well, no," she said, making an astonishing recovery. "I had assumed, quite naturally, I thought, that this would be a traditional celebration—"

"No," Jacob interjected with a firm shake of his head. "My aunt is quite determined to hold a fete on our return to Tunis, and as neither of us has any family in Toledo, it would seem more *practical* to keep things simple here." He watched as his emphasis was comprehended by the older woman, seeing the understanding that he didn't intend to spend much money dawn in her eyes.

"Yes, of course, I see your point. And that only makes sense, as you say, and I should have thought to speak to you before we began making plans."

Amazingly, Berta fell silent for a moment as she mulled this over, and Jacob almost regretted stealing her excitement. But Rebecca was right—there was no reason for a big wedding here and he appreciated her practicality. When he glanced up to find gratitude shining in his fiancée's eyes, he completely forgot about disappointing the matchmaker.

"Perhaps you could excuse us for a moment, Berta," he suggested impulsively, watching Rebecca's cheeks color as the older woman flustered about neglecting her responsibilities as chaperon. Finally, Jacob leveled one pointed glance in Berta's direction and she immediately excused herself.

"You'll have to teach me to do that," Rebecca said admiringly, and he chuckled, taking her hand in his and pulling her a little closer in the soft darkness of the foyer.

"You'll be fine," he assured her, and Rebecca nodded.

"Now that *that's* settled," she agreed with a sigh of relief, and closed her fingers around his.

"Judith would kill me if I didn't let her arrange the festivities," Jacob told her, and Rebecca laughed up at him.

"Don't tell me you're afraid of your aunt."

"She is an indomitable force in her own sweet way," he allowed, marveling at how comfortable he felt here with Rebecca. The sounds of Berta bustling about carried from the kitchen over the incessant patter of the rain; she was still talking to herself, although mercifully he couldn't make out the words. The foyer was falling into shadows, the subdued light softening Rebecca's skin as she smiled up at him.

"How *did* she get you to sign that *ketubah?*" she whispered with that devilish twinkle in her dark eyes, and as something quickened within him, Jacob found himself unable to resist the urge to cup the side of her face. He slid his thumb along the edge of her jaw, watching in fascination as Rebecca swallowed with evident difficulty.

"I'll let her tell you," he teased, bending to brush his lips across hers. The applelike scent of the flowers crushed between them rose to his nostrils as Rebecca leaned against his chest and he kissed her gently, his gesture as much an apology as his words had been earlier. At the sound of Berta bustling with renewed vigor, he lifted his head, seeing his own reluctance to end their embrace mirrored in Rebecca's luminous eyes.

"Until Friday then, unless you need me for anything else." Her lips twisted mischievously and Jacob intuitively guessed the thought that had darted through her mind. He grinned wolfishly at the way his loins tightened in response, chuckling when Rebecca flushed scarlet.

"Actually," she admitted with difficulty as she sobered, "there is one more thing."

Jacob sensed her nervousness, that protective instinct sending his thumb to rhythmically stroke her jaw.

"The worst I can do is say no," he teased to encourage her, and won a tentative smile for his efforts.

"I'd like to buy a new kirtle for Friday," Rebecca confessed after a moment's hesitation, her words falling quickly once she loosed them. Jacob's heart leapt at the import of what she was saying, her embarrassment telling him beyond a shadow of a doubt that she still had her other wedding kirtle, her desire not to wear it pleasing him more than he would have believed possible.

"I can appreciate that," Jacob mused, and her chin shot up in apparent surprise in a gesture that wrenched his heart. Had Rebecca had so little success in requesting something for herself as that? It was true that he had never seen her dressed lavishly, but the circumstances had scarcely required it. Had she never had the luxury to indulge herself, at least once in a while?

What did he really know about her marriage to Ephraim? Judith's gossip had called it a love match but Jacob hadn't noticed any particular emotion when Rebecca had spoken about her deceased spouse earlier. Was she particularly adept at hiding her emotions? Or had things not been that good between herself and Ephraim?

"Bad memories?" he inquired in an impersonal tone designed to make it easier for her to answer.

"Bad omens," Rebecca supplied quickly, which neither confirmed nor denied his question, and Jacob held her gaze for a long moment before deciding to take a light interpretation. She would tell him when she was ready and the wisest thing he could do now was to promote that solid new beginning he had promised them both. The sooner she trusted him, the sooner the air would be cleared between them.

"I'll assume that you're planning to keep me for more than two years," Jacob teased as he reached into the pocket of his tunic, and she swatted him playfully across the shoulder.

"Beast!" Rebecca accused laughingly, and Jacob swooped down to steal a kiss while she was within range.

"Temptress," he retorted, folding her fingers firmly around a pile of gold coins. "Enjoy yourself," he told her when her eyes widened at their number, and he flicked his fingertip across the tip of her nose.

"But..." she began to protest his generosity but Jacob had no intention of listening to it.

"Friday," he asserted firmly as he stepped back to the door, his pulse pounding at the smile that she sent after him. Jacob's pack was still on the floor in the foyer and he scooped it up in passing, stepping resolutely out into the rain in spite of his urge to stay.

Only four days. Jacob swung his pack over his shoulder, whistling to himself as he went in search of the inn.

If Berta's busy chattering and the bustle of fittings kept Rebecca from thinking during the three days that followed, the nights were an entirely different matter. As she lay in the darkness Thursday night and contemplated the ceiling, Yusuf's words returned to haunt her yet again, making her question the wisdom of this decision she had made. Wedding nerves, Berta had blithely told her when she had been jumpy all day, but Rebecca suspected there was more to her growing trepidation than that.

As much as she hated to admit it, she really had only Jacob's own word as to who he was and what he did, and in the middle of the night that fact seemed to attain huge significance. Something about the shadows and the silence of the house encouraged wild speculation as to Jacob's motives, and Rebecca roundly cursed the Berber for putting such errant thoughts into her head. She should be mentally reviewing the vast array of food or thinking about her dress or imagining the expression on Jacob's face when they met for the first time the next afternoon. Instead she was worrying about intrigue.

But Yusuf was right in his assertion that Rebecca would be naive to put her trust in a letter of introduction from someone she had never heard of, as enchanting as Judith sounded. For all she knew, Jacob might have written that letter himself, and that thought, entirely her own, didn't sit very well, either.

But to what purpose would he deceive her? In marked contrast to Jacob, or at least the person who he presented himself to be, Rebecca knew that she was not a terrific catch. No dowry, widowed and not the most physically stunning woman in the world. And there *was* that other liability that she didn't even like to recall herself. She squirmed under the weight of her guilt at deceiving Jacob about her pregnancy, telling herself that that alone would not compel him to take her hand.

No matter what Yusuf said, Rebecca couldn't believe that Jacob did anything he didn't want to do, which brought her to the question that inevitably ground her thoughts to a full stop. Why on earth would he, or anyone else for that matter, want to marry *her* so badly?

Yusuf had said she had something people were willing to kill for. She shivered in the stillness of the quiet house and rolled over yet again, knowing that her lack of sleep was going to show under her eyes at the wedding, but powerless to do anything about it. By this time tomorrow, she would be married.

Again. She closed her eyes and pressed her fingertips to her temples, praying that this time things would work out differently. She had had so few expectations when she had married Ephraim, but even they had been doomed to disappointment. Rebecca hadn't expected a wildly passionate love to bloom from an arranged match, but she had hoped for companionship, something she had had precious little of with Ephraim. Indeed, he had simply continued with his life, closeted in his study, making her think that the sole change to his universe was the fact that she cooked and cleaned instead of a hired woman.

Her life had always been a fairly solitary existence and it had continued in that vein in marriage. At the time she had taken it in stride, but now, on the eve of her second wedding, she was afraid of the future.

This time she had real expectations and she was terrified not only of being disappointed but of the price that disappointment would exact. Could their lovemaking continue at such a fever pitch? Would Jacob really continue to be concerned with her feelings? His apology had been a novelty to her, but one to which she could readily adjust. Was this all just part of the courting game? Rebecca threaded her fingers through her hair and tried to imagine living with a withdrawn and taciturn Jacob, knowing that he was capable of so much more but being denied it.

Was she expecting too much? Possibly, but the fire that sparked to life when Jacob touched her was so much more than she had ever dreamed possible that it seemed fitting somehow to expect more. More? She wanted *everything:* she wanted to know his every thought, to spend hours if not days in his company, to learn everything about his past and his dreams for the future, to taste his passion for the things he loved, to open herself and her most secret thoughts to him.

Was she being terribly unrealistic? Did they really have a hope of making something magical together, or would everything settle into domestic mediocrity by the time they reached Tunis?

Tunis. Rebecca rolled over and groaned, her doubts and suspicions making that town seem forbiddingly far away. Yusuf's insinuations about the solitude of the road tormented her until she sat up and punched a pillow determinedly.

This was ridiculous. What was the difference after all between Toledo and Tunis? Rebecca had no family in either place and probably about as many friends. Hadn't she taken care of herself for as long as she could remember? At least marriage promised the possibility of a husband to protect her, even if her experience had shown that that promise could be an empty one.

Rebecca tucked up her knees and hugged them to her chest, trying to sift her own thoughts from the tangle of Yusuf's suspicions. It was true that there was no one else to back up Jacob's story, just as it was inescapably true that he was in a perfect position to take advantage of her, but she marveled that she wasn't afraid of him. Just as she wasn't afraid when Jacob was angry with her, although Rebecca admitted with a smile that that usually was because he made sure that *she* was angry, as well.

She trusted Jacob, it was as simple as that. Instinct told her that he was a good man and there was no reason to stop trusting her instincts at this point.

But there remained the issue of what Yusuf thought she had that he insisted other people wanted so badly.

Rebecca pursed her lips thoughtfully, recalling that she had only one week to find whatever that intruder was going to come back to retrieve. Undoubtedly, she and Jacob would be long gone by then, but she was curious, and as sleep was being so elusive, she had plenty of time to reflect on the puzzle. The intruder could only be talking about the same thing Yusuf referred to, but unfortunately she had no idea what it was.

Her mind drifted to the book that had been hidden in the fountain and she frowned to herself. As unimportant as it looked, it *had* been wrapped with tremendous care. Could it be the key that everyone sought? It seemed impossible, but the only way she would know for sure would be to find out what it said.

Rebecca slipped out of bed on silent feet and padded down the stairs, making her way stealthily to the library. She found the book despite the thickness of the shadows by touch alone, relieved when Berta's snoring continued undisturbed as she trotted back up to her room.

In the privacy of the moonlit balcony, she fanned the pages and squinted at the script, trying to make a reasonable guess at the language. It should be Arabic, Rebecca told herself. If only Ephraim had taught her to read other languages as he had taught Yusuf, she thought crossly, lifting her head with surprise as she realized the import of her thoughts.

Of course. It was the perfect solution. She would ask Yusuf what the text said and then she would know whether the book was important or not.

Chapter Ten

If Jacob had had any prenuptial trepidation himself, running into Berta in the *souk* on Thursday had summarily dismissed it.

"She's not sleeping," the older woman had confided in a worried tone, launching that damnable protective instinct of his yet again. Though she said no more than that, Berta's murmured words also confirmed every suspicion Jacob had had that Ephraim had been a less than ideal mate.

No wonder Rebecca was worried.

His own reservations were forgotten as he tried to think of some way to reassure her in the short term. To be sure, time would tell that he and Ephraim were vastly different creatures, but that fact would hardly set Rebecca's mind at ease by the time they stood before the rabbi.

Despite Jacob's concentration on the problem, an appropriate solution eluded him until just before Friday's dawn, when he recalled a memento of his own mother's that Judith treasured above all else. If only it weren't in Tunis. Unfortunately, there was no way he could get his mother's *aljofar* for Rebecca, but under the circumstances a new one would suffice just as well.

And as a talisman of luck, it would be a singularly appropriate gift.

* * *

Rebecca had just completed her ritual bath when Yusuf answered her summons. Berta appeared in her doorway to announce his presence downstairs, her voice dripping with disapproval and her brows drawn together in a tight frown.

"Surely you don't intend to meet with him now?" Berta demanded as Rebecca showed signs of doing just that.

"It would be rude not to," Rebecca responded pertly as she swung a surcoat over her shoulders, unaccustomed to the levity of heart that had plagued her all morning.

"I should think it was rude enough of him to come here on the day of your wedding that you wouldn't do any offense in refusing to see him," Berta retorted huffily. "After all, it's not exactly tradition, but it would seem to me that the first man you greet on this day should be Jacob, if only for the sake of propriety, not some disgruntled and rejected former suitor."

"Oh, Berta, don't be ridiculous." Rebecca brushed aside the older woman's objections. "I sent Yusuf a message and asked him to come."

"You *what?*" Berta asked in horror.

"It's perfectly proper, just business," Rebecca continued undaunted as she brushed past the stunned matchmaker. "He'll be gone before anyone even knows he was here."

"*I* know he's here and that should be enough for you, young woman," Berta challenged as she recovered herself, but Rebecca was already tripping lightly down the stairs, oblivious to her criticism. Berta darted after the bride-to-be, muttering her recriminations in a low voice so that the waiting Berber wouldn't overhear.

"Never have I seen such nonsense, and on the very day of the wedding, in sight of the *huppah* no less, and what is the world coming to that a young woman can think that she can do such a thing without consequence? You are testing Jacob's patience too far with this, young woman, and I won't stand for it, no I won't."

Rebecca spun abruptly on her heel and confronted Berta at the bottom of the stairs, her gesture bringing their faces so close that their noses almost touched.

"You will say nothing of this to Jacob," she hissed, but Berta drew herself up to her full height, taking advantage of the fact that she still stood on the bottom step.

"I would be shirking my moral responsibilities if I did not," she retorted indignantly.

"Then shirk them," Rebecca shot back, but Berta tossed her head defiantly.

"I see no reason why I should look the other way if you are determined to start your marriage off on the wrong foot, despite Jacob's generosity. You know, I wouldn't have pointed this out, but you have forced my hand and I will tell you now that you would have a hard time on the open market making a good match, despite your looks, for most men are looking for a little something to line their purses, as well, and throwing this match into jeopardy as you seem to insist on doing is a less than clever move on your part. Even I have to admit that Jacob is a much finer match than..."

"Berta," Rebecca interrupted impatiently. "I give you my most solemn word that I did not summon Yusuf with any romantic intentions."

"It doesn't matter what you intended, child, only what it will *look* like you intended."

"It won't look like anything if no one knows he was here," Rebecca shot back firmly. "Please, Berta," she added more softly, and the older woman studied her features for a long moment before her lips thinned and she glanced away in a gesture that could have been acquiescence. Satisfied, Rebecca turned to continue into the courtyard, wishing her nerves weren't strung so tightly.

Yusuf stepped out from the shadows, his expression as inscrutable as always, and Rebecca extended her hand to him before he could drop to one knee. He smiled and kissed her knuckles, a twinkle lighting his green eyes, and Rebecca heard Berta scurry into the kitchen behind her.

"I know enough to understand my position," he commented dryly in apparent understanding of her gesture. Rebecca stiffened at his admonition, biting back the urge to remind him that he hadn't apparently understood that several days past.

"I am sorry to bother you so early this morning," she began, but Yusuf swept her objections aside.

"The hour is of little import," he insisted gallantly. "Obviously something has disturbed you and that alone is adequate reason for my presence." Rebecca saw the flicker of hope in his eyes and decided to make her position clear right from the beginning.

"I haven't changed my mind," she said solemnly, and that flicker faded away right on cue. To his credit, Yusuf showed no other signs of disappointment. He shook his head in understanding and Rebecca nervously plunged on. "I simply wanted to ask your advice," she confessed in a tumble of words, and Yusuf nodded in graceful acceptance.

"By all means, do so." He spread his hand in an eloquent gesture. "And I shall do my best to honor you with some small measure of wisdom."

Rebecca nodded and took a deep breath to calm herself as she sought the right words. "I was thinking about what you said the other day and I was wondering whether you had any idea what exactly Ephraim might have had in his possession."

Yusuf's jaw tightened and he leaned toward her, his face taut with anticipation. "You have found it?" he demanded sharply, and Rebecca took an involuntary step backward in response to his avid interest. In that instant, his features seemed to have changed, the eagerness burning in his eyes making him look like a far different man from the relaxed Berber she knew, and Rebecca was suddenly, unexpectedly, afraid.

Was Yusuf among those who would kill for what Ephraim had had?

"I simply was curious," she equivocated, desperately trying to assimilate these new and frightening suspicions.

"You have found it," Yusuf breathed in excitement, and Rebecca's heart began to pound. Why had she summoned him here like this? What had compelled her to do something so foolish?

Why hadn't she simply asked Jacob for his advice?

"I don't even know what it is," she snapped defensively, but Yusuf shook his head slowly in disbelief.

"No," he insisted with a telling waver in his voice. "No, you may have doubts, but your instincts tell you that you have found the *Emerald Tablet* itself."

Rebecca tried not to show how much Yusuf's words had surprised her. What was he talking about? She had found a book, not a tablet, and it was red, not green. Before she could decide whether or not to demand an explanation, Yusuf smiled victoriously and squeezed her hands tightly between his.

"You must show it to me," he hissed with shining eyes, and she automatically shook her head in denial, still unable to understand the chord of fear his uncharacteristic animation struck deep within her.

"I don't know what you're talking about," she maintained stubbornly, and her apprehension must have given her tone an edge of conviction, for a frown flitted across Yusuf's brow.

"What game are you playing?" he demanded with an impatient shake of her hands. "Do not be a fool, Rebecca. What you have found is tremendously valuable and can cost you dearly."

"I haven't found anything," she repeated stonily, but Yusuf continued undeterred.

"Fine. Do not show it to me. Perhaps it is better this way, a sign that you have taken my warnings to heart." He stared into her eyes for a long moment, then stepped away with deliberation, still holding her gaze.

"By all means, do not be so foolish as to show this foreigner your treasure," he warned, and by the time Rebecca realized that he was talking about Jacob, Yusuf was gone.

The house had been transformed over the past few days and Jacob marveled at the work Rebecca and Berta had done. The *huppah*, a canopy of red silk, had been erected in the courtyard over a dais, the structure virtually filling the small tiled space with its splendor. Berta greeted him effusively, bringing a wave of warm cinnamon-scented air from the kitchen with her and blushing like a young girl when he complimented her on the preparations.

"Berta, could you help me with this veil?" Rebecca asked from above, her words bringing their exchange of pleasantries to an abrupt halt. Jacob glanced up the stairs and caught his breath at the sight of his intended resplendent in crimson, her brows tightened into a frown as she struggled to make some order of a length of sheer gold silk.

He would have to ensure she wore more brilliant colors than the dark hues he had previously seen her wearing, Jacob resolved just before Rebecca glanced up and caught his eye. She gasped in surprise and he smiled, seeing his own response in her eyes.

Everything was going fine, he told himself, reaching to offer her his hand. He closed his fingers over the softness of hers, giving her hand an encouraging squeeze when he felt her tremble ever so slightly.

"I didn't think anyone was here yet," she said, defensively raising her other hand to her uncovered hair.

"Luckily for you, it's only me," Jacob teased, but his jest fell inexplicably flat.

Berta snorted indignantly and he glanced to the older woman in surprise, almost missing the look of alarm Rebecca sent in her direction. He glanced between the two women in confusion, wondering what he had missed, disliking the way Rebecca's color rose at the lull in the conversation.

"I wanted to give you something before the others arrived," Jacob continued determinedly, noting Rebecca's nervous glance toward Berta before she granted him a thin smile. "Is something wrong?" he asked uncertainly, and Berta drew herself indignantly up to her full height.

"I'll not be telling any tales, that's for certain, so there's no need for you to keep looking at me as though you expect *me* to tell him what you've been up to in his absence." She spun on her heel and stomped self-righteously to the kitchen, muttering to herself all the while, her words doing little to reassure Jacob.

"Far be it for me to spoil the mood of a wedding, even if she insists on seeing *that* one on the very day of her nuptials, and at such an hour. I cannot imagine what the world is coming to and can only be glad that *my* days are coming to an end..."

Berta's voice faded into an incomprehensible murmur and Jacob noticed that Rebecca was looking decidedly uncomfortable.

"Yusuf was here this morning," she confessed breathlessly, and before Jacob could voice any one of the hostile thoughts that rose to the fore, she continued in a rush. "I know that it was horribly inappropriate and you have every right to be angry with me."

"I thought he understood his place," Jacob interjected hotly, unable to contain his annoyance. What was the Berber thinking of, coming to disturb Rebecca on her wedding day? As if Jacob's finding them together the other day hadn't been enough, Yusuf had to persist with such scandalous and inappropriate behavior. Didn't he have any idea what light he cast Rebecca in with his insistence?

To Jacob's surprise, Rebecca winced at his words.

"Well..." She dragged out the word as though she had something to confess, and Jacob braced himself unwillingly against her next words. "Actually, I sent for him," she admitted in a small voice, and Jacob almost exploded on the spot.

"What?" he demanded furiously, but Rebecca laid the flat of her hand in the middle of his chest, her imploring expression effectively stopping his fury in midstorm.

"Please, don't say anything until I'm done," she begged softly. "Just give me a chance to explain. I know it was wrong and I should never have done it, but he said something the other day that confused me and I wanted to know what he meant."

"And you had to know this morning?" Jacob asked acidly, unable to contain himself any longer.

Rebecca pursed her lips for a moment while she considered the question, then glanced up to meet his eyes. "I thought it would be best to know as soon as possible."

"You couldn't have waited until I was here?"

"Well, no," she answered reluctantly, adding hastily, "but you must believe me that it had nothing to do with this wedding."

Jacob sighed and paced impatiently across the courtyard, pausing to finger the silk draperies on the *huppah* and settle his churning emotions before he turned to face her again. Could he believe her? Rebecca looked as forlorn as a little girl caught pinching a chunk off the sugar loaf and his anger melted at the sight of her obvious contrition.

"What did you have to ask him?" he demanded in a low voice, and Rebecca fidgeted.

"I can't tell you," she admitted, shrugging helplessly as she toyed with her gossamer veiling, and Jacob's rage reared its head again. She couldn't tell him? What nonsense was this? They were going to be married and it was time enough she learned that she would have to trust him.

"I made a promise," Rebecca added quickly, giving Jacob's anger a fatal blow before he could voice his objections.

Keeping a vow was something he could understand, although he wished that her promise hadn't been one that would keep him in the dark. And to whom had she made the promise? To Yusuf? He shot a glance in her direction to find her looking as miserable about the entire business

as he felt, y̵̶
In fact, he was ̵̶
becca wasn't prepa̵̶
would they manage to ̵̶

Jacob wanted more than̵̶
more than a mutually tolerant ̵̶
as they stood speechless and on op̵̶
courtyard just how much he had been̵̶
getting to know Rebecca, how much he ̵̶
ravel all her mysteries and inconsistencies. ̵̶ ̵̶was
blocking him before they even started by putti̵̶ wall
where their trust should have been.

The silence grew between them and the first ray of watery winter sunlight stretched its fingers into the courtyard before Rebecca cleared her throat.

"Jacob," she said unexpectedly, and he glanced up to find her closing the distance between them with rapid steps. "I know what I did was wrong, but I can't undo it now." Jacob caught a paralyzing whisper of her scent as she tentatively put one hand on his arm, and he closed his eyes against the inevitable tide of desire that rose within him.

"I'm sorry," Rebecca murmured, and he dared to look into her eyes, catching his breath at the shimmer of tears he saw there. Was it possible that she understood how much she had shaken his confidence?

Wanting only to ease her distress, Jacob found his hand rising to cup her jaw, his heart twisting when Rebecca closed her eyes against his touch and her tears splashed onto his hand. He found himself nodding in acceptance even though he knew she couldn't see his gesture, his fingertips straying of their own volition to tuck her loose hair behind her ear.

"We all make mistakes," he said quietly. Rebecca sighed with exasperation and impatiently jammed her hair behind her other ear, anguish in her eyes as she looked up at him again.

"I wish I could tell you what it was all about, but I promised." She shook her head helplessly. "I wish I hadn't

can't be undone." Jacob nod-
on her bottom lip, impaling him with
when she looked up again.

"I guess I'm asking you to trust me," Rebecca said finally, her words hanging in the air between them.

Could he trust her? Jacob stared down at the woman standing within the circle of his arms, the woman who had deliberately lied to him, the woman he would shortly take to wife, and shook his head slowly. History was not in her favor, that much was clear.

But wasn't that what new beginnings were all about? Jacob cleared his throat awkwardly, daring to place a measure of trust in his instincts once more.

"Can you tell me why he was here the other day?" Jacob inquired in a low voice, relieved when Rebecca's lips twisted.

"Yusuf proposed to me some weeks ago," she confessed, and he saw how uncomfortable she was with the telling. "It was after I had signed the *ketubah*, but I wasn't sure whether you would come, so I asked for some time to think about it. He came back the other day for my answer."

"I'm hoping you declined," Jacob teased to dispel some of her embarrassment, and that dimple he liked made a surprise appearance.

"Of course!" Rebecca feigned shock and he chuckled, cupping her shoulders in his hands as he felt the balance restored between them.

"And then he said something that confused you?" he prompted.

"Yes," she confirmed with a curt nod.

"Hmm." Jacob watched her expression, knowing he had to ask one last question to set his mind at ease. "Will you be seeing Yusuf again?" he demanded quietly, eminently reassured when Rebecca shook her head.

"No, I—" she began, but Jacob slipped one finger over her lips to silence her.

"That's enough explanation for one day," he murmured, his pulse accelerating when her lips parted in surprise beneath his fingertip. "After all, it would be rude of me not to trust my new wife," he added just a heartbeat before his lips replaced his finger. Rebecca sighed in capitulation and leaned against him very satisfactorily, the discarded veiling catching the sunlight as it fluttered slowly to the ground.

"We mustn't," she objected breathlessly when he finally lifted his head, and Jacob stared down into her flushed face with affection.

"No, we mustn't," he agreed, kissing Rebecca again and savoring the way she arched against him as if she were helpless to do otherwise. He pulled away from her with difficulty and slid his thumb across her softened lips as if to seal them, watching her lashes flutter to her cheeks beneath his caress.

Knowing he had to stop now while he still could, Jacob cleared his throat and took a half step backward. "I brought you something," he reminded her, and Rebecca's eyes flew open in surprise.

"Oh," she said, and smiled suddenly. "I forgot."

Jacob grinned himself. "So did I," he admitted, and they chuckled together. Rebecca's smile died on her lips when he pulled the small velvet pouch from his tunic, her eyes flying to his as she realized that it could be nothing other than a jewelry pouch.

Her fingers trembled slightly with excitement as she took the sack from him, the quick looks she kept sending his way feeding Jacob's conviction that this woman needed to be spoiled a little more. Rebecca's astonishment appeared complete when the misshapen pearl and its accompanying gold chain tumbled out into her palm.

"An *aljofar*," she breathed in shock, sending Jacob a look of astonishment that warmed him right to his toes.

"Didn't you have one before?" he asked as he hooked one finger under the chain and lifted the pearl before her amazed eyes. Rebecca shook her head silently and touched the gem's glossy surface as though she needed to convince herself that it was real.

"They're so expensive," she whispered, and Jacob smothered a smile.

"You'd best put it on then," he suggested, passing the chain over her head, unable to help noticing how the pearl fell right against the cleft between her breasts before Rebecca launched herself into his arms.

"Oh, Jacob, thank you so much," she enthused with sparkling eyes, giving Jacob no time to answer before she kissed him soundly. Her embrace took him completely by surprise and he found her tongue in his mouth before he even had his arms around her waist, some part of him enjoying the fact that she had taken control.

"Rebecca!" Berta cried in shock, and Rebecca pulled reluctantly away, her breathing unsteady and her eyes filled with promise.

"You're welcome," Jacob murmured under his breath, and she giggled, rubbing the pearl between her fingers and thumb before she bent to scoop up her veiling.

"It's such good luck," she whispered in undisguised delight.

"Why do you think I bought it?" he asked pointedly, and she smiled sunnily, blowing him a kiss from across the courtyard as Berta chided and hustled her back upstairs.

The afternoon passed in a daze for Rebecca, the bustle of activity emptying her mind of thought as it had on a similar afternoon more than two years past. This time, however, it was Jacob who had met her at the foot of the stairs once the guests had arrived and Berta had pronounced her appropriately veiled and bangled. Jacob, whose eyes lit with some nameless flame when she met his gaze, a flame that warmed her heart and buoyed her through the long hours of sitting silently on the dais alone while the guests indulged themselves.

Time and again she found her fingers straying to the enormous *aljofar* hanging from its delicate chain, her mind still unable to accept that Jacob had spent such a sum just to please her. How she had longed for such a pearl for her first wedding, its powers reputed to bring good fortune, but funds had been meager and, knowing that, she had never even mentioned her desire to anyone. And now, as if by magic, she had a finer and larger *aljofar* than she could ever have imagined possible.

Would the gem really bring them luck? Rebecca watched Jacob surreptitiously as he mingled with the men from the community, shaking hands and accepting the good wishes of her neighbors, and a glow of pride lodged itself around her heart. As if sensing her perusal, he glanced in her direction and their eyes locked for a long moment before Rebecca dragged her gaze away, her color rising as she heard the murmured comments of their guests.

It was a dream come true and she could only hope the *aljofar* would hold the spell.

But perhaps they had no need of spells. Perhaps there really was something wonderful at work here. Perhaps she wasn't wrong to have trusted her instincts in summoning Jacob.

Perhaps she could trust him over this matter of the book. He would most assuredly know what to do and would ensure that it was done. There was the issue of her promise to Yusuf, but wasn't it unseemly of her to refuse to put her trust in her husband? And hadn't Jacob agreed to trust *her* over the matter of Yusuf's visit?

And wasn't she bound to destroy that fragile trust when she confessed that there was no baby coming in the spring?

That thought almost made Rebecca weep and she cursed her own stupidity as she sat silently on the dais with the happy chatter of the guests floating around her. She was doomed to set Jacob against her and it was all her own fault. Surely she had seen enough to know that he was a man of ethics and a lie of this magnitude could not be slipped under the rug without repercussions. Soon enough, he would notice that she wasn't gaining weight or rounding out as she should and the truth would make itself clear.

Despair welled up in Rebecca's heart and she realized how much she had been hoping that theirs would be more than a match of convenience, that they would share more of each other than she and Ephraim had. She had been looking forward to knowing more about Jacob and she realized with a start that she *liked* the man.

She must tell him the truth, and the sooner the better. But there was no good reason to do it before the ceremony and make it easy for him to abandon her.

Finally, the rabbi stepped up onto the dais and the guests fell silent as a frisson of awareness tripped over Rebecca's skin. The tall candles were lit before her and she felt Jacob's presence behind her. She didn't dare to glance up as he knelt beside her, but she gratefully seized on the warm solidity of his hand when she saw his palm rise out of the corner of her eye. His fingers closed over hers and Rebecca took reassurance from his grip, slipping her other hand on top of his and taking a deep breath to dispel her nervousness as the rabbi cleared his throat.

The holy man opened his sermon by stressing the importance of family and Rebecca immediately felt a fraud. He drew the parallel between the *huppah* canopy and the home and she fidgeted. He extended his hopes that theirs would be a fruitful match, and when Jacob's grip tightened on hers for the barest instant, Rebecca felt his pride and her innards positively writhed.

Was she right not to make her confession now?

The ethics of that question plagued her throughout the ceremony and the remainder of the rabbi's words washed over her unheard as she clung to Jacob's hand, unable to argue with how right it felt to be here with him. She simply couldn't put that in jeopardy and she shot a glance at Jacob as though trying to discern his response before she even uttered the telling words. He spared her an encouraging smile, evidently thinking she was nervous about the nuptials, and Rebecca somehow managed to conjure up an answering smile before she dropped her gaze to their entwined fingers.

"Be thou sanctified unto me with this ring in accordance with the law of Moses." Jacob's deep voice resonated close to her ear and Rebecca watched transfixed as he slipped the plain band of gold onto her finger.

Was she doing something that he would be unable to forgive? She had asked for his trust and received it this very day, and now she was forced to break it. The rabbi broke a glass beneath his heel for them, the crunch of glass echoing Rebecca's thoughts so accurately that she shivered despite herself.

Jacob helped her rise to her feet, her legs all pins and needles after kneeling for so long, and she held his hand more tightly than was necessary, wishing she could hold his trust so easily. The assembled group applauded them and Rebecca spared them a smile, letting her eyes drift over the familiar faces and wishing for the hundredth time that she hadn't made that ridiculous lie.

"Are you really under there?" Jacob asked, and Rebecca turned to find him looking pleased as he tentatively touched her gold veiling. A pang of guilt wrenched her heart, but she summoned a smile for him.

"Of course."

"I'm not convinced," Jacob murmured, and Rebecca smiled genuinely at the twinkle of mischief that lit his eyes. "All I can see are your eyes and hands."

"Maybe that's all you need to see for now," she teased, and Jacob grinned.

"Oh, no," he admonished her softly, and the intent in his gaze made her pulse quicken. "I mean to kiss my bride."

Rebecca felt her cheeks heat at his open declaration, but she reached for the veiling that was tucked around her face and hair. "Then you'll have to help me," she whispered huskily, and felt Jacob deftly remove one of the pins that held the veiling to her hair.

"It would be my pleasure," he whispered as he made short work of the sheer silk, and a tingle shot through her.

He framed her face in the strength of his hands when the veiling had been dispatched, and Rebecca melted against him, oblivious to the murmur of approval that rippled through the assembly of guests when his lips closed gently over hers.

Soon, a voice echoed persistently in the back of her mind. She would have to tell him the truth soon.

But maybe not tonight.

Chapter Eleven

Of course it was only a matter of time before something went dreadfully wrong.

When Yusuf arrived, purportedly to extend his congratulations, Jacob gritted his teeth and greeted the Berber politely, telling himself that he had imagined the quick look that Rebecca exchanged with the man. His sense that more than one person was watching the interchange with interest was purely a figment of his imagination, of that much Jacob was certain, but still he bit back the urge to show the Berber to the door.

When Isaac cornered him and demanded to know the date he would be selling the house, Jacob demurred and congratulated himself on neatly sidestepping the impertinent question, at least until the elderly man turned and began to badger Rebecca about the same matter. She shot Jacob a look of such confusion that he wondered fleetingly whether she had even thought about leaving her home in the hectic pace of the past few days and he regretted not having discussed such practicalities with her.

"As you can see, we have yet to decide on the matter," he informed the older man stonily, capturing Rebecca's hand within his, grateful that she seemed uncharacteristically content to stand silently beside him.

"As you know, we're most interested," Isaac began, but Jacob stemmed the tide of his words with one look. Had the man no tact at all? Wasn't it obvious that the very idea

of leaving her home was new to Rebecca and the subject
was better left until she had the chance to come to terms
with it?

"So you've already made clear, but this is hardly the time
or the place for such a discussion." He bit out the words
and Isaac indignantly drew himself up to his full height.

"Jacob!" Rebecca admonished under her breath, but
Jacob tightened his grip on her hand, hoping against hope
that she would hold her tongue just this once.

"I should think you would be grateful for the assistance
of the elders in this matter," Isaac retorted huffily. "Especially as this is shaping up to be such a lean winter for us
all and it is unlikely that there will be many interested in
purchasing a home."

In fact, it seemed to Jacob that an enormous number of
people were inexplicably interested in acquiring this particular domicile, but he wisely refrained from saying so,
wishing he knew what the attraction was.

"I've already given you my word that you would be the
first to know our plans," Jacob explained in precise tones,
fancying that Rebecca fidgeted uncomfortably beside him
when he continued. "Surely a man's word is worth something even here."

"Even the word of a foreigner has value," the old man
conceded with poor grace, and Jacob squeezed Rebecca's
hand briefly when he heard her sharp inhalation. Despite
his innocent expression, it seemed that Isaac was trying to
provoke him, although Jacob could not imagine why.

"Today, however, there are more important matters
afoot," Jacob concluded smoothly, having no desire to
continue the conversation. He held the older man's gaze for
a long moment before Isaac turned to Rebecca.

"Quite so," Isaac agreed with evident reluctance. "I
don't really mean to trouble you about such tedious matters on your wedding day, my dear," he continued, and
Jacob noted with interest the almost deliberate transition
to his usual wheedling tone. "But I was wondering whether
you had seen any sign of my book?"

Rebecca shook her head and Jacob dismissed his impression that her denial came too quickly to be sincere. "No, I haven't," she declared, and the older man studied her for a long moment before he nodded and made to move away.

"I wish you a blessed match," he said without enthusiasm, but Jacob had already turned to greet another guest.

"What was that all about?" he asked Rebecca in an undertone moments later when that guest had also moved away, instinctively disliking the sharp look she granted him before she spoke.

"Nothing," she responded, but she looked away and Jacob was not fooled.

"Rebecca," he murmured. "We cannot start with lies between us." She gave him a look of such outright fear that he was taken aback, but in the blink of an eye, her features were composed again and he dismissed the fleeting expression.

"He's just a harmless old man," she commented uneasily. Jacob touched his fingertip beneath her chin and forced her to meet his eyes.

"What book was he talking about?" he asked, knowing that she could hear his determination to get to the root of this when she frowned quickly.

"It was nothing really, just a book he had misplaced and thought might be here." She shrugged and her features softened as her glance drifted to Isaac on the other side of the courtyard. "He's getting old and he doesn't remember everything. You have to feel sorry for him really."

Jacob followed her sympathetic gaze and wondered whether the explanation was as simple as that.

The shadows of night had fallen and the air had turned chilly, the candles flickering in the gusts of wintry wind when Rebecca tiredly made her way into the kitchen. She leaned against the table for a long moment, savoring the break from the festivities, certain she had never been so exhausted in her life. Her cheeks ached from smiling endlessly, her feet were sore, and she wanted nothing more than to have all these merrymakers leave so she could crawl into bed and sleep for a week.

Well, maybe not *just* sleep.

A mischievous smile made her lips twitch and she pushed away from the table with renewed energy, intending to return to the fray when a furtive sound brought her steps to a sudden halt.

She listened carefully and the sound came again. It was more of a rustle actually, and was coming from Ephraim's study.

Mice. The conclusion came quickly and Rebecca gritted her teeth, cursing the winter weather that brought the rodents indoors. Next they would be into the rice and the flour, if they hadn't already, and all the dry stores would have to be destroyed. It would be a shocking waste and she wished too late that she had remembered to set the traps in the fall despite the disorder in her life.

Without another thought, she crossed the room and shoved open the door of the library. The resulting breeze made the flame of the lantern on Ephraim's desk dance uncertainly and cast the room into an eerie kaleidoscope of orange and black. A man on the opposite side of the room spun on his heel and clutched something to his chest, his horrified expression made surreal by the strange light.

Rebecca's heart leapt at the unexpected sight and she had an instant to regret her impulsive intrusion before she recognized Isaac with relief. Her pulse skittered to a slower pace as the older man's face fell into its customary helpless expression, making her wonder whether she had imagined the flicker of terror in his eyes.

"Oh, my dear, you've given me such a fright!" Isaac gushed as he recovered himself, his left hand resting limply over his heart as though he would slow its pace. His other hand fell to his side and Rebecca barely caught a glimpse of red beneath his palm before he slipped his hand into his tunic. "Oh, my heart, I must sit down for a moment," he gasped, but Rebecca could not erase the image of his fear upon being discovered.

"What are you doing here?" she demanded more sharply than she intended, and Isaac shot her a quick look as he sank weakly into Ephraim's chair.

"I wanted to have a look at Ephraim's books," he replied in his defense, gesturing vaguely to the jammed bookcases. "I wanted to know what he had in case you decided to sell them."

"But you looked at them all a few weeks ago," Rebecca reminded him, noting how uncomfortable he looked for the barest instant.

"But I was so busy looking for *my* book then that I didn't pay attention to the others," he complained, and she saw that both of his hands were now empty. She frowned. He had been holding something, she was sure of it. Something red.

And the book from the fountain had been bound in red leather.

Her eyes flew to the shelf where she had placed the book only to find a small space between the adjacent volumes. Her gaze flew back to Isaac in time to catch a flash of something smug in his expression before his look of innocence again returned. She blinked and he still regarded her calmly, his breathing unnaturally loud in the small room.

"You had something in your hand when I came in," she charged, feeling a flicker of fear herself when Isaac's eyes narrowed briefly before he spread his hands.

"I have nothing," he asserted boldly.

"I saw something in your hand," Rebecca challenged, determined that he would not steal this book from her before she knew what it was. "Something red."

"Something?" Isaac questioned innocently.

"It must have been a book," she suggested wildly, curiously loath to give any indication that she knew about this particular book, but Isaac simply looked puzzled.

"I was only scanning the shelves when you came in," he insisted mildly. "Perhaps it was a trick of the light."

Rebecca almost gasped aloud at the audacity of his lie, the self-satisfied look in Isaac's eyes telling her that he had no intention of surrendering the book. They both knew that he had been holding it when she came in and that she had seen him secrete it in his tunic, but short of calling him a liar and demanding to examine his clothes, Rebecca had no way to prove it.

And he knew it.

Isaac sat back in the chair, wheezing more quietly while he watched her with his lips curved into a smile that seemed slightly disdainful. The confidence with which he had made his assertion that he had taken nothing sank in, and Rebecca wondered whether she *had* imagined that he had held a book. What possible reason would Isaac have to try to steal it? His eyes seemed much colder now than they had before but she wondered whether that was only a figment of her imagination, as well.

Suddenly she wished she had summoned Jacob before she had barged in here to investigate. As if he sensed her trepidation, Isaac rose smoothly to his feet, and it seemed to Rebecca that he stood taller and straighter than he had before.

"I should return to the celebration," he murmured, the expression in his eyes daring her to prevent him from doing so, and Rebecca felt her frustration rise. She stood motionless as he stepped toward her, struggling against her certainty that he was stronger than she had thought, fighting against her own unwillingness to make an accusation against an elder of the community and her own irrational certainty that he meant to steal that book.

"What are you going to do with it?" she demanded when he drew alongside her, and Isaac shot her an amused glance.

"With what?" he inquired guilelessly, his smile knowing, and the very way he made his denial decided the matter for Rebecca.

"Liar!" she charged, and Isaac must have seen the intent in her eyes for he bolted toward the door with surprising agility.

Jacob extricated himself from Berta's ceaseless monologue, his curiosity as to what was taking Rebecca so long getting the better of him. It had been ages since she had disappeared into the kitchen and he wondered whether she had sat down for a moment and inadvertently fallen asleep. Her exhaustion had been showing as the night ripened and he had begun to wish that some of their guests might take note of her state and politely be on their way. For the sake of the baby if not herself, Rebecca needed to get some sleep.

A grunt carried to Jacob's ears, followed by the sound of something heavy falling, and he hastened his steps, coming to a halt in the middle of the unexpectedly empty kitchen. Rebecca was nowhere in sight and he hesitated momentarily, her soft cry drawing him to the poorly lit study with his heart in his throat.

His first thought was that she had fallen and injured the baby, his fear so intense that the sight of Rebecca tussling on the floor with a man took him completely by surprise. Jacob watched in astonishment as the two rolled over, glimpsing the rage in the older man's eyes, and he recognized Isaac just as the older man raised his hand to strike Rebecca.

Jacob leapt into the room, stunned to see Rebecca bare her teeth and bite the arm that held her captive before the blow could fall. Isaac howled in pain and seemingly forgot to strike her, twisting away with herculean strength and struggling to his feet. He tossed Rebecca aside when she gave chase, both of them still unaware of Jacob's presence, and she lost her balance even as she grabbed for the older man. Jacob stepped forward to catch her but she clutched Isaac's cloak, dragging him to his knees as she dropped heavily to her own. Isaac cursed vehemently at her interference and something fell to the floor with a thud.

"The book!" Rebecca cried victoriously, and Isaac's eyes lit with fear as they both dived after the volume that seemed too small to be worth the trouble of a scuffle.

"No!" Isaac protested, and their hands collided as they reached for the book, sending it scuttling straight toward Jacob. They lunged after it of one accord, both pairs of eyes widening in shock when Jacob planted his foot squarely atop it.

He saw fear flicker across Rebecca's features and wondered what she was up to this time, barely catching the malice that briefly lit Isaac's eyes before the older man began to moan. Rebecca shot Isaac a look of such disdain that Jacob almost laughed, the impulse quelled when she seemed momentarily uncertain whether to accept his own assisting hand. He felt her fingers tremble as he hoisted her unceremoniously to her feet.

"What is this all about?" Jacob asked, doubting whether he would get a straight answer but determined to try. He had no doubt that Rebecca knew but had little intention of telling him, her first words making that fact painfully clear.

"Nothing," she said hastily, pulling her hand abruptly from his and averting her gaze.

"Nothing," insisted Isaac at the same time, and Jacob surveyed them both skeptically. Rebecca ought to be better at lying for all the practice she'd had, he mused to himself, watching for their reactions as he bent and deliberately picked up the book.

"Then what's this?" he asked conversationally.

"A book I loaned to Ephraim," Isaac said firmly, extending one hand for the slim volume.

"Liar!" Rebecca charged, and the older man shot her a look of outright hostility before he shook his head sagely, his manner changing so abruptly that Jacob felt as though he had imagined the first gesture.

"She doesn't know what she's talking about," Isaac murmured confidentially. "You know how women are. If you'll just give me the book, I'll be on my way and you can get back to your nuptials."

"Oh," Rebecca gasped in outright indignation, turning on Jacob with blazing eyes. "He's trying to steal this book."

"How can a man steal what already belongs to him?" Isaac demanded reasonably, his manner that of a man forced to endure the company of idiots.

"This book doesn't belong to you—it belongs to me," Rebecca shot back.

"Nonsense," Isaac countered, dismissing her with a wave of one hand. "Just give me the book, Jacob, and we'll be done with this little matter."

"Don't let him talk you into this," Rebecca warned, and one glance in her direction was enough to convince Jacob that she was certain she was in the right.

Jacob spared a glance to Isaac and once again had that disturbing sense that things were not all they appeared to be. He looked down at the book and was struck again by how singularly unspectacular it appeared to be. Isaac inhaled sharply when he nonchalantly flipped through the pages and Jacob noted the gesture, wondering only briefly at its import before one word caught his eye.

Idrîs, he read, and needed to see no more, the whole thing suddenly making sense to him. Jacob skimmed the rest of the pages as leisurely as though he hadn't had a revelation and closed the book, tossing the slight weight of it in one hand as he met the thinly veiled avarice in Isaac's gaze.

Yes, he could well imagine that some people might want this book very badly.

"Perhaps it's best if I keep it for now," he suggested smoothly, flicking a deprecating glance at the book. "We'll sort this out when Ephraim's books are valued."

"But it's *my* book," Isaac insisted.

"I can't imagine that it's worth all this excitement," Jacob countered quietly. "After all, it could hardly be a valuable text by its size. Let me see . . ." He scanned the spine as if he didn't read Arabic and held it out in Isaac's direction with a puzzled frown. "Doesn't this mean Ovid?" he asked, watching scorn flicker in the old man's eyes before he nodded quickly in agreement.

"Exactly. It's a book of poetry that was a gift to me," Isaac claimed, and extended his hand once more.

"He said he wanted it for the inscription," Rebecca interjected, her voice colder than Jacob had ever heard, and he turned to Isaac to find the old man nodding agreement.

"Precisely," he said enthusiastically, evidently thinking events had turned in his favor. "Sentimental value, you know. When one gets older, little things mean more than they ever did."

Jacob held his gaze for a long moment, then opened the book. The endpaper was completely devoid of notation and he smothered a smile, making a mental note not to try to slip anything past his astute wife.

"But there is no inscription," he informed Isaac calmly, watching the man's face fall. "Apparently you have mistaken this book for your own. Undoubtedly they were quite similar and it was an honest mistake."

Isaac's mouth opened and closed a few times, his eyes widening in disbelief when Jacob tucked the book into his tunic.

"I was so looking forward to reading some of the poetry again," Isaac commented plaintively, and Jacob had to admire the man's perseverance. "And now I have no idea when I'll find my own book again," he sighed, his eyes brightening as he looked up, and Jacob braced himself for the inevitable. "Do you think I could perhaps borrow the book?"

"To tell you the truth, I'd rather keep all of Ephraim's things here until we do an inventory. I'm sure the books will be sold shortly and I'll remember that you're particularly interested in this one."

"After all, you've waited this long," Rebecca interjected, and Jacob knew he didn't imagine the venomous look the old man dispatched in her direction.

"Yes, I have waited a *long* time for my due," he agreed under his breath, encompassing Jacob in that same glance before he turned to hobble to the door. "No matter if these old bones up and die before the week is out. No matter if I search for a poem for years and then am denied it for no good reason. Don't let it concern you."

"Well, I'm glad that's settled," Jacob concluded with mock cheerfulness, returning to the role of gracious host despite his feelings to the contrary.

Would Rebecca tell him what was going on when they had a chance to talk? Did she even know? He took her hand and tucked it over his elbow proprietarily, seeing from the wariness in her eyes that she knew this issue was not closed between them.

"Perhaps it's time you bid our guests good night," he suggested calmly, and the way her lips set mutinously told him that she wasn't fooled by his apparent concern. Jacob sighed, wondering what lies she was already concocting for his ears.

No matter how frustrating the man could be, Rebecca had to admit that Jacob was showing real signs of thoughtfulness. As she washed the carmine from her lips, a glow of appreciation filled her. Discarding the hundreds of thin gold bracelets that covered her forearms, she shrugged out of the heavy dress, draping it over the chest against the far wall and unbraiding her hair. Clad only in her chemise and fingering her *aljofar,* she dropped heavily onto the soft cushions and closed her eyes gratefully, struggling not to speculate on why he was being so considerate of her.

The sounds of crockery being gathered and voices exchanging best wishes rose from the courtyard, then faded as Rebecca lay back and let the exhaustion filter through her body. Berta's voice carried through the night air and she heard the new bolt Jacob had insisted on buying shoot home as she faced the truth.

Jacob was being kind to her because of the baby he thought she carried.

She winced and rolled on to her stomach, knowing that she had to tell him the truth tonight. He was going to be upset, that much was beyond doubt, and she could only hope that she had the strength to deal with his reaction. She was so tired that she was likely to become emotional or lose her temper. More than likely she would say the wrong thing.

Her eyelids drifted closed and Rebecca wondered absently whether it would make that much difference if she waited until tomorrow. At least then she would do a better job of it, although the end result would probably be the same.

Because Jacob was going to leave her when he knew the truth, she concluded sadly as she drifted off to sleep.

An awareness that she wasn't alone awoke Rebecca and she rolled over at the sound of a boot hitting the floor, easily picking out Jacob's silhouette against the shadows as he undressed in the darkness. She murmured a greeting and he glanced up in surprise.

"I thought you were asleep," he commented in a low voice, and Rebecca nodded.

"Pretty close," she admitted, unable to stifle a yawn. "I'm sorry I'm so tired, Jacob."

"Berta said you didn't sleep this week," he acknowledged matter-of-factly as he hauled his tunic over his head, and Rebecca felt some of her exhaustion slip away at the sight of his nudity. Her pulse quickened and she rolled over to watch him, completely unselfconscious as he disrobed before her. "Am I that frightening?"

Rebecca propped herself up on her elbows, astonished by the question. "No," she replied, watching his smile flash in the darkness.

"Well, that's good." Jacob bent to untie his chausses and Rebecca averted her gaze, suddenly embarrassed by the intimacy of the situation. And why? she scolded herself. There were hardly any mysteries between the two of them at this point.

"How about Ephraim? Was he frightening?" Jacob demanded softly, and Rebecca's gaze trailed unwillingly back to him, only to find him watching her intently. She swallowed with difficulty under his perusal and felt a flicker of desire at the sight of his bare, broad chest. Ephraim... She forced herself to follow the thread of the conversation. Why on earth was he asking about Ephraim all the time?

"No," she conceded, hearing the waver of awareness in her tone.

"You can tell me," he assured her in a low voice as he discarded his chausses, but Rebecca shook her head in confusion. Tell him what? That Ephraim was deadly dull in bed?

"There's—there's nothing to tell," she stammered, and he crossed the room in three businesslike strides. He dropped to the cushions beside her and braced his hands on her shoulders, leaning over her with an intense expression in his eyes that rendered her as motionless as a butterfly on a pin.

"Rebecca," he said huskily, and her heart tripped at the way he said her name. "If this is going to work, we have to trust each other. I understand that you might not want to talk about Ephraim, but I think you should."

Rebecca studied Jacob's features for some clue as to what he was talking about, knowing from his serious manner that this was not about sex but unable to perceive anything more than that.

"There's nothing to tell," she insisted, helpless to stop the disappointment that clouded Jacob's eyes.

But what did he want to know? That Ephraim read too much? Or mumbled in Arabic? Nothing she could recall about her first husband seemed worthy of this sort of interest and she scanned her memories wildly, trying to figure out what Jacob wanted her to tell him.

"Fine," he said quietly, and it seemed his voice was even deeper than usual. "Tell me when you're ready." Jacob shot her a piercingly bright look. "You do know that I'll listen to you, whenever you decide to tell me?"

Rebecca nodded in agreement. "You always have," she admitted, liking the fact that she had been able to say something to make him smile. He leaned on one elbow and fingered the loose strands of her hair, letting it slip over his hand as he watched.

"This afternoon, you asked me to trust you," Jacob mused, and Rebecca's pulse accelerated guiltily. "And I did." He met her eyes again and she held her breath, certain that somehow he had found out the truth and was going to accuse her of lying about the baby. Or worse. His expression was without censure, though, and she regarded him with confusion, not daring to anticipate his next words.

"I guess I'm asking you to trust me now," Jacob added huskily, and a wave of relief coursed through Rebecca.

"But I do," she breathed quickly, gratified when he grinned outright.

"Good," he whispered just before his lips closed over hers. His fingers wound into her hair and imprisoned her beneath his caress even as the weight of his chest held her captive. Rebecca welcomed him, gripping his shoulders giddily as his touch awakened her drowsy desire, feeling the wiry curl of his chest hair against her tender nipples even through her sheer chemise.

All too soon he lifted his head and she sighed with satisfaction, stretching up to run the tip of her tongue along the outline of his lips. Jacob growled and ducked to nibble her earlobe, the words he whispered dismissing the mood as surely as water doused the embers of a fire.

"What do you know about Isaac's book?" he whispered, and Rebecca almost sat bolt upright, struggling now against the burden of his weight.

"It's not his book," she hissed indignantly. "It's mine and he was trying to steal it." Jacob rolled to his back beside her and regarded her with narrowed eyes.

"Are you sure?" he demanded calmly, and she almost spit at him for looking so cool and collected. What kind of game was he playing with her?

"Of course I'm sure," she shot back, her temper more than adequately fueled by the abrupt change in the romantic temperature of the room.

"Why on earth would he want that book badly enough to steal it?"

"I don't know," Rebecca retorted testily, drawing her chemise higher around her neck with an impatient gesture.

"Well, what is the book?" Jacob asked mildly, and she looked at him in surprise.

"You said it was Ovid's poetry," she accused, and something about the way he nonchalantly shrugged made her wonder if Jacob knew more than he was letting on.

"I asked if it was," he corrected, and she regarded him in amazement.

"Then you can't read it, either," she breathed, immediately realizing that she had revealed too much. She sat up quickly, intending to move away, but Jacob laid a restraining hand on her arm. Reluctantly she turned to meet the question in his eyes.

"What is so special about the book?" he demanded quietly, but she only shook her head, sensing his disapproval. "You said you trusted me," he reminded her, and even though his voice was low, Rebecca could hear that thread of determination making its presence known.

"I don't know," she equivocated, but Jacob gripped her chin and turned her to face him.

"You know more than you're telling me," he insisted, and Rebecca hated the way her gaze wavered from his. His eyes hardened and she knew he had guessed the truth. "Tell me," he urged, but she shook her head again.

"I can't."

"Can't or won't?" Jacob asked sharply. Rebecca hesitated only an instant before she replied.

"Both." As soon as the word was out she closed her eyes against the wave of Jacob's anger, hearing him shove himself to his feet and pace across the room.

"You said you trusted me," he repeated angrily, and she knew she had pushed him too far again.

"I made a promise," she protested in frustration.

"To whom?" he demanded, and Rebecca set her lips mutinously. The news that this was the promise she had made to Yusuf would not improve matters in the least and she was determined not to impart that information.

"Well?" Jacob prompted when she remained stubbornly silent, and Rebecca dared to glance in his direction. With his feet planted wide and his arms folded across his chest, Jacob was the very picture of carefully controlled fury and there was no way she was going to make things worse.

"I can't tell you," she insisted quietly, and his eyes blazed.

"I walked in here this morning and found you with a former suitor," he pointed out in that dangerous tone she was getting to know, "but you asked me to trust you and I did. Now you claim to trust me, but you won't even tell me what you know about a book that someone, by your own admission, wants badly enough to steal." He squatted down before her and Rebecca felt the tension emanating from him. "It would seem that you and I have a vastly different definition of trust."

Rebecca swallowed with difficulty beneath the weight of her guilt. When she said nothing in her own defense, Jacob muttered something under his breath.

"We took a vow today," he growled. "A vow that I thought meant something to both of us."

He picked up her left hand and her gaze fell to the ring he had placed there as he traced its curve with a surprisingly gentle touch. He exhaled shakily and Rebecca dared to glance at his face, only to find his anger had faded.

"There is something magical between us," Jacob mused in a low voice as he folded her hand between his. "I don't know what you've been through in the past, but you have to take a chance this time, Rebecca. You have to reach for this and so do I, or it isn't going to work. And the first step is trusting each other." Jacob cleared his throat and shook his head as if amazed by what he was going to say.

"I trust you," he asserted, "despite your best efforts to convince me otherwise. Now you have to decide to trust me." He lifted her hand to his lips and kissed her fingertips before he rose to his feet and walked to the door. He hesitated on the threshold and spared a glance over his shoulder.

"I know what it means to give your word," he continued so softly that she had to strain to hear him. "But sometimes you have to decide which is the greater good." He sighed and ran one hand through his hair and she realized he was almost as tired as she. "I'll be downstairs if you need me," he said, and with that his silhouette moved out of the doorway.

"But, Jacob," Rebecca protested, not wanting to see him go, half convinced that she should confide in him now and dismiss her promise to Yusuf.

"Hush," he said, ducking his head back around the door frame. "Enough for tonight. Get some sleep, for your sake and the baby's."

Any words she had been intending to say died in her throat and she nodded mutely, her eyes filling with tears as she heard Jacob's footsteps on the stairs. He said he wanted the truth, she thought miserably as she curled up like a child among the cushions and let her tears flow.

But would he feel differently once he knew what he was asking for?

Chapter Twelve

The days dragged by at a snail's pace and Rebecca was uncomfortably aware of Jacob's speculative assessment of her each morning when she made her way downstairs. It didn't help matters that she was still having trouble sleeping, the question of what to do plaguing her throughout the night, while he appeared to be supremely well rested.

Although she had known in some corner of her mind that they would be moving to Tunis, it was difficult for Rebecca to come to terms with the reality of selling the house. It had been her security for so long, her place of refuge, that she couldn't imagine being without it. In her more logical moments, she knew that the house had been severely compromised when it had been broken into so easily and often, but it was her home, as much as any place had ever been, and she was reluctant to leave it.

Maybe she was just afraid of the unknown, she chided herself, knowing that this had never been an issue with her before. Hadn't she ridden boldly to the strange and distant town of Toledo to her wedding? Hadn't she been self-sufficient all these years, even after she and Ephraim had bought this house? When had she ever depended on anyone or anything? And why was she starting now?

She stood in the wintry sunlight and looked around the courtyard, admitting that she had grown to depend on this place and that the thought of being without it frightened her. The thought that dependency on a mere house could make her so weak had even more terrifying implications.

What if she dared to depend on Jacob and was forced to give him up? Or what if she simply lost him, the way she had lost so many others?

She felt his presence and turned to find him watching her from the door to the foyer, his expression as speculative as if he had guessed her very thoughts and wondered himself what decision she would make. The irony of it all, Rebecca realized with a start as she watched him, was that she could only prove to herself that she wasn't dependent on a silly house by giving it up, which meant that she would have to count on Jacob.

"I didn't realize it would be so hard to leave the house," she said tonelessly, and Jacob nodded slowly, scanning the courtyard with an appraising eye.

"It is a pleasant place," he agreed, shoving his hands into his pockets as he came to stand beside her. He had just shaved and she closed her eyes against the smell of pumice, wishing in that moment that he would hold her close and reassure her.

"And I suppose you have a lot of memories," Jacob commented instead, leaving a discreet distance between them. Would that distance always be there? Would there always be something unspoken holding them apart? Rebecca frowned to herself, the alienation she felt from Jacob making her decision to put her life in his hands all the more difficult.

"I suppose," she agreed, and folded her arms across her chest, knowing that that wasn't the root of her problem.

"You get to take your memories with you," Jacob pointed out, and Rebecca looked up with surprise to find compassion and a flicker of humor in his eyes. "They pack very light." She realized that he was trying to make this easier for her and took some measure of comfort in the thought.

"Yes," she agreed, still unable to summon a smile, and she looked around the tiled expanse once more. How would she tolerate living in this politely restrained relationship? She wanted so much more from this marriage, and once again, she wondered whether she expected too much. She felt Jacob watching her for a long moment before he cleared his throat, but still she didn't look up.

"I haven't told you much about Tunis," he said, his tone conversational. "It's warmer than here, of course, but right on the sea so there's always a breeze. It looks beautiful when you come into the harbor, all the white buildings piled against the hills where they rise out of the sea." Rebecca turned to watch Jacob as he spoke, his eyes focused on some faraway point as if he saw the city spread before him, the half smile that curved his lips convincing her as much as his words of the beauty of his recollections.

"The hills aren't quite as steep as here, but the buildings are whitewashed like here, with tiled courtyards like this. The minaret on the mosque is the highest point in town and I think you'll like the huge *souk.*"

Jacob made it sound so lovely and Rebecca could almost visualize the town from his description, his evident affection for Tunis making her suddenly want to see it. She had never been to the Mediterranean and her curiosity sparked at the knowledge that Jacob had seen so much more of the world than she.

"Tell me about your house," Rebecca prompted, and Jacob pursed his lips as he studied the courtyard again.

"It has a courtyard like this," he said, turning to check the distance to the other wall. "But I think it's a little bigger and the tiles have more blue in them. And the fountain is square with turquoise tiles on the bottom," he added thoughtfully, sparing her a mischievous wink, and she felt unexpectedly closer to him.

"Last summer, Judith bought two goldfish for it, but the water got too hot under the sun and they died. I didn't want her to be disappointed, so I bought two more before she saw them." He struggled not to smile and Rebecca felt her lips curling in response.

"They died, too?" she prompted, and Jacob grinned.

"That very day," he confirmed, and rolled his eyes. "So I rushed out and found two more."

"You didn't?" Rebecca demanded incredulously, and laughed when he nodded. "How many did you buy?"

"I have no idea," Jacob said, shaking his head in amusement. "Then, after this had been going on for a while and the man selling the goldfish knew me by name, Judith commented that she wished those silly fish would die because their dirt was clogging the fountain. Can you believe it?"

"No more fish?" Rebecca guessed as she stifled a giggle, and Jacob shook his head ruefully.

"Not a one. It was a relief, but it ruined the goldfish seller's business, I'm sure."

"Your aunt never guessed?"

"Not a clue."

Rebecca smiled to herself, her smile fading as a thought struck her. "Do you think she'll mind having another woman in the house?" she asked timidly, surprised when Jacob gathered her into a loose hug without hesitation. She tipped up her chin in time to see him smile ruefully.

"Judith's been trying to marry me off for years," he confided, and gave her a little shake. "This was her idea, in case you've forgotten, so don't worry about Judith."

Rebecca smiled and leaned against him, closing her eyes against the sound of Jacob's heartbeat beneath her ear and the soft brush of his cotton shirt against her cheek.

"Everything will be fine," he whispered into her hair, and Rebecca nodded, relaxing under the soothing sweep of his hand stroking up and down her back. This was what she had needed, she admitted, inhaling deeply of Jacob's scent and linking her fingers behind his waist.

"I've never had the chance to trust anyone before," she confessed in a low voice, a tear squeezing out of her eye when Jacob's arms tightened around her.

"There's no time like the present," he reminded her, and she hugged him even tighter. He was right, and who better to trust than this man who persisted in showing himself worthy of it?

"How soon can we sell the house?" Rebecca asked, suddenly anxious to be on their way.

"Judging by the local interest, probably in a matter of moments," Jacob commented dryly, and Rebecca pulled back to look up at him in surprise. He brushed away her errant tear with his thumb, but she frowned in confusion at his words, oblivious to the caress.

"What are you talking about?"

"The synagogue elders were very anxious to have first chance to bid on the house and Ephraim's books," he informed her.

Rebecca couldn't imagine why. "But it's a perfectly average house," she protested, noting the assessing gleam in Jacob's eyes.

"That's what I thought, but they told me that it would fetch a good price."

Rebecca took a step back and fixed him with a skeptical eye. "This close to the public baths?" she demanded, and Jacob shook his head in apparent agreement.

"I thought there must be something I didn't know about the house," he concluded, and Rebecca's gaze fell automatically to the fountain.

"Maybe there's something neither of us knows," she muttered under her breath, and Jacob evidently didn't hear her words.

"Rebecca?" he asked, but she shook her head, her mind buzzing with possibilities.

"Let's wait a few days," she suggested, ignoring the way Jacob arched one brow in inquiry. "I need to think about this."

So close and yet so far.

Jacob strode down to the *souk* in poor humor, disliking his sense that Rebecca had come within a hairbreadth of confiding in him before inexplicably changing her mind. She was keeping something from him, that much was beyond dispute, although he cared less for that fact than the barrier it seemed to have erected between them.

He had been crazy to think that marriage would solve anything. And how bold he had been to play his card on their wedding night, certain that the desire Rebecca had shown in the past would compel her to trust him and that he would be back in her bed before the dawn. Evidently that desire was no longer an issue, for he had become well acquainted with the uncompromising hardness of the straw pallet in the kitchen. At least these past few sleepless nights had given him the opportunity to do some very interesting reading, but even that thought did not draw his mind away from the problem at hand.

Had Rebecca's passion been another of her lies? Jacob shook his head in answer to his own question, knowing without a doubt that her response had been genuine. Then what had changed? Did the fact that they were married take the spice out of their lovemaking for her? Or was she simply too tired because of the baby growing within her?

That last thought calmed his fears as it always did and Jacob even managed to smile when he concluded his business with the spice vendor. He ought not to be so hard on her, he reminded himself sternly, trying to recall everything he had ever heard about childbearing. Women were more emotional during their confinement, that much he knew, and Rebecca's concern about traveling and making a new home seemed to coincide with that.

Jacob recalled their conversation and only briefly congratulated himself for easing her fears before he clenched his hands in memory of the way she had withdrawn suddenly at the end. How he wished he could shake the truth from her once and for all so that they could get on with their lives.

And what had he ever done to give her doubts about trusting him? Nothing. Jacob cursed Ephraim once more for destroying Rebecca's faith in men. Her loyalty to the man's memory in the face of that was astonishing to him, and he wondered for the hundredth time how he could encourage her to lay her cards on the table. If he had a better idea of what Ephraim had done to her, he knew he could ease her fears.

"Good morning." A familiar melodic voice interrupted his thoughts and Jacob looked up with a start, a wariness gripping him as he met the faint amusement in those green eyes.

"Good morning, Yusuf," he returned, eyeing the man standing before him speculatively. Surely they had nothing more to say to each other?

"Perhaps you would join me for a glass of tea," the Berber invited, and Jacob agreed, curious as to what the man wanted to talk to him about.

He didn't have to wait long to find out.

"I understand a certain volume has come to light," Yusuf said abruptly once they were seated in what was apparently his favorite café, steaming glasses of mint tea set before them. Jacob's mind tripped through the possibilities and he decided to play dumb in the hope that he would learn more.

"I beg your pardon?" he inquired.

"I had understood that a small red book was found amongst Ephraim's possessions, but perhaps I was mistaken," Yusuf commented smoothly, his casual tone belied by the intensity of the interest gleaming in his eyes. Jacob met his eyes and the Berber discreetly dropped his gaze.

"Oh, yes, the book of Ovid's poetry," Jacob supplied nonchalantly, knowing full well that the book was anything but that.

"Yes, Ovid," Yusuf agreed hastily, apparently unable to keep his lips from twitching. "I am prepared to make you an offer for the poetry volume," he continued, and Jacob barely kept from showing his amazement before he recalled the real subject of the book. He had known there would be many people interested, to say the least, so why was he surprised to have yet another approach him?

"I'm afraid Isaac has already requested the opportunity to bid first," he demurred, and this time Yusuf could not restrain a smirk.

"Yes, Isaac has a great fondness for *poetry*," he confirmed silkily, and Jacob fancied that the other man gritted his teeth.

"Rather unexpectedly," Jacob commented, and Yusuf laughed dryly.

"Perhaps not that unexpectedly," he muttered under his breath.

"At any rate, I have promised him first chance at the volume, in the event that it is offered for sale," Jacob concluded, meeting the challenge in Yusuf's gaze. When the Berber seemed disinclined to comment, he nodded and rose to his feet, fully intending to be on his way.

"Perhaps Rebecca would be more amenable to selling it to me," Yusuf suggested in a low voice, and Jacob shot him a sharp look.

"Just what are you implying?" he demanded, but the Berber only smiled very slowly.

"Let us simply say that Rebecca and I have had, shall we say, an understanding in the past and she may have a soft spot in her heart for my desires." Yusuf calmly took a sip of his tea while he watched Jacob's reaction.

Jacob struggled not to show one, but the man's words shook him to the core. He had believed Rebecca's tale, but this seemed to cast new light upon whatever relations she had had with Yusuf. Had she glossed over certain details? Had she really been more interested in wedding Yusuf but had felt obligated to honor the *ketubah* she had already signed? Jacob sank back into his seat, ignoring the satisfied gleam in the Berber's eyes as he tried to make sense of it all. He cleared his throat and took a sip of his tea while he decided how to continue.

"There seems to be a lot of interest in this book," he commented finally, looking sharply at Yusuf. "I don't recall Ovid being so popular." This time the Berber was completely unsuccessful in hiding his smile.

"There is somewhat of a shortage of this particular translation," he contented himself with saying, and Jacob acknowledged the truth in that statement. "And it is a prized one among people who have an interest."

"Really?" Jacob feigned surprise. "Perhaps I should have it valued then before I sell it at too low a price in my ignorance."

"No!" Yusuf's vehemence was not a surprise to Jacob but he looked up in apparent astonishment, waiting with interest for what explanation the Berber would use. "You are not familiar with the volume," he clarified quickly, his words tripping over themselves in their haste to be heard. "A bookseller could trick you and steal the value of the work himself."

"Surely there are reputable book dealers in Toledo," Jacob scoffed politely, vastly enjoying the other man's dismay.

"It is best to avoid temptation," Yusuf argued, his composure falling back into place. "If you entrust the volume to me, I will see that it is fairly evaluated for you."

Jacob smiled slowly. "I would think that might conflict with your own interest to purchase the volume," he commented, and the Berber had the grace to look discomfited.

"I was only trying to assist," he claimed.

Jacob almost laughed aloud. "Of course," he agreed, "but perhaps it would be best if I handled the matter myself." Yusuf met his eyes with unconcealed hostility, evidently displeased that he had been unsuccessful in persuading a mere foreigner to fall in with his plans.

"Rebecca will undoubtedly feel differently," he countered, returning with a vengeance to the one ploy that had netted him a response. Jacob met the knowing expression in those eyes, determined not to fall so easily into the trap this time.

"Perhaps she would," he commented easily, "but the fact is hardly relevant." He leaned across the small table and continued in a confidential tone. "You see, it is I who knows where the volume is, so it is I with whom you will have to conduct business.''

Jacob rose to his feet, fully intending to leave now that he had made his position clear, but the Berber's next question brought him up short.

"I had thought you were planning to leave Toledo?" he demanded.

"Certainly, we intend to return to Tunis before Hanukkah," he confirmed, not liking the way Yusuf's eyes shone at the news.

"That seems doubtful," the other man commented as he swept to his feet, his lips curved in a disdainful smile as he imperiously summoned the keeper to settle the tab.

"What do you mean?" Jacob demanded in confusion, and Yusuf smiled.

"The gates were sealed this morning by the Castilians," he supplied, watching while his news sank in. "No one can enter or leave the city until we acknowledge Alfonso as king."

"Is there any chance of that happening?" Jacob asked, and Yusuf shot a mocking glance over his shoulder as he turned to leave.

"The streets will run with our blood first," he hissed, his eyes narrowing for an instant and reminding Jacob unaccountably of a tiger poised to spring, then the Berber spun on his heel and stalked out of the café.

"You can take your time deciding about the house," Jacob said flatly as he strode into the kitchen. Rebecca looked up from her sewing in time to see him toss his turban aside impatiently and run his hands through his hair. He dropped into the chair opposite, leaning his head back and closing his eyes in frustration.

"What are you talking about?" she asked, noting how his lips tightened when she spoke. What had she done now?

"Toledo has been surrounded by the Castilians until the *taifa* surrenders," he supplied tersely, and Rebecca frowned at her work. There had been rumors that the army encamped outside of town would restrict entry and departure from the city at some point, but most had expected the invaders to wait until the spring when another season of crusading would begin.

"What are we going to do?" she dared to ask, not encouraged when Jacob shot her a sharp look. He leaned forward and folded his hands on the table very deliberately, his expression so intense that she couldn't tear her eyes away.

"We are going to get to know each other better," he vowed softly, and Rebecca's heart began to pound in her ears. "Beginning right now."

She licked her lips nervously, the way Jacob watched the gesture doing little to ease her trepidation.

"What do you mean?" she asked, her voice sounding like a squeak. Jacob traced a vein in the wood grain with his finger and frowned slightly as though he were searching for the right words.

"I want there to be no secrets between us," he said finally, and Rebecca's mouth went dry.

He knew about the baby, she was sure of it. This was it. She folded her hands together on top of her work to keep them from shaking and forced herself to face the truth. He had found out that she lied and everything would be over in a matter of moments.

And then he would be gone. Something caught in her throat as she tried to imagine being without him. Even as discordant as things had been between them for the past few days, she couldn't begin to draw the picture in her mind. She was losing him and there wasn't a damn thing she could do about it now.

Jacob glanced up and must have seen the fear in her eyes, for his own grew puzzled as he studied her. "What is it?" he whispered, and Rebecca closed her eyes against the compassion in his tone. A chair scraped the floor and she felt him beside her, a tear escaping her eye when the warmth of his palm cupped the side of her face. Jacob made a sound deep in his throat and suddenly she was in his lap, his arms wrapped tightly around her. She huddled against his chest and buried her face in his shirt, her heart aching at the sweet agony of his tenderness.

"Don't hate me," she mumbled, and felt his lips brushing away her tears.

"Never that," Jacob murmured, and as his words sank in, Rebecca looked up in amazement. "Tell me about the book," he prompted, and her astonishment could not have been more complete. Was it possible that he didn't know about the baby?

Should she tell him?

"I don't know much about it," Rebecca found herself confessing instead, the light of approval in Jacob's eyes making it impossible for her to change the subject now.

"Where did it come from?" he asked, and she suddenly wanted to tell him all about it.

"I found it in the fountain," she explained, and when Jacob looked confused, she heard herself laugh with delight. "Come here and I'll show you." She dumped her sewing on the table and took his hand to tug him to his feet.

Jacob's bemusement changed to admiration when she showed him the hidden compartment and how it opened, and Rebecca basked in his approval. He slipped his fingers into the space and felt around experimentally, but there was nothing else hidden there. Rebecca watched as he examined the hinge with interest.

"Do you know what the book is?" he asked with a quick glance in her direction, and she shook her head.

"No, I can't read it. Is it Arabic, do you think?" she inquired, and Jacob nodded.

"Yes, it is in Arabic," he confirmed. "Like most alchemical texts." Rebecca's eyes widened at this last comment and she grabbed his arm in her excitement.

"You can read it then?" she demanded breathlessly, and Jacob shot her a grin.

"Of course," he responded easily, her expectant air evidently a source of amusement to him, for a twinkle appeared in his eyes.

"Well?" she demanded impatiently, and Jacob smiled.

"I'm not sure I should tell you," he teased, and she gasped.

"You have to tell me—it's my book," she countered indignantly, and Jacob laughed.

"Maybe you should convince me," he suggested playfully, and Rebecca smiled herself. Maybe she could at that. After all, they hadn't really celebrated their nuptials yet.

"I thought you didn't want to consummate the marriage," she charged softly, the flare of heat in Jacob's eyes catching her off guard and simultaneously emboldening her. She took a step closer, watching as his jaw tightened.

"I thought you were too tired," he countered, and her smile widened at both his thoughtfulness and what that restraint had cost him.

"You thought wrong," she whispered, sliding her hands up his arms and interlocking her fingers behind his neck. Jacob pulled her close as their lips met and his arousal imprinted itself on her stomach, giving her a heady sense of power even as she lost herself in his caress. When Jacob lifted his head, neither of them was breathing steadily and Rebecca took heart from the evidence that he was as shaken by their embrace as she. She ran her tongue along the line of his jaw, feeling him shudder when she reached his ear.

"Maybe you'd like to tell me about that book," she whispered mischievously, but Jacob shook his head stubbornly. His fingers spread across her buttocks and he lifted her to her toes, molding her pelvis to his so that there was absolutely no doubt as to the state of his arousal.

"It'll take more than a kiss to get that out of me," he murmured suggestively, and Rebecca felt warm all over.

"Is that a threat?" she demanded, enthralled when Jacob shook his head slowly.

"Definitely a promise," he confirmed, bending to kiss her with tender thoroughness once more.

"It's the middle of the afternoon," she protested when she came up for air, but Jacob only grinned.

"And perfectly legal," he reminded her. "Don't tell me you'd rather be sewing," he whispered into her ear, and Rebecca undulated her hips against him, smiling to herself when he gasped.

"You're right, I should finish that kirtle for Berta," she began to tease, but got no further before his lips closed unceremoniously over hers. Jacob's desire was infectious and Rebecca felt her blood heat, her heart racing when his tongue dived between her teeth. She gripped the hair at the nape of his neck and pulled him closer, marveling that she had lasted four entire days without his touch.

She realized her kirtle was gone when her nipples beaded in the cool air. The warmth of Jacob's mouth closing around one sent her arching helplessly against him. Determined to feel his skin against hers, she made short work of his tunic and shirt, liking the way he stiffened when she tasted his nipples in turn. She shivered when Jacob's fingers unerringly found the sweet spot between her thighs and he hesitated until she opened her eyes to meet the concern in his.

"It's too cold here," he murmured, the expression of wonder on his face as he stared down at her so irresistible that Rebecca reached up to kiss the corners of his mouth gently.

Jacob groaned and gathered her up in a tangle of loose clothes, but she gave him no quarter, teasing him with her tongue and caresses even as he stumbled into the kitchen with her clutched to his chest. They tumbled to the straw pallet together and he tickled her until she laughed aloud, the warmth of the fire welcome on her chilled skin. She rolled on top and straddled Jacob's chest, her hair falling over them in a tangle. Grabbing his wrists in her hands, she pinned them to the straw on either side of his shoulders.

"Are you ready to tell me yet?" she teased as though she were really restraining him, and he chuckled.

"Maybe if you slide down a bit," he suggested, and Rebecca complied slowly, her eyes widening at the sensation of his chest hair rubbing against her private softness. Jacob's eyes gleamed and she suddenly understood his intent when she felt his hardness against her buttocks.

"Go ahead," he urged softly, and Rebecca's hands trembled at the thought, the encouragement in his eyes the only thing that gave her the nerve to try. She lifted her hips and let his bulk slide beneath her, a thrill running through her when he closed his eyes as she sat atop him. She slid back and forth experimentally, savoring the way Jacob's nostrils flared at her gesture.

Amazed that she could provoke such a response from him, she knelt over him and let the tip of his masculinity slide inside her. Jacob's eyes flew open and he flicked his wrists free, interlacing their fingers with a quick gesture. Feeling exquisitely in control, Rebecca accepted another increment of his length, leaning over to tease one of his nipples to a peak with her teeth and tongue as she did so. Jacob gasped, lifting his hips involuntarily to push further into her.

Rebecca retaliated by raising herself up so that she held only the tip of his manhood once more and he chuckled under his breath. "Tell me," she prompted with a grin, and Jacob laughed outright.

"Not a chance," he retorted, and she saw the gleam of anticipation in his eyes as she accepted another thumb's width of him within her and his lids dropped in response.

"Tell me," she urged, enjoying their game more than she would have believed possible.

Jacob's grin flashed while he deftly unlinked his right hand from hers, his fingers diving without preamble into her nest of curls and finding the tender pearl hidden there. Rebecca gasped as he caressed her gently, his touch sending such waves through her that she lost any pretense of control and sat down abruptly atop him. Jacob gasped in turn but Rebecca couldn't even think of teasing him further, her hips bucking against him in her own search for that elusive goal.

She set the pace and Jacob followed suit, his grip tightening over her hand, which he now imprisoned against his chest, his heart pounding beneath their tangled fingers. Suddenly they cried out as one and she collapsed against him, barely aware of his arms closing around her or the sweet words he murmured into her hair as the spasms shook them both to the core.

Chapter Thirteen

Jacob let his hands slide over Rebecca's curves as she dozed atop him and he filled his lungs with the welcome scent of her. He turned his head, and as the softness of her hair trailed across his lips, he allowed himself to smile, feeling that he had been waiting forever for this moment.

Rebecca had actually talked to him. She had trusted him with what she knew about the book. Jacob couldn't check the buoyant sense that all that was amiss between them would shortly be laid to rest. She stirred and he noticed suddenly the chill in the air. Reaching down carefully to retrieve the blanket, he pulled its weight over both of them without disturbing her. She snuggled against him and Jacob found himself grinning like an idiot.

Silk and honey. And she was all his. How had he kept his hands off her this week? He cupped the side of her face and kissed her forehead, feeling her lips curve into an answering smile beneath his palm before her lashes reluctantly fluttered open.

Their eyes met and held for a charged moment, then Rebecca stretched as leisurely as a cat, somehow managing to keep from dislodging him. She braced an elbow on his chest, propping her chin on her hand as she regarded him, her dark eyes sparkling with promise, her cheeks flushed.

"Are you ready to tell me yet or do you need more convincing?" she demanded huskily, and Jacob felt himself harden anew at the thought of more lovemaking. Rebecca's eyes widened in momentary surprise when she felt his response and he cupped her buttocks to pull her even closer.

"Do you like it this way?" he demanded, enjoying the way he had shaken her composure. Rebecca smiled seductively, an impish gleam in her eye, then rocked her hips, and he found himself lost in turn.

"Yes," she whispered, pressing a flurry of kisses across his chest. "Don't you?"

Jacob chuckled under his breath, feeling as though he had the world by a string. "Can't you tell?" he asked softly, watching that dimple appear in her cheek before she reared back and knelt above him with her arms stretched high over her head.

His blood rose instantly at the vision of her arched before him, her breasts swaying gently, her nipples hard and dark, and he closed his hands around her waist as he strained toward her. Rebecca rotated her pelvis in a rhythm that drove Jacob to distraction, her eyes flashing victoriously when he increased to a furious tempo until she moaned aloud.

Jacob's climax came quickly and emptied him more thoroughly than he would have imagined possible. For an instant he feared he had left her behind, but Rebecca's satisfied grin when she tumbled into his arms summarily dismissed his doubts.

"Tell me," she prompted again, and Jacob grinned weakly at her insistence.

"It's an alchemical text," he murmured, struggling against the wave of exhaustion that threatened to overwhelm him. "A translation of something called the *Corpus Hermeticum*."

"I've never heard of it," Rebecca commented brightly, clearly more wide-awake than he could hope to be. Jacob sighed sleepily as he pulled her closer and let the languor steal through him.

"Very few people have outside the Art," he told her, hearing his voice drop to a drowsy monotone. "It's considered secret knowledge for initiates only, a revelation from Hermes Trismegistus himself."

"I've never heard of him, either," she complained pertly, and Jacob smiled as he tucked her proprietarily into his shoulder.

"Don't worry about it," he urged. "Just go to sleep for a while."

Even through the haze of his own fatigue, Jacob sensed that Rebecca was not ready to abandon the subject. He could practically hear the wheels turning in her mind and he struggled to retain consciousness in anticipation of yet another question.

"If it's secret knowledge, that would explain why so many people want it so badly," she mused almost to herself, and he realized that she knew he was fading away.

"That and the fact that the volume is extraordinarily rare," he confirmed, wanting to tell her as much as possible but frowning with the effort. Jacob stirred himself with difficulty and opened his eyes to find Rebecca's features brightly inquisitive.

"We alchemists are a suspicious lot and seldom trust such things to paper," he informed her dryly. "After all, you never know who might get their hands on them," he added, and watched her nod in understanding.

Satisfied that he had answered his inquisitive wife's questions adequately for the time being, Jacob closed his eyes with relief and let sleep carry him away.

We alchemists?

Rebecca didn't immediately catch the reference, and by the time she did, Jacob was out cold, the sound of his even breathing filling the kitchen. Suddenly aware that the room was no longer warm, she disentangled herself from his sleepy grasp and rekindled the fire, her mind whirling with what he had told her.

We alchemists. Secret knowledge for initiates. Rebecca spared a thoughtful glance to Jacob's sleeping form as she carefully replaced the poker beside the hearth. It would seem that he had recognized the text immediately and she frowned, disliking the conclusion that forced itself into her mind.

If Jacob was an alchemist, he was undoubtedly one more person who would want the text. She chewed her fingertip, wondering just how badly he wanted it.

And why had he come here prepared to marry her sight unseen that first day? He had said that he had known nothing of the *ketubah,* but she found it increasingly hard to believe that this methodical man would sign anything without reading it. And even she knew that alchemists kept in touch with one another throughout the West. And Jacob's aunt was Ephraim's distant cousin.

There were too many things fitting conveniently together for her taste. Had Jacob known that Ephraim had this text before he came to Toledo? Was the desire to put his hands on that little hermetic whatever the entire reason he had proposed?

Unable to contemplate the matter further, Rebecca retrieved her kirtle, finding it inordinately difficult to fasten the neck with her shaking hands. Jacob stirred and she hastened to start dicing onions, hoping the tears they prompted would disguise the very real tears threatening to spill.

That the climate in the kitchen had changed dramatically by the time he awoke was an understatement to say the least, and Jacob had a difficult time adjusting to the change. Rebecca seemed determined to avoid meeting his eyes, refusing his offer of assistance with preparing dinner, and he dressed slowly, watching her nervous movements with puzzlement.

"Did I hurt you?" he asked finally, unable to believe that was the case but incapable of finding any other explanation. Rebecca shot a look over her shoulder that made him think of a doe on the run before she turned quickly back to her work.

"No," she responded flatly. Jacob walked across the room and stood behind her, unwilling to let their closeness disappear, ice lodging around his heart when he placed his hands on Rebecca's waist and she stiffened.

"Is the baby all right?" he asked, and it seemed to him that she froze midgesture before returning to slice a pepper with renewed vigor.

"Yes," she confirmed in a very small voice. Was she simply more emotional because of the baby? Perhaps she needed reassurance, he told himself, unwilling to believe that that wall could have been reconstructed between them so quickly.

"We should probably start being more careful," he mused, twining his fingers into her hair and playing with its soft length, thinking his touch might soothe her, but she stood ramrod straight.

"If you say so." She bit the words out and Jacob looked down at her with surprise. Had they really taken one step forward only to take two steps back?

"Rebecca, what's wrong?" he asked, determined to get to the root of the matter, but she only shook her head.

"Nothing."

He was being shut out again, there was no doubt about it, and Jacob felt a flicker of panic even as he wondered what to do to reassure her.

"Are you sorry you trusted me?" he demanded quietly, stunned when Rebecca made a helpless gesture with one hand and he heard the tears in her voice.

"I'm not sure," she confessed shakily, and Jacob turned to walk away, unable to believe that she could possibly feel that way. It was inconceivable to him that things should be awkward again after the sweet intimacy they had just shared. He sat down heavily on the table opposite as he tried to make sense of it and glanced up to find Rebecca watching him warily out of the corner of her eye.

"I don't know what to say," he confessed helplessly, watching in amazement as her lips thinned with what could only be anger.

"Why don't you start by telling me when you found out about the book?" she demanded sharply, making a dangerously vicious jab into another pepper with her knife.

"When I found you and Isaac—" he began, but the way Rebecca was adamantly shaking her head in denial halted his words in his throat.

"No," she insisted with a hot look in his direction. "I want to know the *truth.*"

"That is the truth," Jacob asserted tersely, the unexpectedness of her attitude the only thing that kept his anger in check. His confusion mounted when she stubbornly shook her head once more.

"I don't think so," she contradicted him to his astonishment. "You see, it all fits together too easily now. You're an alchemist, you knew Ephraim, you knew what the book was as soon as you saw it, you were willing to marry me without having ever laid eyes on me."

"What are you saying? That I married you to get the book?" Jacob demanded, incredulous that she could have come to such a ridiculous conclusion.

"Did you?" Rebecca's question shot across the kitchen, her chin lifting in challenge, and Jacob held her gaze for a long moment. Clearly she believed that was the case and he wished desperately that he had some idea how to convince her otherwise.

"I told you I didn't know anything about the *ketubah,*" he protested, his heart sinking when she appeared unmoved.

"And Judith is conveniently not here to corroborate your story," she countered, and Jacob leaned back against the heavy table for a moment.

"Rebecca, I didn't marry you for the book," he claimed in a firm voice, wishing he could make a stronger argument, his heart wrenching when she turned to confront him with tears shining in her eyes.

"Then why *did* you marry me?" she demanded unsteadily, and the answer rang in Jacob's mind as he helplessly watched two tears make a path down her cheeks.

"What possible reason did you have for taking someone you barely knew to wife? I have no dowry, no prestigious bloodline, not even virginity to offer you. Why, Jacob? Give me one reason why."

Rebecca's voice broke and Jacob felt more powerless than he ever had, knowing that she wouldn't tolerate him coming any nearer in her distraught state. She sniffled and he waited, determined to be sure she was listening when he confided what he had just realized himself.

Finally, Rebecca looked up expectantly through the shimmer of her tears and Jacob smiled softly at her beauty in disarray, amazed that she could even begin to wonder why he would want her.

"I married you because I fell in love with you," he informed her calmly, knowing as he spoke the words that they were absolutely true.

Rebecca wavered on her feet, something softening in her eyes, and Jacob started purposefully across the room toward her. But as he drew close, she backed away and the spark in her eyes died, her tears spilling now in profusion. He wanted nothing other than to gather her close and soothe her hurt, but her frosty demeanor stopped him in his tracks.

"Don't you *ever* lie to me like that again," she demanded shakily, her eyes narrowing in hostility as she backed away, and Jacob stared at her in amazement.

She raised one hand as though she would say more and he wondered who had hurt her so badly that she couldn't believe something so marvelously simple. Her hand wavered as her emotion got the better of her and she abandoned anything she might have said, shaking her head helplessly before she turned and fled the kitchen.

"Rebecca!" Jacob followed her to the courtyard, the open fear in her eyes when she looked back from the top of the stairs effectively eliminating any impulse he had to follow her further. He hesitated and heard her door slam, his heart in his mouth as he glanced up and scanned the darkening sky unseeingly, willing himself to think logically despite the turmoil churning in his gut.

Jacob closed his eyes for a moment against the sound of her tears, letting disappointment wash over him. How could he teach her to trust him and open her heart to his love? Was this match doomed to failure because of something unnamed in her past? The thought was sobering and Jacob made his way back to the kitchen on heavy feet, unable to summon any interest in finishing the preparations for the meal.

Perhaps it would be better if he left Rebecca to herself for a while.

Miserable wretch!

Rebecca had expected a pretty excuse or two, but never would she have anticipated that Jacob might confess to *loving* her. How dare he sully such a thought with his lies! How could he say such a thing in a deliberate attempt to wring her sympathy? Especially when it was obviously untrue!

Curse him for coming here and curse him for marrying her, whatever his reasons. She pounded her pillows in frustration to punctuate every thought against Jacob ben Solomon, gasping for breath between her sobs. Curse him for kissing her that way that made her forget everything except him, and curse him for being so impossibly understanding.

She rolled to her back at that thought, her tears losing their fury but still streaming over her cheeks unchecked. A plague on him for demanding her trust, she thought sourly, for that thoughtful smile, for those gentle but strong hands. A slight weight rolled unevenly across her chest to fall against the cushions and her tears rose anew even as her fingers wrapped around the misshapen pearl.

And curse him for buying her an *aljofar* and making her believe for one tantalizingly brief moment in the impossible once again.

* * *

Jacob was still lying awake beside the hearth much later when he heard an unmistakable creak coming from the study. He dismissed it as an echo of his overwrought imagination as he closed his eyes and fought insomnia again, but the whisper of voices that followed shortly thereafter couldn't be dismissed as anything else.

He rolled to one side and watched with dawning incredulity as a pair of shadows became discernible in the darkness of the study. But how had anyone gotten past him into the study? He had been wide-awake all evening and he knew there had been no one in there earlier. The room was too small for hiding.

To his amazement, the heavily cloaked figures slipped bonelessly into the kitchen and Jacob lay completely motionless even as he struggled to come to grips with their presence. It was clear that they were unaware of him not a dozen steps away and also that they knew exactly what they were here for. Without a word or a gesture of discussion they headed into the courtyard, and as Jacob caught the sound of their footfalls on the stairs, he panicked.

Rebecca was alone upstairs.

He rolled silently to his feet and found a knife in the shadows before he crept out to the courtyard to find that the pair had disappeared. Jacob took a deep breath and started up the stairs, Rebecca's muffled yelp making his blood run cold.

He listened for an instant before he dashed upstairs, a whispered exchange and the sound of footsteps making him glad he had. Jacob realized they were heading back out onto the balcony and he dived into the shadows of the foyer in the nick of time. He held his breath and distinguished three sets of footfalls, his heart leaping when the trio burst into the foyer an arm's length before him.

The men pushed Rebecca ahead of them, but as far as Jacob could tell she was unhurt, her hair falling around her in an incoherent dark tangle, her feet bare beneath the hem of her chemise. They went into the kitchen and Jacob saw her glance at the pallet by the hearth, her fright when she found only empty space almost tangible. They continued into the study beyond and Jacob followed cautiously, detecting the tremor in Rebecca's hands when she struck a flint and lit a lamp.

The men were after that damned book unless he missed his guess, and he had half a mind to give it to them for all the trouble it had caused. Jacob leaned back into the protection of the shadows shrouding the doorway while he watched and waited to see what would happen next.

The hairs were pricking on the back of his neck and he schooled himself not to react too quickly as he had the last time he had confronted intruders in Rebecca's house. That thought gave him pause and Jacob wondered whether the two events were linked, or even whether these were the same two men.

They had been looking for something then, too, he recalled, feeling as though a veil had been lifted from his eyes. And Rebecca had not been surprised to see them that night, either. He watched her across the room, wondering yet again how much she knew that she wasn't telling him. Why hadn't these intrusions continued in the interim? There had been no one in the house since he had returned to Toledo, he was sure of it.

And how had they gotten into the house without him knowing? There wasn't even a window onto the courtyard in the study, no windows at all in fact. Something didn't add up, and Jacob wished for once he wasn't so certain that Rebecca held more than one of the missing pieces to the puzzle.

Rebecca had reassured herself with the knowledge that Jacob would be downstairs, and now that he wasn't, she couldn't even think of what to do, her sleep-dazed mind paralyzed with the fear that leapt to new heights in his absence.

Had Jacob left because she saw through his lies?

One of the mysteriously cloaked men shoved her unceremoniously forward and she almost tripped on the threshold to the study, her heart pounding in her ears as she realized the precariousness of her situation. How was she going to get through this without surrendering the book to these thugs? Or worse, would she even manage to survive this interlude?

And why hadn't she remembered to tell Jacob about that nocturnal visit and the man's threat to return? A niggling voice demanded whether she would have told him even if she had remembered, especially since that was the night she had created the lie about her pregnancy, but Rebecca shoved such questions aside.

After all, there were more important matters afoot, she reminded herself, wishing her heartbeat would slow just a little so she could think. One man kept turning a long silver blade so it flashed in the meager light, a gesture no doubt intended for her benefit, and she took a shaky breath to try to compose herself. She lit the lantern on the desk at the leader's imperious gesture, hating how her trembling hands so thoroughly betrayed her nervousness.

It wasn't the least bit reassuring to realize that she had been counting on Jacob being in the kitchen to resolve this problem. That thought smacked of dependency and Rebecca was certain that she wasn't going to depend on Jacob for anything. She had learned that lesson a long time ago.

But where was he? She suddenly was afraid for him, afraid that these thieves might have found him first and done something unspeakable to keep him out of the way. Had she endangered him by not telling him the truth?

"Where is it?" one of the intruders demanded impatiently.

She looked up with surprise, the muttered words bringing her back to the present with a jolt. Unfortunately both men were so thoroughly cloaked and masked that she couldn't even begin to guess at their identities, their muffled voices completely unrecognizable. The second man flashed that knife again and she swallowed nervously, the implicit threat making her decision easy.

It was only a book after all, and even a secret text wasn't worth dying for. She would have liked to have kept it for Jacob, if anyone was going to have it, but she had little choice in the matter now. She glanced at her two companions and wondered whether producing the book would affect her survival one way or the other.

Were they going to kill her?

Now that she was faced with the imminent possibility of her own death, everything suddenly became crystal clear to Rebecca. If only they spared her life and Jacob's, she would tell him everything. No more secrets. Jacob was right: trust between them was what was important, not a secret book or even a baby that never had been. They would make one if he wanted, she resolved, feeling that things were much simpler than they had appeared to be for quite some time. After all, if they had each other, what else could they possibly need?

She reached automatically for the spot on the shelf where she had placed the book, her fingers faltering when she saw that it was empty.

Of course! She hadn't seen the book since Jacob had tucked it into his tunic after her fight with Isaac! She glanced at the two mysterious shadows and felt her palms go damp.

Now what was she going to do?

"Well?" the man growled, and she folded her hands together carefully while she desperately tried to think of something.

Anything at all would do.

"I forgot that I moved it upstairs," she said in a small voice, not in the least encouraged by the vulgarity vehemently expressed by the henchman. The other silenced his companion with a single menacing gesture.

"Are you quite certain?" he inquired silkily, and Rebecca took an involuntary step backward when he advanced toward her, his dark silhouette towering over her. "Or is this just a little game of yours?" he hissed.

"It's upstairs," she insisted, wishing her voice could ring with more conviction in this moment. "I forgot that I moved it there for safekeeping."

The man stood before her for a long moment as he apparently assessed her sincerity. Rebecca's mouth went dry and she barely dared to breathe as she waited for his decision. Without preamble, he made an impatient gesture to his companion.

"All right—back upstairs it is," he growled, leaning closer to Rebecca as the second man preceded them into the kitchen. "For your sake, I hope you're not trying anything foolish," he warned, and she shivered, no doubt in her mind that he would make her regret any impulsiveness.

Rebecca could only swallow mutely, her heart pounding in her ears as she meekly followed the man with the knife toward the courtyard. What was she going to do? She had no idea where Jacob had put the book and there was absolutely no way that she could overcome two men to gain her freedom. Her gut twisted as she realized that death was much closer than she had anticipated.

There came a soft sound behind her and she flicked a fearful glance over her shoulder, astonished to find the menacing shadow that had been there a moment past gone. She glanced ahead to the man who preceded her but he had detected nothing amiss. Another backward look weakened her knees as she caught sight of a very familiar man holding one finger to his lips not two steps behind her.

Jacob! It was all she could do not to launch herself into his arms and tell him everything right then and there. He was all business, though, his expression stern as he silently urged her to continue on, and Rebecca curbed her exuberance, knowing that the job was only half-done. Her relief betrayed her in the very moment that she turned to do Jacob's bidding and she tripped on the threshold to the courtyard.

Her toe cracked and she cried aloud in pain, the sound setting the man ahead reeling on his heel. He swore and trotted quickly down the first few stairs to grab her by the hair and haul her to her feet when she stumbled. Rebecca gasped at the pain as the roots were pulled, barely having the chance to wonder if he intended to haul her up the stairs before she glimpsed a moving shadow from the corner of her eye.

Not a heartbeat later it was over and the man was sprawled on the tiled patio, his face still showing signs of the surprise that had flickered across his features when Jacob had loomed unexpectedly out of the shadows. Rebecca wasted no time throwing herself into Jacob's arms and he held her tightly, murmuring incoherently into her hair as his strong fingers gently massaged her scalp.

"I thought they had killed you," she mumbled through her tears, and his arms tightened around her as he leaned down to whisper into her ear.

"And you weren't glad to be rid of me?" he murmured, the deep tone of his voice telling her that he was as relieved as she. Rebecca gazed up at Jacob in wide-eyed surprise, astonished that he could even tease about such a thing.

"Oh, no," was all she managed to whisper before his lips closed decisively over hers. She pressed herself against the reassuring solidity of his chest and held him close as she ardently returned his embrace.

"I have to tell you something," she began when Jacob finally lifted his head, then she closed her eyes as he dotted an intoxicating row of kisses across her cheekbone and nibbled on her earlobe.

"It can't wait?" he whispered seductively, and she shivered at the flutter of his breath fanning her ear.

A furtive sound from the kitchen brought them both abruptly back to the present.

Rebecca looked up in time to see a shadow separate itself from the darkness around the hearth and dart into the study. The lamp still flickering on the desk illuminated the cloaked figure as he reached out to touch the far wall. She gasped against Jacob's shirt when the bookcase there swung outward to reveal a dark crevasse, barely hearing Jacob swear under his breath as he bounded into the study in pursuit.

Jacob reached the wall too late, the bookcase swinging closed in the wake of the fleeing figure with an audible click, and he ran his hands searchingly over the wall. Rebecca joined him without a word, sliding her fingertips over the smooth expanse in the hope of finding whatever triggered the door.

"I was sure he reached over here," Jacob muttered unsuccessful moments later, and Rebecca could only nod in agreement. She fetched the lantern and held it close so he could see the wall better, and he shot her a grateful smile that warmed her to her bare toes. "Wasn't it here?" he demanded softly, and she nodded again.

"I thought so, but I can't see anything." The walls were indeed as smooth as silk and whatever latch there might be was visually undetectable.

Just when they might have given up in defeat, a heartfelt groan carried to their ears from the courtyard and their eyes met over the flickering flame.

"Put it out," Jacob rasped, but Rebecca had already licked her fingertips to pinch the wick. As the sounds of the man stirring carried to their ears, Jacob unceremoniously urged Rebecca under the desk, touching his finger to her lips for one moment before he slipped away. Rebecca gripped her knees tightly, trying to hold herself absolutely still in the confined space, praying that her heart wasn't pounding loudly enough that anyone would be able to hear it.

Footsteps shuffled on the stone floor of the kitchen, and Rebecca held her breath impatiently, wondering where Jacob was and what he intended to do. She closed her eyes and prayed with all her might that he wouldn't be hurt as the footsteps grew increasingly louder.

She stared at the floor as the man crossed the room, a mere arm's length away from her, and she shivered despite the protective darkness that hid her presence from him. He paused and it seemed that the sound of his breathing filled the room. Rebecca strained her ears, fancying she heard his fingers scrabbling against the plaster, and she jumped when that distinct click shattered the relative silence of the room. Something creaked and his footsteps echoed in the room once more, their sound fading away before the creaking started again, this time much slower.

The door was closing! Rebecca shoved Ephraim's chair out of the way and scrambled to her feet, but Jacob was at the wall ahead of her.

"Ha!" he cried victoriously, and Rebecca couldn't help but giggle when she saw his grin flash in the darkness. Her smile faded quickly, however, when he jammed a book under the door to hold it open and darted into the kitchen, returning with his burnous swinging over his shoulders.

"You're not going down there?" she demanded, knowing all the while that that was exactly what he intended to do.

"Absolutely," Jacob confirmed flatly, cupping her chin in his hand and brushing his lips over hers as casually as if he were headed to the *souk* for the afternoon.

"You can't do this," she protested weakly, but Jacob only nodded.

"I can and will," he affirmed. "And you will pack whatever of your belongings you can easily carry while I'm gone. Find my pack and bring it here, as well."

"But..."

"Simply do as I say," he instructed as he laid a finger against her lips, but Rebecca shook her head in confusion.

"I don't understand," she insisted despite the weight of his fingertip, and Jacob studied her silently for a moment, his eyes glowing in the darkness.

"Trust me," he said simply, then he turned and disappeared into the dark space behind the bookcase.

Rebecca stepped to the edge of the abyss, the stone steps suddenly visible when Jacob struck a flint and lit a lamp far below. He looked up at her, grinning with a mischievousness she was far from feeling.

"Be careful," she urged, and he nodded.

"I will," he responded, giving her a jaunty wink before he stepped around the last corner, only the faint glow of the lamp shining back on the stairs in his wake. "And don't close the door." His whispered admonishment carried to her ears as the light faded.

Rebecca nodded in understanding even though she knew he couldn't see her gesture, and she clutched her chemise around her as the earthy smell from the cavern below filled her nostrils. Even after the stairs had fallen into darkness again, she stood silently, waiting until the last echo of Jacob's footsteps had long faded from earshot before she reluctantly turned away.

Chapter Fourteen

It seemed that forever had come and gone before Rebecca heard something at the foot of the stairs.

She had packed as Jacob had requested, blindly jamming whatever came to hand into a leather satchel and rushing back downstairs to be ready for his return. But there had proved to be little need of haste. Rebecca had no idea how much time had passed, the darkness seeming as impenetrably black as it had when Jacob disappeared, but her legs were cramped from being tucked beneath her for so long. Although the coldness of the night air settled more heavily around her as she sat in Ephraim's chair waiting, she didn't rise to kindle the fire, certain that Jacob's arrival was imminent.

Now she huddled a little deeper into the chair as the footsteps below grew increasingly louder. Fingering her *aljofar* nervously, a thousand horrible questions crowded into her mind. What if Jacob had run into those two thugs? What if something had happened to him? Her mouth went dry and she briefly considered hiding or fleeing, when a dark silhouette appeared in the opening.

What if it wasn't Jacob but somebody else?

"Rebecca?" came a familiar murmur, and she was on her feet in an instant in her relief.

"Jacob!"

He smiled tiredly when she approached, his preoccupation with setting the flickering lamp down without spilling the oil making it impossible for her to hug him impulsively in welcome. Feeling like a child deprived of an anticipated treat, she stood before him, painfully conscious of the way her hands were twisting together nervously, wondering whether his avoidance of her embrace had been deliberate.

"I didn't want to frighten you," Jacob explained in a low voice, and she nodded, feeling his attention shift away from her with disappointment. He was all crisp efficiency and her heart drooped at the decided lack of encouragement in his tone. Had she finally pushed him too far with her accusations and destroyed any possibility of making this right?

"Do you have everything you need?" Jacob demanded over his shoulder as he brushed past her into the room. He picked up the two packed satchels and checked their weight almost absently, scanning the room with a frown as if he wanted to ensure that he didn't forget anything himself.

"I don't know," Rebecca answered, realizing only now why Jacob must have asked her to pack.

They were leaving Toledo. She swallowed and studied the shadowed familiarity of the small room as if she would memorize every detail, wondering how she could have missed that salient point. Worry about Jacob had blotted out all other thoughts and Rebecca marveled silently at this not entirely welcome change in her thinking. She looked up to find Jacob watching her speculatively and she licked her lips carefully before she spoke.

"Where are we going?" she asked in a voice that seemed curiously small, and Jacob spared her a dry smile.

"Tunis, of course," he responded easily, although Rebecca suspected he was watching her reaction more carefully than he let on.

"Tonight?"

Jacob grinned outright at that. "I doubt we'll make it the entire way before sunrise," he commented, his teasing tone doing nothing to ease her trepidation.

"But I thought we couldn't leave Toledo because of the Christian crusaders," she pointed out wildly, feeling that the moment of decision she had dreaded was upon her, if not already past.

She was going with Jacob and leaving her home. The time had arrived unexpectedly and just when she thought she had been granted a reprieve. Rebecca felt panic rise within her, even as she knew without a doubt that she would go with him. For the first time, she considered that it might be fear of the unknown that disconcerted her and not a fear of trusting her spouse, but there was no time now to reflect upon that thought.

"So did I," Jacob countered calmly, and gestured to the stairs. "But now I know differently."

"But—" Rebecca protested one last time, only to have Jacob shoot her a quelling look.

"We have a long way to go before sunrise," he informed her bluntly.

"We could go tomorrow night," she suggested hopefully, but Jacob shook his head.

"You know as well as I do that it's not safe here anymore. Who knows whether those two will come back tomorrow night? And we might not be as lucky a second time."

Rebecca dropped her gaze, knowing he was right but still afraid of what they might encounter ahead. She jumped when the weight of Jacob's hands settled on her shoulders, and she glanced up to find him watching her steadily.

"We have a chance to get out of Toledo before Alfonso's troops descend on the city, Rebecca," he said carefully. "What do you say we take it?"

With that gesture, all of her doubts were swept away. The very fact that he had asked her opinion, even though they both knew that there was no real choice, made the decision to go an easy one for her.

"It would be crazy to stay," she whispered, breaking into a smile when he grinned and crushed her against his chest for a heady instant. She closed her eyes and let the smell of him fill her lungs, completely certain of the wisdom of her decision to trust him.

"Did you bring any bread?" he demanded abruptly, returning to practical matters all too soon for Rebecca's taste. She shook her head, not having thought about food, and Jacob spared her a teasing frown as he scooped up his pack and headed purposefully into the kitchen.

"As if it's not enough to go without sleep, the woman expects me to walk all the way to Algeciras with nothing to eat," he grumbled good-naturedly, and Rebecca giggled, picking up her own pack and trailing him into the kitchen to empty the larder.

Rebecca tightened her grip on the lantern when Jacob pulled the book from underneath the door, certain her sweating palms would have it slipping to the floor and plunging them into darkness at any moment. It was one thing to have to follow an underground tunnel that led who knew where, and quite another to shut the only door out that they knew of. A door that neither of them had any idea how to open from either side.

Jacob's arguments that there was no reason to leave their path of escape obvious made perfect sense, but still Rebecca couldn't help the claustrophobia that washed over her when the door began to creak. Jacob tossed the book onto Ephraim's desk and stepped onto the stair above her, both of them watching transfixed as the secret door swung closed at a leisurely pace. At the last instant, Rebecca stifled an almost overwhelming impulse to dive forward and jam open the door, her hand even rising with intent before Jacob's fingers firmly captured hers.

Their eyes met over the flickering flame as that distinct click filled the silence of the cavern and the sound launched an army of goose pimples across Rebecca's skin. She shuddered involuntarily, knowing that they were now locked into the cavern for better or for worse.

Jacob's grip tightened reassuringly. "This way," he urged as he took the lamp from her unreliable fingers, his grip moving to close surely around her elbow as they made their way down the twisted stairs. "Watch your step," he warned softly. "They're not very even."

The earthy smell grew stronger as they descended and Rebecca saw with dawning amazement that the stairs had been hewn out of the rock and soil directly below her home. And to what purpose? She shook her head in wonder that she had never had any idea that this space was here. Where did the tunnel lead? It must go somewhere as the two thugs had chosen this as their route of escape.

Were they going to encounter them in the darkness below?

The stairs ended and the pathway bent sharply to the right. The lamplight suddenly seemed much dimmer as they rounded the corner and entered a large room with a high ceiling that diffused the light. Rebecca gasped at the unexpected sight before her.

A veritable Aladdin's cave greeted her eyes, the flickering golden light dancing off a vast array of gleaming objects in the cavern, making them seem like half-buried treasure awaiting her discovery. But there were no jewels or riches of customary shape and design; closer examination revealed a strange mélange of uncommon articles constructed from fine materials interspersed with the most mundane.

The light twinkled on the curved bellies of hundreds of tiny glass jars and vials arrayed along the shelves that lined the wall. Each appeared to contain a minute amount of some substance either metallic or woolly, wildly colored or looking exactly like dust from the road. Foreign-looking brass objects with odd markings gleamed golden from their perches on these same shelves, intermingled with the vials, and the gold lettering on the leather covers of a few heavy books stacked on the table on the far side of the room also glinted in the light.

Rebecca advanced into the room slowly, intrigued by the unfamiliarity of the shapes of what were apparently vessels. A great brass tool of some kind dominated one corner, looking like a long-legged water bird cast in metal. As she drew closer to the table she saw tongs and ladles that reminded her of kitchen utensils, and spotted the pots that were stacked beside a narrow fireplace tucked into the end of the room. It was as though she had stepped into a different world. She tentatively picked up a tool of some kind, unable to fathom a guess as to its purpose.

She lifted her hand experimentally to the flue of the fireplace and felt a cool waft of air, turning to confront Jacob in amazement, but he merely shrugged. The flue must open out somewhere into the street, she reasoned, taking in the scorch marks on the pocked earthen floor with puzzlement. What a strange and remarkable place. She let her eyes run once more over the room, noting now the heavy wooden door opposite her, its broken bolt dangling uselessly and some half erased symbol etched in chalk on the wood panel.

"What is it?" she whispered, curiously unwilling to raise her voice in this room. Jacob folded his arms across his chest so matter-of-factly that she realized the room hadn't surprised him either now or when he had visited it earlier.

"It's a laboratory," he supplied simply. "An alchemical lab."

"But what for?" Rebecca asked, his answer not enlightening her in the least.

Jacob sighed and pursed his lips as if trying to think of a short explanation for something moderately complicated. "Alchemists," he said finally, "are concerned with transforming the common into the exception, or more specifically, turning dross into gold."

"Surely that's not possible?" she demanded skeptically, but Jacob only shrugged again.

"There are those who claim to have done it," he informed her, spreading his hands wide as he continued. "And who knows what is really possible? Yesterday you might have claimed it impossible that there was a room like this beneath your home, let alone a tunnel like the one beyond that door. The world is full of wonders that we cannot even guess at."

"A tunnel?" Rebecca asked, seizing on that single word.

Jacob nodded and quickly surveyed the room. "It seems your house is not unique."

Rebecca followed his gaze as she tried to think things through. It was incredible to consider that this room had been here all along, maybe even longer than the house, and she had had no inkling of its presence in two years. And now Jacob seemed to be implying that there were others like this connected by subterranean tunnels. It was almost too much to believe.

"But why would anyone bother?" she asked when she turned back to Jacob, her brows drawing into a frown. "This must have taken years to construct," she mused, gesturing to the marks on the wall where the stone had been hewn away.

"I told you that alchemists are a secretive lot," he reminded her, his words making Rebecca recall something else.

"You said 'we alchemists' before," she pointed out. "Do you have a lab like this under your house, then?"

Jacob smothered a smile and shook his head. "No," he said, and she thought for a moment that he might not say more, but he continued. "I belong to the school of alchemical thought that follows a less literal ideal."

"I don't understand."

"The text says that the basest substance can be turned to gold," Jacob explained softly as he strode to the large table. "This is the workshop of one who believes the words should be taken literally. You see..." He poked at a few of the vials in sequence and Rebecca came to stand beside him, noting the contents of each bottle he touched. "Lead, tin, earth, pebbles from the bed of the Tagus. Someone has been trying to find the formula to turn these into gold."

"But that's not what you do?"

Jacob spared her an indulgent smile. "There are those of us who find the words a metaphor for the perfection of the spirit."

Rebecca thought for a moment, then looked up at him. "Then the basest matter is the human spirit?"

"Unrefined, yes," Jacob agreed soberly.

"And how is it turned to gold?" she inquired, and he grinned down at her.

"If you keep asking that, you might one day discover the secret," he teased, and Rebecca smiled in turn, losing herself in the warmth of Jacob's regard.

"Do you think Ephraim knew about this room?" she asked in an effort to get back to matters at hand, and the way Jacob cocked one eyebrow answered her question more eloquently than mere words.

"Without a doubt," he affirmed, and Rebecca folded her arms across her chest in turn.

"Do you think he knew how to turn things into gold?" she asked skeptically. If he had, he certainly could have used that particular skill around the house a little more, she thought with no small measure of irony.

"I don't know," Jacob responded with a frown. "But I wonder whether someone *thought* he had found the *lapis exilis.*"

"The what?"

"*Lapis exilis,* the philosopher's stone, the supposed key that makes the transformation possible if not inevitable," Jacob supplied automatically, but it was clear his mind was on other things.

"Well, what is that?" Rebecca demanded when he didn't continue, and he smiled.

"That's hidden knowledge. Whoever possesses the *lapis exilis* has the ability to turn dross into gold."

"Oh." She hesitated for a moment before she asked the inevitable question, feeling as though this alchemy were altogether a very mysterious business. "Do you know the secret?"

Jacob shook his head. "I'm not entirely sure that anyone does," he conceded, frowning as he stared down at the floor. "'This is the stone which was set at naught of your builders, which is become the head of the corner,'" he continued slowly, evidently quoting something, and Rebecca regarded him in puzzlement.

"What does that mean?"

"Perhaps that something precious may be found where it is least expected," he explained, cocking his head as he regarded her thoughtfully, and Rebecca had an uncanny sense that he wasn't talking about alchemy anymore. For some reason she couldn't meet the intensity in his eyes and she struggled to think clearly. For being so deep in the earth, it suddenly seemed warm in this laboratory.

"If someone thought Ephraim had found the *lapis* whatever, maybe that's what they were looking for in the house," she reasoned haltingly, and Jacob nodded in businesslike agreement despite the warmth still lurking in his eyes.

"I suspect so."

"It would be pretty valuable to know how to turn things into gold, wouldn't it?" she concluded, glancing up in time to see that Jacob had been through this logic already.

Rebecca nodded to herself as she understood the implications. Was this the secret Yusuf had declared that some would be willing to kill for? Was this what the intruders had desired?

And it was written in the book. In that instant everything became crystal clear to Rebecca and she turned back to the stairs impulsively.

"Where are you going?" Jacob demanded, and she heard him behind her as she started up the darkened stairs.

"We have to get the book," she explained impatiently. "Bring the lamp—I can't see where I'm going."

"Forget about the book, Rebecca," Jacob responded tersely. "There isn't time and we don't know how to open the door." She paused and glanced over her shoulder to find him staring up at her with his hands propped on his hips.

"We need to get out of town before sunrise," he reiterated firmly, and Rebecca dropped to sit on the dank stairs as she recognized the truth in what he said. They could spend hours or even days looking for the latch on the hidden door, but still she didn't like the idea of leaving such a valuable book behind for just anybody to find.

"But someone else will get the secret," she hissed, surprised when Jacob shook his head.

"You don't even know whether the secret is in that book," he reminded her.

Rebecca frowned down at the hard-packed dirt, wishing yet again that she could read Arabic.

"I thought you read it," she recalled suddenly, wondering whether Jacob had really hesitated in midgesture as he extended his hand to her.

"I only glanced at it," he said quickly.

Rebecca pursed her lips in frustration, wishing she didn't have to leave the book behind, and accepted his assistance in getting to her feet. She glanced up into the darkness above her and recalled the brightness in Yusuf's eyes when he warned her about Ephraim's knowledge. She thought of the knife catching the light just hours before and shivered as she stepped quickly toward Jacob.

He was right. They should get out of Toledo while they had the chance.

"Maybe some things are better left unknown," she whispered, and he nodded in agreement.

"Maybe so."

But had they already tarried too long? Were the intruders planning another foray into the house while she and Jacob stood and discussed alchemy? She swallowed with difficulty and glanced up at Jacob, wishing his face wasn't thrown into shadow so she could have a better idea of what he was thinking.

"Perhaps we should go now," she suggested with her heart in her mouth, and he nodded again.

"The sooner the better, I think," he said ominously, his words doing little to reassure her as she picked up her satchel again.

* * *

Rebecca felt that flicker of panic once more when they stepped out of the room and the walls of the tunnel closed so tightly around them that Jacob had to stoop slightly as he walked. There was no room to walk abreast and she clutched Jacob's hand as she trailed behind him, unable to see the way ahead for his shoulders, unable to see the path they had already transversed in the scant light that made its way around him and back to her.

The silence was oppressive, every footfall echoing eerily in the distance until they both mastered the trick of walking more quietly. The air was dank and stiflingly stale, the hard-packed dirt floor uneven and marked occasionally by deep pocks, but Rebecca matched Jacob's pace stubbornly, determined not to be the one who forced them to endure this any longer than necessary.

She thought she imagined the first narrow opening off to the right and glanced over her shoulder to check, but whatever she had seen had disappeared into the shadows that trailed them. One on the left followed shortly thereafter and Rebecca felt the space an arm's length away more than she saw it. Now she started watching for them, her eyes adjusting to the relative darkness and picking out the intermittent openings on either side of what was apparently the main tunnel.

Jacob stayed resolutely on the wider path and Rebecca was loath to disturb the eerie stillness by asking him any questions. The openings must lead to other cellars, other labs, other houses, and she marveled at the complicated network being revealed to her now, her imagination running wild as she pictured the entire hill beneath the city rife with holes and tunnels.

The pitch of the path changed abruptly as they rounded another curve and inclined sharply downward. Jacob placed her hand on his shoulder then gripped the wall as he felt his way forward, the change in angle giving Rebecca a chance to see the path ahead clearly over his shoulders for the first time. It wound on endlessly, seemingly without

change other than the irregularly spaced openings carved
out of its walls. She tried to calculate how far they had
walked and could only conclude that they must be nearly
out of the Jewish quarter, the slope of the tunnel obviously heading down to the Tagus.

Jacob stopped so abruptly that Rebecca ran into him, her
gesture setting the flame in the lamp to fitful dancing even
as he held up his hand for silence. She listened, straining her
ears against the darkness, catching her breath when she
heard the faint but unmistakable sound of men's voices.

Voices that were growing louder.

Jacob ducked into one of the nearby doorways, gesturing for silence just before he pinched the wick and plunged
them into darkness. Rebecca shivered involuntarily, painfully aware as the smell of the earth filled her nostrils that
she was standing beneath the weight of the city. The darkness seemed to fuel her claustrophobia and she imagined
the entire city crumbling down on top of them, leaving
them helplessly buried beneath enormous mounds of rub-
ble.

Her heart raced when she felt Jacob's presence move
away and she almost screamed aloud in her fear until she
caught the subtle scrape of the ceramic lantern settling on
the ground. Rebecca's eyes began to adjust and she sensed
Jacob straightening back up from his crouch. She sagged
against him with relief when he pulled her into his arms as
though he sensed her terror.

For a moment she could hear only his heart beneath her
ear and she breathed deeply of his scent, driving out the
image of the dark tunnel from her mind. Faintly then, she
caught the sounds of the approaching men, feeling Jacob's arms tighten around her as their words gradually
became clearer. He touched his thumb to her lips un-
necessarily and she nodded mutely against his chest, barely
daring to breathe as they stood as still as statues and waited
for the threat to pass.

"Well, of course there was a man there," someone berated in an irritable hiss, and Rebecca's eyes widened in

surprise. It couldn't be him, it just couldn't be. "There was a wedding last week, for goodness' sake. Don't you pay attention to anything?"

"But he wasn't upstairs," a second voice argued. Jacob stiffened and Rebecca knew that he had recognized the voice of the intruder who had seemed to be in charge.

"So now a man doesn't have the right to wander around his own home at night?" spat the first. "Incompetents, both of you, and God only knows what I was thinking of to give you this simple task. How could you possibly make such a mess of retrieving a simple book?"

"You didn't do so well yourself," the second man shot back, earning himself an indignant humph.

"At least I got my hands on it—you haven't even seen the blessed thing," the first man snorted in disgust. "Not that you'd know it if it jumped up and bit you on the end of the nose. Now you've frightened the woman, alerted her husband to the problem *and* made it clear that it's the book we want."

He growled incoherently under his breath. Rebecca's eyes widened as his tirade continued and she acknowledged in amazement whose voice she was hearing. It was Isaac who was drawing near, she was certain of it.

"I doubt you could have made more of a mess of things if you had tried. Now there's no chance that he'll sell the book to anybody, if he has a drop of blood in his veins. Who would? If people are willing to steal it, it's obviously something of tremendous value, and I'd take the purchase price out of both your hides if I intended for a moment to pay it."

"So what are we going to do?" the other man demanded, and Isaac snorted with impatience.

"We'll do what we have to do, probably what we should have done in the first place."

"I don't understand," the third man finally piped up, and Rebecca could almost feel the scorn dispatched in his direction.

"The widow and her new husband are going to mysteriously disappear tonight," Isaac continued, and Rebecca's heart seemed to stop. "After all, they said they were going to Tunis and it will be months before anyone thinks anything different might have happened. By then, we'll have ripped that house apart and found the book. If you hadn't been so impulsive with that miserable thief Ephraim—" someone stumbled as he was apparently dealt a blow and the light cast on the opposite wall flickered "—we would have had it months ago."

"I don't know how he guessed about the poison," the man whined.

"It doesn't matter," Isaac snapped. "He realized what was happening and knew he had only to hold his tongue until the poison did its work. Sneaky bastard probably even knew what it was and how long he had to live."

The voices drew almost alongside them and Jacob pulled farther back into the shadows as the light bobbed brighter on the opposite wall. Rebecca's mind reeled from what she had learned and she tried desperately to assimilate all of the pieces despite her fear. She wanted nothing better than to break and run, to put Toledo as far behind her as possible, but Jacob was as immovable as the rock walls themselves. The light grew brighter and she squeezed her eyes shut, gathering fistfuls of Jacob's shirt in her hands as she willed the trio to pass them by.

"What's that?" Isaac demanded hoarsely, and Rebecca's pulse took off at a run.

"What?"

"Smell it, you fool. I can smell a snuffed wick. Haven't you a dot of sense in your head? Someone has been here recently."

"I used a candle on my way down," the third man confessed, but Isaac tut-tutted dismissively under his breath.

"No, this is recent—check the passages," he commanded, and Rebecca trembled as she heard the men's footsteps scatter in different directions.

Jacob eased a little deeper into the passageway they occupied and Rebecca moved silently with him, her heart in her throat with every step they took. She felt him draw his knife from his belt and knew they hadn't a chance against three if they were found. Would anyone ever know that they had perished here in the tunnels below the city? She thought suddenly of Jacob's aunt and worried about the older woman being left alone, unaware of her nephew's fate.

A silhouette loomed in the entranceway to the main tunnel and Rebecca cringed as Jacob straightened and pulled her deeper into the shadows. She was certain that they would be discovered in an instant. She recognized the profile of the third man when he peered intently into the shadows to his right and her heart positively stopped. He looked to his left with the same piercing scrutiny and took another step into the passageway.

This was it. They really were going to disappear mysteriously tonight and never be heard from again. Rebecca's mouth went dry and she drew away imperceptibly from Jacob, giving him the room to defend them as best as he was able.

"Forget it!" Isaac called suddenly, and the figure in the doorway hesitated as he glanced over his shoulder in surprise. "We haven't the time for this now," Isaac continued impatiently.

Rebecca thought her knees would give out beneath her from the relief. She clutched at the wall and felt Jacob's tension ease minutely. "It's not long until dawn and I want this business finished tonight," Isaac added tersely, no hint of his usual cajoling tone in evidence, and the other two men mumbled in assent.

Rebecca clutched Jacob's hand as the sounds of the men's progress faded into the distance, barely daring to believe that they had been so lucky.

"We have to get out of here," Jacob whispered into her ear when the men's footsteps were no longer discernible, and Rebecca nodded.

"They'll come back this way when they find us gone," she said, unable to keep a thread of panic from her tone.

"Exactly," Jacob confirmed flatly, and she felt him bend down. A flint was struck and the lamp flared to light again, giving her a glimpse of the concern in his eyes.

"They killed Ephraim," she murmured incredulously, only now coming to terms with the revelation, and Jacob's lips thinned.

"We don't need to give them the chance to repeat the offense," he muttered, and Rebecca nodded in whole-hearted agreement.

"Let's get out of here," she urged, and after sparing one careful glance down the tunnel in the wake of the trio, Jacob stepped out of the passageway and set a brisk pace in the opposite direction, Rebecca scrambling behind him.

They had to crawl on all fours toward the light at the end of the tunnel, but Rebecca was never so glad to see the dawn as she was that morning. The sky was barely tinged pink far ahead of them when they gained the narrow ledge that marked the end of the path, the swollen Tagus raging just below them. Rebecca looked up and saw the outer walls of Toledo above them.

Jacob dropped to sit on the ledge and pulled off his turban. He ran one dirt-encrusted hand through his hair as he, too, surveyed the scene before them. Far to their right and almost out of sight around the curve, the Alcántara bridge spanned the river, the opposite bank jammed with hundreds and thousands of gaily colored silk tents, all eerily silent in the predawn light. Rebecca retrieved a loaf of bread from her pack and they sat quietly for a few moments as they took sustenance and considered the task before them.

Jacob stood restlessly and frowned into the distance in either direction, kicking at the scrub on either side of the ledge until he apparently found something. He squatted down beside Rebecca and pointed off into the distance across the river.

"See that gray line far behind the crusaders?" he demanded softly, and Rebecca squinted as she followed the direction of his gesture, nodding when she picked out the sliver of color. "That's the old Roman road that leads to Granada and on to Algeciras. That's where we need to be."

"But it comes right up to the Alcántara," she pointed out as she traced its path from the horizon, earning a curt nod from her spouse.

"Right, and we can't go that way."

She looked up at him in confusion. "Then how are we going to cross the river?"

"I don't know," Jacob admitted, gesturing to the scrub he had kicked aside to their left. "But we're obviously not the first to come this way and there's a path of some kind along the bank here." He met Rebecca's eyes and she saw that he, too, was worried. "We'll just have to hope it leads to a ford or a crossing of some kind."

Rebecca held his gaze and nodded slowly, packing up the remnants of their impromptu meal. It wasn't as though they had many options. Back to the house would mean almost certain death, the Tagus was running so high that they couldn't risk crossing here, and the Castilians held the bridge closed. They would have to try the path and take their chances.

"We should go before it gets any lighter," she agreed calmly, knowing she didn't imagine that quick smile of approval that lit her spouse's eyes.

"Watch your step" was all he said, though, and he turned onto the narrow path, Rebecca close on his heels.

Chapter Fifteen

It was a fortnight later when Jacob caught Rebecca as she stumbled from the boat that had ferried them across the straits of Jebel Tariq. She was dead on her feet and he could only admire the perseverance she had shown on this trip. If he had known how difficult it would be, he would never have insisted they leave Toledo, and he worried now whether he had pushed her too hard and risked the health of the baby.

The deed was now done, however, and its consequences would have to be borne, whatever they were. And the more Jacob listened to fellow travelers, the less certain he was that they might have fared better if they had stayed in Toledo. For there was bad news beside the threat of Isaac and his henchmen.

Already there were tales of the surrender of the city to the Castilians and whispered rumors of Toledo's Jews enduring harassment. The synagogue had been lost to the mozarabs, and Jacob, for one, was glad he didn't have to watch the conversion of that holy place to a temple of another faith. Heartily glad to be back on the civilized side of the Mediterranean, he tucked his arm around his wife and virtually carried her and both of their satchels through the deserted streets.

They had walked miles, unable to purchase a horse or even a donkey until they reached Granada, undoubtedly due to the unusually harsh winter. It had been cold and windy the entire way but Rebecca had never complained, much to her credit. Jacob had seen the exhaustion in her face and done what he could to make the unaccustomed travel easier for her, but the fact remained that it had been a hellish journey and she had endured it better than most seasoned travelers would have done in her place.

Even more remarkable to Jacob's mind, there seemed to have been some minuscule adjustment in Rebecca's attitude toward him. He couldn't put his finger on the change, but more than once he had caught her watching him or felt her sidle up beside him like a little cat, as if she had forgotten or was at least reconsidering the accusations she had hurled at him that last day in the kitchen.

Was she coming to trust him? The very thought filled him with anticipation, but he would not jeopardize such a fragile thing when it was so close to being within his grasp. He wanted Rebecca's trust too badly to push her now and possibly clip its wings before they were even tried. She would come to him in time, Jacob reminded himself, resolving yet again to be patient with her and simply wait.

Even if the tension of waiting was nearly killing him.

"Can we sleep soon?" Rebecca murmured, and he wished he could somehow manage to carry her as well as their belongings. But it was only a little farther now.

"As soon as you eat something hot," Jacob confirmed, smiling when she looked up at him skeptically.

"Hot food is not a joking matter," she pointed out, but he saw a faint twinkle in her eye.

"We're almost there," he promised, and she snuggled tighter against him. "Smell," he instructed as he lifted his own nose to the air, then watched her smile as she followed suit and caught a whiff of Fatima's cooking.

"Mmm," she purred. "Does this mean we don't have to sleep on the ground tonight?"

"Cushions thicker than you can imagine," Jacob promised, feeling a twinge of doubt at the destination he had chosen. But Fatima's cooking was the best in town and he hadn't the energy himself tonight to find another place to stay. It was late, they were both exhausted, and Husayn would tell no tales, that much he knew for certain.

"I could sleep for a week," Rebecca confessed through a leonine yawn as they crossed the quiet *souk,* and Jacob grinned.

"You'll have that chance once we find passage to Tunis," he promised, her grateful smile warming his heart as they reached the threshold of the tavern.

Rebecca rolled over sleepily, savoring the delightfully thick cushions while she scanned the room lazily for her husband. She must have fallen asleep, her stomach full of something spicy, delicious and nameless, for darkness had fallen and a number of candles had been lit around the room. She really would have to take a better look at Ceuta tomorrow, she mused, only vaguely recalling the unfamiliar and ghostlike white silhouettes of the buildings they had passed on the way here.

She smiled at the scent of the beeswax candles and the misty recollections it summoned from the dark corners of her mind, closing her eyes for a moment against the emotions those memories carried with them. It had been so long since she had thought of her childhood, she mused, her grandmother's careworn features swimming slowly into focus in her mind.

"And what are you smiling so mysteriously about?" Jacob asked softly from somewhere to her left. Rebecca snuggled deeper into the covers at the sound of his disrobing, like the intent she heard in his deep tones.

This companionship that had sprung up between them on the journey was so comfortable that she could only hope it would be the keynote for their marriage. She smiled even wider in anticipation of their first night together without stones pressing into their backs, and hoped that this mood would lead to further intimacy, something in Jacob's voice telling her that his thoughts had turned in the same direction.

"My grandmother," she responded easily, not even thinking of keeping anything from him. Her heart took a little leap as she felt the cushions shift under his weight. Jacob's leg brushed hers and she turned instinctively to his warmth, giggling when he groaned in satisfaction at the softness of the bed.

"I knew there was something missing on the road," he commented as he stretched and made himself comfortable.

"Mmm. This is marvelous." Rebecca shifted so Jacob could slip his arm beneath her and cuddle her up against his chest. Perfect, she thought with a sigh as she settled against him with satisfaction.

"Tell me about your grandmother," he prompted in a low voice, and the words dispelled Rebecca's sleepiness. How long had it been since she had permitted herself to remember? A barrage of memories seemed to loose themselves in her mind, the good times and the tragedies, even the worst of them unable to mar the glowing memory of her grandmother's reassuring smile. She propped herself up on one elbow and looked down at Jacob to find his eyes bright with interest.

"You really want to know," she commented, not without a trace of surprise, and he nodded slowly as he held her gaze.

"Yes, I want to know all about you," he murmured, and a tingle tripped down her spine as his hands slid to cup the back of her waist.

The softly spoken words hung between them for a moment and Rebecca watched her fingers tracing patterns on Jacob's shoulder as she felt her color rise beneath his perusal. Perhaps it would be best if she told him all of it now, she mused, flicking a glance at his attentive features and knowing she owed him this.

There had been some change between them, and although she had realized it, she hadn't been able to pinpoint its source until this moment. The rigors of the road had permitted little speculation once the exhaustion had taken possession of their bones, yet even so, she marveled now that she had reflected so little upon the change.

She had decided to trust Jacob in Toledo. It was as simple as that. And although he seemed to know it, Rebecca appreciated that he was letting her set the pace, almost as though he understood that this was difficult for her. But when had he ever let her down or proven her trust was misplaced?

She looked up and met Jacob's eyes, smiling when the corners of his mouth tipped encouragingly, and she suddenly felt tingly all over. He was waiting for her to tell him whatever she wanted to, and Rebecca decided that she owed him as many explanations as he would endure.

"She was wonderful," she admitted finally, prepared for the inevitable when her eyes glazed with tears of recollection. So many funerals. Why had they always been such a part of her life? Why had everyone she had ever cared about left her behind? She tensed and Jacob seemed instinctively to understand, for his grip tightened on the back of her waist, that gesture alone making her tears rise all the faster.

"Unfortunately, she died when I was five," Rebecca added huskily.

"I'm sorry," Jacob murmured, and it seemed to her that he truly was. His fingers traced soothing circles on her back and Rebecca closed her eyes, letting the smooth rhythm of his touch ease away the hurt that still filled her at the memory.

"What about your mother?" he asked softly when she didn't continue.

"She died in childbirth," Rebecca told him, hearing the break in her voice as she anticipated Jacob's next question. She glanced up at him before she dropped her gaze again, ashamed of the confession she had to make. "She never told anyone who my father was."

There it was, out in the open, that dirty little secret of illegitimacy that she knew she would have to confess sooner or later. She was halfway relieved to have spoken, even as she dreaded Jacob's response. For who wouldn't be ashamed to have a wife of uncertain heritage? She was certainly ashamed of its taint herself.

Instead of the censure she had expected, Jacob pulled her close, the compassion in his touch almost starting Rebecca's tears anew, but she couldn't accept his sympathy just yet. It was time to set everything right.

"Where did you go?" Jacob asked quietly, and she winced in recollection.

"A distant cousin took me as a ward," she said tonelessly, unable to believe that his judgment wasn't still to come. "They had three children of their own who were already grown." A quick glance at Jacob found him still listening attentively and Rebecca tried to school her features, knowing how perceptive he could be.

"They were good to me in their way," she added carefully, the way Jacob snorted under his breath telling her that she hadn't succeeded in fooling him.

"So you were always alone," he mused, tenderly tucking a strand of hair behind her ear, and Rebecca couldn't bear to look into his eyes.

"Yes," she mumbled in assent, startled when Jacob cupped her chin and forced her to meet his gaze.

"So that's why you were afraid," he said, his words more a statement than a question, and Rebecca nodded hastily.

"I've not had much luck depending on people," she whispered shakily, and Jacob rolled her easily beneath him, his eyes alight with something that made her melt inside.

"I think we can change that streak of bad luck," he murmured, and Rebecca found herself without anything to say.

Jacob's eyes darkened and she guessed his intent, stretching toward him as he bent to kiss her with a lazy thoroughness. Her heart sang as his hand closed possessively over her breast, his embrace telling her in no uncertain terms that he didn't hold her past against her. This was her future, this man and his compassion, and she could only be grateful that she had been granted this opportunity for happiness. When Jacob lifted his head and ran his fingers through her loose hair, Rebecca felt that she was positively glowing beneath his touch.

"Your grandmother must have loved you very much," he said unexpectedly, and she looked up at the abrupt change in subject. Jacob smiled and touched the tip of her nose affectionately. "She taught you how to take care of yourself," he continued softly, "and I'm sure she would be proud of the woman you've become."

There was no checking Rebecca's tears now and Jacob pulled her close as she cried. She acknowledged that she loved him with all her heart and soul when he rocked her and murmured unspeakably sweet things into her hair. She was right where she belonged, no matter how convoluted a road she had taken to be here, and it was more than time for her to clear the slate with Jacob.

"Jacob?"

"Shh. You don't need to say anything more," he urged in a throaty whisper, his hands doing magical things that weren't at all soothing.

"I have something I have to tell you," she insisted, fighting desperately against her body's intuitive response to his touch.

"It can wait until the morning," Jacob demurred, and she gasped involuntarily as his fingers meandered between her thighs. "We've had enough confessions for one night."

"But—" Rebecca barely saw the glimmer of mischief in his eye before he captured her lips for a long, heart-stopping kiss. The taste of him was intoxicating as always and she allowed the universe to drop into a slow spin around her as she savored his touch. When he finally lifted his head, she was limp with desire, but still she managed to grit her teeth with determination.

She simply had to tell him the truth about the baby and she had to do it now.

"It can't wait any longer," she insisted, and Jacob smiled, evidently thinking she was being coy.

"Neither can I," he teased as he leaned toward her, obviously intending to kiss her into agreement, but Rebecca dodged his embrace.

"It's probably waited too long already," she added breathlessly, seeing that she had finally gotten his attention with those last words.

"You're quite serious," Jacob commented when he paused, scanning her features in confusion, and Rebecca nodded.

"I lied to you about something," she confessed all in a rush, and he nodded in easy agreement.

"A lot of things," he clarified with a wry smile, and Rebecca felt herself color. He wasn't taking this seriously and she had no idea how to convince him of its import without blurting out her news.

"I'm not pregnant," she said quickly, and when his brows pulled together in concern, she shook her head wildly before he could ask. "I never was. Ever. I lied about the baby because I was afraid you wouldn't come back otherwise."

"You were never pregnant?" Jacob repeated slowly as though he didn't understand the words, and Rebecca cringed inwardly at the sound of that dangerously controlled tone.

"No," she responded meekly, unwilling and unable to retract her statement of the truth now.

Jacob's eyes flashed, and then he was abruptly on his feet, his fury clear from his thunderous expression. He glared at her as though she were a complete stranger, then paced the length of the room and back so quickly that Rebecca was suddenly alarmed. What if she couldn't make this right? Was she doomed to lose Jacob, too?

"You *lied* about the child?" he demanded tersely once more.

"Yes," she admitted, getting slowly to her feet, well aware of the tension in his stance even as she sought to explain. "But you have to understand, I was frightened and I knew that you could help me..."

Jacob's lips curled scornfully. "So you deliberately *lied* to me?"

"Well, yes, but I was going to tell you..."

"*When* were you going to tell me?" he demanded acidly. "You certainly didn't tell me when I asked you in Toledo whether you were telling the truth. In fact, if I remember correctly, you looked me right in the eye and *swore* that you were carrying my child."

The air positively crackled between them and Rebecca licked her lips, trying to choose the next words with care.

"Well, yes," she conceded uncomfortably, knowing that this was not going at all as she had hoped. Where was that understanding man of a few moments past? He was furiously, blindingly angry and her words seemed to be having no impact at all on him.

"But I needed help and I trusted you," she explained, trying desperately to avoid losing her temper, as well, but Jacob showed no such control.

"Whether or not you trust *me* is not the issue here," Jacob practically shouted, the anger in his eyes making Rebecca take a tentative step backward. He inhaled shakily in an apparent bid for self-control and continued in that low tone that always brooked trouble for her. "You may trust *me*," he observed, "but I can't see any reason why I would ever trust *you* again."

"You have to trust me," Rebecca countered in panic, knowing the color had drained from her face at his assertion. "You said that you trusted me."

"That was before I knew how deceitful you were," he charged, pacing across the room again and jabbing his finger through the air in her direction to punctuate his points. "You have lied to me over and over again and every single time I've made allowances for you. But this is it, Rebecca. This time you've gone too far."

"But I'm telling you the truth," she insisted, uncertain what he intended to do but not liking the direction his words seemed to be headed.

Jacob sneered. "And how am I supposed to know that?" he demanded icily, his words hitting too close to home for her comfort.

"I'm telling you that this is the truth," she declared wildly, but his expression became only more intimidating.

"Like you told me you were pregnant?" he retorted coldly, his eyes narrowing so that she saw once again the hostile stranger who had stood on her doorstep, judging her, that afternoon so long past. In that chilling instant, Rebecca was certain that Jacob was going to walk right out of her life.

Just like everyone else. Just when she had begun to depend on him.

"Won't you give us one more chance?" she begged, hearing the desperation in her own tone, telling herself that she wouldn't beg but not at all certain that she could restrain herself.

Jacob stared down at her and she held his regard despite the coldness in his eyes, knowing now that she would give anything to keep from losing him, wishing she hadn't been so terribly stupid. How could she have lied right to his face about something so important?

"I've given you a chance to be honest so many times already," Jacob finally said, and Rebecca fancied she heard regret in his tone. "What possible justification is there to try again now?"

The words that echoed in her heart stuck in her throat right when she needed them and she stared wordlessly back into Jacob's eyes. He held her gaze for a long moment, then hauled on his chausses and scooped up his shirt, turning to stride out of the room and leaving a trembling Rebecca in his wake.

"Because now I know that I love you," she whispered when she finally recovered her voice, but the confession came too late, the empty hall echoing with silence as tears began to roll down her cheeks.

* * *

How many times would she push him so? How many times would she demand that he give her a chance? Jacob exhaled noisily as he made his way down the stairs to the common room of the tavern, the jingle of the *tars* carrying to his ears. He didn't know which way to turn anymore. His conviction that Rebecca just needed a little more time to come to him had been disproved so often, and now he felt only that he had backed down over and over again.

And each time the revelation she dealt him in response had been a harsher blow. She was taking advantage of his gullibility, or at least it was beginning to feel that way.

But what could she possibly have to confess that was worse than what she had told him tonight? Surely the worst must be over.

To be illegitimate was no small matter, although it didn't bother Jacob particularly and he knew that he could keep it from being an obstacle to Rebecca in Tunis. Of far more concern was the issue of her pregnancy, for not only had she lied about it on the *ketubah* but she had looked him in the eye and reiterated that lie when he had challenged her.

Jacob had *known* she was lying and still she had managed to convince him, which didn't bode well for his understanding of his new bride. Would he ever be able to believe anything she told him from this point onward? Or would he always wonder? That would be the worst of it, for he knew without a shadow of a doubt that Rebecca could convince him she spoke the truth while she was in his presence, but later, when he was alone, he would question her word. And that uncertainty would drive him mad.

Had Judith been right? Had he made the mistake of falling in love with a woman who would use him and abuse his trust? A woman who would unscrupulously destroy him? He couldn't believe that was the case, but at the same time, he had believed Rebecca's lie. He closed his eyes and saw her once again before him all those weeks ago, boldly asserting that she bore his child, and he shook his head.

And there was the issue of the child. Only now Jacob realized how much he had been looking forward to seeing Rebecca round with his child, with their child. It had seemed a sign that this match was somehow blessed, and now the disappointment of finding it all an illusion tasted bitter on his tongue. Half of him wanted never to see her again, the other half not to let her out of his sight until their union was genuinely fruitful.

"Your bride is shy?" Husayn demanded with a knowing smile that drew him out of his introspection, but Jacob could only shake his head.

"I wish it were as simple as that," he muttered wryly, accepting a shot of *eau-de-vie* and feeling the liquor burn down his throat under Husayn's assessing eye.

"You cannot be fighting already," the portly keeper chided, wagging one finger at Jacob. "Not with such a pretty one as that."

"We were fighting before we even met," Jacob replied flatly, staring down at the tiled counter as he struggled to come to terms with the warring emotions within him. His heart sank as he heard Husayn settle the bottle on the counter, dreading whatever his friend might have to say.

"It can be hard for a woman to adjust to such changes in her life," he commented mildly, but Jacob shook his head again.

"It's not that," he insisted, looking up when Husayn inhaled with politely expressed surprise.

"Oh, you know this to be so?" he demanded skeptically, and Jacob met his eyes in confusion. "Foolish is the man who thinks he understands a woman, especially his own," Husayn added with a wise chuckle, making a great pretense of wiping the counter now that he knew he had Jacob's attention.

"What do you mean?"

"What do I mean? You have taken her from her home and brought her to a completely foreign land. You do not think this is difficult for her?" Husayn leaned confidentially across the counter and dropped his voice to a whisper. "Women care about hearth and home. She has her home no longer and has yet to see yours. Do you not think this bothers her?"

"But that's not what we argued about," Jacob protested, his words brought up short by a curt shake of Husayn's head.

"What is *not* said is as important as what *is* said," he insisted, refilling Jacob's glass amiably. "What is she thinking now that you have left her alone upstairs in this foreign and unfamiliar place? Is she worried about what she will do in this strange land if you do not return?"

Jacob frowned into the amber liquid, wondering whether there was something of merit in Husayn's words. Rebecca had seemed distressed about leaving the house that one afternoon, he conceded, but he still couldn't get past his annoyance at her lying.

"She keeps pushing me," he insisted, and Husayn tuttutted under his breath.

"Perhaps she wants to see what you are made of," he suggested, and Jacob threw back the second shot.

"It's hard to believe it's worth it," he muttered, not liking the gleam that came into his friend's eyes.

"And when have things worth having not required some effort to obtain?" Husayn demanded archly, turning on his heel with an elegance that belied his weight to leave Jacob pondering this last thought.

As if to emphasize Husayn's assertion, Jacob looked up and recoiled at the determination shining in the kohl-lined eyes of the dancer who advanced upon him, her hips swaying rhythmically in an indication that she would be easy to come by.

Dross into gold, he thought suddenly as his gaze landed on the coins girding her hips. What was he made of, indeed? The dancer was immediately forgotten, a frown appearing between his brows as he had an unexpected thought. It was Rebecca who had given him the chance to show his gentler side, Rebecca who brought his passion to a pitch, Rebecca for whom he had trusted his long-disregarded instincts, Rebecca who had taught him that love could recolor his perspective of the world.

Jacob smiled to himself and quaffed the rest of his drink, savoring the simplicity of the inevitable conclusion. There was no other explanation for the way Rebecca made him feel as though he could conquer the world when things were good between them, as though he were more than he had known himself to be. And indeed, he felt he had won the fight when she gifted him with that rare smile, as she had when he gave her the *aljofar*.

No matter what she had done or what she had said, his conclusion was unassailable. Loving Rebecca refined his spirit as nothing else had done. The past was behind them now, if he could only leave it there, and Jacob decided in that instant that the ends definitely justified making the effort. One more chance was all she had asked for and he would be a fool to deny her something so simple. There was too much at stake to let it all slip away.

"Jacob," a woman called seductively, and as he made his way to the stairs, Jacob spared a glance over his shoulder to the forgotten dancer. He recognized Alifa now with some measure of disinterest, fully intending to return to Rebecca as quickly as possible. Husayn was right: Rebecca might well be worried that he wouldn't return.

"Good evening, Alifa," he answered stiffly. "If you'll excuse me?"

"Oh no, Jacob," the dancer purred, locking her hands around his elbow with unexpected tenacity, and Jacob scowled in anticipation of an unwelcome scene.

"I hardly think we have anything to talk about," he hedged. "Perhaps Husayn has told you that I'm here with my bride." Alifa's eyes narrowed quickly, then she arched one brow, her next words bringing Jacob's efforts to extricate himself to an abrupt halt.

"Then perhaps you'd like *me* to tell your new wife about the pox that's been going around Ceuta," she hissed.

"What?" Jacob demanded in shock, Alifa's satisfied smile doing nothing to reassure him.

"Don't worry," she soothed as she patted his arm reassuringly. "There's a cure and the physician is in the back room, if you'd like to speak to him."

Completely stunned by this revelation, Jacob found himself halfway to the dancers' hideaway before he knew what he was about, his mind finally engaging as a terrifying thought occurred to him.

Had he unwittingly passed an infection to Rebecca?

Was Jacob ever coming back?

That thought precluded any possibility of sleep despite her exhaustion, so Rebecca reluctantly rose and shrugged into a relatively clean chemise. She had to find Jacob, she resolved. She had to force him to listen, to beg if she had to, because she simply couldn't let him walk out of her life.

At least not before she had told him she loved him.

If that didn't make any difference, well, she would cross that bridge when she reached it. She rummaged in her satchel, then frowned at the pack and tossed it aside impatiently, certain she had brought a second kirtle but not finding it there. Fatima had graciously offered to wash the filthy one she had been wearing, but she had to wear something to pursue Jacob down to the tavern.

Maybe it was in his satchel, she reasoned, bending to unfasten the buckles and feel around in his belongings. Jacob's scent rose from the garments within, mingling with the smell of the worn leather, and Rebecca closed her eyes against her longing for him, her heart stopping cold when her fingers encountered a hard shape.

She pulled it from the pack, knowing what it was before she laid eyes on it, the sight of the little red book launching a tide of anger through her.

Jacob had lied to her!

The nerve of that man! After telling her that they would have to leave the book behind, he had had it all along! Talk about a travesty of trust—after all, it was *her* book! And now he berated *her* for lying! The cheek of the man and his sanctimonious attitude! One set of rules for her and another for him!

She practically growled as she found her errant kirtle and hauled it over her head in one vicious gesture. She jammed the book into one of her pockets and stuffed her feet into her well-worn shoes, wrapping a veil around her hair with a cavalier sweep as she gritted her teeth in determination.

Jacob ben Solomon had something to answer for now, of that there was no mistake, and Rebecca was looking forward to this exchange. Oh, he was not going to slip out of this one easily, she promised herself. She would make sure of that.

Chapter Sixteen

"Alifa, there is no one here," Jacob declared when they stepped into the back room and he saw that it was empty.

"He must have stepped out for a moment," the dancer declared offhandedly as she swept past him, trailing one fingertip down his arm.

Something wasn't quite right, Jacob thought, watching dispassionately as Alifa draped herself across the cushions and patted the embroidered one beside her invitingly.

"Come and sit," she purred seductively, but Jacob shook his head. What had he ever been thinking of to get involved with such a creature? It was impossible to imagine that her superficial sexuality had ever satisfied him in any way.

"No, I think this will have to wait," he said, seeing the dancer's expression harden slightly.

"Surely you want to know about this infection?" she demanded coyly, and Jacob couldn't deny that he did. This was his worst nightmare come to life, some indiscretion from his past not only making itself known to Rebecca, but possibly endangering her health, as well.

"I understand it has quite serious repercussions," Alifa supplied, evidently having seen his indecision, and Jacob knew he had no option but to talk to the physician.

"Perhaps you could let me know when your physician returns," he said, and Alifa smothered a smile.

"Don't tell me you're afraid to stay here with me?" she asked, reaching for a sweet from the tray that seemed to be perpetually filled. She selected a confection delicately between finger and thumb, catching an errant drop of honey with her tongue before she met Jacob's eyes again.

"I remember a time not that long ago when you were very comfortable in this room," she mused, but Jacob folded his arms stubbornly across his chest. He was not going to let Alifa drag him into some sort of unsavory assignation with Rebecca right upstairs. What kind of man did she think he was?

"I've told you those days are gone," he said flatly, watching as Alifa arched one brow skeptically.

"So you have," she agreed easily, the tip of her tongue darting out to lick the remains of the sweet from her rouged lips. "That said, what do you think I intend to do?"

She was not going to goad his imagination. Jacob knew this trick of Alifa's and it wasn't going to work anymore. Clearly it was time for him to go.

"I have no interest in finding out," he maintained stonily, turning to leave the room. There was a heavy silence behind him but Jacob refused to glance over his shoulder, even as he dreaded Alifa's next words. She had something on her mind, he knew her well enough to sense that.

"I could come up to your room when the physician returns," Alifa suggested softly from the other side of the room, and Jacob closed his eyes against the effectiveness of her countermove. "I'm sure your wife would be *most* interested in his diagnosis."

"Damn you, Alifa," Jacob rasped, the privacy curtain clenched in his hand. He was torn between the misleading appearance if he stayed back here and the inevitable confrontation between Rebecca and Alifa if he left. A confrontation that was certain to be an ugly one, if he had any understanding of the dancer's character.

"You should have told me earlier," he growled, hating the position she had put him in as he turned to meet those catlike eyes once again. Alifa smiled slowly and Jacob knew that she thought she had him cornered.

"I didn't know," she maintained, patting the cushion one more time as her eyes narrowed slightly. "Don't worry, Jacob. I'm sure he'll only be a few moments and then you can get back to your little wife."

Not knowing what else to do, Jacob reluctantly released the curtain and watched it shimmer as it fell into place once more, feeling that he had been forced into doing something he would regret.

"Rebecca!"

Rebecca checked her stormy descent into the smoky tavern at the melodic call of her name and frowned into the shadows as she sought its source. It couldn't have been his voice, she told herself. Not in Ceuta, so far from home.

Much to her astonishment, it was indeed Yusuf who stepped out of the haze, his eyes filled with an unspeakable sadness as he dropped to one knee before her and brushed his lips across her slipper.

"Yusuf!" she breathed in amazement, taking his hands in hers and urging him back to his feet. "Yusuf, what are you doing here?"

The Berber merely shook his head as though he couldn't find the words and cast his gaze down to the floor in silence. Filled with concern when he refused to answer, Rebecca reached up to touch his cheek.

"What is wrong?" she demanded softly. "You must tell me."

"I cannot speak of it," Yusuf declared quietly, his lips thinning for an instant before his gaze flicked to hers, his eyes bright with some purpose. Without another word, he took her elbow and threaded a path across the crowded tavern floor.

"Where are we going?" Rebecca demanded, coming to a full stop when Yusuf still did not answer her. She twisted out of his grip in frustration and faced him with her hands propped on her hips. "What is going on here? You must tell me." The traffic in the tavern dipped and swayed around them, but she paid the patrons no mind.

Yusuf sighed heavily before he spoke and she saw that he would have preferred to say nothing at all. "It is my solemn duty to show you the kind of man you have wed," he said, a new melancholy in his melodic tone. A flicker of panic tripped through Rebecca but she refused to indulge it.

"You're talking in riddles, Yusuf," she declared flatly. "Now, tell me what you're doing here and what you're talking about."

"I would not speak of it," he hedged, but Rebecca fixed him with a sharp eye.

"Then I will wish you the best and return upstairs," she countered, watching while Yusuf fought some inward struggle. Finally he met her eyes, the intensity in his own almost compelling her to take a step backward.

"You know that I still hold you in high regard," he began, and Rebecca nodded, not having been certain of any such thing but unwilling to question him and interrupt the flow of his tale. Yusuf frowned down at the floor for an instant. "I was concerned at your nuptials that all was not as it should be, and as I told you before, I had doubts about your spouse's tale of his origins."

Understanding dawned suddenly on Rebecca and she regarded the Berber with horror. "You followed us," she hissed, and Yusuf looked down at his mud-encrusted boots with some measure of embarrassment.

"I did," he conceded softly, lifting his chin to continue before Rebecca could launch into a tirade against him. "But you must forgive me. I did it only because of my concern for you and these concerns have borne fruit in what I have seen tonight."

Rebecca shook her head in disbelief but Yusuf gripped her hands with such force that she was compelled to look into his eyes once more.

"I wished only to know that you were happy and that he intended to care for you honorably." Yusuf swallowed with difficulty and Rebecca admitted to herself that he seemed to be speaking the truth.

"Tonight I intended to ask you whether you were indeed satisfied with your match. If so, I would have returned to Toledo with the dawn." Yusuf looked down at their entwined hands as if dreading what he had to say next.

"What is it?" Rebecca prompted, and when he lifted his gaze, there was agony in those green depths once more.

"I would not hurt you with this news, Rebecca, for I fear that you may have already granted your heart to this man, but I must tell you the truth."

"Go on," she urged, that very heart nervously taking up residence in her throat.

"Your Jacob came down these stairs not long ago," Yusuf began, and Rebecca nodded impatiently until his eyes met hers once more. "And disappeared into the back room with one of the dancers."

"Dancers?" she demanded uneasily, schooling herself not to jump to conclusions.

"A belly dancer," Yusuf clarified with a sad shake of his head. "They are all whores, Rebecca. Do not even imagine it to be otherwise."

Rebecca tore her hands from Yusuf's grip, everything within her recoiling in revulsion at what he had told her. Not Jacob. Jacob would not do this to her. It was unthinkable that he would leave her to visit a whore.

"I don't believe you," she countered indignantly, feeling the pity in the Berber's gaze as he regarded her for a long moment.

"I feared you would feel this way," he said quietly, and Rebecca's heart sank like a stone when he calmly took her hand. "That was why I originally intended to let you see the truth with your own eyes.

Yusuf turned to walk directly toward a doorway hung with a glittering violet silk curtain and Rebecca was suddenly afraid that he was right.

* * *

"Alifa, your physician doesn't seem to be coming," Jacob pointed out with annoyance as the dancer leisurely indulged herself with another sweet.

"You are so terribly impatient these days," she commented, and he suddenly had the sense that she was being evasive.

It was unusual that no one had come or gone from this room all the time they had been here, and now that he thought about it, it was strange that none of the women were dancing at this hour of the evening. And where were the young boys who normally trotted in and out, fetching veils, *tars* and sustenance for the dancers? In fact, the only time Jacob could recall this room being so quiet was when Alifa had specifically decreed that it be so.

"Where are the other dancers?" he demanded suspiciously, and the way Alifa lifted her shoulders in feigned nonchalance fueled his newfound doubts.

"I'm not my sisters' keeper," she retorted quickly, sucking the honey off the tip of one finger and releasing it with a resounding smack. Jacob held her gaze for a long moment, his conviction that she was lying growing with every instant that passed.

"There is no physician, is there?" he asked, advancing toward her when he noted the flicker of fear that danced through her eyes.

"What are you talking about?" she asked lightly, obviously trying to brush off the question, but Jacob was not deterred. He was right, he knew it. This was all some elaborate ruse of hers for who knew what purpose, and he wasn't going to play along any longer.

"There's no physician because there is no pox. Isn't that right, Alifa?" He leaned over her impatiently, certain that she had some other trick up her sleeve.

"I don't know what you mean," she argued, but the conviction was gone from her tone.

"What is this all about?" Jacob fairly roared, and Alifa's eyes flashed defiantly.

"I've told you already," she cried, but Jacob shook his head adamantly.

"No," he insisted, his eyes narrowing as he guessed her game. "You're trying to destroy my marriage and I won't stand for it." He turned to leave the room but Alifa launched herself after him and hauled him to a stop.

"I won't let you go," she declared as her arms latched around his neck, and Jacob spun on his heel angrily.

"You haven't got a choice," he informed her, trying to disentangle himself from her embrace, trying to pull back when she planted her lips hard against his. Jacob recoiled in disgust, shoving Alifa away from him, the triumphant gleam in her eyes making him wonder what he had missed.

"It's true," whispered an achingly familiar voice from behind him. Jacob's heart sank when he spun to see the tears shining in Rebecca's eyes, and he immediately reached for her.

"Rebecca!" he breathed, taking a step toward her, but she was gone, shoving her way past Yusuf, of all people. Jacob regarded the other man in stunned amazement for an instant, watching in confusion as the Berber sadly shook his head, before he forced such trivialities out of his mind and rushed out of the room in pursuit of his wife.

She was on the stairs at the far side of the room already and Jacob's heart wrenched as he saw her trip on her kirtle, one hand raised to her cheek. How could he have made her cry yet again, and this time without even trying? What must she think of what she had seen?

He darted through the tangle of tables and patrons, desperately trying to gain the stairs before she had the chance to reach their room and lock him out. He had to explain himself before she closed her heart and mind against him. He had to set the record straight before more damage was done, and he could think of nothing else.

He heard Husayn call his name and fancied the keeper's tone held a warning, but he was too bent on his task to turn around. A hand clamped on his shoulder and he glanced back in annoyance, but didn't have time to make out the person who restrained him before lights exploded in his head and everything faded suddenly to black.

Rebecca stumbled into their room, blinded by her tears, and slammed the door behind her, unable to believe the scene that had confronted her in the back room. Jacob with a whore. It was almost too much to be believed, but she had seen the proof with her own eyes, as much as she hated to admit it.

There was no denying the evidence of that woman draped across Jacob, or her profession, her ample curves almost spilling out of her sheer costume. How shocked he had been that she had interrupted their little liaison; how shocked she had been that he would cavort so with her only footsteps away. She dashed her fingers ineffectively at her tears, knowing that Jacob was right behind her and steeling herself now against his inevitable pleas for her understanding.

"Just the woman we have been waiting for," came a smug voice, and Rebecca's chin shot up, her eyes widening in fear when she saw Isaac leaning casually against the far wall. She pivoted to run out of the room, only to find a tall, unfamiliar man firmly planted in front of the door, his arms folded across his chest.

"We meet again," he drawled, and Rebecca recognized the voice of one of the intruders.

How could she have not noticed that the room was occupied? She cursed her tears and scanned the room quickly, seeing now how her and Jacob's belongings were haphazardly scattered, not packed neatly as she had left them. Isaac blocked the arched window that overlooked the courtyard, while the other man stood between her and the door, and it was clear that there was no way she could slip from the room.

A quick glance at Isaac revealed the malice gleaming in his eyes and Rebecca felt a shiver of trepidation run down her spine. She recalled too easily the declaration of his intentions in the tunnels in Toledo and tried desperately to keep her pulse from racing out of control.

"What are you doing here?" she gasped, breathless, wishing her fear wasn't so evident. She glanced warily between the two men and wondered what had happened to the third.

"It seems you have something of mine," Isaac declared softly, and Rebecca turned slowly to face him, unable to believe that she had ever thought this vibrant and determined man to be old and feeble.

"I don't know what you mean," she responded unevenly, willing herself not to reach for the book hidden in her pocket.

Isaac smiled and shook his head sadly. "I think you do know, Rebecca, but if your memory needs prompting, I'm sure Zachary will oblige."

Rebecca shot a wild look over her shoulder and the tall man in the doorway nodded with apparent enthusiasm. She swallowed carefully and turned back to Isaac, determined to know the truth before she met her fate.

And maybe if she stalled long enough, Jacob might appear. Hadn't he called after her in the tavern? She had been certain he was right behind her, but now she acknowledged a niggle of doubt. He should have managed to climb the stairs by now if he had been pursuing her. Rebecca's heart drooped at that revelation but she willed herself not to reflect upon her husband's apparent lack of regard for her now.

"Surely you didn't follow us all the way from Toledo for a little book of Ovid's poetry?" she asked innocently, and Isaac snorted under his breath.

"Ovid," he spat with disgust. "You've chosen a fool for a husband once more, my dear, for not only did he not know what he had, he didn't take advantage of an excellent opportunity to profit from its possession."

"I don't understand," Rebecca insisted, enduring Isaac's level assessment of her unflinchingly.

"Maybe you don't," he mused thoughtfully, shoving away from the wall and coming to stand right before her. She watched him warily but didn't back away.

"You see, that was no book of poetry," Isaac murmured confidentially, and Rebecca forced her eyes wide in mock surprise even as she felt a shadow of dread at the threat underlying the older man's tone.

"Then what is it?" she asked guilelessly.

"Something I have waited all my life for." He bit out the words, his eyes narrowing into hostile slits. This time when he stepped forward, Rebecca couldn't stop herself from taking a step away from him, and his lips tightened as he noted her gesture.

"Yes," he said grimly. "That book is rightfully mine because I alone am the most deserving of its secrets." Isaac's eyes narrowed so that the avaricious gleam was partially concealed, but Rebecca noted it nevertheless. "Not Ephraim, foolish child that he was. He tried to trick me and almost succeeded, but I knew the book was in that house and that sooner or later it would make its presence known." He leaned closer and Rebecca saw that wildness in his eyes again.

"They have forces of their own, you know, these secret texts," he whispered theatrically, and Rebecca shivered. "And they will not suffer being hidden for long. It is not the way of the great works and I knew that this one, too, would assert its presence. It was only a matter of time before it appeared and I was determined to be ready and waiting for the sign that must come."

"But why did you try to steal it?" Rebecca managed to ask, earning herself a deprecating glare in response.

"Steal it? Surely you jest, foolish child. Is it thievery to take what is destined for your hands alone?" Isaac demanded, and Rebecca knew in that instant that he would stop at nothing to get the book. "That book is mine, it always was mine, and it will be in my hands where it belongs very shortly." He eyed her assessingly. "Unless, of course, you would prefer to martyr yourself to the cause," he hissed, and Rebecca's eyes widened.

"You killed Ephraim," she charged softly, her heart taking off at a gallop when Isaac threw back his head and laughed.

Where *was* Jacob?

"Oh, yes," Isaac confirmed readily, his eyes glowing as he leaned closer. "What is a life in exchange for universal truth, after all? Ephraim wasn't the first, my dear, and I heartily doubt that he'll be the last."

He made a quick gesture and Rebecca didn't have a chance to turn before she felt her wrists clasped from behind in an iron grip. She cried out when her arms were twisted behind her and she was lifted painfully to her toes, her entire field of vision filled with Isaac's mad eyes.

"Now make your choice," he challenged, dismissing the room with one sweep of his hand. "Tell me where the book is hidden or join the ranks of those who have died for its secrets." He chuckled to himself, evidently finding humor in his remark. "It makes little difference to me whether you hand it to me or Zachary searches a corpse or two."

"It's hidden," Rebecca insisted, but Isaac shook his head dismissively.

"It's not hidden here or in the house in Toledo. And I heartily doubt that you abandoned it on the road, so either you or your clever husband has taken it."

"I don't know where it is," Rebecca lied, hoping the desperation in her voice made her sound as if she were telling the truth. "I haven't seen it since that day in the library." That was almost true, after all. Isaac's eyes narrowed in recollection and he nodded slowly, as if to himself.

"He took it, then," he muttered under his breath, shooting a sharp glance at his companion. "He must still have it."

"Carlos will have him downstairs," the man holding Rebecca captive confirmed, and her fright only increased.

What had they done to Jacob? Was that why he hadn't appeared? Had this Carlos already killed him? Rebecca felt panic settle within her at the thought of being without Jacob and wished with all her heart that their last encounter hadn't been so awful. The knowledge that she had sent him away because of her own lies would haunt her for the rest of her days.

Isaac stepped forward in that moment and gripped her chin tightly, forcing her to look into his eyes as he spoke.

"No tricks from you," he hissed, "or we'll kill you both."

The conviction in his tone told Rebecca that he wouldn't even hesitate, and she nodded weakly in acquiescence, feeling that there was no way they would manage to escape this ordeal, if indeed Jacob still had the opportunity.

Jacob drifted groggily back to consciousness and opened his eyes to find the terra-cotta tiles of Husayn's establishment right beneath his nose. He almost grunted before he sensed the presence of someone close beside him, recalling in that instant that he had been hit from behind. A man's hand landed heavily on the back of his neck and Jacob hastily closed his eyes again.

Apparently his assailant was intent on ensuring that he didn't leave anytime soon. Jacob did his best to breathe slowly as though he were still unconscious, even as his mind raced forward. How was he going to get out of this? And what had happened to Rebecca? Rage boiled in his chest, and he knew that if anyone had hurt her, he would tear the offender from limb to limb.

The man beside him stood abruptly with a muttered oath and Jacob had to take the meager opportunity for what it was. Counting on the element of surprise, he leapt to his feet and watched the hazy room swim giddily around him before it settled reluctantly into place.

A stocky man stood before him, his mouth mercifully open in shock, the way he was raising one fist indicating that he was quickly recovering from his surprise. Jacob instinctively lashed out with his right hand and caught the man across the bridge of his nose. He heard a resounding crack and the man grabbed at his face with a wince as Jacob danced backward and out of range.

A shout echoed in the tavern and the patrons on the far side of the room were on their feet, but Jacob had no time to turn and look at the source of the commotion, for his opponent was still standing. The man dabbed at his bleeding nose in disbelief, lifting his gaze to meet Jacob's as if he could not believe the insult he had sustained.

Jacob had time to scan his build and recognize him as a formidable opponent before the man bellowed like a disgruntled bull and launched himself in Jacob's direction. Jacob sidestepped his assault but the man spun and came up with a knife, its blade gleaming evilly in the lamplight.

The gesture reminded Jacob of that night in Toledo when he had watched one of the intruders threaten Rebecca the same way, and his mind froze at the connection. Had Isaac and his henchmen followed them all the way to Ceuta? That could only mean that Rebecca was in far worse danger than he, for there were still two others unaccounted for.

Seized with a new panic for his bride, Jacob grabbed the only object within range, a flickering lamp. He balanced the weight of its round bowl carefully in one hand, feeling the heat of the flame near his skin and wondering what he was going to do with it.

The men circled each other warily, each assessing the other's choice of weapon and kicking stools out of their way. Suddenly the shorter man lunged forward. Jacob leapt out of the path of the blade in the nick of time and threw down the lamp as the man shot past. He squeezed his eyes shut against the unexpected flare of flame as the vessel shattered explosively on the man's back and the fire spread immediately to gobble the spilled fuel.

His attacker shrieked as he dropped his knife and fell to the floor, desperately trying to extinguish the flames. He rolled into a group of patrons and spread the fire to them, their cries of panic alerting the others in the tavern to the danger, while Jacob watched in horror.

* * *

Men shouted and Rebecca heard a woman scream as her companions forced her out onto the stairs. Someone tripped over a number of *tars* and their discordant jingling seemed woefully out of place as chaos erupted in the tavern.

Within an instant, growing flames made their presence known, glowing orange in the darkness as they leapt even higher, smaller flares igniting all around the room from the lamps spilled in the confusion of patrons trying to escape. Rebecca could smell the oil that gleamed on every surface, but as the light of the flames grew brighter, she could only scan the shadows for another sight of Jacob. Finally she spied him, his turban gone and clothing dirty but otherwise unscathed. He looked stunned at the pandemonium erupting around him and Rebecca permitted herself to exhale shakily.

Jacob was alive.

"There he is," Isaac growled beside her. Zachary forced her up to her toes once more and pushed her toward the stairs.

"Where's Carlos?" he demanded, and the thought that Jacob might have dealt with one of the thugs encouraged Rebecca that they might yet survive.

"It doesn't matter," Isaac spat. "Our business is with Jacob ben Solomon."

"What are you going to do?" Rebecca demanded breathlessly, needing to hear the worst. Her question earned her a sharp glare from the older man she had once thought benevolent and harmless, a shiver slithering along her spine at the coldness in his eyes.

"We're going to persuade him to give us the book," Isaac hissed, arching one brow as he continued. "One way or the other."

Rebecca's shoulders arched from the way Zachary was twisting her arms, but that was nothing compared to the jolt of fear that tripped through her at Isaac's apparently grim intention. Her gaze flew back to Jacob, her heart contracting at the frown that etched his brow as he turned toward the stairs, evidently meaning to seek her out.

She lifted her chin stubbornly and gritted her teeth, determined not to let these men steal Jacob away from her if there was any way that she could prevent it. She had the book that they wanted, and somehow there had to be a way that she could save Jacob's life with it.

Jacob could think only of Rebecca as everyone around him fought to gain the door. He turned toward the stairs, heading purposefully in that direction to seek her out.

Husayn shouted to him from the other side of the tavern but Jacob waved off his friend, even as he acknowledged his concern. If they didn't get out of the building soon they never would, and Jacob knew it, but he had no intention of leaving without Rebecca. He touched his left hand and saw Husayn nod in understanding even as he noted Fatima's silhouette behind her spouse. Husayn hesitated and Jacob gestured impatiently to the door before he raced toward the stairs.

He had to find Rebecca.

"Jacob!"

Rebecca's call seemed to have come as much from his own thoughts as anywhere else and Jacob froze in his steps. His heart leapt into his throat when he made out her figure at the top of the stairs and he gestured to her to jump before he noted that she was held captive between two men.

He stepped forward instinctively, but the way the man on her left waved a knife in his direction threateningly brought his footsteps to an uncertain halt once more. It was Isaac, Jacob saw with amazement, his gaze drawn back to Rebecca's frightened look. He had to do something and soon, but that knife and its proximity to Rebecca seemed to eliminate most of the possibilities.

"Make one move and I'll kill her," Isaac cried wildly, confirming Jacob's worst fears. The flames sizzled behind him and he cast a glance over his shoulder to see the tapestry on the far wall leap to life. It wouldn't be long now before the entire place burned to the ground and he wished he could just scoop up Rebecca and get them both out of danger.

"What do you want?" Jacob demanded hoarsely, hating his helplessness when the other man forced Rebecca a step forward and she grimaced in pain. Her arms were twisted behind her, he saw now, and he vowed silently that Isaac and his friend would pay dearly for any bruises she sported as a result of their rough handling.

"The book," Isaac shouted, the blade wobbling unsteadily in his hand. Jacob saw that the madness had completely taken him and wished Rebecca were farther away from the older man.

"What book?" Jacob demanded. He didn't have the book, he thought in puzzlement, unable to understand why they hadn't found it in his satchel. Surely they had searched the room. Jacob looked to Rebecca but she was wisely watching the path of that unpredictable blade.

"You know what book," Isaac cried, the blade flashing as he tucked it under Rebecca's chin. She recoiled but the other man kept her from stepping backward and Jacob cursed the fact that he could only watch. "I'll trade you the book for her life!" the old man bartered.

Chapter Seventeen

Before he could summon a response, a shadow leapt from the top of the stairs. A flaring crimson cloak revealed the man's identity before he landed with a resounding thud on top of the man holding Rebecca.

Yusuf! Never had Jacob thought he would greet the Berber's presence with enthusiasm, but now he thanked all the powers that be for this small mercy. His heart leapt in relief as the tall man released Rebecca with a cry and he and Yusuf rolled down the remaining stairs in a tangle of black and red.

Jacob grabbed a discarded blade and jumped forward to help the Berber when the men's tumbling came to a halt at the foot of the stairs. Yusuf reared back unexpectedly and Jacob saw the gleam of a dagger clenched in his teeth, knowing in that moment that the tall man was as good as gone.

He glanced up to see Rebecca darting down the stairs in the wake of their tumble, her wide eyes flicking to his for an instant before she stopped abruptly and fell back with a cry of pain. Isaac had recovered his wits in time to grab a fistful of her hair and haul her to a stop, his victorious leer making Jacob's hopes plummet once more. Rebecca twisted futilely, rummaging inexplicably in her pocket as she regained her balance.

"Take the book!" she cried, and Jacob was stunned to see the little red book hurling through the air toward him.

He caught it with a snap of his wrist in amazement, trying to make some sense of her gesture.

Why hadn't she just given Isaac the book?

Jacob glanced to her in confusion and she mouthed the words "take it" once more. He shook his head slowly, unable to believe the only explanation that came into his mind.

She hadn't surrendered the book because she knew it was important to him. There could be no other reason. Although that one defied logic to Jacob's mind, the soft glow in Rebecca's dark eyes told him that he had guessed right.

She had risked her life to keep something that he desired and his amazement was quickly followed by the urge to shake her. Didn't she have the sense to know that she was far more important to him than a book? Isaac shouted an obscenity at that moment and Jacob instinctively tightened his grip on the slim volume.

"Give it to me!" the older man commanded, and Jacob was torn as to what to do. He felt the Berber's gaze upon him and licked his lips nervously, knowing what he had to do. He gripped the book in one hand and slowly offered it to the madman.

"Come and get it," he demanded quietly, the fingers of his other hand curling more tightly around the handle of the knife concealed behind his back.

Isaac's eyes flashed and apparently the sight of victory within his grasp clouded his thinking, for he forgot about Rebecca for the barest instant. Jacob held his breath but Rebecca saw her chance. He silently praised her quick thinking as she twisted abruptly away and darted out of reach. At least she was safely out of harm's way, however this encounter might end.

The tavern filled with an unnatural silence as the two men faced each other, the crackling of the flames filling Jacob's ears. He flicked his glance away from Isaac to find Rebecca huddled against the wall beside Yusuf as she struggled to catch her breath, one hand clutched over her heart as she watched him with fear in her eyes.

Jacob felt Yusuf's gaze upon him, too, but didn't spare the Berber a glance, turning back to meet Isaac's gaze steadily as he dared the man to come closer. Isaac took each step more deliberately as he grew near, seeming now to wonder about Jacob's intentions as the book loomed temptingly closer. His gaze flicked to the left and the right when they stood two paces apart, almost as though he had just realized that he stood alone now, and Jacob willed himself to wait for the perfect moment.

When the book was within an arm's length, Isaac could stand it no longer and leapt forward to grasp the volume to his heart. Jacob had anticipated the gesture, though, and quickly pulled the book out of range once more, greeting Isaac with his bare blade instead. The older man's eyes boggled at the glint of the dagger and his gaze rose to Jacob's in confusion.

"It's just a book of poetry," he wheedled one last time, but Jacob only smiled.

"Do you really think that I could trade on this sea without reading Arabic?" he whispered softly, and understanding dawned in Isaac's eyes.

"You know what it is," he charged in quiet amazement, and Jacob nodded once.

"It would be wrong to let you have it," he vowed, but Isaac smiled now with maddening certainty.

"Don't imagine that I will rest as long as you possess it," he asserted coldly, gesturing in vague dismissal to his fallen companions. "This day may not have gone in my favor, but I will find you again, Jacob ben Solomon of Tunis." Isaac leaned forward, his last words sending a chill down Jacob's spine. "I will find you," he threatened, "or your wife, or your children, or your ancient grandmother, and I will have that book for my own. You cannot hide from me forever."

And he would not try. Jacob's grip flexed on the small book and he weighed Isaac's words in his mind, knowing that Isaac would not be the only one who would stop at nothing to know the *Emerald Tablet*'s secrets. Who knew how many other lives this innocent-looking book had claimed beside Ephraim's? It would never stop and Jacob couldn't begin to imagine allowing his family to live in such danger.

No secret was worth living the life of a hunted animal.

Jacob stared into Isaac's knowing eyes and deliberately tossed the small book into the raging flames. With satisfaction, he watched Isaac's expression turn to horror, then the older man cried out like a creature in pain. The fire flared as if devouring something it found particularly delectable, the gold lettering on the book's cover gleaming unnaturally in the depths of the flames.

"No!" Isaac screamed, and launched himself into the flames in pursuit of the book. Jacob grabbed at the older man's surcoat but the cloth tore away in his hands, leaving him with a handful of rent cloth as Isaac's figure disappeared into the blaze. Rebecca gasped in shock behind him as the pitch of Isaac's scream rose. Jacob turned away as both man and book were engulfed in the flames.

Something soft shone in Rebecca's eyes when they met his and Jacob held out his hand to her as he walked to the bottom of the stairs, knowing in that instant that all that had been between them could be resolved. Now they could begin to trust each other fully. He saw an answering sentiment reflected in his wife's eyes and his heart began to pound in anticipation as he reached for her outstretched fingers.

To his astonishment, Yusuf stood up suddenly and blocked his path. Rebecca uttered the Berber's name indignantly but he did not move, his features impassive as the two men's gazes met and locked. Those green eyes were cold beyond compare and Jacob almost took an involuntary step backward at the condemnation he saw there. Yusuf offered his hand to Rebecca as he stared Jacob down and she hesitated for a moment until the Berber shot her a sharp look.

"He is not worthy of you," he said tersely, and Jacob's optimism sank as Rebecca closed her eyes in apparent agreement.

"But—" Jacob protested as his wife slipped her hand in Yusuf's, the other man's frosty expression stopping his words in his throat.

"There is nothing to explain," Yusuf fairly snarled. "A woman of quality does not need a whoremonger for a spouse."

With that, the Berber led Rebecca quickly past a dumbfounded Jacob and hustled her out into the street to safety. Jacob watched them go, not knowing what he could possibly say to defend himself after the damning scene Rebecca had witnessed with Alifa. He coughed and squinted his eyes against the growing smoke, covering his mouth with his hand as he raced out of the burning building in their wake.

Husayn had made accommodations for Jacob and Rebecca in his own home, and Rebecca had tried to settle herself there, although Jacob had not appeared throughout the long night. Fatima had reassured her when the moon was at its zenith that he was fine, but she had still been unable to sleep, plagued by worries in turn that he would come to her in the night before she had figured out how to make things right between them. Perhaps it was just as well he had stayed away, Rebecca reflected sourly as she paced the street between the house and the remains of the tavern the next morning, for she had no idea how she could have faced him.

In that one instant when they had confronted each other and she had seen the love in his eyes, she had forgotten completely about the incident with the dancer. Relief that he was alive and whole had apparently clouded her thinking, relief and a curious glow of pleasure that he had chosen to destroy the book. She couldn't begin to understand what had compelled him to do that, but something in Jacob's eyes in that moment before Yusuf interfered had told her that his reasoning had something to do with her. That heady thought left her feeling warm all over and she wondered if she would have the nerve to ask him about it when their paths did cross.

She supposed she should be grateful to Yusuf for recalling her to her senses, but at the time she had greatly resented his interference and even now found it hard to believe he had done her a favor, however noble his intentions had been. Yusuf's open disapproval of her tears after he had dragged her from Jacob's side had done little to endear him to her and she pursed her lips in disapproval.

Just where had Jacob gone, anyway? Was he going to avoid her for the rest of her life? Or was Yusuf standing guard somewhere to ensure that Jacob couldn't come and talk to her?

Rebecca sighed and watched with disinterest as young boys began to pick through the still-hissing remains, evidently seeking souvenirs or trinkets of value within the debris. One shouted victoriously and picked up something that reflected the sunlight like brass, dropping it an instant later with a holler of pain. Served him right, Rebecca thought, folding her arms across her chest, the gesture releasing a waft of smoke from her kirtle.

She winced at the smell and acknowledged that she would have to talk to Jacob, at least so that she could get something else to wear. Her fingers found the reassuring curve of her *aljofar* and she shook her head at her own foolish hopes for the future. What would become of them now? Would they ever be able to have that trust Jacob had so long insisted upon pursuing?

"You are Rebecca," a woman with a husky voice pronounced, and Rebecca glanced to her side to find the dancer Jacob had been embracing standing beside her.

"Yes," she responded crisply, taking a step away as she had no intention of talking to the woman. "If you'll excuse me?"

To her surprise, the woman caught at her sleeve. Rebecca looked up and the dancer forced an apologetic smile. "I would speak to you for a moment," she explained, but Rebecca shook her head adamantly.

"I can't imagine you have anything to say that I need to hear," she said curtly, and something flashed in the other woman's dark eyes before she shook her head.

"You are mistaken," she asserted softly, arching a brow toward the other side of the small crowd that had gathered around the burned-out husk of the tavern. Rebecca looked up, surprised to find Yusuf watching their exchange intently, his arms folded across his chest, his expression forbidding.

"It seems the *gentleman* is quite insistent that I explain what you saw last night," the dancer continued, and Rebecca shook her head in confusion.

"But he took me there," she protested, and the other woman shook her head.

"Like you, he misinterpreted." She frowned to herself, her delicately arched brows pulling together in consternation before she continued. "It seems Jacob explained what happened to him and the Berber feels obligated to ensure that you hear the truth."

Rebecca half smiled to herself. "He would," she agreed, and the dancer's expression hardened for an instant.

"Yes. He is *most* persuasive." Her lips thinned momentarily and Rebecca hadn't the nerve to ask what sort of terms Yusuf had dictated. It was clear that the woman was not enamored of her task and it would be easier for both of them if this ordeal were over sooner rather than later.

"You must understand that I was very angry with Jacob when he ended our liaisons the last time he came through Ceuta," the dancer said quickly, and Rebecca examined the woman's features with surprise. "Oh, yes," she confided with a wry smile. "It is long since he warmed my bed, and I fear I was never more than a sexual release for him." The dancer shrugged nonchalantly. "It is that way in this business," she maintained matter-of-factly, and something in her manner made Rebecca wonder whether she regretted the choices she had made.

"At any rate," the dancer continued with a sigh, "I never thought I would lay eyes on him again, and when he came into the tavern last night, so proud to have you on his arm, I saw red." Her dark eyes turned away from Rebecca's nervously as though she were reluctant to continue.

"What did you say to him?" Rebecca prompted, not daring to hope that there really was a reasonable explanation for what she had seen.

"I told him that I had a pox and that there was a physician in the back he should talk to," the woman confessed, and Rebecca regarded her in shock.

"A pox?" she repeated, horrifying images flooding her mind until the dancer quickly shook her head and laid one hand on her arm reassuringly.

"It was a lie." She made the assurance hastily, the concern in her eyes telling Rebecca that she was telling the truth. "I just wanted to get even with him somehow and that was the first thing that came to my mind." The dancer sighed theatrically and rolled her eyes. "And, oh, was he angry," she breathed, and Rebecca almost smiled at the mental image that popped into her mind.

"I can imagine," she murmured, watching as the other woman took a deep breath to finish her tale.

"At any rate, when you and that *thug* came in—" she cocked her head to the ever vigilant Yusuf "—Jacob had figured out that I was lying and was calling my bluff." She shrugged and spared Rebecca an apologetic smile. "I saw you and took the last chance I had."

The two women's eyes met and Rebecca knew that this was as close to an apology as she would get. She noted the bitterness pulling the corners of the other woman's mouth and knew that she wasn't in any position to judge her, not having any idea what the dancer had been through to reap the meager rewards that she had.

Who knew how she would act in her place? Who knew where she would have ended up herself without her grandmother and at least a few years of love? Rebecca had been lucky and she knew enough of the world to recognize that. She placed her hand over the other woman's where it still rested on her arm and gave those slim fingers a squeeze.

"Thank you for telling me," she said quietly, and their gazes held for a long moment before the dancer nodded once and turned. Rebecca silently watched her walk away, her hips swaying gently in a provocative rhythm. She turned back to Yusuf, but the Berber had disappeared without a trace into the crowd.

Rebecca tipped her head back and looked up into the morning sky, her fingers finding her *aljofar* of their own volition. She took a deep breath of clean morning air, knowing without a doubt what she had to do.

The hour was late when Jacob returned to Husayn's home, for he had deliberately endeavored to make it so, but he couldn't help a twinge of disappointment when he found only his friend in the kitchen. He dropped to a seat in exhaustion and the two men sat in awkward silence for a few moments, Jacob still struggling with the realization of what a terrible financial blow Husayn must have sustained the previous night.

"I'm sorry about the tavern," Jacob said finally, stunned when his friend merely shrugged good-naturedly.

"So was I," he confessed, his dark eyes twinkling as he glanced up to meet Jacob's perplexed gaze. "Until Fatima straightened out my thinking on the matter."

"What do you mean?"

Husayn sighed and shook his head as he trimmed a lamp wick. "It seems she was tired of the business but was afraid to tell me so."

Jacob raised his brows at the irony of that, and Husayn fixed him with a telling look, giving a significance to his next words that Jacob couldn't fathom. "She wants to cook just for me."

"So, you won't open another tavern or rebuild this one?" Jacob demanded, and his friend shook his head adamantly.

"I am told that it is an unhealthy atmosphere for young ones," Husayn admitted with a grin.

"But you have no children..." Jacob began to argue before he made the connection. "Oh," he said simply, sitting back for an instant as he realized the import of the words, and Husayn grinned even wider at his surprise. Grinning himself, Jacob extended his hand to the other man. "Congratulations." Husayn shook his hand and turned back to the lamp.

"That will be a big change," Jacob commented, uncertain of his friend's feelings on the matter until Husayn chuckled.

"Oh, yes," he agreed easily, putting down his blade and meeting Jacob's eyes with a wry smile. "You know, I had thought after all these years that there would never be little feet pattering around my hearth, but sometimes—" he grinned almost to himself and picked up the knife again "—sometimes it is good to be wrong."

Jacob chuckled and watched his friend work for a moment, a sadness rising in his chest at the reminder that Rebecca was not pregnant after all. He had been looking forward to their child, although he hadn't realized how much until he saw Husayn's happiness. Jacob frowned to himself, wondering whether he and Rebecca would have had a better chance of coming to an understanding if there really had been a child to hold them together.

"We missed you today," Husayn commented with apparent idleness, his words drawing Jacob out of his own thoughts. He made a great production of trimming a lantern wick and Jacob spared him a wry smile.

"I'm afraid I wasn't very good company," he admitted, thinking that little had changed over the course of the day.

"Fortunately your wife is a charming companion," the older man pointed out, and the resulting pang of jealousy that shot through Jacob caught him off guard. So he had been wrong to trust Yusuf with the truth of what had happened between Alifa and himself, he mused, reasoning that there could be no surer sign that Rebecca held him in little regard than for her to be in fine spirits while he was moping around the *souk* all day.

"Yes, she is," he agreed with no great measure of enthusiasm, fancying that Husayn shot a smug glance in his direction. Jacob looked up only to find his friend innocently adjusting the wick.

"Then perhaps you should avail yourself of her company," he suggested, and there was no mistaking the twinkle in his eye this time. Jacob sighed heavily and frowned at the glowing coals on the hearth, uncertain he had the confidence to seek Rebecca out tonight.

"I had thought I might sleep here and let her get her rest," he explained, but Husayn shook his head in adamant denial.

"I will not hear of it," he protested. "If that is the case, Fatima and I will sleep on the hearth and you can take our room."

"I couldn't do that," Jacob objected immediately, unwilling to put his host out more than they had already.

Husayn spread his hands wide in concession. "Those are the only options I will tolerate, I'm afraid," he concluded pertly, something in his manner giving Jacob the distinct sense that he was being toyed with.

"But Fatima is pregnant and I really don't mind sleeping here," he tried one last time, but the older man fixed him with a sharp eye.

"But I do, and it's my home and my hospitality you'll be insulting if you do," he maintained firmly. "Go talk to your wife," he urged in an undertone when Jacob didn't move, and Jacob took encouragement from his tone as he got to his feet.

It was, after all, ridiculous for him to be afraid of Rebecca. And he couldn't spend the rest of their lives avoiding her.

It was undoubtedly best to get this over with sooner rather than later.

That decided, Jacob bade his friend good-night, catching the last half of another of those enigmatic grins as he slowly climbed the stairs.

He tapped once on the door of the room they were supposed to have already shared, Rebecca's muted response almost dismissing his determination to put this unpleasant encounter behind them. What was he going to say to her? he thought in panic, forcing himself to take a deep breath and push open the door.

The sight that confronted his eyes took Jacob by such surprise that he stood for a moment as if frozen on the threshold, completely dazzled by the warmth of Rebecca's welcoming smile.

There must be some mistake, he thought dazedly, taking in the hundreds of flickering candles that lined the window ledge overlooking the starlit courtyard. More filled the low tables and were clustered in groups on the floor, casting the room in a golden glow. He smelled the sweetness of beeswax, his mouth going dry at the richness of the cushions piled in the far corner atop a thick and ornately patterned rug, the arrangement evidently made for a liaison. With him? Surely this couldn't be. A *rebab* was plucked in the courtyard below, its plaintive strains wafting through the air on the breeze that ruffled the fringed window shades, and Jacob dared to look at his wife again.

Her hair was brushed out and hung in a gleaming ebony curtain over her shoulders and down her back, the slim golden curves of her figure picked out by the candlelight through the sheer gauze of her pale chemise. He met her eyes and caught his breath at the promise he found there, unable to believe the way her lips curved into a smile at the sight of him, bringing that delightful dimple into view.

"Come in and close the door," she chided softly, and Jacob realized he was still standing on the threshold like an idiot. Remarkably Rebecca didn't seem to understand what a fool he was, for she gifted him with another of those bone-melting smiles as she drifted toward him when he couldn't move.

His pulse raced as she drew near, the warm scent of sandalwood rising from her skin as she laid one hand on his arm and reached past him to close the door. Her breast brushed across his arm and Jacob gritted his teeth at the feel of the hardened nipple against his skin, his mind supplying an image of that dark nub when he closed his eyes.

He felt Rebecca lean her cheek against his shoulder and knew she was looking up at him but couldn't meet her eyes. Why was she tormenting him like this? And what was he supposed to say or do? All he could think about was putting this romantic setting to good use, for it seemed forever since he had tasted her, but there was too much left between them to cast aside cavalierly.

"Liar," she charged quietly, and Jacob knew then that she was trying to drive him crazy. This was her vengeance for his lie about leaving the book behind.

"I had no idea you would even think of bringing it," he maintained stonily, the flutter of her breath across his chest when she chuckled pulling his nerves as taut as a bowstring. If he touched her, he would be lost, and he clenched his hands at his sides, unable to think straight enough even to fathom a guess as to what Rebecca wanted from him.

"If you wanted it so badly, why did you burn it?" she asked softly, and Jacob closed his eyes in recollection of the feelings that had surged through him in the tavern.

"He said he would hunt it down," he explained, his tongue as dry as sandpaper at the thought. "And I knew he wouldn't be the only one." Jacob stopped for a moment and tipped his head back to stem the tears he felt gathering behind his lids. "I couldn't do that to you, to us, for the sake of a book."

"But you had read it already?" she demanded, and Jacob shook his head quickly in denial.

"No. I was waiting until we were home in Tunis." He gestured vaguely with one hand, feeling the inadequacy of his reasoning even as he voiced it, unable to explain exactly what had stayed his hand on their sleepless wedding night when he had sat down to read the little volume. Some sense that it was not his to read had assailed him and he had found himself putting it aside in favor of another text.

"I guess I needed my reference books," he added with a shrug, and Rebecca fell momentarily silent. With his eyes closed, her soft scent seemed even stronger, more bewitching, and he wished he had some idea what she was thinking.

"Do you regret losing it?" she asked in a small voice, and Jacob shook his head without hesitation.

"There was no choice," he stated flatly. "He was going to kill you for it."

The room was silent once more and Jacob cringed at the realization of how much of his feelings he had revealed. Evidently Rebecca was embarrassed by the implication because he knew how uncharacteristic it was for her to be so quiet.

"The dancer came to talk to me," she whispered, and Jacob's eyes flew open in shock. He looked down at her and she nodded slowly, her eyes glowing with some unspoken emotion. "I'm beginning to think I'll have to keep making up lies to maintain your interest," she teased, and Jacob exhaled unsteadily, reaching tentatively to cup the side of her face. Was it possible that she was not furious with him?

"She told you?" he demanded hoarsely, feeling ten years younger when Rebecca nodded quickly in agreement.

"Everything," she confirmed, and Jacob raised his brows in mock surprise.

"Not *everything*, I hope," he teased in his relief, loving the way Rebecca laughed at his change of mood. "I still wanted to teach you about a few things."

"You'll just have to figure out what I don't already know," she informed him pertly, and that dimple danced in her cheek as she darted a few steps away, peeling off her chemise with a flourish. Her skin glowed golden in the light and Jacob found himself grinning as he followed her. Threading his fingers into the soft mass of her hair, he tipped her face up to his.

"I accept your challenge, wife of mine," he whispered, seeing the flash of Rebecca's smile before he tasted the sweet honey of her lips once more.

Epilogue

Tunis was as lovely as she had imagined, Rebecca acknowledged as they sailed into the harbor. The rows of whitewashed buildings in front of the craggy wall of mountains and the bright blue of the sky reflected in the turquoise waters of the Mediterranean were just as Jacob had described.

He came to stand beside her at the rail and she tucked her hand proprietarily into his elbow, her heart taking another one of those little leaps when he closed his other hand over hers and slanted her a smile. She leaned her cheek on his shoulder and realized that she would be completely happy if she knew just one last thing.

Jacob had not said that he loved her since the day she had called him a liar for making that claim. Yusuf braced his hands on the rail on her left and she glanced up to meet the knowing glint in his eyes, realizing that he hadn't missed the distinct warming between Jacob and her this past two weeks. He smothered a smile and studied the coastline, as well, his lips pursing in what Rebecca could only assume was approval.

"Well, what do you think?" Jacob asked good-naturedly, and Rebecca marveled at how accommodating he had been of the Berber's insistence to see her well settled.

"It seems a moderately affluent town with a pleasant climate," Yusuf conceded with mock reluctance. "Although things could prove much different on closer inspection."

"I think it looks lovely," Rebecca enthused, and Jacob's fingers tightened briefly over hers.

"Well, you are somewhat more susceptible to this merchant's charm than I," Yusuf acknowledged matter-of-factly, and Rebecca felt her color rise at the accuracy of that remark.

"I should hope so," Jacob muttered under his breath, and the Berber actually grinned.

"You should appreciate the interest I am taking in Rebecca's situation," he chided gently, and Jacob smiled in turn.

"I'm sure it's reassuring to Rebecca to know that someone from Toledo is concerned about her circumstance," he allowed, and Rebecca watched as the two men met each other's eyes in that newfound camaraderie.

"It certainly is wonderful," she agreed, looping her other hand through Yusuf's elbow. Over the past few days he had been as protective as the older brother she had never had, and Rebecca appreciated his concern. "I hope you approve of his lodgings," she teased the Berber, and he shot her a speculative glance. "I just might want to stay here."

"Then let us hope they are adequate," Yusuf commented with a regal nod, refusing to admit to anything before he had made his assessment.

Jacob made some barely audible sound beneath his breath and Rebecca tightened her grip on his elbow. He shot her a confident smile that made her briefly wonder what he was up to. Nonsense, she told herself, he was simply glad to be finally coming home. After all, their arrival here had been in doubt on more than one occasion.

And he must be looking forward to seeing his aunt again, she realized, that familiar trickle of fear jolting along her veins. Make that two last things she was worried about.

For what would she do if Judith didn't like her?

Jacob could barely restrain himself that afternoon from hustling Yusuf and Rebecca impatiently along the quiet streets. It seemed to him that they wanted to stop and peruse every single shop while he couldn't wait to get home. Finally, he cajoled Rebecca out of the *souk* with the promise that he would bring her back the next morning, a concession that would undoubtedly cost him dearly, and he heaved a sigh of relief as at last they climbed the winding street to the house.

This was it, Jacob thought to himself as he opened the door, giving Rebecca a smile of encouragement so that he would have an excuse to be watching her reaction as the interior was revealed.

"Congratulations!" shouted Judith from the foyer, her arms spread wide as she closed in for a hug in front of the dozens of guests crowded behind her.

"Congratulations!" came the cry from the rest of the assembled friends and family. Rebecca's mouth fell open in astonishment and Jacob knew without a doubt that she had been completely surprised.

"Welcome home, sweetheart," the older woman enthused with a wink for Jacob as she gathered his dumbfounded bride close, and Jacob permitted himself to grin. "I'm so glad to meet you, dear. Look at this lovely face, everyone. Isn't she the most precious thing? Jacob has certainly done us proud. And don't you worry, sweetheart, he's written all about you and I know we'll get along famously. Now, we thought it would be just as easy for you to meet everyone at once, dear, and you know, it looks like there are some wonderful gifts for you to open later. Now, this my cousin..."

Just when it seemed that Rebecca was doomed to be swept along with his aunt's enthusiasm, she cast a glance over her shoulder and smiled at Jacob. He grinned back, watching as she politely extricated herself and headed purposefully toward him. Judith's greeting stopped amiably in midstream when she noted the look that passed between the new couple and Jacob knew they had an audience but he didn't care.

He saw the gleam in Rebecca's eye and realized her intent in time to brace himself for her attack, laughing as she jumped on him and he caught her against his chest.

"You knew!" she accused, and he chuckled at the sight of that dancing dimple.

"Of course," he responded. "How else would they know when we were coming?"

"Oh, Jacob, it's so marvelous," Rebecca whispered to him in delight, and Jacob held her close.

"I wanted you to feel welcome here," he murmured back, tipping her chin when her eyes glazed with joyous tears.

"I do," she managed to whisper just before he kissed her soundly. His heart began to pound as she pressed against him and he fervently hoped that it would always be thus between them. The guests applauded the gesture and Jacob lifted his head reluctantly, something in Rebecca's dark eyes convincing him that it would be, just before Judith determinedly tugged her new niece into the fray. Rebecca blew him a kiss from her fingertips before she disappeared, and he smiled to himself.

Maybe it would be an early night for everybody.

"Good trip, Jacob?" inquired another merchant from town, and Jacob shook his hand gratefully, turning back to indicate the Berber standing politely behind him.

"Absolutely. Zebediah, I'd like you to meet a good friend of mine. This is Yusuf Khudabanda." He met the Berber's eyes steadily for a moment, noting the way Yusuf almost permitted himself a smile at the choice of words before turning his attention to the other man.

"Pleased to make your acquaintance," Zebediah declared as he shook Yusuf's hand, and Yusuf inclined his head elegantly.

"The pleasure is mine," he maintained smoothly.

"Yusuf is one of the best chess players I know," Jacob supplied conversationally, and this time Yusuf did smile as he met Jacob's eyes.

"But it was you who ultimately won the match," he conceded softly, their gazes holding for a long moment before Jacob smiled in turn.

"I was lucky," he maintained, knowing it to be so. "And I had some help with the last move," he added, and the Berber inclined his head in acknowledgment before turning his attention back to the enthusiastic Zebediah.

"Now, I like a good game of chess myself," the merchant commented, obviously having taken to the Berber and the possibility of a challenge. "Maybe you and I could play a little game one of these days before you leave. How long are you staying in Tunis?"

Yusuf met Jacob's eyes again, an enigmatic smile playing over his lips. "Not long now," he said. "I simply needed to check on something." The two men's gazes lifted in unison to pick out Rebecca, the sunlight glinting on her veil in the courtyard past the foyer, her laughter carrying easily to their ears.

"You're welcome to stay," Jacob offered once Zebediah had excused himself, but Yusuf shook his head slowly.

"There is no need," he said, a hint of sadness in his eyes. "She is happy and that is all I needed to know."

Jacob reached out to grasp his shoulder and the Berber spared him a surprised glance. "Somewhere there is a woman for you," he insisted in an undertone, and Yusuf nodded once.

"One can only hope so," he agreed, forcing a smile as he turned to shake Jacob's hand. "I would offer you my congratulations, as I have not done so before," he said stiffly, his eyes narrowing as he scanned Jacob's features one last time. "Mind you always take such care of her."

"I will," Jacob promised. "I wouldn't want to answer to you for anything."

Yusuf's teeth flashed white for an instant. "We made a good team in Ceuta," he acknowledged, and Jacob nodded.

"You could stay," he suggested once more, but Yusuf shook his head determinedly.

"Not now," he reiterated with a frown, and Jacob watched his eyes lift to the courtyard once more. He followed the Berber's gaze, but Rebecca had slipped out of sight.

"She would want to say farewell," Jacob added when he sensed the other man intended to leave, but Yusuf shook his head quickly.

"No, it is better this way," he said simply.

"Thank you for talking to Alifa," Jacob said in a low voice, and one of Yusuf's brows arched before he spoke.

"My error hurt Rebecca," he admitted tersely. "I had no choice but to make it right." With that, Yusuf looked Jacob steadily in the eye for a long moment before he turned and swept abruptly out the doorway.

Jacob watched him make his way down the narrow cobbled street, the red burnous swirling in his wake, but Yusuf did not look back, and all too soon he passed out of sight.

"What took you so long to bring her back?" Judith chided at his elbow, and Jacob granted his aunt an apologetic smile as he returned to the present.

"What do you mean?"

"She's absolutely charming, Jacob, and I don't understand why you didn't simply snap her up the first time you went to Toledo. Now come in here and say a few words."

Jacob spared one last glance down the street but Yusuf was long gone, and he turned back into the melee of happy guests. Gradually he worked his way through hearty handshakes, claps on the back and sticky kisses to Rebecca's side, the happiness on her face making him glad he had thought of this welcoming celebration. Someone pressed a glass of red wine into his hand and he smiled down at his wife as he took her hand in his.

Jacob felt something firm within his grip and glanced down to find himself fingering the gold band he had placed upon her finger. His wife. His Rebecca. She was looking down at their entwined hands, and as he watched, she glanced up at him, her lips curving into an infectious smile again. Was it possible that she was as happy as he?

"I want to thank you all for coming to welcome us home," Jacob began as he gave her fingers a quick squeeze.

He cast a glance over the assembled guests and the sight of so many faces that he knew and loved made a lump rise in his throat. They were so lucky, not just to have each other and Judith but all these friends surrounding them. Here Rebecca would find the love and acceptance she had missed all her life. He would make sure of it. That thought brought the words so readily to his lips that Jacob could only marvel that they were his own.

"I especially want to thank you for making the effort to make my new bride Rebecca feel at home here in Tunis," he continued easily. A few of the guests cheered enthusiastically, but Jacob waved his glass to catch their attention again.

"And finally, I would like to propose a toast." This suggestion was met with a murmur of approval and a bustle of activity as everyone ensured that they had a full glass. When the courtyard had settled once more, Jacob held his own goblet aloft as he lifted Rebecca's hand and brushed his lips across her fingertips. He met her eyes for an instant and knew exactly what he had to say.

"To life," Jacob declared, pausing while the assembly repeated his words. "To love, and to all of you. May you be so lucky to find the *lapis exilis* that will turn your dross to gold before your very eyes."

The group roared their approval and drained their glasses along with Jacob and Rebecca, excited chatter breaking out around them as Jacob handed over his empty goblet and cupped Rebecca's face in his hands.

"I can't turn dross into gold," she chided with a twinkle in her eye, and Jacob shook his head.

"Not literally," he confirmed, watching understanding dawn on her face. "You make me more than I am, Rebecca, better than I am alone." Her eyes glazed with tears and she shook her head mutely as though she couldn't find the words.

"Oh, Jacob," she whispered shakily, and Jacob gently kissed away an errant tear that escaped her brimming eyes.

"I love you, Rebecca," he told her solemnly, and she smiled up at him in delight.

"I love you, too," she murmured back, and his heart took an unsteady lurch at the sound of the words he had longed to hear.

"Then we have everything we need," he said with conviction, ignoring the press of people around them as he bent to taste the wild honey that would fill his senses for the rest of his days.

* * * * *

Harlequin® Historical

FIRST IMPRESSIONS THAT ARE SURE TO ENDURE!

It's March Madness time again! Each year, Harlequin Historicals picks the best and brightest new stars in historical romance and brings them to you in one exciting month!

The Heart's Desire by Gayle Wilson—When the hunt for a spy pairs a cynical duke with a determined young woman, caution is thrown to the wind in one night of passion.

Rain Shadow by Cheryl St.John—A widower in need of a wife falls in love with the wrong woman, an Indian-raised sharp-shooter more suited to a Wild West show than to a farm.

My Lord Beaumont by Madris Dupree—Adventure abounds in this tale about a rakish nobleman who learns a lesson in love when he rescues a young stowaway.

Capture by Emily French—The story of a courageous woman who is captured by Algonquin Indians, and the warrior whose dreams foretell her part in an ancient prophecy.

Four exciting historicals by four promising new authors who are certain to become your favorites. Look for them wherever Harlequin Historicals are sold. Don't be left behind!

HHM94

Take 4 bestselling love stories FREE

Plus get a FREE surprise gift!

**A SON OF BRITAIN, A DAUGHTER OF ROME.
ENEMIES BY BIRTH, LOVERS BY DESTINY.**

Lynn Bartlett
Defy the Eagle

From bestselling author Lynn Bartlett comes this tale of epic passion
and ancient rebellion. Jilana, the daughter of a Roman merchant,
and Caddaric, rebel warrior of Britain, are caught in the clash of two
cultures amid one of the greatest eras in history.

Coming in February 1994
from Harlequin Historicals

Don't miss it! Available wherever Harlequin Books are sold.

When the only time you have for yourself is...

Spring into spring—by giving yourself a March Break! Take a few *stolen moments* and treat yourself to a Great Escape. Relax with one of our brand-new stories (or with all six!).

Each STOLEN MOMENTS title in our Great Escapes collection is a complete and never-before-published *short* novel. These contemporary romances are 96 pages long—the perfect length for the busy woman of the nineties!

Look for Great Escapes in our Stolen Moments display this March!

SIZZLE by Jennifer Crusie
ANNIVERSARY WALTZ
by Anne Marie Duquette
MAGGIE AND HER COLONEL
by Merline Lovelace
PRAIRIE SUMMER by Alina Roberts
THE SUGAR CUP by Annie Sims
LOVE ME NOT by Barbara Stewart

Wherever Harlequin and Silhouette books are sold.

HARLEQUIN®

Don't miss these Harlequin favorites by some of our most distinguished authors!
And now, you can receive a discount by ordering two or more titles!

HT#25409	THE NIGHT IN SHINING ARMOR by JoAnn Ross	$2.99	☐
HT#25471	LOVESTORM by JoAnn Ross	$2.99	☐
HP#11463	THE WEDDING by Emma Darcy	$2.89	☐
HP#11592	THE LAST GRAND PASSION by Emma Darcy	$2.99	☐
HR#03188	DOUBLY DELICIOUS by Emma Goldrick	$2.89	☐
HR#03248	SAFE IN MY HEART by Leigh Michaels	$2.89	☐
HS#70464	CHILDREN OF THE HEART by Sally Garrett	$3.25	☐
HS#70524	STRING OF MIRACLES by Sally Garrett	$3.39	☐
HS#70500	THE SILENCE OF MIDNIGHT by Karen Young	$3.39	☐
HI#22178	SCHOOL FOR SPIES by Vickie York	$2.79	☐
HI#22212	DANGEROUS VINTAGE by Laura Pender	$2.89	☐
HI#22219	TORCH JOB by Patricia Rosemoor	$2.89	☐
HAR#16459	MACKENZIE'S BABY by Anne McAllister	$3.39	☐
HAR#16466	A COWBOY FOR CHRISTMAS by Anne McAllister	$3.39	☐
HAR#16462	THE PIRATE AND HIS LADY by Margaret St. George	$3.39	☐
HAR#16477	THE LAST REAL MAN by Rebecca Flanders	$3.39	☐
HH#28704	A CORNER OF HEAVEN by Theresa Michaels	$3.99	☐
HH#28707	LIGHT ON THE MOUNTAIN by Maura Seger	$3.99	☐

Harlequin Promotional Titles

#83247	YESTERDAY COMES TOMORROW by Rebecca Flanders	$4.99	☐
#83257	MY VALENTINE 1993	$4.99	☐

(short-story collection featuring Anne Stuart, Judith Arnold,
Anne McAllister, Linda Randall Wisdom)
(limited quantities available on certain titles)

	AMOUNT	$
DEDUCT:	**10% DISCOUNT FOR 2+ BOOKS**	$
ADD:	**POSTAGE & HANDLING**	$
	($1.00 for one book, 50¢ for each additional)	
	APPLICABLE TAXES*	$ _____
	TOTAL PAYABLE	$ _____
	(check or money order—please do not send cash)	

To order, complete this form and send it, along with a check or money order for the total above, payable to Harlequin Books, to: **In the U.S.:** 3010 Walden Avenue, P.O. Box 9047, Buffalo, NY 14269-9047; **In Canada:** P.O. Box 613, Fort Erie, Ontario, L2A 5X3.

Name: _____

Address: _____ City: _____

State/Prov.: _____ Zip/Postal Code: _____

*New York residents remit applicable sales taxes.
 Canadian residents remit applicable GST and provincial taxes.

HBACK-JM